THE GOL DEN S

THE GOLDENS

LAUREN WILSON

HARPER
FIRE

First published in the United Kingdom by Harper Fire,
an imprint of HarperCollins *Children's Books*, in 2025
HarperCollins *Children's Books* is a division of HarperCollins*Publishers* Ltd
1 London Bridge Street
London SE1 9GF

www.harpercollins.co.uk

HarperCollins*Publishers*
Macken House, 39/40 Mayor Street Upper
Dublin 1, D01 C9W8, Ireland

1

ISBN 978–0–00–868752–6
WTS ISBN 978–0–00–878515–4

Lauren Wilson asserts the moral right to be identified as the author of the work.

A CIP catalogue record for this title is available from the British Library.

Typeset in Adobe Caslon Pro by HarperCollins*Publishers* India
Printed and bound in the UK using 100% Renewable
Electricity at CPI Group (UK) Ltd

MIX
Paper | Supporting
responsible forestry
FSC™ C007454

For my parents. Thank you for everything.

'Hell is a teenage girl'
Jennifer's Body, *2009*

Prologue

I always think of her during summer storms.

The dark, sultry heat, the violet skies and petrichor in the air; all of it transports me back to that July morning.

The bonfire was still smouldering on the lawn, a stark pile of blackened logs and ash reminiscent of a funeral pyre, when I followed Clara out of the orangery. The air was smoky, full of the fragrance of dying, rotting things, and thunder rumbled in the distance.

I was still wearing the stained white satin dress I'd worn the night before, and I was barefoot. The morning dew chilled my toes, and wet grass brushed against my calves as we walked across the lawn towards the woodland at the end of the garden. Neither of us spoke.

The ground gradually sloped downhill, the trees growing denser the closer we got to the river. To the temple. It was there that Clara led me, strands of her blonde hair snagging on branches as we passed, sticks snapping underfoot.

I've always known that friendship is a powerful force in young women. In the muddy, tumultuous waters between

1

adolescence and adulthood, those impatient years of not-quite-independence, we embrace friendship with our whole hearts. Whether that's for better or for worse.

Any loose bonds without passion, those with old classmates just barely held together with cancelled breakfast dates and belated *happy birthday* texts, fade quickly, replaced by new friendships that are intense, beautiful, all-consuming. Friendships in this strange, in-between age are more blood pact than pinkie promise, living the very best moments of your lives together alongside the very worst. You hold hands and make drunken, fervent vows in the early hours. You would die for each other, kill for each other.

In my experience, by the age of eighteen, every girl knows another girl that she would follow to the very ends of the earth.

For me, that girl was Clara Holland.

It started to rain, warm droplets running down my face, my arms, my back.

When we reached the overhang at the water's edge, in the shadow of the crumbling temple, Clara stopped. Silently, she looked down into the rushing torrent, the shallows choked with reeds and vegetation. She tilted her head, indicating something that I should see. I followed her gaze.

There was a body in the water.

Chapter 1

It was only through coincidence, really, that I ever became involved with the Goldens at all.

At eighteen, I had a mild anxiety disorder and a fondness for books over people. In maths, science and art, I was average but hardworking – yet in literature I shone.

I'd spent two years at my shabby, underfunded sixth form being complimented and encouraged, pushed and praised. I would never be a public speaker; I physically trembled whenever I had to read in front of the class, even more so when I was reading my own work. But that didn't seem to matter. My grades were good enough to get me an interview at Dern University, and for me that was all that counted.

I had it all worked out. I'd read English and Creative Writing, with the long-term goal of becoming a prize-winning novelist. For over a decade, I'd imagined myself one day striding through an enormous, glittering city – London, Paris, New York – in a pair of thick-heeled boots, leaving lipstick stains on paper coffee cups as I sought inspiration for my next bestseller. Later, I imagined, I would settle down at my writing desk, which would sit in the corner of my tiny but cosy apartment, and the words would flow from my pen like water.

My interview for Dern was to be over video call, which was a relief – for both me and my parents. I was already unsure how I'd afford the train fare there and back every term.

I barely slept the night before, as reflected by the bruise-like shadows beneath my eyes, but I knew in my heart that it would all be worth it. I'd taken the morning off so that I could sit at the kitchen table with my laptop while my parents were at work. I carefully angled the screen for the best lighting, filled a glass with water to set beside it and tried not to let the anxiety buzzing in my veins get the better of me.

I was eight minutes early signing into the meeting room. As I waited for my interviewer to join, I flicked through the Dern prospectus. I was awestruck by the stone buildings, the willows hanging over the chamomile-green banks of the river. Every glossy photograph called my name, conjured visions of a new wardrobe that would complement my classical surroundings: penny loafers and Mary Janes, tweed and houndstooth, white shirts with crisp collars.

The academic who I was speaking with signed in at precisely ten o'clock. She introduced herself as Dr Huntsman, a poet and poetry scholar at the university. My heart sank. I, a novelist through and through, knew a bit about poetry – but hardly enough to impress somebody who'd committed their life to writing and studying it.

I fumbled my way through the answers to her first

questions – what was I currently reading? How much of an impact did I think the form of a text had on the overall experience of reading it? – all the while dreading the inevitable moment that she asked me a poetry-related question. When it came, I answered haltingly, wracking my brain for any knowledge of the poet she'd mentioned, even a snippet of one of their poems, but came up utterly blank.

Dr Huntsman smiled kindly, but I could feel my future slipping away from me. Everything that I'd worked so hard for was disappearing, and I knew that I had to hold on to it tightly, to grasp it with both fists. If I didn't, my dream would be over before it had even started.

It was her final question that turned things around.

'If I said to you "the grass in the field is green", would you define this as poetry?'

I cleared my throat, and then took a sip of water, stalling for time. 'I don't think so,' I said eventually.

Dr Huntsman nodded at me in an encouraging way, her eyebrows tilted with curiosity above her modern, thick-rimmed glasses. 'Why is that?'

The stalling hadn't helped. My nerves were fraying. And, when it came, my answer sounded more like a question.

'Poems rhyme,' I said, the words falling from my lips in an anxious rush. 'They rhyme, or they have rhythm. Or both. Or there's a story. But that – well, that's just a sentence. I think?'

'So you think this being outside the conventions of poetry is what makes it *not* a poem?'

'Yes,' I said. Then, an idea blossoming, I added, 'I mean, no. How important are conventions in poetry, really?'

I was beginning to warm to my theme, slowly regaining my confidence. 'Traditional poetry has conventions, but does all poetry? Maybe a sentence *could* be a poem, if we loosen the rules. It's all about perspective, right?'

Dr Huntsman was smiling now. 'And what about you?' she asked. 'What is your perspective?'

'My perspective is that it isn't a poem,' I said. 'It's just a sentence. It's a fact – it doesn't say anything except for what it says, and isn't that the whole point of poetry? To say something beyond the words on the page – to tell the truth about the world?'

At the end of the interview, I thanked her for the opportunity and she logged off, leaving me staring at my own blurred reflection in the black, empty screen. It was impossible to know how I'd done. The beginning had been rough, but I'd saved it by the end. Hadn't I? I shut my laptop and allowed myself a deep breath.

One way or another, my fate was sealed.

Dern University, Havington. A campus of old, light stone, traditional latticed windows and cobbled alleyways, home to a student body of just under six thousand, all specialising in arts and humanities to some extent. And, as of the second of September, that would include me.

'I'm so proud of you,' Mum had said as I'd clutched the torn white envelope in both hands, stunned. 'I didn't doubt you for a second.'

'Your mum's right,' Dad had agreed. 'We knew you'd get in. They'd be missing out big time if they turned you away.'

My parents had always believed that I would be accepted, but I hadn't been so certain. I'd remained quietly hopeful that my interview performance had been enough to secure my place. And it had.

Every year, my sixth form boasted about its results-day successes online – and this year was no different. Mid-morning, a slideshow of my year group's higher achievers appeared on the website, a collection of school portraits with each student's name, grades and their onward destination. *Chloe Hughes*, mine read in bold, undeniable lettering. *AAB. Dern University.* I read it over and over again, relishing the fact that I'd done it. I'd *really* done it. I was going to Dern.

And so on the morning of the second of September I finished packing up all my things and boarded the early train, laden with two suitcases and a backpack.

My first glimpse of Havington came just as the sun crept over the hills, turning them a blazing shade of late-summer gold. It felt like an eternity before the train that I'd been on for the better part of three hours – spending the time alternately reading and gazing out of the window as the pre-dawn landscape flashed past in a blur – creaked into Havington Station, releasing me and four other passengers unceremoniously on to the minute platform.

As the train pulled away, I checked the map on my phone. I had a fifteen-minute walk ahead of me. That was nothing, on any other day. But now, with my nerves fizzing and the caffeine levels in my system severely depleted, it was going to be a struggle.

At this time of the morning, the market town of Havington was quiet and still. The streetlights were still on: a series of glorious, old-fashioned lamps, their glow reflecting off each glass-fronted shop as I passed. There was a bakery, a butcher's, a hairdresser's, a shop selling antiques, a greengrocer's, and even a haberdashery. I'd only ever seen high streets like this in films; at home, our high street was populated with charity shops and betting shops, and we bought our groceries from the supermarket. And now I'd be able to buy fresh pastries and fruit and flowers whenever I wanted, as a treat – as long as they weren't too expensive.

My heart was lighter by the time I reached a picturesque bridge, buoyed by my imagined future lifestyle. The river beneath was wide and flat, and everywhere there were trees, their leaves crisping up and turning yellow in the early light, preparing themselves for autumn. Up ahead was a beautiful clock tower I recognised from the prospectus: a beacon, guiding me on.

The students' union was an old stone building like all the others. Just outside, there stood an imposing bronze statue of a man with a solemn expression. *Joseph Dern*, a plaque beneath his feet read. *Founder of Dern University. 1808–1894.*

Inside, the students' union had glossy hardwood floors, which contrasted sharply with the shabby interior paintwork. There was only one other person there: a girl, slouched in her seat behind the welcome desk, drinking coffee from a paper cup. She seemed irritated to encounter somebody so early.

'Welcome to Dern University,' she said, pushing her fringe out of her eyes to get a better look at me. 'Can I take your full name?'

I swallowed. 'It's Chloe Hughes.'

I'd always expected to arrive at university as a transformed version of myself: a butterfly having finally escaped its cocoon. The new me would be calm, collected, elegant, intelligent. She would let nothing faze her. Instead, I'd arrived as my present self: eternally uncool, and caring far too much what others thought.

The girl looked at a sheet of paper on the desk in front of her, running a pen down it. Her name tag said *Rebecca*. 'And your middle name?'

'Alice.'

Rebecca nodded, struck a line through my name on her list, and then spun her chair round so that her back was to me. Her hair was pink at the ends, and a deep brown at the roots.

'This is your welcome pack,' she said as she turned back round, slapping a thick plastic wallet down on the desk between us. 'It contains your student ID, which gives you access to the buildings on campus. There's also a campus map, your class schedule and two sets of keys for your assigned first-year residence. Try not to lose them. If you do, the fee to replace them is pretty hefty.' She smiled conspiratorially. 'There's also a card in there for the student launderette – you just top it up at one of the machines using your student ID.'

'Okay,' I said slowly, trying not to look as overwhelmed as I felt. 'And which accommodation have I been assigned to?'

Rebecca peered down at the welcome pack. 'Ivy House, by the looks of it.'

I frowned. 'I requested Poppy or Willow.'

'They were probably full by the time you filled in your application,' she said. 'They're the two newest buildings, so they're always in pretty high demand. But Ivy House is great! It's actually the oldest student accommodation on campus, so it's got *history*.'

In my mind, the word *history* was synonymous with *leaks*, *spiders* and *cracks in the ceiling* when it came to living accommodation. But, then again, I *was* an aspiring novelist; I lived for romanticising my surroundings. At the very least, the building might be somewhat picturesque – even if it was falling apart.

'Okay,' I said. 'Thanks so much for your help.'

'You're welcome!' Rebecca grinned. 'I hope you enjoy your time here.'

'Me too,' I said. Then, quieter, just to myself, 'Me too.'

Ivy House was similar in style to the rest of the buildings on campus: brown stone with latticed windows, and a small, shaded space outside dotted with flowerbeds. The remnants of summer blooms were bright between the evergreen bushes, but this was where any semblance of beauty ended.

I fumbled with my keycard, and opened the main door with a shove. Inside, it was dark and cool, and it took a moment for my eyes to adjust. It had the air of an old school: dim fluorescent lights buzzed above my head, the paint was an unwelcoming beige and stained grey linoleum covered the floor, overlaid in places with shabby carpet.

The flat that I'd been given was on the second floor and there was no lift. My backpack was feeling heavier by the minute, and I groaned internally at the thought of lugging it, and my suitcases, up multiple flights of stairs. But, I told myself, I'd come this far. This was the last hurdle.

By the time I'd reached the second-floor landing, luggage in tow, I was panting, sweat beading on my temples. I leaned against the wall for a moment to catch my breath, frankly exhausted and not at all prepared to see another human being just yet. Which was unfortunate because, at that moment, I became acutely aware that I was being watched.

One of the doors along the hallway had opened, and three girls were peering out, craning their necks. They emerged, stepping out one by one like a girl band.

'We thought we heard someone,' the tallest of the three said. She had a blonde, choppy bob, smudged eyeliner and sharp cheekbones, and she spoke in a bored, drawling kind of way.

I was conscious that they were all assessing me. My plain jeans and blue jumper felt suddenly wanting. 'I guess you did,' I said. 'I'm Chloe. Hi.'

'Hi,' one of the other girls, both brunettes, said. She had a lilting Irish accent, which gave her words an almost musical quality. 'I'm Skye. That's Amelia and that's Vanessa.'

'Hi,' I said. 'Again.' There was an awkward pause, which, as the new arrival, I felt obligated to break. 'So. Where are you all from?'

'Vanessa and I are both from London,' Amelia said. 'Skye's from Dublin.'

'Near Dublin,' Skye corrected. 'What about you?'

'You've probably never heard of it,' I said. 'It's just a little town up north. *Way* up north.'

'So *that's* why you talk like that,' the blonde girl, Vanessa, said, her tone dripping with derision as thick as honey. 'I thought you just weren't very well educated.'

Such a pointed jibe from a complete stranger stung. A biting retort left my lips before I could stop it. 'We're all at the same university,' I said. 'If I'm not well educated, then neither are you.'

The already tense atmosphere soured further, and Vanessa's expression turned icy, her mouth a thin line. She shoved past me without another word. After an uncomfortable pause, Amelia and Skye followed her, clearly having chosen their side. They didn't so much as glance over their shoulders.

Alone in the hallway, I listened until their footsteps faded, until I could hear their voices in the courtyard outside, laughter echoing off the walls. No doubt they were already discussing me.

Eyes stinging, I unlocked the door to my room and dragged my suitcases across the threshold. I let the door fall closed behind me, and sank down on to the bare mattress. And, when the tears came, I didn't try to stop them.

Chapter 2

Over the next few days – that empty swathe of time allotted for us to settle in before the semester officially started – I hoped that my flatmates would warm to me, that perhaps we'd get past our initial altercation and maybe even begin to understand each other.

Unfortunately, nothing changed. I would go into the kitchen whenever I heard the girls in there, ready to try to make amends, only to be met with abrupt, stubborn silence as they waited for me to leave. They'd start talking again the moment the door swung shut behind me, muffling their laughter, and I'd flush with humiliation.

I'd always been more of a background character – especially at school. I was clever, yes, but I was also mild, inoffensive and bookish, with a group of similarly quiet friends who were more like acquaintances, the kind of girls you'd sit with at lunch, but who you'd never really speak to outside of school. I'd never been particularly popular, but I'd also never been excluded. And never quite so deliberately.

They'd dress up in wonderful sparkly clothes and go for

drinks, or for brunch, or to a student night. I was never invited. I began to look forward to the times when they'd leave, the slam of the door behind them and the jingling in the hallway as they tucked keys into handbags, signalling my freedom. I'd emerge from my room and wander along the hall into the kitchen in my socked feet, just because I could, or I'd curl up on the sofa in the living room with a blanket and a book I'd brought from home. Sometimes, I'd take one of my notebooks and write for a while, allowing my feelings to transform into words on the page.

By the end of the third day, I'd ordered an electric kettle online to keep in my room, to limit how often I had to encounter the three of them. Already, I was looking back at the Chloe of just a few weeks earlier – hopeful, dreamy, excited – with a sort of embarrassed sympathy.

If only she'd known, I thought.

But then, if I had known, what would I have done? I'd only applied to Dern. My choices were to stick it out, or go home. And maybe once lectures and seminars began, I told myself, I'd make friends.

My first lecture was the next day at one o'clock, and I was committed to dressing as nicely as I could. Clearly, first impressions here counted for a lot. I spent so long overthinking my hair (loose and wavy), make-up (mascara and a hint of sheer red lip balm) and clothes (light jeans, lilac knit jumper), that I was very nearly late, stumbling into the lecture hall with a minute to spare.

Despite the shabby and somewhat disappointing interior of Ivy House, the lecture hall lived up to expectations. It had a high, vaulted ceiling, like something you'd see in a church. The semicircular seating rose up in stages to look down on the speaker, old-medical-school style, and the walls were panelled with glossy wood. Jarringly, a modern smartboard now hung where the blackboard once would have been.

I made my way up the central aisle, trying not to look too hard at the other students milling around and taking their seats. There seemed to be a few groups already deep in conversation, and I wondered how they all did it. How did they melt into friendship, or at least acquaintanceship, so seamlessly?

It was then that I noticed one girl sitting alone, her deep red hair pinned back into a high ponytail, vivid against the black hoodie she wore. She had been furiously scribbling something in a notebook, but, catching my eye, she smiled in a friendly, vaguely hopeful kind of way. An invitation if I'd ever seen one. I sidled along her row, hoping that I didn't look as embarrassingly grateful as I felt.

'Hi,' I said. 'Is it okay if I sit here?'

'God, yes,' she said. 'I don't know anybody, and I'm so nervous.'

'I don't know anybody either,' I said, relieved that somebody, at least, wasn't part of the weird clique situation that Dern seemed to have going on. 'I'm Chloe.'

'Olivia,' she replied. 'Hey, have you seen the required-reading list yet?'

I shook my head, and she slid a piece of lined notebook paper across to me. Her handwriting was impeccably neat, to the point where it was practically calligraphy. Every 'y' or 'g' was adorned with a little curlicue, and there were a lot of them; the list was easily thirty books long.

'You've got to be kidding,' I said, all at once forgetting my shyness. 'Where did you get this?'

'One of the lecturers emailed us about it on Friday morning,' she said. 'You didn't get it? Don't stress – just check your junk mail when you get a chance. That's where mine went to begin with.'

'Thanks so much – I wouldn't have even thought of that,' I said honestly, and she beamed.

The room quietened then, all chatter ceasing as a grey-haired man entered through the double doors. The smartboard came to life, revealing today's topic of discussion: an introduction to Gothic literature from the nineteenth century to today.

I poised my pen attentively, waiting for the lecture to begin. Olivia leaned over. 'Want to go and check some of those books out after this? Get a head start?'

'I'd love to,' I whispered back.

Olivia, as it turned out, was from a village not too far from mine – less than twenty miles – which, considering we were so far from home, I found pretty remarkable. For that reason, and because of her light wit and warmth, it didn't take long for me to relax around her.

After the lecture had finished, we strolled across campus to the library, which was housed in a wonderful old church complete with stained glass windows. Sunlight flickered in red, blue and yellow blurs on the stone walls as we discussed Daphne du Maurier, bought milky takeaway coffees from the little refreshment cart, and spent a happy two hours buried in the stacks and circling the mezzanine floor hunting down copies of the various books we'd need to read and study for the rest of the semester.

I was pulled back to reality when, her tote bag loaded with battered volumes, Olivia said, 'I suppose I'd better be getting back to the flat.'

My heart sank. I'd been so absorbed that I'd all but forgotten the cold atmosphere that would no doubt be waiting for me at Ivy House. 'I might stay here a bit longer,' I said.

'Cool,' Olivia said, hitching her bag higher up on her shoulder. 'See you tomorrow, though, yeah? I'll save you a seat.'

I smiled. 'Definitely,' I said. 'See you tomorrow.'

Once she was out of sight, her Doc Martens thudding on the stairs as she descended, I slumped down at one of the lamp-lit reading tables. I couldn't stay here all evening, I knew, but I also had no desire to go back to the flat to see Vanessa and Amelia and Skye and hear their laughter in the kitchen as I sat in my room, alone.

As I pictured the scene, a wave of steely determination came over me. *No*, I thought. I wasn't going to let them ruin this. This was my *dream*. I'd enjoyed my first lecture, and I'd already made a friend – and it was only my first proper day! I wasn't going to let my flatmates dampen any more of my university experience.

As I stood up, ready to go back to the flat, something slipped from my chair and fell on to the floor beside me – a scarf. I picked it up. It was impossibly soft, a pink, grey and cream pattern crafted from an expensive wool. Cashmere? Maybe. It was easily the most luxurious item I'd ever held.

It was then that something caught my eye: monogrammed in thick cream thread on a light pink square were the letters *C A H*. My initials. I frowned, then glanced around. There was nobody else on this side of the mezzanine, and only a couple of girls with their heads close together on the opposite side.

'Excuse me,' I called, holding up the scarf. 'Is this yours?'

They both looked up, then shook their heads. I lay the scarf back down on the table, and ran my fingertips across it with admiration. It was awfully coincidental, wasn't it, that I'd come across a scarf monogrammed with my initials? Maybe it was a chance initiation into some sort of scarf-wearing secret society – the kind that I'd read about in books, where particularly erudite students were welcomed into an inner circle. If that was the case, I thought, they'd made a mistake. And yet I imagined secret tunnels running deep beneath the campus, lit by firelight, their walls glinting wet with moss, myself running along them . . .

More likely, of course, was that it wasn't a coincidence at all. Perhaps somebody I knew had planted it. But, then again, who could even be responsible for such a thing? My parents would've sent any surprise gifts to my accommodation. My flatmates certainly wouldn't have bought me such a lovely scarf, and Olivia was an unlikely suspect as we'd only met for the very first time today. Besides, she'd already left when I'd sat down at the reading table.

Perhaps it was a sign, something from the universe to tell me *hey, you belong here.* As my mum always said, signs were everywhere; it was up to us to interpret them. I didn't necessarily believe that the universe cared about me, that my future was a long, pre-planned rope woven by fate, but, just this once, I was willing to try.

I glanced around furtively, and then slipped the scarf into my bag. It was too nice to leave in the library. I would find out where to hand in lost property, I decided, and then take it there tomorrow. For now, it would be my lucky charm. My hidden weapon against the girls who so clearly wanted to see me fail. I lifted my chin. I wouldn't give them the satisfaction.

The first thing Olivia said to me the next day was, 'Wow! Love the scarf.'

I had planned to hand it over to the girl at the students' union welcome desk, but the way that she eyed it as I approached, like a crow assessing a particularly sparkly pebble, unnerved me. I'd ended up keeping it, wearing it to the coffee shop where I'd arranged to meet Olivia before our next lecture, somewhat self-consciously, in the hope that its owner would recognise and claim it – preferably with enough time for me to explain why, exactly, I had it in my possession.

I told Olivia about how I'd found the scarf. When she saw the beautifully stitched letters, her mouth fell open into a little O.

'You don't think this was intentional, do you?' she asked. 'A surprise?'

'I thought about it,' I said. 'I mean, don't get me wrong, I *know* it's a weird coincidence, but I just don't know who would do something like this.'

Olivia's brow crinkled. 'It's odd,' she said. 'I swear I've seen a monogram like that before, but I have no idea where . . .' She trailed off, her gaze fixed on something over my shoulder.

I shifted in my seat, trying to see what she was looking at so intently. And then I did.

There was a girl standing at the counter, ordering a coffee. She was around my age, and tall, with the glowing skin of the wealthy: sun-kissed from years of tennis lessons and summers in the south of France. Even at a glance, she was incredibly elegant, giving off cool-girl chic in light jeans and a thick-knit cream jumper, with loose, honey-blonde hair cascading in waves past her shoulder blades.

She'd captured the attention of everyone in the café, myself and Olivia included, although she seemed to be unaware. That, or she was very good at pretending she was. Her head tilted nonchalantly as she glanced up at the menu and then back to the barista, and then tapped her card against the machine.

She had a white leather satchel slung over one shoulder, and as she turned slightly I spotted something that made my heart beat faster. Monogrammed on the satchel's flap in gold were the letters *C A H*. It matched the monogramming on the scarf exactly, even down to the slightly italicised tilt of the letters.

'Do you know who that is?' Olivia murmured, although we were well out of earshot.

'Someone who dropped her scarf,' I replied, equally quietly, nodding towards the girl's satchel.

It took Olivia a second, but, once she clocked the monogramming, she gaped at me. '*No,*' she said. 'You do not have *Clara Holland*'s scarf!'

I looked over at the girl again. Her attention was focused on her phone as she waited for her coffee, and everyone else's attention was on her.

'Clara Holland,' I repeated. 'Who is she?'

'She's not, like, *famous* famous,' Olivia said. 'But she's one of those girls that does *everything*: she's an influencer, she's done some modelling work. Her dad's this huge fashion photographer, and her mum designs clothes – high-end stuff, boutique. She's *huge* on Instagram too. Clara, that is, not her mum. She's got probably half a million followers, maybe more.'

As Olivia spoke, I watched Clara from the corner of my eye. She collected her coffee from the barista and took a sip, leaving pink lipstick on the white plastic lid. She stood to one side of the counter, looking for something in her satchel with one hand, and I could see it in the way that she carried herself, her posture.

I got up without thinking about it, the legs of my chair scraping against the floor.

Olivia stared at me as I peeled the scarf from round my neck. 'What are you doing?'

I didn't answer her. I feared that if I said the words out loud, any semblance of courage in my veins would completely dissipate. Instead, I held up the scarf, briefly, before walking across the coffee shop to where Clara was standing, still rifling through her satchel.

'Hi,' I said. 'I'm so sorry to bother you.'

Clara looked up. I'd expected the warm but somewhat tired expression of the well-known: the gratitude for a fan's support, combined with the fervent wish that you'd just *go away*. But Clara was smiling as if we knew each other, as if she was genuinely delighted to see me.

'Hi,' she said, light, friendly. 'You're not bothering me at all. What's up?'

I held out her scarf. 'I found this in the library yesterday.'

Clara took the scarf in both hands, clutching it to her chest. 'Thank you so much!' she said. 'I had no idea where it had gone. It was a birthday present too – I was *so* upset. Where in the library was it?'

'Up on the mezzanine,' I said. 'Tucked down the side of one of the reading table armchairs.'

Clara sighed, the sound almost musical. 'I should've known,' she said. 'The *one* place I didn't check. Typical, right?'

'Typical,' I echoed. Her presence was so easy, so warm, that I felt comfortable adding, 'I thought it was a surprise, actually. For me.'

Clara tilted her head slightly to one side. 'Why's that?'

'We have the same initials,' I said. 'I'm Chloe Alice Hughes. See?'

A smile crept across Clara's face. 'Clara Annabelle Holland,' she said. 'God, what a coincidence!'

'I know, right!' I said. 'How weird is that?' Then, a bit awkwardly, 'Well. I'll let you get back to your coffee, or whatever.'

'Cool,' Clara said. 'Hey, thanks again, Chloe. Seriously, you've made my day.'

I gave her a quick smile before I headed back to my table, where Olivia was watching me, hands clasped round her mug, looking considerably awed.

'What did you say?' she asked as soon as I sat back down.

I gave her a quick overview of our conversation, that we had the same initials, and she sighed dreamily.

'What?' I asked.

'She's just so *cool*,' Olivia said. 'I want to be her.'

As I watched Clara leave, her coffee in one hand, I knew that Olivia was right. Clara was different from us. She was *better*.

And I wanted to be better too.

Chapter 3

In the weeks that followed, I saw Clara everywhere. It was like thinking about a red car, or a specific insecurity: now that I knew Clara existed, she was all that I could see.

I saw her behind the wheel of a white Mini Cooper, her face half covered by an enormous pair of dark sunglasses. I saw her sitting in the library, chin resting on one slim, manicured hand as she flicked through an old textbook. I saw her walking across campus, effortlessly elegant in a white wool coat and leather trousers, her long hair and gold jewellery gleaming bright in the late-September sun.

Clara was an amalgamation of every girl I had ever envied, that painful twist of jealousy and adoration. I remembered that salt-stung feeling from my first year at secondary school as we, fresh-faced and in too-big jumpers, looked up to the older girls. We idolised all of them: the rebellious ones who wore dark lipstick and smoked cigarettes, the ones with the high ponytails who were on the netball and hockey teams, the ones who always hung around with the boys and would wink at you conspiratorially as you passed them in the hallways. We adored them from a distance, collecting stories and rumours about them, which we traded in whispers. They were our goddesses, our worship as habitual to us as detentions and tartan school-uniform skirts.

And, clearly, I wasn't the only one who found Clara mesmerising. Whenever I saw her on these occasions, there were other people looking at her too, fixated on her every movement. It was impossible to tell whether it was because they knew who she was, or because they felt what I did: a strange kind of magnetism, like gravity pulling me into her orbit.

In November, our paths finally crossed again. I'd taken my laptop to the campus coffee shop, bored by the four unfriendly walls of my room at Ivy House, and in need of an amount of decent coffee that the library couldn't provide. I'd tucked myself in a corner that, after nearly two months at Dern, I'd begun to think of as mine: a single table, placed perfectly between a window and a radiator. I'd got into the habit of sipping my coffee, warming my feet, and hammering out reading reports and essays until the coffee shop closed for the evening.

I'd just ordered a third caramel latte in the hope that the sugar rush would power me through the last quarter of the essay I was writing on *Carmilla*, and I was letting my mind drift to the sound of the espresso machine, when the door opened and let in a burst of wintry air.

'Back again!' the barista, a woman in her fifties who

reminded me of my mum, said with a chuckle. 'What can I get you?'

'You can't blame me – it's the best coffee on campus,' a warm, familiar voice replied. 'I'll have a grande iced vanilla latte, please. For here.'

I glanced up, hardly daring to hope. And yet there she was, her knee-length camel coat and cream turtleneck and blue jeans both cosy and on-trend in a way that I'd never been able to achieve. My own cold-weather style, as a rule, could be described in two words: *Arctic expedition*.

Clara spoke first. 'Hey,' she said slowly as she turned to me. 'Do I know you?'

'We saw each other here a couple of months ago,' I said. 'I found your scarf in the library.'

Her expression brightened. 'Yes! That's it. I *knew* I recognised you.'

Clara Holland recognised *me*. Olivia was going to die. 'I'm in here pretty often,' I said. 'I'm surprised we haven't seen each other before now.'

Clara laughed. 'I know, right? I basically live here.'

The barista slid my mug across the counter. 'Caramel latte for Chloe,' she said.

I picked it up. 'Thank you,' I said. I hesitated for a half-second, decided that I had nothing to lose and went for it. 'I'm over there, in the corner, if you want to come and sit for a bit or anything.'

My expectations were low, since she was probably on her

way to a lecture or to the library for a study session, but Clara nodded with a smile. 'Sure,' she said. 'I'd love to. I'll be over in a sec, okay?'

I tried not to let the burst of excitement I was feeling show on my face. 'Cool.'

I took my coffee back over to my table, and shuffled my battered paperbacks and notebooks around to make some room for Clara. I remembered this feeling, the specific, heady glow of receiving attention from someone I admired. Aged eleven or twelve, even the most offhand compliment – *I like those trainers, cute butterfly clips, I wish I had freckles like yours* – would give me a burst of confidence that lasted for hours. In the years since then, I'd learned that external validation shouldn't be the basis for self-esteem.

And, yet, who didn't rely on it just a little bit?

'What're you working on?' Clara asked, surprising me, as she pulled out the chair next to me and settled herself into it, her back to the rest of the coffee shop. I imagined that that was the way she liked it.

'An essay,' I said. 'It's on *Carmilla*.'

Clara looked thoughtful. 'That's about vampires, isn't it?' she asked. When I nodded, she added, 'I take it you're studying English?'

'Yep,' I said. 'English and Creative Writing. What about you?'

'Well, I started off in Art History,' Clara said, 'because it sounded cool. But I just wasn't engaged, so I've switched to

Journalism. It's only the basics this year, but hopefully next year I'll be able to specialise. I want to pursue fashion.'

'That makes sense,' I said. At her slightly confused frown, I added hurriedly, 'It's just . . . you look like you work in fashion already.'

'Oh! I don't know about that,' Clara said, looking down at herself. 'I try.'

We sat in companionable silence for a minute or two, sipping our drinks.

'So,' I said eventually, 'why did you want to come to Dern?'

'Well, I got offers from Oxford and Cambridge.' She sniffed. 'Dern was always my first choice, though. My parents' summer home is near here, and I just love the campus.'

'It was my first choice too!' I said, delighted. 'How did you find the interview? Tough, right?'

Clara took a sip of her drink, the ice cubes tinkling in the bottom of the glass. 'Oh, I didn't need an interview. My parents made a donation.'

I nodded, but my mind was filled with snapshots from my own application: the essay, the preparation for the interview, the anxiety of the interview itself, the way that I'd had to think on my feet as best I could. My smile grew tight. I'd clawed my way into Dern, but, for Clara, they'd held the door open. Envy welled up in me. I wanted life to be that easy, to have victories handed to me without having to fight for them.

'Look,' Clara said, and I knew she could tell, 'I'm a big believer in destiny. The universe, fate . . . whatever you'd like to call it. I like to believe that we're all on our own predetermined path, and, no matter what choices we make, we'll always end up where we're supposed to be. One way or another.'

'And we're supposed to be here?'

Clara smiled. 'And we're supposed to be here.'

I laughed, my envy suddenly gone. 'You should be a motivational speaker.'

Her smile widened into a full-blown grin. 'What do you think I *do* on social media?'

And all of a sudden I remembered who she was. She wasn't just a kind girl offering her encouragement; she was Clara Holland, influencer and model, who certainly didn't need to be here, talking to me. It occurred to me then that if she was here, it was because she wanted to be, and it filled my chest with a warm glow.

At that moment, Clara glanced down at her dainty gold wristwatch. 'I've actually got to go. It's been so lovely talking to you, though. Really.' She reached into her satchel as she stood up, and pulled something out: a white card, barely bigger than her palm. 'Here,' she said, sliding it across the table towards me. 'I'll see you soon, okay?'

'Definitely,' I said, not caring that I sounded overly eager.

She gave me a wink as she tossed her satchel over her shoulder and headed towards the door, weaving through the lunchtime crowd with practised elegance.

Once she was out of sight, I picked up the card.

Later, the tabloids would say that this was the moment

that everything changed for me. If I hadn't taken the business card, if I'd just left it sitting there on the table, I would have continued on with my perfectly normal, perfectly safe life. I would have read about what had happened in the newspapers a year later, along with everybody else.

But I didn't know that then, as I studied the card in my hand. It was crisp and white, a business card, with handwritten-style lettering in gold foil. It read:

Next event: Saturday 29 November, 8pm
Location: Deneside Manor
Dress code: Sparkles

There were no other details. I glanced around furtively, unsure what exactly I'd been handed, and tucked it into my pocket.

Later, at the beginning of our lecture, I showed it to Olivia. 'What do you think this is?' I asked her in a whisper.

She studied it, and a smile crept on to her face. 'I'm pretty sure that's an invitation to Clara's inner circle.'

Chapter 4

I booked a taxi for seven thirty on the twenty-ninth of November, anxious about being late. It arrived dead on time, but, foolishly, I hadn't considered the fact that I didn't actually know where Deneside Manor was.

We took the main road out of Havington, the market town's streets giving way to winding country lanes. At this time of year, the last breath of autumn was cool in the evening air. The trees leaned in close on either side of the road, their remaining leaves brown and sparse in the glare of the headlights.

An eternity seemed to have passed by the time the taxi slowed to a stop at a set of electric gates. I checked my watch; it was just before eight.

'What's your name again?' the driver asked, glancing at me in the rearview mirror.

'It's Chloe,' I said. 'Chloe Hughes.'

Before I could ask why, he leaned out to press a button on the intercom. As it crackled to life, he cleared his throat, then said, in a faintly questioning voice, 'I'm here to drop off Chloe Hughes?'

The gates buzzed open.

As we passed through and began to roll steadily up a long driveway, I leaned forward to try to get a glimpse of the house itself. And there it was, atop a slight hill with a view of the valley below.

I didn't know at the time, but eventually just the sight of this house – in a grainy photograph on the front page of a newspaper, or a drone shot used on the evening news of the garden – would be enough to make me nauseous, to nearly bury me under a torrent of memories.

But, that night, it was only glorious. A square Georgian manor built from a creamy stone, it glowed in the darkness as if lit from within. It was like the setting of a period piece, something beautiful and heart-wrenching and incredible. It was difficult to imagine anybody *living* there.

As we grew closer, the taxi driver whistled. 'Your friend lives *here*?'

'I think so,' I said. It began to occur to me that I might be the victim of some kind of long-thought-out prank: about to knock on a complete stranger's door, and then be bombarded with the video of my own humiliation on Clara's social-media accounts tomorrow morning.

The taxi stopped beside a bone-dry fountain, lights illuminating the mossed statue of a woman at its centre. The driver kept the engine idling as I paid and nodded his thanks, still gaping at the house.

'I'll wait till you're in,' he said gruffly.

'Thank you,' I said. Apparently, even he thought something was awry.

I almost *wanted* it to have all been a joke so I could run back to the taxi, go back to Ivy House and hide in my room. But when I knocked at the door, the great brass knocker echoing somewhere inside like a distant rumble of thunder, it was Clara who opened it with a smile. She looked radiant, dressed in a short white dress embroidered with tiny golden stars.

'You came!' she said.

I realised that, in my shiny silver top and black jeans, I was thoroughly underdressed. Nevertheless, Clara was here. I turned and waved at the taxi driver, who beeped his horn and pulled away.

'Of course I did,' I said. 'Do you *live* here?'

'This? No, I just rented it for the party.' Clara paused for a moment, saw my bemused reaction, then burst into laughter. 'Yes, I live here! It's my parents' summer house. The one that I told you about. They stay in it when they're not travelling here, there and everywhere.' She rolled her eyes. 'Come on in.'

She held the heavy oak door open for me and I followed her into the entryway. The door slammed shut behind me with a groan of its hinges.

And then I simply stared.

The entrance hall alone was bigger than my flat at Ivy House; it was probably bigger than my parents' whole downstairs. The tiled floor beneath our feet was glistening marble, set out in black and white squares like a chessboard. A staircase with a beautifully carved banister curved up to the first floor, rounding a glittering crystal chandelier. Tiny rainbows reflected on to portraits of grim-faced men and women, all in period clothing. The scene was strangely alluring, like something out of a historical novel, the sort with a mansion and a mystery.

'It's really something, right?'

As I gazed around, awed, Clara had started along the hallway. I followed her, meek as a mouse, marvelling at the effortless way in which she inhabited the space. I couldn't imagine living somewhere like this, somewhere so *grand*; I knew that I'd find myself somehow wanting, like when you buy a daring new outfit and it ends up crumpled at the back of your wardrobe because you're too insecure to wear it. I could never belong in a place like this.

Clara stopped at an open doorway, and through it I could hear talking, laughing, the clink of glasses. She glanced at me over her shoulder, winked and then cleared her throat.

'Everyone,' she began, and the people in the room quietened. 'I'd like you all to meet Chloe. Please give her a warm welcome.'

As we stepped inside, there was a chorus of greetings. I smiled, more than a little overwhelmed, and a dozen or so faces smiled back at me. Every single one of them was absolutely perfect.

My fellow guests were spread around the room, all of them women, all of them young. They lounged on enormous cream cushions and white leather beanbags, their bare toes warmed by plush rugs strewn across the polished hardwood. The eggshell-cream walls were covered with pink roses, fairy lights dotted in between. On low tables between the cushions and the beanbags, candles flickered, giving off a light, floral musk. The effect was like stepping into a fairytale grotto, a magical forest filled with beautiful elves.

Clara plucked two champagne flutes from a shining silver tray, handed one to me and then expertly flopped down on to one of the beanbags without spilling a drop.

The closest girls had turned to face us, like flowers following the sun. I slid down on the beanbag beside Clara, suddenly feeling both intently observed and significantly lacking.

'We're just relaxing in here for a while,' Clara explained to me. 'Until the chefs bring out the food.'

I spluttered on my drink. 'Chefs?'

Clara laughed. 'It's literally just charcuterie,' she said.

One of the other girls, in a sequinned minidress, her legs long and coltish, leaned across from where she was lounging on an overstuffed cushion. 'She says that, but it's the best charcuterie you've ever tasted,' she whispered.

Clara waved the compliment away, although I could tell she was pleased. 'You guys are easily impressed,' she said.

'No, Clara,' the girl in the minidress said. 'You've *seriously* outdone yourself with the decor this time.'

'It is beautiful,' I agreed. 'I love the flowers.'

'It looks like the theme of Sophia Vandenberg's wedding,' the girl continued dreamily. 'She and Max had the ceremony in this huge villa in Provence, and it was decorated like this.

Only your version is way prettier because you don't have all the lavender. And the bees. But don't tell her I said that.'

This time, Clara preened. I watched as she raised her glass and took a sip of champagne, her eyes sparkling.

'Didn't Sophia just win a Grammy?' another girl piped up.

'Yes, but it's her third,' Minidress Girl said. 'So it, like, practically doesn't count.'

So these girls knew – were *friends* with – someone who had not only won a Grammy, but who had won *three*. It was beginning to dawn on me, sitting cross-legged in the luxurious surroundings of Clara's home with her party guests, that I was in way over my head. What could I possibly bring to this group of people?

As the conversation moved on, Clara leaned in to me. 'See that girl over there? That's Alessandra Greene. She's a model – you might've seen her on that *Vogue* cover, the one with the forest? The Italian one, I think.'

Never in my life had I purchased *Vogue*, Italian or otherwise, but I nodded indulgently. Clara's arm grazed mine.

'That girl,' she continued, her voice low, 'is Dove – *just* Dove, no surname. She's a campaigner and activist. And the girl in the shimmery tulle dress, that's—'

'Ayanna Lynch,' I whispered. 'I know her.'

At least, I knew *who* Ayanna Lynch was: an up-and-coming actor – I'd double-tapped one of her Instagram posts only a day earlier.

'Perfect,' Clara said. 'Come with me.'

Gracefully, she got to her feet, and gave the girls we'd been sitting with a smile. I trailed a few steps behind her as she moved across the room, depositing her empty champagne flute on a tray without so much as slowing down. As we got within earshot of Ayanna, she reached out and took my hand.

When I realised what she was doing, I tried to back away. But her fingers gripped mine, vice-like.

'*Ayanna,*' she said in a singsong voice. 'I have a present for you.'

Ayanna looked up. Unlike the other girls we'd spoken to, smiles spreading across their faces like sunshine whenever Clara addressed them, Ayanna seemed more reserved. She excused herself from the girls she was speaking to and came towards us. She and Clara kissed each other on both cheeks in greeting. It was surreal to see somebody I'd previously only seen on my Instagram feed right in front of me. I understood now why Olivia had been so star-struck the first time we'd seen Clara together.

'Ayanna, this is Chloe,' Clara was saying. 'She's a *huge* fan.'

My cheeks burned, but Ayanna just laughed. 'You're the worst,' she said to Clara. Then, to me, 'Ignore her. She just loves to embarrass me.'

'That was supposed to be embarrassing for *you*?' I said.

'Oh, yes,' Ayanna said, with a good-natured eye-roll. 'Clara's *very* jealous of me.'

'Ayanna's just signed a contract for the lead role in the film adaptation of a dystopian trilogy that's predicted to make hundreds of millions of dollars,' Clara explained, deadpan. 'Obviously I'm jealous.'

'Wait,' I said, forgetting my shyness in my sudden excitement. 'Is that the *All My Stars* trilogy? I saw the announcement. Are you going to play Grace?'

Ayanna's face lit up. 'Yes! It is – and I am. You've read them?'

'Only about a million times,' I said. 'Grace is just amazing.'

'I love her too,' Ayanna said. 'What did you think of her arc throughout the second book?'

As we talked, Clara drifted away to mingle with her many other guests. By the time Ayanna politely excused herself to get a refill of champagne (but not before taking my phone number and promising to wrangle me a set visit), I couldn't see Clara anywhere.

I found her in the orangery, which was on the other side of the kitchen. All stainless steel and marble, the kitchen was chaotic in the practised way of caterers, people carrying enormous dishes to and fro and calling out instructions to each other.

The orangery, by contrast, was far quieter. It was beautifully wild, a dimly lit wonderland of hanging vines and glowing lanterns, the sound of trickling water emerging from somewhere in the artificially dense undergrowth.

Despite all the friends gathered just inside, Clara was sitting alone on a wicker couch. She hadn't seen me yet; she was gazing out into the dark garden beyond the glass, where I could see fairy-lit trees shivering in the November wind.

'Hi, Clara,' I said. 'Is everything okay?'

She turned to face me, blinking, as if I'd pulled her from a daydream. 'Oh, hey,' she said. 'I'm just having a moment.' She patted the couch. 'Come on, sit. Are you enjoying the party?'

'It's incredible,' I said as I sat beside her. 'Seriously, Clara. How do you know so many amazing people?'

'Oh, from here and there. School, holidays, events in London. Or modelling stuff – that's how I met Ayanna.' She gave me a sideways glance. 'You two looked like you hit it off.'

'I think so,' I said. 'I mean, we were talking about books mostly. But she's lovely.'

There was a burst of laughter inside, which seemed to pull Clara fully out of the reverie within which she'd been lost. 'Cool,' she said. Then, 'Why'd you come out here, anyway?'

'I was looking for you.'

Clara was quiet. She looked surprised, genuinely touched, that anybody would have thought to do such a thing, which surprised me in turn. She was loved, adored; of course her friends would want to check on her. But, then again, I was the only other person out here. I was the only person who'd thought to come looking for her.

'Let's go back inside,' she said eventually.

I shrugged. 'Sure.'

We stood up, together, and as we returned to the party – the lights and voices blinding after the quiet cool of the orangery – Clara transformed. The electric quality she had that attracted people like a magnet re-emerged, her charm and sparkle directed full force at each and every guest.

But, as we once again joined the crowd in the sitting room, it was me that Clara sat beside, my hand that she reached out and squeezed with her own.

I interpreted it as a thank you.

For the rest of the night, I stayed close to Clara. I watched how she engaged with the people around her, the way that she exuded confidence in every interaction. A contrast to the Clara I'd got a glimpse of in the orangery.

Once the food was served, the party spread into the dining room. People milled in and out, helping themselves to wafer-thin prosciutto, chorizo cooked in red wine, acorn-fed Iberian ham, cheeses of every variety, black and green olives stuffed with pimento peppers, and crispy bread drizzled with olive oil. The champagne flowed and conversations buzzed, all of us buoyed by the food and the knowledge that we were here, surrounded by fantastic people, which surely meant that we were fantastic too.

I couldn't help but imagine my flatmates' faces if they could see what I was doing. One moment, I was sharing olives with a swimmer who'd won two Olympic gold medals. The next, I was helping an artist choose a dress to wear to her cousin's wedding, none of which cost less than three thousand pounds. It made something warm curl in my stomach, a deep satisfaction in knowing that, for once, I was undoubtedly having more fun than them.

Somebody flicked the lights off and synced their iPhone

up to Clara's surround-sound system. As Bleachers blasted throughout the whole of the downstairs, I danced in the candlelight without any self-consciousness. I watched everyone's shadows move on the walls, linked fingers with Clara as we scream-sang the lyrics at each other, until, breathless, we broke apart to get more to drink.

As the evening passed into the early hours, the music became more mellow. Some of the guests booked taxis, and left in a rush of hugs and compliments and fervent promises to keep in touch. It didn't matter if they were empty promises; it was the intention that mattered, and this seemed to be something that all of us, as one, understood.

Once they'd left, the remaining guests, eight or nine of us, stretched out on beanbags and the floor. I recognised a Mazzy Star song playing softly over the speakers, and I was dazed with happiness.

'You can stay over if you like,' Clara said. She was lying on her back, staring at the ceiling, and it took me a moment to realise she was speaking to me.

'I didn't bring anything with me,' I said. 'Toiletries and stuff. Otherwise I'd love to.'

'That's okay.' Clara stretched, then rolled over to face me. 'There's, like, ten bathrooms. They've got spares of everything.'

I wanted nothing more in the entire world. But I also didn't want to break the spell that the night had cast over me, the veneer of confidence that was sure to disappear in the dawn light. I didn't want to stumble out of one of Clara's guest bedrooms tired and dull, no longer the girl that she believed I was, the girl that her party had made me: Chloe, the social butterfly.

No. It was better to make my escape before the metaphorical clock of my confidence struck midnight and I transformed back into my insecure self, any semblance of the girl I'd so briefly been faded into nothing.

'Maybe next time,' I said. 'I'm kind of tired.'

'What makes you think you'll be invited back?'

The coolness of Clara's tone surprised me, and I rolled on to my side to look at her. Her lips, stained pomegranate red, quirked to one side. She had a dimple that I hadn't noticed before.

'You won't be able to stop me,' I said. 'I'll sneak in here disguised as a caterer.'

Clara's smile bloomed, and she stretched her arms up above her head. 'I actually think you're my best friend,' she said. 'Did you know that?'

I laughed. 'We've met three times.'

'So what?' Clara said. 'What's the phrase? When you know, you know.'

'I'm pretty sure that only applies to romantic relationships,' I said. 'As in, "How did you know you'd get married one day? How did you know he was your soulmate?"'

'I think friends can be soulmates,' she said. 'What's more romantic than friendship? You haven't made any commitments, but there you are. Together.' She didn't look at me when she added, 'Not many people see me as a person, you know. They don't see past the social-media following. But I think you do.'

'Yeah,' I said. 'Of course I do.'

Clara reached out and squeezed my hand, the same way she had earlier. She didn't say anything. She didn't have to.

Chapter 5

'Tell me *everything*.'

Olivia flopped down in the seat beside me, breathless. Our Monday-morning lecture had officially started five minutes ago but, luckily for her, the lecturer hadn't yet arrived. Dr Brock was widely suspected to be a bit of a fraud; he had no obvious passion for literature, and often wouldn't answer even the most reasonable questions, prompting us to re-read the text instead. So, all things considered, nobody was particularly concerned whether he turned up or not. At this stage of the semester, we'd covered the majority of the material needed for our two exams in January. We were now at the reviewing stage, where we spent the majority of our time outside of lectures poring over notes, writing them up semi-legibly and memorising as many quotes and contextual references as possible.

I remained nonchalant. 'What do you mean?'

'You know exactly what I mean,' Olivia said. 'Clara's *party*.'

'What if I didn't go?'

Olivia scoffed. She set her phone on the table between us. It was open on Clara's Instagram page. She tapped on to one of the posts – Clara, eyes sparkling, posing in front of a wall of roses with a flute of champagne – and then pinched the screen to zoom in on it. And, in the background, there I was: a glass in my own hand, looking at something off-screen and smiling fit to burst.

'So that's not you?' she said.

I laughed. 'Okay, okay. *Obviously* I went. It was amazing.'

Olivia nudged me. 'Amazing *how*? Come on, I need *details*.'

I glanced towards the front of the lecture hall. There was still no sign of Dr Brock.

I described Clara's enormous house in the same awed way that the tabloids would later, painting a picture of the long, gravel driveway lined with trees, the elegant sitting room with its luxurious cream furnishings and the tropical night-time air of the orangery. I described the party décor and the bustling kitchen, the charcuterie platters and the endless glasses of champagne served on silver trays. And then I described the guests: the athletes, the artists, the activists, the actors.

Olivia had seemed impressed throughout, but now she gaped. 'You're kidding,' she said. 'Ayanna *Lynch*? Did you talk to her?'

I nodded emphatically. 'We had a full conversation about *All My Stars*,' I said. 'She's in the adaptation.'

Olivia clamped both hands over her mouth. 'No way.'

It was at this moment that Dr Brock deigned to arrive, more than fifteen minutes late. 'Sorry, everyone,' he said, although his tone sounded anything but. 'Let's get back to reviewing the Gothic, shall we?'

The lecture hall quietened as all of us shifted our attention to the front of the room where Dr Brock was setting up. I opened my notebook and flipped to the page where I'd summarised our Gothic set texts, noted down the key themes and talking points. I tried to focus on the discussion, the group analysis of the environment in *Rebecca* versus *Jane Eyre*, but adrenalin was thrumming in my veins. For once, I didn't want to lose myself in the novels; finally, my real life was beginning to match the fantastical stories that I dreamed about.

I hadn't encountered my flatmates since the party. I'd arrived home by taxi at four o'clock in the morning and had expected them to still be awake and in the kitchen, ready to either pointedly ignore me or pepper me with vaguely resentful questions – *Chloe*? With a *social life*? – but there was no one in the kitchen and their lights were off.

I returned home after my lecture to find the three of them sitting on the high stools at the kitchen breakfast bar, each nursing a hot drink.

Vanessa spun on her chair. 'Chloe!' she said warmly. 'Hey.'

'Hi,' I said. I knew my voice betrayed my wariness. Was this a trap?

'Come sit,' Vanessa continued.

I stayed standing.

'We heard you went out the other night,' Skye said. 'Did you have fun?'

'It was good,' I said.

47

There was a silence.

'Do you think you could get us an invitation?' Amelia asked.

The other two girls groaned.

'Amelia!' Vanessa said. 'You're such an idiot.'

Amelia looked confused. 'Sorry?'

It dawned on me what was happening. 'You want me to get you invitations to one of Clara's parties,' I said. It wasn't a question.

Vanessa was cringing. 'If it's not too much trouble,' she said. 'We saw you on her Instagram, see? You were gorgeous, obviously, and the party looked . . . well, it just looked incredible.'

'Out of this world,' Skye agreed.

'We'd love to go,' Amelia echoed.

I had two choices here: the high road, where I gently dissuaded them, or the low road, where I called them out for excluding me until they wanted to benefit from my connections, then took their mugs of tea and tipped them over their heads.

I took the high road, but just barely.

'They're not really open parties,' I said, despite not knowing if this was entirely true. 'Everyone who attends is personally invited by Clara, so it isn't really my place to invite you.'

Vanessa nodded, slowly. 'That makes sense.'

Skye, though, wasn't so easily dissuaded. 'Are you sure?' she asked. 'You could ask her, right?'

'I could,' I allowed. Silently, I added, *But I'm not going to.*

To her credit, Vanessa looked embarrassed. 'It's okay,' she said, casting a warning look at the other girls. 'We just thought we'd ask.'

At that moment, my phone began to vibrate in my pocket. I glanced at the caller ID and held back a smile as I lifted it to my ear.

'Hey, Clara.'

'Hey, girl.' Clara was bright and cheerful on the other end. 'Are you up to much?'

I turned away from my flatmates. 'No, I'm not doing anything. Why?'

'Do you want to come over? I've never been so bored in my *life*.'

'I'd love to,' I said.

'Great! I'll come and pick you up. Ivy House, right?'

'That's the one.'

'Cool! See you in a few.'

I hung up. I couldn't keep the satisfaction out of my tone as I said, 'So . . . I've got plans. Can we talk about this later?' I didn't wait for an answer.

I left the girls sitting in the kitchen in silence. It felt like a victory.

Back in the relative safety of my own room, I allowed myself to briefly worry over any potential backlash. But then, I thought, what more could they do to me? I'd already been excluded from every activity, even from most conversations. They could hardly exile me even further. *And*, a tiny voice in the back of my mind said, *you wouldn't even mind if they did, as long as you still had Olivia and Clara.*

I dug out my overnight bag from the bottom of the

wardrobe and hastily packed my essentials, including a couple of vaguely Clara-like outfits. This time, if Clara asked if I'd like to stay over, I'd be prepared.

I couldn't hear anything from the kitchen as I left. I tried not to enjoy just how good it felt.

Chapter 6

By the time I'd made my way to the narrow road at the far side of Ivy House, Clara had arrived. I could see her scrolling on her phone with one hand as she waited, the other on her Mini Cooper's white leather wheel.

She glanced up when I opened the door. 'I know I'm early. I was already on my way.'

'I'm glad,' I said as I squeezed into the passenger seat, tucking my bag under my feet.

It was a bright autumn day, the sun a pale slice of lemon. Clara opened the car windows and let in a burst of searing cold air. It felt like sinking my face into iced water. With her hair blowing in the breeze, her dark sunglasses and tiny gold hoop earrings teamed with an oatmeal turtleneck jumper, Clara looked every bit the icon that she was.

As we left Havington behind, I recounted my interaction with my flatmates. I gave her the background, the way that Vanessa had immediately decided I wasn't worth her time, the way that, as a group, they'd excluded me from the very first day. I was slightly self-conscious, but I needn't have worried. At first, Clara was shocked. And then, when I told her what they'd asked me, she spluttered with scandalised laughter.

'*Bitches,*' she gasped. 'They wanted an invitation to my party that much?'

'Apparently,' I said. 'Enough to actually speak to me.'

Clara gave me a sideways look as she manoeuvred us along the twisting country roads. 'They don't deserve you,' she said. 'Shall we invite them to a party, and make it the worst one they've ever been to?'

My heart fluttered, both at the compliment, and at the way she'd said *we*, as if we were a team.

'Nah,' I said. 'Honestly, I don't think they're worth the effort.'

Clara switched on the radio, and a country singer's voice crackled to life, the twangs of his guitar marred by static. It sounded alien in the landscape of British greenery that surrounded us, but I found myself warming to the mournful timbre of the man's voice all the same.

At the house, Clara parked her Mini beside the fountain. In daylight, I could see that, even though it wasn't running, there was still water in the bottom. It was mottled with moss and algae, tiny insects flitting around in their underwater world, unbothered by the pale oval of my face peering down at them in the murk.

Clara didn't bother to lock the car doors before we went inside, a statement of carelessness that strangely impressed me, then tossed her keys on the table in the hallway.

I realised that now I was going to see the house in its natural form, unadorned with all the decorations of one of Clara's parties. But, really, it wasn't much different. The hanging roses were gone, and the cushions and beanbags were back in their rightful places on the sofas and at the edges of the sitting room. It was still beautiful, if neither cosy nor immaculate. The chessboard tiled floor in the entryway was marred with dirt, the kitchen countertops dusted with crumbs and smears of greasy butter. Even the sink was piled high with plates.

I tried not to stare as Clara disappeared through a frosted glass door marked *Pantry*, and returned with a tall glass bottle of chilled orange juice.

'Oh,' she said, waving a hand at the mess. 'Ignore all that. Our housekeeper quit. No doubt there'll be a new one next week.'

'They quit?' I asked. 'What happened?'

'Party clean-up.' Clara rolled her eyes. 'I told her I'd just hire an outside cleaning company to do it, but she insisted. And then she was all *your parents are my employers, not you* and pretty much just stormed out. Isn't that the worst?'

'The worst,' I echoed.

I took the glass of orange juice that Clara proffered. It was tangy and sweet, and tasted of summer. 'Where are your parents?' I asked.

'At their other house, mostly,' Clara replied coolly. 'Their main one, in London. But if they're not there they're out of the country – either for work, or just on holiday.' She paused. 'Let's go through to the orangery.'

I nodded an agreement that she hadn't really waited for, and followed her through the glass doors I remembered from the party. The orangery was even more wonderful in daylight, a true Victorian-style winter garden with a tangle of vines stretching across the ceiling, umbrella-like trees in enormous clay pots and deep green cacti that were taller than me, stretching their thick, spiked limbs towards the glass roof above. It was filled with the aroma of sun-baked soil and citrus, which I inhaled gladly. Clara sat on the wicker couch, and I perched on the armchair across from it. A loose straw dug into my back.

'Where do they go on holiday?' I asked. 'Your parents, I mean.'

'Where *don't* they go on holiday would be more of a question,' Clara said. 'I used to go with them, but it got quite boring. It was all places like Marbella, the Maldives, Dubai, Bali, over and over again. And like, *constant* seafood. God, I hate seafood.'

Jealousy bubbled up in my chest, viscous and thick. I'd only been abroad once, and it was to see my grandparents after they'd emigrated to Spain when I was six. I couldn't even begin to imagine travelling so much that I got bored with it.

Nevertheless, I sympathised. 'I don't like seafood either,' I admitted. 'My limit's pretty much fish fingers and battered cod from the chip shop.'

Clara looked at me as if I was speaking another language. 'I was thinking like . . . oysters,' she said. 'Paella.'

I refused to let myself be cowed. 'You haven't lived until you've had a fish-finger sandwich. Trust me.'

And then, unexpectedly, Clara began to laugh. She set her orange juice on the glass table beside her and just laughed, her eyes glistening with tears. Somehow, her laughter set me off and I started to laugh too. I couldn't stop even if I'd wanted to; it was as if all the anxiety, all the alienation that I'd been feeling since I'd started at Dern was sputtering out of me in peals of laughter and tears, to the point where I was doubled over, holding my stomach.

'Chloe,' Clara said once she'd calmed down, wiping her eyes carefully so as not to ruin her eye make-up, 'you are something else.'

It didn't feel like an insult. It felt like a compliment.

We spent the rest of the afternoon in the orangery, my studies far from my mind. We lounged on the wicker seats and flipped through old *Vogue* and *House Beautiful* magazines, all the while feasting on a box of cherry-liqueur chocolates that Clara had dug out and which filled my mouth with tart flavour when I bit down on them.

When the light started to fade, Clara offset the lengthening shadows by flicking on a tall, curved brass lamp. I knew it was time to offer to leave.

'I really should get going,' I said. 'Thank you so much for inviting me over again, though. You have a very beautiful home.'

My mum had taught me to always say thank you after being

invited somewhere, and to always compliment someone's home upon leaving. But for the first time it didn't feel false; I genuinely meant every word. I would have quite happily stayed in Clara's home forever, given the chance. I thought longingly of my overnight bag. I'd abandoned it in the hallway, overlooked by the vaguely sinister portraits.

'I'll go and ring a taxi for you,' Clara said. 'I'd drop you off, but I'm a bit tired. And I think I've had too many of those chocolates.'

Once she'd disappeared through the orangery doors, I leaned back in the armchair and gazed out at the garden, the sun setting hazily over the rolling hills in the distance. Outside there was a bit of a patio – great, grey flagstones with a rusty white bistro set perched unsteadily at the edge of the steps that led down to the lawn. The lawn was enormous, really more of a meadow of coarse overgrown grass, knee-length at least, which sloped gently downhill to what looked like a dense band of woodland at the far end. Strangely unkempt, I thought. Surely they would have hired a gardener as well as a housekeeper? Or had they quit too?

'The taxi'll be here in about twenty minutes,' Clara said when she returned a moment later. 'It's paid for. Obviously. I'm going to go up and run a bath if that's okay. Help yourself to another drink or whatever while you wait.'

Her tone surprised me. It was cooler than it had been all afternoon, and there was a thin layer of ice to it. *Proceed with caution*, it said. *You don't want this to crack.*

'Thank you so much,' I said carefully. 'I'll pay you back.'

'It's fine,' she said. 'We should do this again. I'll text you before the weekend, okay?'

'That'd be great. I've loved today.'

Clara smiled, but it was distant, her eyes clouded and faraway. 'Me too,' she said. 'See you soon.'

She went back into the kitchen.

I was confused by Clara's personality change, and also somewhat taken aback that she was just going to leave me alone. For a start, it didn't seem like good manners – and hers were usually impeccable. Then there was the fact that I was completely unobserved, and she lived in a house with well over a dozen rooms. I could steal her antiques, slash her cushions and scatter feathers across the floor, set her candles alight and leave the sitting room in flames. I could smash every plate in the kitchen, every window in the orangery, glass and porcelain falling at my feet like so much blossom. Clara wouldn't even know what had happened until she returned downstairs from her bath, perhaps in her pyjamas, her hair wrapped neatly in a fresh white towel, and stepped on a shard. I could see it before my eyes: the way she lifted her bare foot, inspected it, plucked out the glass. The droplets of blood spattering on the tile, becoming a stream that seeped across the chessboard floor, sticking to the specks of dust.

And then I shook my head to clear it, disturbed by my own imagination. I'd never hurt Clara, nor would I ever want her to *be* hurt. But there was something horribly satisfying about the thought of causing such destruction, of knowing that I could ruin Clara's house and our friendship in one fell swoop, in one moment of madness. It was like the intrusive thoughts I always experienced when I was in a high place, walking over a bridge or along a pier. *You could jump*, they would say. *You could hop over that railing right now.* And, yes, I *could*. But of course I wouldn't. It was an exercise in preparation, in assessing danger; that was all.

Despite this, I was slightly unnerved by my uncharacteristically violent thoughts, and decided to go and hover in the entrance hall. I lingered beside the coat rack until I heard the crunch of tyres on the driveway outside, the sound as the taxi slowed and rounded the fountain. I heard Clara's footsteps padding across the landing, the faint running of the taps.

'Bye,' I mouthed to the empty hallway, and let the door behind me fall shut with a thud.

Chapter 7

The following week, Clara was back to her usual sparkling self.

We met for coffee twice, Clara fielding the stares and the whispers around us with little more than a good-natured eye-roll. It was strange how quickly I grew used to it, pretending that I couldn't see the subtle nudges, the tilts of the head, the occasional phone camera pointed in our direction.

It did lead me to a sudden realisation, though, which was this: although I'd first been introduced to Clara as an influencer, courtesy of Olivia, I'd never actually looked her up online. Of course, I'd seen the pictures that Olivia had shown me, the ones with me in the background, but I hadn't visited any of her profiles myself. It was a clear oversight on my part, to not internet-stalk my internet-famous friend.

Perhaps, though, that was why. I'd really started to consider her my friend, albeit a somewhat changeable one, a friend who was miles out of my league. The idea of other people knowing about Clara without actually having met her struck me as absurd.

So I decided to do it. I was waiting for Clara at the campus coffee shop the Friday after our afternoon together at Deneside Manor. I'd intended to use the time to try to coax out the threads of a book idea that I'd had, to try to weave them into something with an actual form, but I was struggling. In need of procrastination, I reached for my phone. Clara would be here, with me, in less than an hour. Really, there was no better time to become familiar with her online presence. I wanted to know the girl that the people around me knew.

I found her right away, and, although I'd expected her to have a relatively large following, the actual numbers dumbfounded me.

Posts: 1,228

Followers: 684K

Following: 1,341

Clara Holland, said her profile in bold lettering. *Entrepreneur. Model. Influential speaker.*

Entrepreneur? Of what, exactly? I wondered. Spontaneous entrepreneurship seemed to be a common trait of the wealthy, attractive and well connected. After all, any business that they set up didn't actually have to succeed. I imagined that, in Clara's world, it was a coating of prestige to be able to declare yourself 'an entrepreneur' – even if the only brand you'd created was your own. And, I had to admit, Clara was very good at that.

She had multiple different highlights at the top of her feed, each one signposted with its own unique combination of emoticons. *Outfits. Maldives. Girls. Monaco.*

I tapped on *Girls*. It was in this highlight that I appeared;

there were more than a hundred different images in it, photo after photo taken at parties, sometimes with a Polaroid camera, the edges blurred and soft, captions scribbled on in permanent marker; more often not. They showed scenes exactly like the ones I'd encountered at her party, but styled for every season: girls in dresses and strappy heels, dusted with glitter; girls in bikinis, lounging in the orangery holding pink and lilac cocktails, each one dotted with sprigs of wildflowers and herbs; girls dancing in the moonlight in the garden, their heads thrown back in ecstasy.

I tapped back, and then scrolled further down her feed. Clara's face gazed out at me from the square icons, dozens and dozens of them, every image impossibly perfect in its execution. Clara posing in a white swimsuit, her slim, tanned figure reclining on the grass beside an azure pool, a vineyard stretching into the distance behind her. Clara, glowing at sunset, holding a glass of red wine, a heart-shaped locket perfectly placed just below the hollow of her throat. Clara reflected in the mirror of a magnificent ornate bathroom in a white towelling robe, her skin free from make-up and blemishes, pouting. Even in her robe, her hair wet, she exuded a magnetism.

It was odd, I thought, how none of these strangers, almost seven hundred thousand of them, knew who Clara was outside of this carefully curated version of herself. They didn't know what she looked like walking across campus, a breeze blowing strands of hair across her face like threads of gold, or what she looked like when she ordered her coffee, her warm, practised smile. They probably didn't even know how she liked her coffee: a grande iced vanilla latte, even when it was snowing.

But, then again, what did it matter? Weren't we all just presenting a version of ourselves to the world?

As I refreshed the app, Clara uploaded a new picture. She was in what looked like the orangery, luscious greenery behind her, wearing a satin pyjama top edged with lace. Bare-faced and serious, yet effortlessly stunning. The caption read: *When you're out of champagne and strawberries on a Friday* and was accompanied by a little broken-heart emoticon.

As I watched, the comments rolled in, one after the other.

You're so beautiful!

I wish I was you.

Love, love, love!

Gorgeous girl xo

There were hundreds of them, all loaded with compliments and praise. I couldn't even imagine what it must be like to be so universally adored.

And yet it was me who Clara had added to her guest list, me who Clara had invited to spend the afternoon with her, me who she met for coffee.

Out of the nearly seven hundred thousand people who hung on her every word, Clara had, apparently, chosen to befriend me – a stranger who'd come across her scarf in the library, who she'd spoken to once.

Why? What was so special about me?

* * *

When Clara arrived, strolling in with cheeks pink from the cold and trailing an Acne Studios wollen scarf behind her, she had one thing on her mind.

'We need to plan our New Year's Eve party,' she said. 'Do you have any ideas for a theme?'

'That's lovely,' I said. Then, 'Hold on. *Our?*'

'Obviously,' Clara said. 'You're one of us now.'

She sipped her iced vanilla latte nonchalantly, as if she hadn't just dropped an arguably life-changing bombshell. 'Anyway, I always feature some floral elements – you'll learn that soon enough. It's more of a challenge during winter, though. We just need . . . I don't know. It has to be something really special.'

I didn't have much practice when it came to organising events, with florals and aesthetics, but coming up with ideas? That I thrived on. In fact, I spent more time adding to my list of potential book ideas than I did actually working on any individual project. And then a theme flashed in my mind.

'What about *The Nutcracker*?'

'The what?'

'*The Nutcracker*,' I repeated. 'The ballet? The main character is called Clara, after all.'

I'd wanted to write a retelling of *The Nutcracker* for a while, something that took the ballet's reflection on the end of girlhood, of the transition to womanhood, and twisted it into something new.

Clara stared at me, excitement spreading across her face

63

like the light of dawn, her eyes gleaming. 'Yes,' she said. '*Yes.*
Go on.'

'Picture . . .' I scrambled, desperate to impress. 'Exquisite
dresses made from silk and satin, thick faux-fur stoles, ballet
slippers.' I glanced up; Clara was listening, spellbound, her lips
slightly parted. I *had* her. 'White candles, themed cocktails
with silver stirrers and dry ice. Snow, glitter. Decadence.'

'Decadence,' she repeated in a whisper. I wasn't sure if I was
supposed to hear. 'I love it.'

My smile in response was part joy, part relief. 'Really?'

'Really,' she said. 'It's decided. Our theme this year's going to
be *The Nutcracker*. There'll be ballerinas, glamour and spectacle.
And, of course, just a little bit of *me*.'

'Perfect,' I said. 'It wouldn't be a party without plenty of
Clara.'

'Here's to that,' Clara said. She picked up her coffee, and I
picked up my own. We clinked them together. 'Okay,' she said.
'Let's plan.'

Chapter 8

Autumn faded into winter, which brought with it a flurry of snow and a mass of deadlines. The increase in my workload meant spending less time with Clara in her beautiful mansion. I would've been lonely if not for Olivia, whose company I was grateful for. It became our habit to sit together in lectures, and then hole up in the coffee shop or the library afterwards. Sometimes, we discussed our dreams: mine, to be a writer. Olivia's, to be a respected editor at a big publishing house. But, more often than not, during the long hours of studying, our communication was silent. Our affection for each other was shown through the companionable sliding of a book across the desk, a coffee set down next to a laptop. We took it in turns to buy lattes and snacks, to read over each other's essays and suggest improvements, both of us determined to succeed together. I wondered whether Clara was studying as hard for her Journalism exams, but I thought I knew the answer to that.

In the flat, the single radiator in my room was placed unhelpfully beneath the draughty window. When it did rattle and cough out soupy heat, it was only for minutes at a time and usually only after a carefully angled kick. I filed a repair ticket with the accommodation office, but when the maintenance person arrived, he didn't even bother to take out his tools. 'It's these old buildings,' he said, with a sympathetic shake of his head. 'They need a whole new heating system, really. If I were you, I'd buy one of those portable heaters. It's the only way you're going to keep this place warm.'

I thanked him, feeling somewhat defeated, but searched for fan heaters online all the same. I selected the cheapest option: a squat, heavy thing made from grey-white plastic. I set it on my desk, facing the bed, and irresponsibly left it on for as long as I could when I was in my room. I'd curl up with my laptop under my duvet and layers of blankets, luxuriating in the bearable temperature, until the element in the electric fire overheated and it automatically shut off.

Sometimes, I pretended that I was a writer in a cheaply rented garret somewhere exciting, like Paris or Rome, the dismal conditions serving to inspire my muse. Unfortunately, nothing that I wrote was particularly artistic. I started a half dozen short stories and a couple of novels, but the characters I created refused to take any action after the first chapter or so. It was as if they, too, were frozen.

I found the whole process frustrating. I couldn't sing or dance, I wasn't a musician or a painter, but I'd always been able to lose myself in literature. The only way that I would ever be able to make a mark on the world was with my words, and they were, for reasons I couldn't really understand, completely stoppered. All I could do was hope that I found some real inspiration – and soon.

The days passed like this, with me darting to lectures and to the library and back to Ivy House to write, to seminars and to have coffee with Olivia, all the while fielding calls from Clara about preparations for the *Nutcracker*-themed New Year's Eve party that was, now, only a couple of weeks away. My attention was being pulled this way and that as I bounced from one obligation to another like the ball in a pinball machine, and I was exhausted, but deliciously so; I'd never had such a packed schedule, such a full social life. My mind was whirring, focusing on the lecture or seminar I was attending or the essay or story that I was writing or the friend with whom I was spending time, so much so that it drowned out the stream of anxious thoughts that left me with a near-constant sense of uneasiness.

I boarded the train home on the twentieth of December with all the air of a victor, believing that, after only a brief time, I'd conquered the dual battles of university and of having a social life and come out on top. I was self-satisfied and light, keen to spend at least a week surrounded by home comforts.

Mum met me at the ticket barriers, enveloping me in a hug that smelled of cold air and fabric softener. 'I've missed you so much,' she said, her breath warm on my neck.

I hugged her back, surprised at how small she felt in my arms. Had I always been so much taller than her? I'd never noticed.

'I've missed you too,' I said.

She held me at arm's length, looking me up and down. 'You look tired,' she said.

'I have been sitting on a train for three hours,' I pointed out.

'You're right, you're right,' she said. 'Sorry, love. I know I shouldn't worry. But you're my girl.'

She flicked the heater on as we got in the car. I couldn't help but compare our battered Ford Focus to Clara's Mini Cooper with its pristine interior. But that was Clara's, and this was mine. My parents had worked for this, while Clara's had been a gift. They weren't comparable.

As Mum drove us home, happily filling me in on all the latest gossip and the plans for Christmas Day, I gazed out of the window. It had been raining, and the streets glistened, tyres splashing on the road and puddles reflecting the brightly coloured lights. Christmas trees lit up every window in our cul-de-sac. My parents still lived in the 1930s semi-detached house of my childhood, with its neat redbrick facade and pocket-sized front garden. It was nothing special – the majority of my schoolmates had lived in houses more or less identical to this one when we were growing up – but it was home. Just the sight of the porch, adorned with a fresh coat of white paint by my dad every year, was enough to make my heart leap in my chest.

Dad was in the kitchen when we went in, clad in his striped apron and listening to Radio 4.

'It smells good in here,' I said, and he spun round, his lined face transforming quickly from confusion to delight.

'My love! I didn't even hear you come in. Where's your mum?'

'I think she's just nipped upstairs.'

I dropped my bags at my feet as Dad gave me a tight hug, my head pressed against his chest. Then he stepped back. 'Right, then,' he said. 'Out, out! Go and find your mum.'

I rolled my eyes at him. 'I love you too!'

'You'll ruin the surprise,' he said, gesturing towards the arrangement of pans on the hob. 'Go on. I'll see you in a bit.'

'Okay, Dad,' I said. I kissed him on the cheek, and then left the kitchen.

Later that evening, after we'd all eaten the special steak pie Dad had made to celebrate my first evening home, I said goodnight to him – a delivery driver, he had long shifts in the run-up to Christmas and so liked to get an early night – and snuggled up on the sofa with Mum. We sat beside each other, our legs tucked up, holding mugs of strong tea in our laps. The wood burner was lit, and the kitchen door was closed to keep in the heat. An old soap rerun played on the TV, muted.

'I've missed this,' Mum said.

'Me too,' I said.

Mum took one hand away from her mug, and rested it on my knee. 'I know you didn't get off to the best start,' she said. 'I'm so proud of how you've been handling it all. If I were you, I would've been back here within a week.'

I covered her hand with my own. 'I doubt it,' I said. 'You're the most resilient woman I've ever met.'

It was true. Mum had never been able to go to university. Like most of the other women her age in our town, she'd left school at sixteen and got a production-line job at a factory on the outskirts. However, determined to do more, she'd signed up for night classes in typing, then taken on a full-time role as a legal secretary. At times, she'd told me once, she'd been working sixteen-hour days. She was still working now, in her late fifties, at a solicitor's office in town.

I'd always looked up to her, admired her work ethic and her determination to do what she needed to do to succeed. But, at the same time, I also felt a certain level of pressure to make her proud of me, to take advantage of the opportunities that she'd never been given.

'How's your course going?' she asked me now.

'Good, I think,' I said. 'We haven't had feedback for our last assignment yet, but I'm feeling confident. And I'm enjoying it.'

'That's good,' Mum said. She sipped her tea. 'And how's that book of yours coming along?'

'I haven't really had much time to work on it these past couple of months,' I admitted. 'I've got a sentence down here and there, but aside from that . . .'

I didn't want to tell Mum the truth, which was that I'd scrapped that book, and the one that I'd started after that. Even the projects I'd been working on for the creative writing aspect of my course were bland and uninspiring, desperately missing the shine that they needed. I felt like a failure: a writer who couldn't write. I'd kept trying, but eventually it had been easier to let it go, to try to ignore the sting of defeat, and let myself get lost in essays and seminars – and, of course, Clara's world – instead.

Mum squeezed my hand. 'Don't beat yourself up, love. University's hard work. Just don't forget you're there to have fun too.'

I smiled gratefully, but my stomach churned. Mum loved that I wanted to be an author, dreamed of seeing a book I'd written on the shelves one day. How could I tell her that my well of creativity, once so full, had run completely dry?

'Anyway,' Mum said, as if she could read my mind and knew that I wanted to change the subject, 'speaking of fun, tell me about this friend of yours.'

'Olivia?' I bluffed. 'She's super clever, witty – I think you'd like her. She's from Bishop.'

Mum eyed me. 'You know she's not who I meant,' she said.

'You want to know about Clara.'

'Obviously.'

'Well . . . she's Clara,' I said. 'She's really lovely. Very wealthy, very pretty. Kind of famous.'

'And you get on with her?'

'Yeah, I do,' I said. 'I've been to her house a couple of times – it's this gorgeous country mansion – and I've been to one of her parties.' I was warming to my theme, unable to stop myself from getting excited. I'd told Mum about all this briefly, over the phone, but it wasn't the same as being able to describe Clara in person. 'She has these exclusive parties, guest-list only. And she invited me to one.'

'How did you become friends?' Mum asked.

'I found her scarf in the library,' I said. 'Remember? It had her initials monogrammed on to it. Well, *our* initials, actually. They're the same. She's C A H too! Anyway, I saw her a few weeks later when I was getting a coffee, and she sat with me for a bit. Then she just slid this invitation across the table. It was like something out of a spy film. Can you believe that?'

'It's amazing,' Mum said. 'Really.'

There was something in her tone that I was unsure about. 'Mum?' I pressed. 'What are you thinking?'

Mum sighed. 'She isn't using you or anything, is she? I know you didn't really mesh with your flatmates on that first day, and they seemed quite like . . . that too.' I could see her searching for an apt description. 'A bit posh?'

'Clara's different,' I said. 'And, anyway, they're not even posh. They're just snobby.'

'And Clara's not?'

I shook my head. 'Not even slightly. She's just like me or you. Except, you know, more . . . extravagant.'

'Extravagant,' Mum repeated. 'I'd like to be extravagant.'

'You're sorting the work Christmas party this year, aren't you?' I asked, teasing. 'When is it?'

'Friday.'

'Then that's the perfect occasion!' I said. 'Go all out!'

'I'm not sure what Ms Jacobson would think if I turned up in a sparkling ballgown,' Mum said. When I stared at her, she added, 'Oh, I saw the pictures of that last party you went to on Instagram. You looked beautiful.'

'First of all, *stalker*,' I said. 'Secondly – I *wish*.'

'You did!' Mum said. 'I loved how you had your hair.'

'Thank you,' I allowed. 'But I'm really not on Clara's level.'

'You're not on Clara's level because you're already on Chloe's level. And that's the best level, as far as I'm concerned.'

She patted my leg, then reached over and picked up the remote, flicking the volume back up. *Miracle on 34ᵗʰ Street* was starting, one of our favourite Christmas films.

'Love you, Mum,' I said, filled with gratitude.

'Love you too, Chloe,' she replied, flashing me a quick, warm smile.

We both turned our attention to the TV, waiting for Mara Wilson to appear.

Christmas Day came round quickly.

We all rose early, hugging and wishing each other a merry Christmas before we convened in the living room to open our gifts. I hadn't bought my parents anything too big or expensive – I'd had to lug their presents home on the train, after all – but our family were big believers in *it's the thought that counts*, so I hoped they'd be happy. For Mum, I'd tracked down a signed copy of one of her most beloved books online, and wrapped it up with a tube of her favourite hand cream. For

Dad, I'd bought a pair of stainless-steel cufflinks engraved with his initials and a soft tartan pyjama set.

And then it was my turn. I opened each lovingly wrapped present carefully, pulling back the snowflake-patterned paper to reveal a selection of perfect gifts: a gold locket, a shimmery lipstick, two paperback novels and a new thick-knit pink jumper.

I thanked them both profusely, we hugged again and Dad announced he was going to start preparing Christmas dinner. The turkey had been in overnight, but the trimmings still needed to be peeled and chopped and cooked. I offered to help, but was unceremoniously exiled from the kitchen (I had a feeling it was because of the year I ruined the Yorkshire puddings; no one could hold a grudge like my dad), and so I retreated to my bedroom to get ready.

With a soundtrack of Christmas songs playing faintly on the radio downstairs, I styled my hair and then slipped on a pair of jeans and my new jumper. It was as soft as lamb's wool, with wide, flattering sleeves that fell over my wrists. I smiled at myself in the mirror as I applied my new lipstick and then fixed my locket carefully round my neck. It reminded me of Clara's locket, the one of which she'd posted pictures on her Instagram. I wondered if she'd notice it when I next saw her.

We devoured Christmas dinner. The centrepiece, of course, was the enormous turkey, served with crispy roasties, fluffy mashed potatoes, golden-brown Yorkshire puddings, pigs in blankets and a rainbow of vegetables drizzled with olive oil.

After Mum and I had washed up, the three of us settled down to watch yet another festive film. We still had pudding to go, but wisely agreed to let our full stomachs rest before we attempted it.

Content and sleepy, I pulled out my phone and scrolled lazily through the dozens of new posts on my Instagram feed: a kaleidoscope of Christmas dinners, children playing with new toys and couples posing in their matching-slogan jumpers.

And then, just as I was about to close the app, a notification appeared at the top of my screen. It was a message, and it was from Clara.

Hey, girl! Merry Christmas. I hope you're having fun.

It's been nice, I replied. *Thanks! How's your Christmas Day going? x*

My parents are in Barbados, she typed back. *So it hasn't been anything special.*

I glanced at my own parents. Mum, on the sofa beside me, curled up with her feet in her festive socks, squinting at a new crossword book. Dad, fast asleep in his favourite armchair, slippers propped on the pouffe. I couldn't imagine either of them flying off to Barbados for Christmas and leaving me at home alone.

As I wondered what to type back, my fingertips moving absently from letter to letter as I tried to come up with something that was sympathetic but not patronising, a new post from Clara appeared on my feed. Four pictures in a carousel format, one after the other.

In the first, Clara was posing in a red velvet dress, her hair smooth and sleek and tied back with a matching velvet ribbon. Glistening red lipstick outlined her perfect smile. The second photo showed a Cartier gift bag, with the third revealing what had presumably been inside it: a diamond-encrusted bracelet, carefully fastened round Clara's slim wrist.

The caption read: *Opening the door to a courier with Cartier. Can Christmas get any better? #LuckyGirl #MerryChristmas x*

A quick Google search revealed that the bracelet in question retailed for just under a staggering ten thousand pounds. I wondered if Clara's parents often bought her such expensive gifts, or if this particular treat was an apology for spending Christmas so far away. A figure like that, I supposed, was nothing to people who holidayed so often that they barely saw their daughter.

I swiped across to look at the final photo she'd uploaded, which was of her dining room. As it was during her parties, it was elaborately decorated, festooned with twinkling lights and red ribbons, white candles glowing alongside sprigs of holly on the mantelpiece. But the real focus of the image was the table.

Positioned in the centre of the dining room, it was filled with every variety of Christmas food that I could imagine. Plates of turkey, beef, chicken, pork and duck battled for space alongside bowls of stuffing, silver platters of pigs in blankets, great tureens of buttered vegetables, roasted potatoes and parsnips, a gathering of different condiments and sauces – including an enormous jug of gravy – and a huge dish of at least twenty Yorkshire puddings. I zoomed in to count them. Twenty indeed.

The sight of such a veritable mountain of food after I'd eaten my own Christmas feast nearly made me groan. Plus, I couldn't help but wonder who it was all for. After all, we'd already established that Clara's parents were in Barbados – and surely most, if not all, of her friends were spending Christmas with their own families?

She messaged me again a minute later.

Sorry to be so gloomy! Missing our talks. x

The contrast between her messages and the pictures that she'd shared was stark and, frankly, a bit upsetting. Clearly, having a luxurious Christmas that anyone would envy was part of her brand – when, in reality, she was alone, surrounded by more food than she could possibly eat. I mentally filed away a lecture on food waste for later, and typed a reply.

Don't be. I miss you too. x

Not long till it's New Year's Eve, Clara sent back. *And we can go wild. x*

Chapter 9

I arrived back at Dern late in the afternoon on the last day of the year.

The sun had already set when I reached the university campus, moonlight washing over a faint scattering of snow that had fallen while I'd been gone. Havington itself had been quiet, but the campus was even more so – almost to the point of eerie. Most students would still be back in their hometowns, I imagined, before rushing back in the first week of January, refreshed and ready for their exams.

I dragged my bags past the familiar buildings, dark and mysterious with nobody inside them, my locket bumping reassuringly against my chest beneath my collar. When I unlocked the door to my flat at Ivy House, I was surprised to see that the lights were on. I knew I hadn't left them on when I'd gone home – and I'd been the last to leave.

I left my suitcase in front of the door to my room, and crept along the hallway. I was imagining scattered cutlery drawers and smashed plates, the carnage left by a burglar. Instead, when I cautiously opened the kitchen door, I saw Vanessa. She was looking away from me, but I recognised her choppy blonde bob, the pale nape of her neck.

I fully intended to quietly shut the kitchen door, go back to my room and pretend that I hadn't even seen her, but at that moment she turned – and jumped.

'*God*,' she said, a hand to her chest. 'I didn't hear you come in.'

Without her sultry make-up, she looked curiously wide-eyed and innocent, like a little-girl version of herself. It made it difficult to be as spiky with her as I knew she deserved.

'Sorry,' I said. 'I didn't think anyone else would be back yet.'

'Me neither,' she said. 'Did you have a nice Christmas?'

We hadn't spoken since the morning after my first party at Clara's, when she and Skye and Amelia had ambushed me in this very kitchen. 'It was good,' I said. 'Thanks. What about yours?'

She shrugged. I took this to mean that she hadn't had a good Christmas. If she had, I supposed, she probably wouldn't be back here on New Year's Eve, standing in the kitchen alone in her pyjamas and looking positively miserable.

'Where are Skye and Amelia?' I asked.

'Still at home,' she said.

'I think most people are.'

'Yeah.' She sounded tired. She leaned back, her elbows resting on the kitchen counter. 'Why are you back so early?'

'Clara's having a party,' I said.

Vanessa nodded, as if I'd confirmed her suspicions. 'I won't keep you, then,' she said.

'Sure,' I said. 'Sorry I scared you.'

She smiled half-heartedly. 'Oh, don't worry about it,' she said. 'I'll live.'

I was halfway out of the door when I thought I heard her say something else. I stopped, looked back over my shoulder. 'What?'

Her voice was sheepish. 'I said, I'm sorry for being so horrible to you.'

I stepped back into the kitchen. She could barely meet my gaze.

'You were pretty horrible,' I said.

'I know. I shouldn't have been. And I won't be any more.'

I studied her. 'Is that because I'm friends with Clara, or because you actually feel bad about what you said?'

Vanessa visibly cringed. 'Because I actually feel bad.'

'Any reason why?'

She shrugged. 'I suppose I just realised how lonely you must have been here, and how excluded you must have felt. All because of something I said.'

'I did feel excluded,' I said. 'Honestly, if I hadn't made friends elsewhere, I probably would have just dropped out. But that's what you wanted, right? Because northern girls can't be . . . what? Clever?'

'I didn't say that,' Vanessa said, but her cheeks flushed a painful pink.

'You told me that I didn't sound educated,' I said. 'And we'd barely even had a conversation. You judged me by my accent, and my accent alone. You were snobby, and you were elitist.'

'And I was wrong. Clearly.'

'Yes. You were.'

We stood there in silence, just looking at each other. And then, just as I thought she might burst into tears or storm out of the room, I reached my hand out. 'Truce?'

Vanessa looked down at it, then back up at me, a line appearing between her eyebrows. 'What?'

'Truce,' I repeated. 'We don't have to be best friends or anything, but we can live together. Right?'

Vanessa took my hand in her own, and shook it, once. 'Right,' she said.

'Why don't you come? Tonight?'

I'd said the words almost before I'd thought them, and was startled at my boldness. Clearly, Vanessa was too; she stared at me as if I were speaking an alien language. 'What?'

It was a solid olive branch. So I doubled down.

'Come to Clara's party,' I said. 'You're here on your own, so I'm guessing you don't have plans.' Her silence was all the confirmation I needed. 'I'm going over there now to help her decorate, but you could always get a taxi over later on. Give me your number. I'll text you the address.'

'Are you serious?' she asked. It wasn't challenging, or sassy in the way that she'd spoken to me previously. She sounded disbelieving, on the edge of tears.

'Of course I'm serious,' I said. 'Being on your own sucks.'

'Thanks, Chloe,' she said. 'Really.'

'Don't worry about it,' I said. 'I'll see you tonight, okay?'

'Yes,' Vanessa said, her eyes shining with gratitude. 'You will.'

'She said *what*?'

'She apologised,' I said triumphantly. 'She said that she was wrong to have judged me. It came *literally* out of nowhere.'

Once again, I was in the passenger seat of Clara's Mini Cooper as we sped towards Deneside Manor. I'd offered to help her decorate for the party and, while she'd assured me that she'd hired stylists for the occasion, it'd still be fun to spend some time together before the rest of the guests arrived.

She'd looked pale when she'd picked me up outside Ivy House, which I'd attributed to party-planning stress, until she reassured me that she was suffering from the last of a hangover instead. It brought to mind images of Clara rattling around her enormous house for days on end, all alone in the candlelit dark as snow drifted down outside. She must've felt like the world had ended, taking long baths and staring at the uneaten food in the kitchen and drinking champagne until she was sick. And, for the first time since we'd met, I really, truly didn't envy her.

'Next year,' I'd said, consumed with guilt. 'We'll do something.'

'I'd like that,' she'd said. 'Maybe we could go to Milan.'

Now, twenty minutes into the drive, there was no sign that she'd looked anything but perfect, no sign of the drawn, slightly distant Clara who'd managed to tug on my heartstrings. Instead, she seemed completely herself: comfortable in her own skin – and dazzlingly happy on my behalf. 'That's amazing! What did you say to her?'

'I asked her for a truce,' I told her. 'We shook hands and everything.'

Clara laughed, delighted. 'You're so *cute*.'

I knew that she was making fun of me, but something hot and fluttery curled in my gut even so. It felt a little bit like adoration.

I bit my lip, trying to tamp down the feeling. 'I also invited her to your party.'

I'd expected Clara to be furious, to nag me about attendance numbers and exclusivity and table settings, but she didn't even sound surprised. If anything, she sounded impressed. 'Really?' she asked. 'When she was so horrid to you?'

'Yeah,' I said. 'I wanted to make amends. Besides, she looked so lonely I felt awful.'

'Maybe she deserves to feel lonely,' Clara said.

'Maybe,' I said. 'Maybe not. What would you have done?'

'Me?' Clara repeated. 'Whether she apologised or not, I would've ruined her life. Obviously.'

Her tone hadn't changed, still filled with lightness and humour. I side-eyed her. 'You'd never do that,' I said.

'You're right. I wouldn't. I'd make sure she ruined it all by herself.'

The clouds above us, blue-grey and heavy with snow, had parted to unveil thin beams of light, and as Clara grinned at me I noticed that her eyelids were coated with a gold lustre.

'Come *on*, Chloe,' she said, seeing my expression. 'Have you never had a revenge fantasy?'

'I suppose,' I said. 'Maybe when I'm writing. Not so much in real life.'

'There's nothing wrong with it,' Clara said. 'It's *natural*.'

Whether she intended them to be or not, her words were biting, defensive – as if I'd accused her of something and she didn't quite like it.

'Of course,' I said placatingly. 'It's a whole genre of film, right? Girls getting revenge?'

Clara seemed to consider this. I watched the world outside rushing past the car window. When she spoke, the edge in her voice had softened. 'You're so right,' she said. 'Women love a revenge story. Especially if they're getting revenge on a man. Or another woman.'

'So . . . pretty much anyone, then?' I asked, forgetting that I was trying to tread carefully.

But, to my relief, Clara just laughed.

Chapter 10

The dining room table was filled with boxes and bags, their insides spilling out all over the glossy wood.

'I know it looks like a lot,' Clara said, clearly sensing my trepidation, 'but the stylists are coming at three. We're just going to make a start.'

'Thank God,' I said. 'There are, like, fifty boxes here.'

Clara pouted. 'That's an exaggeration,' she said. She reached into the nearest box, and pulled out a bottle of Moët with a pink foil label. She held it up, and wiggled her eyebrows. 'Besides, I'll make it worth your while.'

I sighed. 'Fine,' I said. 'But I'm not being held accountable if my decoration skills aren't up to your standards. *Or* the professional stylists'. Deal?'

She laughed. 'Deal.'

A few hours later, Deneside Manor had been transformed.

The stylists had arrived not long after we'd started, a team of three glamorous older women wearing dazzling jewellery. Clara introduced them to me as Sam, Linda and

Emily, and added that they'd been working together for a long time.

'We've styled many a Clara party,' Emily said with a wink. 'But I hear you came up with the *Nutcracker* theme? Gorgeous idea!'

They surveyed their canvases – the hallway, the living room, the kitchen, the orangery – with an experienced eye, and then determined that they'd each take charge of a room, with Clara and me instructed to decorate the hallway.

'Demoted to my own hallway,' Clara muttered, although good-naturedly, as she pinned white and gold balloons above the door.

'Look at it this way,' I said. 'You want to get your money's worth, right? Besides, the hallway's the part everyone sees first. It's kind of an honour.'

'You're so right,' Clara said. Then, 'Do you want some more champagne?'

I glanced up at her from where I was busy wrapping a string of lights round the banister. 'We've already drunk one bottle,' I said. 'Is that really a good idea?'

Clara's answering smile was crafty. It said, *No, it isn't. But who cares?*

'Okay,' I said, pushing the doubt from my mind. 'Why not?'

Now, two empty bottles of Moët stood on the kitchen counter, rings of moisture at their base. Together, we moved from room to room, clutching each other in our excitement.

Emily had used the marble kitchen island to set up an Art Deco-style bar. It held dozens more bottles of Moët, each one in its own silver bucket of ice, alongside tall glass decanters of bespoke lavender-distilled gin and deep green bottles of crème de menthe. Bowls of different garnishes sat beside fifty or more flute glasses, each one outfitted with tongs to personalise your drink: juicy raspberries, tart lemon slices, fragrant mint leaves.

As if that wasn't enough, more Martini glasses were lined up on the kitchen counter, each one filled with a shimmering pink liquid. These were the special, *Nutcracker*-themed cocktails that Emily had concocted, each topped with a swirl of whipped cream and a sprinkle of glitter.

In the dining room, the boutique chocolates that Clara had ordered from a local chocolatier were arranged on silver platters on the table: pink champagne truffles, dark chocolates with a pinch of Himalayan salt and milk chocolates oozing raspberry fondant. Alongside the chocolates, also on silver platters, were sugar cookies, each one carefully iced by hand to look like a nutcracker doll or a snowflake or – my favourite – a pink sugar plum fairy. Between the platters were tall white candles, their glow cosy and warm, and miniature snow-dusted pine trees, each one in its own gold-painted pot.

More of the same white and gold balloons we'd put in the hallway drifted across the hardwood flooring and plush cream carpets, and Linda had fixed backdrops on the living room wall, each woven from hundreds of crystals. White tulle had been hung from the ceiling and, at its centre, a disco ball hung from the enormous chandelier. Its mirrored surface reflected the flickering light from the white candles placed along the mantelpiece, and turned every wall into a kaleidoscope of sparkles. It looked truly magical, like a winter grotto.

In the orangery, Sam allowed me to set up a space for the DJ Clara had hired, while she fixed a canopy of twinkling lights across the inside of the glass roof. At ground level, the orangery had been transformed into a winter forest: real pine trees lined the walls, each at least six feet high, their branches glittering with fake snow. Faux fur throws in white and grey covered the wicker furniture, and two life-size wooden nutcracker soldiers guarded the door, their uniforms red and glossy and smelling of fresh paint.

Once we were finished, we stood together in the living room, the stylists, Clara and I, and admired our handiwork.

Clara clapped her hands together. 'Perfect,' she said. 'Everything is perfect! Thank you so much.' She turned to the three women, who were all looking very pleased. 'Will you stay for the party?'

'We can't, lovely,' Linda said, adjusting one of her earrings. It was dangly, glittery and shaped like a snowflake. 'We've got another house to get to.'

We followed them to the door, where Clara sent them away with a bottle of champagne each and promised to pay the invoice as soon as it was sent.

Once we were alone, I sighed. 'Do we still have to have a party?' I asked, only half joking. 'I'm ready for a lie down.'

Clara turned to me, her eyes sparkling mischievously. 'I suppose that means you don't want to see the present I got you?'

She knew what she was doing. 'Well, I didn't say that,' I said.

'Come on,' she said with a grin. 'It's upstairs.'

My present, as it turned out, was a dress. Not a specific dress, though: my present was the choice of a dress from Clara's extensive wardrobe to wear to tonight's party. Plus accessories.

I'd worn jeans and a jumper for the drive over and subsequent decorating session, but I'd packed some of my nicer sparklier tops in my overnight bag – along with make-up and two pairs of heels to choose from. When I mentioned this to Clara, she just smiled.

Her wardrobe was enormous, an old-fashioned dresser that evoked memories of *The Lion, the Witch and the Wardrobe*. It had been painted white and sanded, battered vintage chic, and fitted into the bedroom like a spoon into sugar – that is, as if the very room had rearranged itself around it.

Clara's bedroom was twice the size of my own at Ivy House, perfectly square, with a fireplace and a deep-set window looking out over the garden. It was decorated exquisitely: walls washed a subtle cream, pristine white sheets on a four-poster bed with pink silk drapes, a gold-rimmed dressing table complete with enormous mirror, and a beautiful oil painting of a garden bright with flowers above the mantelpiece. It was the sort of room where a little girl would imagine a princess slept, only with a touch that was uniquely Clara. Copies of *Vogue* were spread out on the thick, cream fur rug, and an empty bottle of what appeared to be Prosecco rested on the bedside table, on top of a solitary copy of *The Virgin Suicides*. I knew even without asking that Clara's favourite Lisbon sister was Lux.

Clara made a beeline for the wardrobe, and presented me with dress after dress, each one seemingly pulled from a hanger somewhere in its dark, baby-powder-scented depths.

'I'm not sure which would suit you more,' Clara said.

I felt like a doll, or perhaps a small child, as she puttered around me, murmuring almost to herself. Eventually, she settled on one: a champagne-coloured shift-style dress, cut to mid-thigh, with silver bead detailing. It was in a pattern reminiscent of Art Deco, with blunt-edged triangles and lines.

'Borrow a pair of my heels,' Clara said. 'Silver ones. And, with your colouring and your dark hair, you'll look like a dream.'

I didn't know enough about either of those things to dispute her. 'What are you going to wear?' I asked as she thrust the dress at me. I needed both arms to hold it; it was *heavy*.

Clara winked at me. 'It's a surprise,' she said. 'I'm going to go and let the caterers in, then I'll get dressed in one of the guest bedrooms. Take your time getting ready, okay? The first guests shouldn't be arriving for another hour.'

And then the door closed, and I was alone.

I applied my make-up first: a subtle smoky eye, and a coat of mascara, finishing off with a rosebud-pink tint to my lips, dewy and glowing. Then I focused on my hair, teasing it into slightly smoother waves with a bottle of expensive hair serum that I'd found in the bathroom.

I pulled the dress over my head, but didn't look at my reflection until I'd selected some heels. I picked out a silver pair from Clara's wardrobe as she'd suggested (they were Jimmy Choo, but they had a few scratches already so I wasn't too panic-stricken at the prospect of wearing them), and slipped them on to my feet.

And I stood back to assess myself in the full-length mirror.

I knew that I would never look as good as Clara. I was too pale, knobbly-kneed, with not enough waist. My figure was straight up and down – *like an ironing board*, a nasty great-aunt once remarked. As a result of that, or perhaps just as a result of being a woman, I'd always ranked my own beauty in comparison with that of my peers, an invisible tally chart in my mind that I added to whenever I saw a girl whose looks outdid my own. I knew I shouldn't. I couldn't help it; I was my own worst critic. However, I'd never had to compare myself to somebody as effortlessly perfect as Clara, and the thought of her seeing me in her clothes, of appearing next to her, made me want the ground to swallow me up.

But Clara had been right. I looked like a dream.

The loose fit of the shift dress accentuated my slender figure, and the short cut teamed with Clara's heels made my legs look elegant and long instead of spindly and spider-like. My make-up caught the light, and my eyes sparkled.

For once, I actually believed that I looked *good*.

I truly looked as if I belonged here, standing in Clara's luxurious bedroom, preparing to ring in the new year with her nearest and dearest, a veritable catalogue of the rich and stylish and famous. Plus, I told myself with a little flutter of excitement, *I* was the one wearing Clara's dress, her Jimmy Choo heels.

I heard Clara's voice on the landing outside, and opened the door. She was talking on her phone, pacing back and forth, but stopped when she saw me. A smile crept on to her face as she looked me up and down, nodding in approval.

'Gorgeous,' she mouthed.

I whispered 'thank you' back, hoping that my cheeks didn't betray my gratitude; I could feel the rush of heat flowing to them in response to her words. She gave me a wink, and then turned back towards the banister, looking down to the entrance hall as she listened to whoever was on the other end of the line. I took the chance to look at her properly, to really take in the glamorous girl who'd claimed the title of my best friend.

She looked positively ethereal in a white, calf-length tiered tulle dress, teamed with ivory satin ballet slippers. Her hair was sleek with subtle waves, extending nearly to her waist, and accessorised with an elaborate headpiece. A thin band of silver, it had five tall spires, each one encrusted with tiny crystals and sparkling in the light. She looked like an ice queen, or perhaps an ancient, long-forgotten winter goddess.

I could understand, easily, why so many people worshipped

her, why they hung on every word she said. She was completely, utterly magnetic.

'Okay,' she said into the phone, uncharacteristically subdued. 'Yes. Okay. I will.'

She tapped the end call button with a fingernail, paused for a second, and then turned to face me. If I hadn't seen the put-out expression on her face in the millisecond before she gave me a stellar smile, I would have believed it was genuine.

'You look *incredible*,' she said.

'Thank you,' I said. 'Is everything okay?'

'Of course,' she said. 'That was just my mum.'

'Is she still in Barbados?'

Clara choked out a laugh. 'Oh, no. Of course not. They're in New York now.'

'I hope they come home soon,' I said.

'They won't,' Clara said, matter-of-factly. 'As far as they're concerned, they give me a generous allowance and so they're fulfilling their parental duties.'

'I'm sorry,' I said.

'It doesn't matter,' she said. 'Tonight isn't about them, anyway. It's about us.'

'Not quite,' I corrected. 'It's about *you*.'

Her smile returned. 'I think I can handle that.'

Chapter 11

The guests started arriving around nine. The invitation had specified eight thirty sharp, but being fashionably late was the trend – and Clara's guests were nothing if not on trend.

To my surprise, the first person to arrive was Vanessa. When the bell rang, Clara was still upstairs, ostensibly looking for a specific pink lip gloss. Embracing my role as her fellow host, I smoothed down my dress and opened the door. Vanessa stood there on the step, lightly flushed and practically vibrating with excitement.

'Hi!' she squeaked.

'Hey,' I said. 'Welcome to Deneside.'

She peered past me into the beautifully lit but still-quiet house. 'Am I early?'

'No,' I replied. 'Technically, you're late. But everybody else is later.'

She'd made an effort to impress, I noted, as I propped the front door open – as per Clara's instructions – and then led her through to the kitchen to pour her a glass of champagne. Her silver sequinned dress looked new, and her bobbed hair was dusted with glitter. She made a little toasting motion as I handed her a drink, smiling in a way that seemed genuine, and I decided that, while I hadn't warmed to her enough to be friends just yet, it wasn't entirely off the table for the future.

Together, we retreated to the living room and settled by the window to wait for the other guests to arrive. At first, we sat in silence, just looking out at the driveway and the distant, rolling hills. But, after a while, Vanessa began to make small talk – asking me about my studies, telling me about her own. I was quietly pleased she was making an effort to speak to me, even if it was just because I'd invited her to the party.

It wasn't long before Clara's guests began to arrive in earnest, taxis and cars pulling up by the fountain one by one. Each vehicle was seemingly more expensive than the last: a Mercedes, a Bentley, a bright red Lamborghini, tyres crunching on the gravel.

Guests strolled up the front steps and into the entrance hall like it was the Met Gala red carpet, dazzling in their party outfits, greeting each other with strong handshakes and fervent kisses on both cheeks.

The gossip magazines and true-crime blogs would later note that the guests wore Versace, Givenchy, Yves Saint Laurent, the occasional hint of vintage – and only vintage – Gucci or Chanel. Their shoes were by Prada, Jimmy Choo, Tom Ford, Salvatore Ferragamo; their bags by Hermès, Fendi, Celine. If not the elite themselves, these were the children of the elite – the bright young things with glittering futures, celebrating the beginning of a new year. And here I was: one of them, if only for tonight. A thrill of electricity ran through me.

'I'm just going to get a drink,' I said to Vanessa. 'I'll be back in a minute.'

I left her by the window and went into the kitchen. The caterers had filled the glasses with champagne now, and I selected one, adding a single raspberry to it with a pair of silver tongs. I'd intended to go back to Vanessa to keep her company, but in my absence she'd fallen into conversation with a short, pretty girl with sleek black hair. I decided to leave her to it.

Besides, I was already in demand. I was flattered by how many people recognised me from the first party I'd attended, nodding and smiling or stopping to make conversation, to ask how university was going or to compliment me on my dress. Every time I told them that it was Clara's, I felt a little bit more powerful, a little bit more established in the room full of wonderful people who loved Clara. We all loved Clara, but she loved *me* the most.

I spotted Ayanna the second she walked into the room. She was striking in a white lace jumpsuit, which contrasted beautifully with her deep brown skin, and silver heeled sandals. Clara approached her first.

'Hi, Ayanna,' Clara said, embracing her. 'You remember Chloe?'

'Of course,' she said. 'I was hoping I'd see you here.'

'Likewise,' I said. 'You look amazing!'

96

She did. Her curly hair was voluminous, a halo around her head, and the silver glitter around her eyes had been applied with a delicate hand. It made them, framed by exquisitely long lashes as they were, appear infinitely darker.

'So do you,' she said. 'Love the dress.'

'It's Clara's.'

Clara beamed, evidently pleased. She squeezed my arm, and then darted off to greet somebody else. I watched her go, and then turned back to Ayanna.

Unlike the other guests, Ayanna didn't look envious, or even very impressed that I was wearing one of Clara's dresses. 'I thought I recognised it,' she said.

'Yeah,' I said. 'She let me borrow it, just for tonight. Dress code, and all that.'

'Well, that's Clara.'

I sensed that there was something being unsaid between us. There was a shift in energy, a crackling in the air. I decided to break it by asking a question I thought I knew the answer to. 'So, how did you and Clara meet, anyway?'

Ayanna met my gaze. 'Modelling,' she said coolly. 'Then we dated for nearly a year.'

And there it was: the source of the tension. The word *dated* reverberated in my skull. Clara and Ayanna had *dated*.

'I didn't know Clara liked girls,' I said. I heard the hope in my own voice, and I knew Ayanna did too.

Ayanna studied me. 'Not exclusively,' she said, arching an eyebrow. 'But predominantly, as far as I'm aware.'

I tried not to let the sudden flutter in my chest, a glimmer of something a bit like longing, show on my face. 'Well, anyway,' I said. '*We're* not dating. Just so you know.'

'It wouldn't be any of my business if you were,' Ayanna said. For a moment, she seemed poised to move on, to say goodbye and start up a conversation with someone else. But she hesitated. 'Clara wasn't a very good girlfriend,' she said eventually, her perfect posture only slightly slumping. 'We had a messy break-up.'

It couldn't have been that bad, I thought, *otherwise why would you be here?*

'Oh,' I said. 'But you're still friends?'

'Mostly,' Ayanna said. 'We have mutual friends, so we stay on good terms. I come to her events; she comes to mine.' She snorted. 'When I host any, that is.' Her tone softened. 'Look. I've been there, so I understand. Clara's amazing. She's alluring, she's captivating – she makes you want to be her and be *with* her, all at the same time. But if you let her she'll prioritise herself. She used to push me to skip auditions, you know; she'd beg me to go on holiday with her instead. If it wasn't about her, she wasn't interested. Clara doesn't want an equal; what she wants is an admirer.'

I swallowed at the intensity in Ayanna's gaze, at a loss as to how to respond. 'We're not dating,' I repeated. 'Really. We're just friends.'

'This applies to friends too,' she said. She reached out, put a hand on my shoulder in an almost parental yet surprisingly intimate gesture. 'You're a lovely girl, Chloe. You deserve better than that.'

As I thanked her, trying to find the words to reassure her, I caught sight of Clara. She was standing at a distance, by the open doors to the orangery, a drink in hand. She was watching me and Ayanna, her expression carefully neutral.

Ayanna followed my gaze. 'I'm going to go and get a drink,' she said lightly. 'See you later?'

'Sure,' I said.

As I approached her, Clara became enthusiastically involved in a conversation about Montenegro with another guest – a statuesque, androgynous model type wearing a royal-blue cocktail dress. I hovered on the periphery until the model had moved on, leaving Clara with a kiss on both cheeks.

When she spoke, Clara's voice was breezy, deliberately carefree. 'You and Ayanna seem friendly,' she said. 'What were you two talking about?'

'Oh, just how the film's coming along,' I lied. 'She says they'll be shooting on location soon.'

Clara considered this. 'That's exciting,' she said, warmer this time. 'Is that all you talked about?'

I hesitated. And then I decided to tell her the truth – or, at least, a version of it. 'She said that you two used to date,' I said. 'You never told me that.'

'Oh, yeah,' Clara said. 'For maybe seven, eight months? It wasn't anything serious, really. I didn't think it mattered.'

Maybe that had been the problem. Clara had seen their

relationship as casual, as having fun, while Ayanna had been much more invested. That might, in a way, explain why Clara had chosen to disregard Ayanna's wants and needs to prioritise her own; she hadn't pictured their relationship lasting. I clung to that thought. Clara wasn't a cruel person. Spoiled, occasionally self-centred, yes – but not cruel.

The night spun on, gossamer wisps of core memory forming in my mind like funfair candyfloss in a steel drum. What had started out as an elegant, understated event transformed when the DJ began her set, her fist punching the air in time with the thrumming bass. I could feel it in my chest, through the soles of my feet. The sky was dark, the fairy lights in the orangery twinkling like a canopy of stars, and the doors hung open, people spilling out into the garden. A pile of blankets had appeared from somewhere, and Clara's guests were sitting in small groups, swathes of fleece and knitted wool wrapped round their shoulders over their Oscar de la Renta gowns, their Needle & Thread minidresses, their Tom Ford suits.

Vanessa appeared by my side, startling me.

'Thank you *so* much for inviting me,' she gushed, her eyes bright. I wondered how much she'd had to drink. 'I'm having the *best* time. I still can't believe I'm here! Everyone's just so lovely.'

'Don't thank me,' I said. 'Thank Clara! She's the one who said you could come.'

This, of course, was a lie. But it'd look good on Vanessa's part if she thanked the host who'd made this all happen.

'Isn't she just wonderful?' Vanessa sighed. 'You're so right. I need to thank her.' She squeezed my hand. 'I'll be back in a bit, okay? I'll find you.'

'Okay,' I said.

I watched her walk away, leaving an imagined trail of silver glitter behind her.

Midnight arrived, all of us shouting together. *Five, four, three, two . . .*

As the clock hit twelve, we were screaming, cheering, all of us hugging complete strangers, kissing them on their cheeks, on their lips. Somebody sprayed a bottle of champagne into the air, and somebody else launched into a professional-sounding rendition of *Auld Lang Syne* and we jumped up and down as one, our arms linked.

Then: an explosion. A perfectly timed fireworks display, rockets and sprays of colour launching from the field across the road from Deneside Manor's gates. I swayed with the crowd, all of our faces turned up towards the stars. I knew that they'd rival any display in Havington – they'd probably rival most displays anywhere. And they were just for *us*.

The DJ set another song going, and I noted, absently, that Vanessa hadn't reappeared. She'd been gone a while – she'd only been going to find Clara, hadn't she? Maybe Clara had asked her to leave. Maybe she'd even come to my defence, telling Vanessa that *I* might have forgiven her, but *she* certainly had not. Something like satisfaction curled warm in my chest.

What did it matter? I'd invited Vanessa out of kindness, and she'd come. I didn't owe her anything more than that. I shrugged any concern I'd had for her away. She was an adult; she could take care of herself.

The night continued. Somebody passed around a joint, and, despite never having smoked in my life, I took it from the girl next to me when it was offered. I inhaled deeply, too deeply. I coughed and spluttered, my eyes pricked with tears.

'You have to *hold* it in your lungs,' the girl who'd handed it to me said, laughing. 'Here. Watch me.'

She took the joint back, put it to her own pink-glossed lips, and inhaled expertly. She held it for a beat and then breathed out, slowly. 'See?' she said. She sounded dazed, dreamy. 'Give it another try.'

She held it out to me. I noticed that she was wearing three of the bracelets that Clara had been given for Christmas. Thirty thousand pounds, on one slim wrist.

I took the joint. The party seemed very far away as I breathed it in, the world around me shrinking until it was only me and the air in my lungs. I exhaled steadily through my nose.

At first, I didn't feel anything. And then, gradually, it seemed as if I could feel *everything*. The pound of the music, the wintry chill of the night air against my exposed skin, the tastes of champagne and weed on my tongue. It all combined to create an almost euphoric sense of relaxation. I felt loose-limbed and formless, and stupidly, blissfully happy. The undercurrent of anxiety, ever-present beneath my skin, had dissipated. I hardly knew who I was without it.

'Is this what normal people feel like?' I asked the girl, but she didn't hear me, her head facing the other way. I took another drag, and then pressed it back into her hand.

That, she understood. She grinned, nodded at me in approval, and passed it on.

Distantly, from somewhere outside of my mind, I noted that there were other drugs being shared too – tiny clear plastic bags of unidentifiable pills, of white powder. I shook my head when they were held out to me and continued to dance, leaning my head back so that the night sky spun around me, the stars blurring into a spiral of light.

It was then that Clara found me.

'Where have you been?' I asked. 'Did you see the fireworks?'

'Yes!' Clara said. 'They were gorgeous.' She took one look at me, then another. 'Wait. Are you *high*?'

I considered the question. 'A little bit,' I said.

She started to laugh. In her white tulle dress, the elaborate headpiece perfectly centred on her skull, her make-up glimmering in the light, I thought that she was the most beautiful person I had ever seen.

'You're amazing,' I said.

'I know,' Clara replied. Her pupils were dilated, her irises thin slivers of ice, and it occurred to me that she, too, might be high.

'You're the best friend I've ever had.'

'I know that too.'

She took my hand in hers, and we danced.

Chapter 12

The next day, Clara invited me to live with her.

Later, in court, this would be described by a prosecutor as 'the beginning of the end'. That morning, though, the first of January, all that chaos was yet to come. It was simply a new day, cool and clear: the morning after the best night I'd ever had.

Clara and I had risen long after the sun, yawning and stretching, wiping crescents of make-up from our eyes and combing the glitter from our hair. We lounged on the thick faux fur rugs and cream leather pouffes in the living room, drinking mimosas and Bloody Marys that she prepared with an experienced flourish.

'Why don't you stay here?' Clara asked, out of nowhere, as she lazily swirled a celery stick around the rim of her glass. 'I've been thinking about it. There's plenty of room, and it's way nicer than that dump of a place you're staying in. And you don't have to pay my parents any rent or anything. I don't.'

My tenancy was officially set to end in May, when the spring semester finished. Staying there throughout the winter was a dismal prospect; it was damp and still cold, and I was miserable there. And, although I felt a strange inclination to argue, to insist that it wasn't really *that* bad, I knew that it was. I'd complained about it enough to Clara.

'I'll think about it,' I said. I knew already that I would say yes.

Even so, I left Deneside Manor to go back to the flat that afternoon, my tolerance for alcohol thoroughly tested and my social battery almost completely drained. Clara had booked me a taxi, and I hugged her goodbye as it idled impatiently by the fountain. Somehow, even hungover, she still smelled of peaches and vanilla.

At Ivy House, I climbed the stairs up to the flat and let myself in quietly, but no one seemed to be around. I relaxed and closed the door to my bedroom behind me, flopping down on the bed. I'd missed breakfast, and the light lunch had done nothing to ease the gnawing in my stomach. I knew there was nothing in my kitchen cupboard – I hadn't been to the supermarket since before Christmas – so, feeling irresponsible, I ordered a salmon and avocado breakfast muffin and a green smoothie for delivery from a local café.

While I waited, the radiator started to clank in an ominous way, and my ever-so-brief delusion of grandeur faded. I hurriedly changed into my pyjamas, flicked on the fan heater, and then crawled under the covers to conserve warmth. It wasn't long before the delivery driver buzzed up to the flat, and I asked him to leave the bag outside before tearing down the stairs, still clad in my pyjamas, to retrieve it, blessedly unseen. I got back into bed, set my favourite comfort film, *The Devil Wears Prada*, playing on my laptop and pulled the covers up to my chin as I ate my food. Whatever happened, I reasoned, at least I'd never have it as bad as Andy Sachs.

Later on, I rang my mum. When I told her about Clara's invitation, and my plan to accept it, she was flustered. 'You've only known this girl since . . . what? September?'

'November,' I clarified. 'We met in September, but only for a few minutes.'

Revived by my breakfast muffin and nutrient-packed smoothie, plus a brief nap with the sound of Meryl Streep's clipped voice in the background, I was feeling a lot better. More *myself*. I paced with my phone pressed to my ear, trying to avoid staring at the damp patch on the ceiling above my window. It was beginning to look like a face, and a disapproving one at that.

'November,' Mum said. 'And you want to give up your flat and move in with her? Just like that?'

Her voice rose in pitch with each word, and I realised then just how concerned she was at the prospect.

'It isn't *my* flat, Mum. I share it with three other girls, none of whom actually like me very much,' I reminded her. 'Besides, it costs a fortune to live here, and it's rubbish! Even if I just live with Clara until the end of the semester, I'll be able to save *so* much money if I'm not paying rent every month.'

That, she couldn't argue with. 'Fair enough,' she said, relenting. 'But if anything happens—'

'Nothing's going to happen, Mum.'

'But if anything *does*, if you two fall out, you know you can always come home.'

I pressed the phone a bit closer to my ear, as if that would bring me closer to her. 'I know,' I said. 'Thanks, Mum. I love you.'

'Love you too,' she said. 'Just be careful, won't you?'

'Always,' I replied, confident in the assumption that nothing would, or could, possibly go wrong.

Around eight that evening, I heard a light knock on my door. And then another, this one firmer.

I huffed as I strode across the room to open it. I was expecting to see Vanessa on the other side of it, sheepish and apologetic for disappearing the night before. Perhaps she'd be tearful, eager to tell me how horrible Clara had been to her. Nastily, I almost wanted her to seek me out for comfort, just so that I could sympathise with her and then gently remind her that Clara was only looking out for *me*.

But it wasn't Vanessa. It was Skye and Amelia, together, their faces pinched and pale.

'Vanessa's missing,' Amelia said, in lieu of a greeting.

I blinked at her. 'Missing?' I repeated, the word refusing to sink into my skull.

'Yes,' Skye said. '*Missing*. She isn't answering her phone. Her mum's worried sick, and—'

'Have you seen her?' Amelia interrupted.

'I saw her last night,' I said. 'She came to Clara's New Year's Eve party.'

The two girls glanced at each other, disbelief written across both their faces.

'Clara *Holland*'s party?' Skye asked. 'Why would she go there?'

'I invited her. She was in the kitchen when I got back yesterday,' I explained. 'She said she'd be here by herself all night, so I invited her along.'

Amelia looked doubtful, but Skye nodded. 'We'll have to tell the police,' she said. 'Vanessa's mum's already called them. They'll want to speak to the people who were at the party.'

Considering that I'd just been told that Vanessa was missing, it was this that shocked me the most. 'The police?' I asked. 'You don't think something's *happened* to her, do you?'

'We don't know,' Amelia said gravely. 'But it's not like Vanessa to just disappear.'

The search for Vanessa began in earnest on the second of January.

Volunteers from both the town and the university crawled across the snow-speckled landscape like ants on white icing, peering down the cobbled streets and the dark alleys, inspecting clumps of grass and lifting dustbin lids, eager to find any clues that might lead them to Vanessa.

The police had arrived at our flat just before midnight on New Year's Day, the cold clinging to their dark uniform jackets and their heavy boots. Privately, I'd thought notifying the police was an overreaction. I'd seen Vanessa less than twenty-four hours earlier, so how could she be *missing*? Surely she'd just gone to see a friend, or maybe met someone at the party and gone back to their place, and hadn't thought to check in with her parents – something with a perfectly simple explanation that didn't really warrant this much attention.

I didn't say any of this to the police, though. Instead, I tried to be as helpful as I could, keen to clarify my involvement with Vanessa. It'll all be a misunderstanding, I told myself. The second I finished giving my report, she'd open the door, dusted with snow and wide-eyed, surprised at all the fuss.

'How did she seem when you got back to the flat yesterday?' one of the officers, a woman around my mum's age who'd introduced herself as PC Dugan, asked. 'Was she upset? Worried?'

'She seemed a bit . . .' I searched for the word. 'Unhappy, I guess? Out of sorts.'

'Unhappy.' PC Dugan jotted something down on a little pad of paper. 'Okay. And can you tell us what happened next?'

I described the conversation that we'd had, the subsequent timeline of the night: Vanessa's early arrival at the party, how she'd seemed thrilled to be there, how she was eager to thank Clara for the invitation.

'She went to find Clara,' I said. 'And that was the last I saw of her. I thought she'd probably just got a taxi back. Or gone home with someone, maybe.'

I learned, then, the reason why there was already so much concern over Vanessa's disappearance. While a student going AWOL for a day or so didn't necessarily mean that they were in danger, the fact that Vanessa had been drinking had rung alarm bells for the local police. Only a year earlier, they'd been forced to launch a water-safety campaign due to a series of drunk students stumbling into Havington's central river. While all of them had been swiftly rescued, treated for acute hypothermia and survived their ordeal, the danger of the river was clear.

Once the police had left, we all slunk, silently, away to our rooms. I lay on my bed in the cold and the dark, head spinning, my ears still ringing with the officers' solemn thanks and hollow-sounding reassurances.

Vanessa is missing. The phrase just didn't feel real.

I wanted to speak to someone. I needed to tell somebody what had happened, to try to make some sense out of the situation. But I didn't know who.

I couldn't tell my parents. They'd only worry. Frankly, they'd probably assume that a budding serial killer was somehow responsible and they'd beg me to come home. No; my parents definitely weren't an option.

Olivia? My finger hovered over her name on my contacts

list until I remembered it was almost one in the morning and she was at home. She was probably snug in her bed, fast asleep. I couldn't bother her.

Which left one person.

Hey, I typed. *Can I ring you? x*

My phone buzzed seconds later. 'Hey,' Clara said. I could hear noise in the background, distant conversations. 'Is everything okay?'

I sniffed, my eyes welling up at the sound of her voice. 'Not really,' I said. 'Vanessa's missing.'

'Who?'

'My flatmate, Vanessa. The one who came to the party.'

'Oh,' Clara said. 'What do you mean, she's missing?'

'I mean, she's *missing*,' I said. 'No one's seen her since last night.' I sounded faint, even to my own ears. 'The police are involved. They've been to the flat.'

'That seems a bit premature,' Clara said. 'It's only been, what? Twenty-four hours?'

I explained what the police had told us, about the incidents of almost-drowning. 'And the last place anyone saw her was at your party,' I finished. 'So the police are probably going to want to speak to you.'

'Okay,' Clara said. 'You've given them my number, right?'

'Yeah.'

'Then I'll do whatever I can to help,' she said. 'I'm really sorry, but I've got to go. I'm out right now. Try and get some rest, okay? And, hey – don't blame yourself.'

'Why would I—' I started to ask, but she'd already hung up. The unspoken words echoed in my mind. *Why would I blame myself?*

The following morning, I followed Skye and Amelia across campus to the students' union. The Dern campus was bare and brittle, the stone walls dark and cold. Leftover Christmas lights swung in the breeze, their colours only emphasising the gloominess of the winter day.

I donned a hi-vis jacket, which smelled faintly of old sweat, and fell into step with a gaggle of other volunteers. They all spoke in hushed voices as we made our way across ice-slicked cobbles towards the river. I was glad I'd been assigned to the campus team. Other teams had been instructed to search the woodland and the fields on the outskirts of Havington. I'd read enough pulpy crime novels to be able to visualise the scene: the woods would be cold and dark, the wheat in the field long dead with the stalks snapped. When I was engrossed in those types of books, I hungered for the specifics, the details: the moment somebody stumbles upon a bloated corpse, crime-scene tape flapping in the breeze, the grim-faced police officers delivering the tragic news. The reality was very different, and I desperately wished that I wasn't involved at all.

That evening, after a day of searching that had turned up zero signs of Vanessa – I wasn't sure whether that was a good or a bad thing – I stripped off my cold, damp clothes, turned the shower as hot as it would go and later climbed into bed. I hadn't eaten, but I wasn't hungry. I was too churned up. And Clara's words were still running through my mind. *Don't blame yourself.*

I reached for my phone, and swiped through my contact list. Clara picked up on the third ring. 'Hello?'

'Is it my fault?' I asked. 'Is it my fault that Vanessa's missing?'

'Of course it's not your fault.'

'You told me not to blame myself,' I said. 'But what if it is my fault? I invited her to the party in the first place. If she hadn't come, then maybe she—'

'Seriously, Chloe, I wouldn't worry too much,' Clara said. She didn't sound concerned, like she had the previous evening. If anything, she sounded relaxed. Positively breezy. 'I spoke to the police this morning, and they reckon she's just gone to stay with some friends and broken her phone or something. Or that she's maybe dropped out and hasn't told her parents yet. It happens, you know.'

'Oh,' I said. 'The police really think that?'

'They're looking into a lot of stuff,' Clara said. 'But, honestly, I think they're just following up all these leads to cover their backs. One of them told me they get teenage runaways, like, all the time.'

The certain way she said it made it true. Obviously, Vanessa was safe – this was all a big misunderstanding, the kind of situation that I'd laugh about at parties, drink in hand, in years to come. *Remember when that girl I lived with in first year broke her phone and there was a full-scale police search?*

'Yeah,' I said, feeling better. 'You're so right. Thanks, Clara.'

'You don't have to thank me,' she said. 'They'll find her, okay?'

'Okay,' I said.

And it was, for a short while.

I moved into Deneside Manor a week later, the day that the spring term officially started. Ivy House had never been *comfortable*, but it was infinitely more uncomfortable in Vanessa's absence. I avoided Skye and Amelia, and they avoided me. The atmosphere in the flat was oppressive, inescapable. Skye's phone rang at odd hours; it was usually Vanessa's parents checking in, or else Skye's own parents, but I found myself beginning to tense up whenever I heard the iPhone ringtone, whether it was inside the flat or elsewhere. My heart would leap into my throat at the familiar chimes, every cell in my body readying itself for bad news. It was unbearable. And so I decided that it was time for me to accept Clara's invitation.

I told her at her first and only search-party appearance, on the fifth day since Vanessa had gone missing. She'd arrived wearing cute pink combat boots and a matching sparkly hair band, the neon hi-vis vest that she'd accepted with a wrinkled nose clashing horribly with the rose hues. When I'd explained the situation at Ivy House and asked if it'd be possible to move in one day soon, she'd smiled as if she wasn't surprised at my decision at all.

'What about Monday?' she'd asked, as casually as if she was asking me what I wanted for lunch.

'Perfect,' I'd agreed. And that was that.

I booked a taxi in advance to pick me up early on Monday morning, because while Clara's Mini was utterly adorable it wasn't particularly spacious. Although the semester had officially started, neither of us had any lectures scheduled until the afternoon, and so it was an ideal day for me to escape the confines of Ivy House.

My two suitcases and assorted bin bags fitted easily into the boot and back seats of the taxi, and I settled myself into the passenger seat without looking back. The driver was a friendly, balding man with an accent not too dissimilar to my own and, once he'd clocked the address, he spent the journey telling me all about his fifteen-year-old daughter and how much she loved Clara. He helped me unload my bags and drag them on to the front steps. I tipped generously since I'd no longer be paying so much rent, and promised to pass on his daughter's Instagram handle. He drove away with a cheery beep of the horn.

I texted Clara 'Here!' as we'd agreed, and waited, arms wrapped around myself to keep warm. Deneside Manor, up on a hill as it was, wasn't very well protected from the elements, and a biting January wind had set in. Eventually, I tried the door handle. It was unlocked.

I knocked once, opened it and peeked into the dim entrance

hall. Clara was sitting at the bottom of the stairs, her head resting against the banister railing.

'Hey,' I said, a bit irritated. My cheeks felt raw, my fingers icy. 'Why didn't you answer my text? Or open the door?'

Clara was nonplussed. 'It was open,' she said. 'You *live* here now. You don't knock on your own front door.'

I glared at her. 'I don't have a key.'

She stood up and, in a way that gave me the impression that she'd rehearsed this moment, strode across to me. She held out her hand theatrically, and I opened my own, my chilled palm facing up. Clara dropped a brass key into it.

'Now you do,' she said. 'Welcome home.'

Chapter 13

My first lecture of the semester was at one o'clock, and so we had breakfast (Clara heated up some blueberry pancakes from the pantry, which were *exquisite*) and then we dragged my luggage into the bedroom that Clara had chosen for me. It was twice as big as my room at Ivy House, with a deep-set window and a fireplace framed by ornate tiles. Other than that, it was relatively plain, with a beige carpet and cream walls, but I didn't mind; I was just grateful to be there at all. However, Clara assured me that I was welcome to decorate however I wanted, to put my own personal stamp on the room.

She left me in private to unpack my things, slotting clothes and toiletries where they all belonged. It wasn't long before I spotted the door set into the wall close to the window, which I found led to an en-suite bathroom. My own en-suite! And it wasn't cold or leaky or run-down like the bathroom at Ivy House. No, this bathroom was all mottled marble and shiny surfaces. I couldn't believe my change in fortune, although the excitement was dampened a little when I remembered why I'd so wanted to leave Ivy House in the first place.

I pushed all thoughts of Vanessa from my mind as I rooted through my suitcases and bin bags to find what I needed. Black lace-up boots, jeans, a soft, rose jumper. My faux-fur-lined parka. Hair serum, mascara, lip balm. A sweep of sheer glitter across my eyelids.

'Cute,' Clara said when I emerged. She was waiting by the front door, her expensive satchel in hand. 'Loving the glitter. All settled in?'

'Near enough,' I said as we went out to the car together. 'You didn't tell me I had a bathroom.'

'Didn't I? Don't fret about it; most of the guest bedrooms have one.' She gave me a mischievous sideways glance. 'It's not like you're getting special treatment or anything.'

I rolled my eyes at her, secretly thrilled at the teasing.

Depending on her mood, Clara liked to listen to the radio or a podcast, or sing along to Taylor Swift in the car. I, on the other hand, preferred to quietly catch up with the news, although I indulged Clara by applauding her singing. I was surprised that she'd already posted two updates that day: one of the blueberry pancakes, and another a mirror selfie, satchel slung over her shoulder. *The secret to getting ahead is getting started*, the caption read. *In other words . . . it's the first day of term! #InMyEducatedEra #ElleWoodsEnergy #WhatLikeItsHard.*

We left the Mini in the potholed car park at the edge of campus, right on the bank of the fast-flowing river. It was closer to the library, my lecture hall a further ten-minute walk to the other side of campus, but Clara insisted on walking across with me.

'I need a coffee,' she declared. 'The kind of coffee that only Debbie can provide.'

As we headed towards the coffee shop, the frost on the ground crunching beneath our boots, we passed dozens of posters tacked up on every wall. Vanessa's face smiled blurrily out from each one in black and white, the word *MISSING* pasted above her head in big, bold letters.

It was strange; now that the new semester had started and the majority of students were back on campus, I'd expected a more dramatic response as the news spread. More searches, maybe, or at the very least an increased rate of shares on the #FindVanessa hashtag that somebody had started on Instagram. During those first harried days, my feed had been cluttered with pictures of her, dozens of snapshots of her posing and pouting, friends' cheeks pressed against hers. But people apparently had other concerns now, rushing to their lectures without even glancing at the posters as they passed. Vaguely nauseated, I looked away from Vanessa's happy, hopeful expression.

It was then that I realised that people were looking at me differently. Looking at *us* differently. It started with two girls who were heading towards me and Clara, their arms loaded with art supplies. As one of them caught sight of us, she nudged her friend with her elbow. The other girl, at first at a loss, followed her friend's gaze. Together, they gave us a wider berth than was necessary. I put it down to them avoiding a patch of ice, or perhaps not wanting to smear us with paint from a wayward brush, but the way that they looked at Clara, wide-eyed, just didn't sit right.

'That was weird,' I said lightly.

Clara glanced at me. 'What was?'

She hadn't noticed. I wondered if I'd been reading too much into their behaviour, overthinking the briefest of interactions. It wouldn't exactly be unusual for me, being as anxious a person as I was.

I decided not to elaborate. 'Oh, nothing,' I said instead. 'Never mind.'

And then it happened again when we arrived at the coffee shop, a cosy haven in the bleak afternoon light of January. The bell rang above our heads as we went inside, stamping flakes of frost from our boots, and a table in the corner, which had been loud with laughter, went completely silent.

There were six students crowded around the table, a mess of mugs and textbooks and tote bags spread across its surface, the detritus of exam preparation. It was clear that they were looking at us from the way that they were trying so hard not to, their glances flitting to us and away, their voices low as they leaned in close and murmured to each other. I wondered what they were saying.

'Afternoon, my lovelies,' Debbie said when we reached the front of the queue, her familiar face a soothing balm to my paranoia. 'The usual?'

'Yes, please,' I said.

Clara nodded. 'The same for me too.'

Debbie started preparing our coffees, brewing the espresso and frothing the milk. Clara, relaxed as anything, took out her phone as we waited. I was too distracted.

'Clara,' I whispered. 'That table over there . . . they keep looking over at us.'

I indicated the table with what I hoped was a subtle head tilt.

Clara didn't even look up. 'So?'

'So? It's *weird.*'

'Not really,' Clara said. 'This happens to me, like, all the time.'

'I've been with you on campus plenty of times,' I said. 'It's never been like this.'

It really hadn't. There had always been some glances, nudges, the occasional comment or a 'hi, Clara!' from a passing stranger. A sense of quiet awe instilled into those who recognised her. But this was different. Conversations were ceasing, and people were staring; this wasn't subtle admiration. It was something else. It felt as if there was a light shining on me that I couldn't see, highlighting my every move, making it ripe for comment and criticism.

'Do you think it's something to do with Vanessa?' I asked, careful to keep my voice low. 'Do people know she came to your New Year's Eve party? What if they know I lived with her?'

'They probably do,' Clara said. 'Don't let it get to you, though. People just love gossip. It'll all blow over soon enough, anyway.'

I wasn't so sure. But, before I could protest, Debbie placed our takeaway coffees on the counter with a chirpy 'There you go, dears.' Clara reached into her satchel and presented her card with a flourish, paying for both of us. I nodded at her gratefully.

'I'm going to the library,' she said as we left. 'Text me when you're done, okay?'

'I can get a taxi back,' I said. 'I don't mind.'

Clara shrugged. 'It's up to you. I'm just saying we'll see where we are – if we're both finished on campus, we can go home together.'

Home.

'Okay,' I said. 'Thanks, Clara.'

'See you later, okay?' she said, and I watched her walk away, turning the word *home* over and over in my mind as if I was sucking on a sweet, smoothing away all its uncertain edges.

The odd, searching looks continued as I walked to my lecture. Whether they were related to Vanessa or not, I was more than a little unnerved by the time that I reached the tiered lecture hall. The first to arrive, I sat in last semester's seat with a relieved huff, struck by an odd sense of nostalgia. Had it really only been four months since I'd chosen this seat? In that time, my life had utterly transformed.

I was so lost in my thoughts that I flinched when Olivia sat down beside me, throwing her tote bag on the seat next to her. *Never underestimate the power of a girl with a book – Ruth Bader Ginsburg*, it read, in a swirling black font.

'Hey,' she said with a bright smile. 'Happy New Year!' Her smile faded slightly as she took me in. 'Are you okay? No offence, but you look exhausted.'

I brushed off her concern. 'I'm fine. It's just all this stuff with my flatmate going missing, you know? It's been really messing with my head. I've been volunteering with the search parties, and there's still no sign of her.'

'She's your flatmate?' Olivia gaped. '*Fuck*. I'm so sorry, Chloe. I had no idea – I only found out what had happened when I got back yesterday and saw the posters at the train station.'

'It's okay,' I said. 'We weren't exactly close. She was a bit nasty to me when I first moved in, actually. And then we sort of made up. So it's all feeling a bit . . . complicated.'

'I'll bet,' Olivia said.

I blew out a long exhale. 'It just feels like everyone's been staring at me today.'

To my surprise, Olivia didn't leap to reassure me. 'Well, yeah,' she said with a slightly curled lip. 'But that's nothing to do with your flatmate.'

She must have seen my expression, the sheer confusion written plain on my face, and swore under her breath. She retrieved her phone from her tote, and tapped on an app before sliding it across the desk to show me.

The feed on the screen was filtered to show image results

that corresponded to the search term *Clara Holland*, and there were hundreds of thousands of them. But that wasn't what caught my eye. The newest results all featured a single image, one that I didn't even remember being taken: Clara, Ayanna and me on New Year's Eve, the three of us illuminated by the magical lighting of the orangery. It was slightly out of focus, completely unposed, and I realised that it must have been taken, and uploaded, by a guest. However, it looked like Clara and Ayanna had then both shared it on their own respective profiles, where it had been scooped up and shared further by an assortment of fashion blogs, celebrity gossip outlets and Clara's horde of fans. And now, practically overnight, everybody seemed to know my face, if not my name.

It had nothing to do with Vanessa. Nothing at all. This was all *me*.

A shiver of pleasure rippled through me. At this university, its campus micro-sized, I'd learned that gossip filtered from person to person impossibly quickly; the campus celebrities were the girls' netball-team captain who'd been pegged for stardom; a boy whose short film had won a significant international award. I'd always thought that I wanted to be a novelist purely because I loved words, the joy of stringing them together. But perhaps the recognition – the validation of my talent – was a part of it too.

'Oh,' was all I said.

'Yeah,' Olivia said, emphatically. '*Oh*.'

'What do I do?'

Olivia snorted. 'You don't do anything. It'll die down. Let's be honest – you were a guest at some girl's party. It's not exactly the scoop of the decade.'

There was an undertone of bitterness to her words that made me frown – it wasn't something I'd ever seen in Olivia – but I chose to ignore it. And then something else occurred to me. Were people staring at me because they were *jealous*? Surely not. It was only big news to me, to some of Clara's more dedicated followers and perhaps to a few other people on campus. Nobody else in the world would even care.

Chapter 14

As we left the lecture hall an hour later, Olivia fell into step beside me. She was uncharacteristically quiet as she spoke.

'I need to talk to you about Clara,' she said. 'You're like . . . proper friends now, right?'

'We are,' I said. 'Actually, I live with her now. I took my stuff over first thing this morning.'

Olivia's expression was unreadable. 'Really?'

'Yes! Can you believe it?' I couldn't stop the smile. 'She asked me on New Year's Day – the morning after that picture was taken. I wanted to, obviously, but I wasn't sure when would be a good time. And then all this stuff happened with Vanessa, and I just had to get away from Ivy House.'

'Right,' Olivia said. There was a hardness to her tone.

I peered at her. 'Are you jealous?'

'It's not that.'

'Right.'

'It's *not*,' Olivia said. By now, we were outside, and she glanced around as if she was afraid of being overheard. 'Can we go somewhere? Not the coffee shop, or the library. There's a café in the Art block.'

I'd never been to the café, but I knew of it: it was typically full of sculptors and painters and designers, all of them wired on too much caffeine and who knew what else, discussing their pieces with exhausted pride.

'Okay,' I said. 'But the coffee had better be decent.'

The coffee was not decent. The latte I'd ordered was cheaper than the one I bought in the coffee shop, roughly the same price as the library coffee cart – but far inferior in quality. I'd never been a huge coffee snob, but even I could taste the bitterness of burnt coffee beneath the syrupy-sweet caramel.

Olivia had ordered a latte for herself too, and was fussing with it at the counter in a way that I sensed was to stall: she added two packets of brown sugar, stirring between each one, then added an extra bit of milk, and then a sprinkle of cinnamon. After a minute or so, I took a seat at a nearby table and watched her, wordless, waiting to find out why she'd wanted to talk to me somewhere so secluded. Well, secluded if you ignored the small gathering of artists in the far corner, who were nursing their own coffees and arguing in muted tones about somebody's command (or lack thereof) of digital paint-brushes.

Eventually, Olivia sat down opposite me. 'I know we're both huge fans of Clara,' she began. 'And you know her better than I do. But . . .' She turned her gaze to her coffee cup, clutching it like a life preserver. 'Over the break, I heard some things. About Clara. I don't know how true they are, but I wanted to tell you.'

'Okay,' I said slowly. 'What is it? You know you can't take stuff like this too seriously.' I heard Clara's voice in my head as I added, 'People love to gossip.'

Olivia shifted in her seat. 'Yes, I know. But this is . . . well, it's bad.'

I frowned. 'How bad?'

'Bad enough for me to worry about you,' she said. She finally looked up at me and leaned closer, her voice hushed. 'If I tell you,' she said, 'you can't tell anyone that I told you. Not even Clara. Actually, *especially* not Clara.'

'Okay,' I said. 'I won't tell her.'

'Promise.'

I sighed. 'Fine, I promise,' I said. 'Whatever. What's going on, Liv?'

Olivia paused for a moment, as if she was practising what she was going to say before she came out and said it.

'She poisoned someone,' she said in a rush. 'Another girl, at boarding school. She was thirteen.'

Olivia's words reverberated around my skull. *Poisoned. Boarding school. Thirteen.*

'She poisoned someone?' I repeated. 'What do you mean *poisoned*?'

'She was having a birthday party,' Olivia said. 'She set it up in the school's walled garden, and ordered a picnic from some fancy deli. Anyway, afterwards, this girl keeled over. It turned out that, somehow, peanut oil got into one of the salads. She had an allergy.'

'That's horrible,' I said, 'but it sounds like an accident.'

'They couldn't prove it was anything else,' Olivia agreed. 'According to this girl I know, though, *everyone* knew about her nut allergy. Clara swore up and down that she'd checked the labels, but . . .' She shrugged. 'Apparently, this girl and Clara had butted heads before, multiple times. People were surprised Clara had even invited her to the party in the first place – and then she ended up in the hospital.'

'What happened to her?'

'Clara? Supposedly, she was absolutely inconsolable. They had to call her parents.'

'Not Clara,' I said. 'The girl with the allergy.'

'She was lucky. Someone ran for her EpiPen, and they got her to hospital just in time. But seriously, Chloe, it could have killed her. Nut allergies are no joke.'

I had to clear my throat before I could speak. 'It's just a rumour,' I said. 'It must be. Otherwise somebody would've said something by now.'

'You know who Clara's parents are,' Olivia said. 'They're pretty well-known people in certain circles. And, besides, there weren't any charges, because it was an *"accident"*.' Olivia made quotation marks in the air with her fingers. 'So it would have been her word against theirs.'

'I guess.'

'Come on. Would *you* go to the press about Clara, if she did something like that to you?'

'I don't have a nut allergy,' I said. My evasiveness embarrassed me. It was as if I had a neon sign flashing above my head that said, *I like her too much to even pretend to imagine it.*

Olivia smiled, somewhat pityingly. 'Look,' she said, 'you don't have to believe me, but I wanted you to know. Just keep it in mind, okay?'

I drained my coffee cup, and stood up. 'Okay,' I said. 'I'll keep it in mind.'

That night, I dreamed about a baby-faced, thirteen-year-old Clara – summer dress, white Converse high tops, neat blonde plaits – in a beautiful garden, carefully snipping lilac and cream blooms with a pair of silver sewing scissors. In the dream, she arranged them neatly in a glass vase in the middle of a table, smiling all the while. Each place at the table was set with a floral china plate and cutlery, and in the centre there was a great bowl of salad. In the dream, I knew that there was something wrong with this scenario, something sinister, despite how perfect it all was. I stood there, an invisible bystander, as a group of innocent-looking girls approached, and each of them took a seat. I watched from behind as one of them, this one with deep brown hair like my own, reached out and helped herself to a forkful of salad. An instant later, the fork dropped on to the table as her hands moved to her throat, her eyes widening in panic for a fleeting moment before she collapsed. I ran over to help her, the air moving thick like water around my limbs, slowing down my every movement. And when I finally reached her, kneeling beside her, I realised that it was my own face I was looking into, my own thirteen-year-old lips tinged with blue.

I woke up with a start, my heart pounding. Sweat prickled on my forehead. I sat up, and for a moment I was disorientated by the room around me. It was too big, too empty, too moonlit – nothing like my bedroom at home, or my room at Ivy House. And then I remembered that I'd moved in with Clara.

I leaned back against the headboard to catch my breath, waiting for my pulse to slow. In my mind's eye, I could still see Clara's pleased little smile as she arranged her flowers, delicately, all the while knowing exactly what was about to happen.

It's not real, I reminded myself. *It was just a dream.*

And yet it had disturbed me on a visceral level. Could any part of what Olivia had told me be true? Was this simply jealous rumour-spreading, or had Clara really been capable of such a violent act, of deliberately triggering a classmate's potentially fatal allergy, at such a young age? And, if she *had*, was she likely to do something like that again? I didn't know.

I wanted to trust her. Of course I did. She was my friend, the best friend I'd ever had. And more than that too: I felt something for Clara I'd never felt for anyone else.

But I trusted Olivia. I knew already that Olivia wasn't the

type to deliberately cause trouble; she wouldn't have told me if she wasn't genuinely concerned.

As my breathing returned to normal, or near enough, I lay back down and pulled the duvet up to my chin. I'd speak to Clara about it in the morning, I decided. I'd tell her about the rumour, and I'd ask her point blank if it was true – or if she'd done anything remotely similar, something tiny and inconsequential that could have been taken and twisted into a completely different, far more cruel piece of gossip by somebody intent on destroying her reputation.

But I wouldn't say that it had come from Olivia. Just in case.

We had a late start the next day, with neither of us due to be on campus until three o'clock. I had a lecture scheduled then, and Clara had a seminar.

By mutual, silent agreement, we both had a long lie-in, rising around ten, and then a slow, relaxing brunch. Clara made herself creamy coffee and settled down to read the newspaper in a chair by the Aga, like a little old woman.

Meanwhile, I toasted some crumpets and unscrewed the lid from a glass jar of expensive-looking marmalade. The tastefully illustrated label, displaying oranges plump with juice, said *Seville Orange*, and when I turned it round and saw the price I gaped. This single jar had cost eight pounds. That didn't stop me from smothering my crumpets in it once they'd popped out of the cream Smeg toaster, though.

I joined Clara by the Aga with my crumpets and a coffee.

Despite my surroundings, the quiet winter birdsong outside and the soupy heat of the kitchen, I couldn't relax. Nervous energy thrummed beneath my skin like a current.

'Hey, Clara,' I said as she turned a page, 'can I ask you about something?'

Clara held up a finger, the nail painted pearly white, until she'd finished the sentence she was reading. When she had, she looked up at me apologetically, her smile warm. 'Sorry,' she said. 'I *really* wanted to reach the end of that bit. But yes, of course. You know you can ask me anything.'

Her expression was so open that I hesitated, consumed with guilt.

Two lines appeared between her eyebrows, her lips a pout of concern. 'Chloe? Is something wrong?'

'No, no,' I said quickly. 'Nothing wrong. It's just that . . . well, I heard a rumour.'

Clara set her newspaper gently aside. 'A rumour?'

'Yes,' I swallowed. 'It was about you. And I know it isn't true, but it's just so *cruel*. It's so cruel, and I can't get it out of my mind.'

'What is it?' she asked.

I took a deep breath. 'I heard you poisoned somebody,' I said. 'A girl. When you were thirteen, at boarding school.'

Clara studied me, her expression carefully neutral. 'Did you hear anything else?'

'They said it was at a party,' I said. 'They said that the girl had a nut allergy, and everyone knew, but that there was peanut oil in the salad.'

134

There was a long pause, and then Clara leaned back in her armchair. 'Quite impressive for a thirteen-year-old,' she said. 'Don't you think?'

I felt a stab of sheer horror, like a knife to the stomach. 'Are you saying . . .' I could hardly get the words out. 'Are you saying it's *true*?'

'I am,' Clara said. She was calm and cool, completely unperturbed.

'You triggered someone's allergy?' I said, aghast. 'On *purpose*?'

'I was thirteen! It's not that big a deal.'

'It absolutely *is* that big a deal!'

Clara laughed. 'You're really bothered by this, aren't you? Look at you – you're scandalised! I bet you were so ready to protect my honour too.' Her voice rose, mimicking mine. 'Clara's too lovely! Clara would never!'

I looked away, my cheeks hot with shame.

Clara leaned forward, taking one of my hands in her own. 'I'm sorry,' she said. 'I'm not making fun of you. It's just – I was a total nightmare at thirteen. I was going through a rebellious phase. I'd been reading library books about famous deaths, accidental and otherwise, and that girl and her friends were foul. They bullied me relentlessly.' She shrugged. 'Obviously, it was a stupid thing to do. But didn't we all make mistakes at thirteen?'

I pulled my hand away, but gently. 'Clara, that's not just a mistake. It's not like . . . giving yourself a bad fringe, or wearing an embarrassing outfit. You could've *killed* her.'

'I could've,' Clara allowed. 'But I didn't. She was fine.'

She was fine. I wondered where she was now, this girl, whether she frequented bars in London or sat writing sonnets in libraries or spent hours measuring out chemicals in a laboratory somewhere. In each scenario, I imagined her telling the people around her – her friends, colleagues – that Clara Holland, the influencer, had once triggered her nut allergy on purpose. I could see her in my mind's eye, relaying the story over drinks ('Yes, her! The pretty one!'), able to laugh about it now, years later, but her skin still prickling with horror at the memory of the way that her throat had closed up. And, despite what Clara had told me about her bullying behaviour, I couldn't help a pull of sympathy towards this stranger.

I'd been bullied, once. The girl, Francesca, had originally been my best friend. We did all the things that pre-teen girls do: we had sleepovers, we spent days in the park with ice pops, we sat together at lunchtimes and read our books together at break. When we started secondary school, though, she became integrated with a more popular crowd – and turned on me to gain their approval. I'd been confused, and hurt, and then numb. And then, blessedly, I'd made other friends.

But what if I'd made a rash decision? A stupid, melodramatic decision? Was what Clara had done really that difficult to understand?

She didn't say anything as I mulled it over, just watched and sipped her coffee, waiting for me to come to a conclusion.

'It was only the once?' I asked. I hated how thin my voice sounded, how hopeful.

'It was only the once,' Clara confirmed.

'And you'd never do anything like that again?'

Clara was solemn. 'Never.'

'Okay,' I said. Then, with a sense of finality, 'Okay. Then I guess we can forget about it.'

'Thank you,' Clara said in a rush. 'Really.'

I noticed that her eyes were bright. Tears of relief, I imagined. I wondered at having the power to affect her like that, the way that, for just a moment, I'd held her happiness in my hands, fragile as a butterfly. So easily crushed.

'Don't worry about it,' I said, pleased with my own generosity.

Clara smiled, and picked up her newspaper again, effectively concluding our conversation. And, although her attention quickly turned back to the letters on the page, my own lingered on her, the thrum of bloodlust that I imagined I could hear in her veins, sounding out like a siren.

A warning.

Chapter 15

It seemed only natural that my days became consumed by Clara.

We got up together, ate breakfast together, drove to campus together. If we had afternoon classes, we ate lunch together, hunched over tables in the library or soaking up the atmosphere of the coffee shop, depending on our respective deadlines. We went home together. It was like nothing at all had happened, our bond stronger than ever.

On the other hand, Olivia was distant. She still sat beside me during lectures and seminars, but it seemed to be more out of habit than anything else. She shared her notes with me, made polite enquiries about themes and quotes and analyses when prompted by whichever lecturer we had that day, but otherwise we didn't speak. I knew that she felt betrayed by what I'd done, that I'd chosen to stay close to Clara after what she'd told me. I missed Olivia. But what choice did I have?

With Olivia more or less out of the picture, I spent even more time with Clara, if that was remotely possible. At home –

and I *had* begun to think of Deneside Manor as home – we whiled away the hours, always together.

Often, we were silent, just doing our own thing in the same room. Parallel play.

Meanwhile, Clara's staff – her new housekeeper, and the chef who provided lunch and dinner – moved around us as if they were invisible, spiriting away dirty plates and glasses and replacing them with tasty titbits and refills without a word.

'You don't have to, like, acknowledge them every time,' Clara said to me, once, after I'd thanked the housekeeper. 'It's their job.'

'I'm just being polite,' I said. Clara frowned at me as if that had never occurred to her.

These slow days became a habit. I'd curl up on the sofa in the living room and read, while Clara painted her nails a pastel hue or applied an antioxidant-rich face mask or scribbled in a leather-bound notebook. When I caught a glance over her shoulder one day, I saw that the pages were full of her neat, blocky handwriting: poems, observations, quotes, all her own. Caption fuel for her never-ending series of posts on social-media.

Clara posing with a pouty peace sign, her hair tied up in a bun, her face layered thickly with a deep, pomegranate-red concoction: *I just caught myself in the mirror, looking like this. #ScaredMyself #BloodOfMyEnemies*

Clara in her camel coat in the library, her hair glowing

in the dim, golden light, perusing a shelf of jewel-coloured tomes: *Do you ever wonder where humanity would be if we'd never lost the Library of Alexandria? #MorningThoughts #LibraryLove*

I was already part of her world, and I followed her account, tapping the heart button religiously whenever she posted an update. Sometimes, we'd be in the same room, and she'd blow me a kiss when the notification popped up on her screen. *@ChloexHughesx liked your photo.*

It didn't take long before I became even more involved in the process – something I saw as inevitable.

It was the second week of February, the tiniest green buds only just beginning to swell on the trees in the garden. We'd taken the opportunity to bask in the orangery, as it was unseasonably warm and sunny outside. The glass roof distributed the heat from the sun wonderfully, and the orangery felt positively tropical. It smelled of humid leaves, damp soil, the spritz of perfume that Clara had applied that morning, all intermingling.

I was lying on a sunlounger cushion on the terracotta-tiled floor, the navy-striped fabric warm and slightly musty from improper storage. I had been reading a magazine, but I'd neglected it, opting instead to roll over on to my back and sunbathe, my eyes closed. The light filtered red through my eyelids.

Clara, meanwhile, was on the wicker recliner, a glass resting on the white bistro table beside her. It held a generous helping of champagne, topped up with cranberry juice – a combination that, she'd told me with an all-knowing air, was listed on cocktail menus as a Poinsettia.

'Some people add triple sec, or orange liqueur, or vodka,' she'd said, 'but I think it's perfect as it is.'

Now, I shifted to look up at her, raising an arm across my eyes to block out the brightness. 'What are you doing?'

She was holding her phone at arm's length, the angle awkward and, when I spoke, she let out a frustrated huff. 'I'm trying to take a picture,' she said. 'This light is amazing, but I just can't *get* it.'

I sat up, leaning back on my hands. 'I can take a picture of you,' I said. 'If you want.'

'Would you?' Clara's voice light with hope.

'Of course,' I said. 'Besides, if you can't get the angle, it's easier if I do it. I can just move wherever you want me to.'

I struggled to my feet, my muscles stiff, and took the phone that Clara held out. It was the newer model of my own, covered with a faux marble case.

I paused and looked around. 'Over here might be better, actually,' I said, a little hesitantly. 'With these big leaves in the background?'

The plants in question were jungly and dense, with hanging vines trailing down. Clara stood with her back to them, her hair bright against the layers of deep, mixed greens. She closed her eyes, her face tilted up towards the sunlight, perfectly poised like a flower. The leafy fronds brushed against her forehead and her shoulders as she stepped further back, as if they were enveloping her, claiming her as one of their own.

'Perfect,' I said.

I took pictures from as many different angles as I could, tapping the button over and over in the hope that Clara would be pleased with at least a few of the shots.

'Make sure you get some of my make-up,' she murmured, her lips barely moving.

I nodded, momentarily forgetting that she couldn't see me with her eyes still shut, and then moved closer. And, as I leaned in to focus on her eyeshadow, she opened them. I could see her gaze flitting across my face, and I looked at her in return: her blue eyes surrounded by a sunset-gold shimmer, artfully flushed cheeks, her lips blotted red from the cranberry juice. Her pulse jumped in her throat.

I found myself thinking of my university interview, the one that had earned me my spot at Dern and, as a result, changed my life. *Would you define this as poetry?* the scholar had asked me. Now, I could see that that simple sentence was anything but poetry. *This* was poetry. *Clara* was poetry.

I was only a little bit breathless when I stepped back. Clara reached out to take her phone, her smile widening as she swiped through the selection that I'd taken. Gradually, the tightness in my chest loosened.

'Okay, these are seriously good,' she said when she'd reached the last one. 'You could be a photographer. I'm not even joking.'

'It's absolutely all you,' I said without thinking. 'You'd still look good if somebody took your picture on a flip phone.'

I flushed at my own boldness; I'd always told Clara she was pretty, but never quite so fervently. To my relief, she just laughed.

'Hey,' she said suddenly. 'You haven't got a drink! What do you fancy? Champagne? Green juice? Cranberry without the alcohol?'

'Cranberry would be lovely.'

'One cranberry, *sans* alcohol,' Clara repeated. 'Next time, just help yourself. Okay? This is your *home* now.'

I nodded, chastened. 'Okay.'

I watched her go, then sank back down on to my mildewed sunlounger cushion. She was gone for a while. I slipped my phone from my pocket, and typed a quick message to her.

Everything okay? x

A bubble appeared, followed a second later by her reply.

Hunting for ice! x

I closed the app and switched to aimlessly scrolling through my social-media feeds instead. My eyes scanned over snippets of celebrity gossip, political debates, snapshots of acquaintances posing on their holidays abroad. *How*, I wondered, *do so many people have so much going on in their lives?*

As I refreshed my feed again, a new post from Clara appeared. It was one of the pictures that I'd just taken: Clara gazing dreamily into the camera, her lips slightly parted, her eyes as deep and as wide as the ocean. I watched the comments flood in, and, for the first time, I didn't feel jealous of her online presence at all. Instead, I was strangely flattered, almost satisfied; it felt like her followers were complimenting me, the photographer, as well as her. After all, I was the reason that Clara looked so wonderful – I was the one who'd found the perfect angle, and snapped the perfect picture. I was the person behind the lens, the person that Clara was looking at.

Your eyes!

Beauty. x

I'm in loooooove.

What foundation are you using, babe? You're stunning. xo

Thoughtlessly, I picked at the pencil eraser-sized scab on my chin, the remnants of a spot I just couldn't leave alone. I imagined having skin like Clara's, so smooth and flawless that people genuinely thought I was wearing make-up.

The reappearance of the real offline Clara broke the spell. 'Sorry I took so long,' she said. She placed a glass of cranberry juice, clinking with ice, on the bistro table. And, as she put it down, she caught a glimpse of my screen.

'It's an amazing picture, isn't it?' she said. 'I meant what I said, about you being a photographer. Maybe we should collaborate more.'

I reached for the glass of ruby-red juice. I was surprised to realise how thirsty I was, and took a long swallow. It was sweet, and then tart on my tongue. 'What do you mean?' I asked.

'I mean, maybe we should do some actual work together. You and me.'

'That's an amazing idea,' I said. 'Do you need to check with like . . . a manager or anything first?'

Clara laughed. 'I don't have one. I did, for a while, but I let him go. He was *so* boring. He didn't want me to post *anything* without his approval. I get to make all of my own decisions now.' She raised an eyebrow at me, expectantly. 'So, what do you say?'

'Yes,' I said. 'I'd love to.'

And so the next stage of my life began.

Not only was I Clara's live-in best friend and confidante – I was her live-in photographer. She was a relatively easy-going model, far more so than I'd imagined. The photoshoots weren't planned; we'd be doing something together, cooking breakfast or reading or trying on clothes, and she'd say something offhand, casual, like, 'This would look perfect on the grid, don't you think?'

This was my cue to accept her phone when she passed it to me and snap pictures until she asked me to stop. Sometimes, this was after one or two. More often, I'd take ten, fifteen, twenty pictures, my thumb tapping the shutter icon over and over again as Clara moved smoothly through a series of poses and facial expressions. She was perfect – every coy glance, big smile or hair toss was so well practised that, somehow, it looked completely candid.

Afterwards, I would watch over her shoulder as she deleted any that she thought made her look bad – as if that was ever a possibility – and selected the ones that she liked the most. She would open a photo-editing app and carefully tweak the colour composition or add a filter, ensuring that she was as bright and as glowing in the image as she was in real life.

She'd upload the subtly edited version with all the requisite hashtags, and together we'd watch all the love pour in. It was addictive, almost, watching something that we'd created together receiving such adoration. And I wanted *more*.

'I could help you write the captions,' I offered one day. 'If you want.'

I'd noticed that Clara's most popular posts seemed to be the ones that had witty captions, a quip or remark that was short and sweet. The majority of the time, she just combined a series of emoticons: a pink blossom, a pair of champagne flutes, an ice cream, a rain cloud with a fork of lightning. She'd been lamenting her lack of creativity, stabbing a manicured nail at the profile of a rival influencer who supplemented *her* images with snapshots of her own handwritten poetry.

She looked at me with interest, her eyebrows lifting. 'Really?' she said. 'Are you sure it's not too much? You're basically my photographer already.'

'I know,' I said. 'Seriously, I don't mind. I want to.'

'Well, at least let me pay you,' Clara said. She grinned. 'Hey! You can be my social-media manager.'

And so I had a job title – albeit an unofficial one. *Social-media manager*. It wasn't *writer* or *novelist*. It wasn't *New York Times bestselling author*. But my words were reaching an audience who loved them, adding a new element to Clara's online presence and helping her to gain followers every day.

Sometimes, depending on the PR gifts she'd received in the past week or so, our captions would be specific: gushing endorsements of skin-plumping moisturisers, of hair oil imbued with honey, of a crystal-beaded bustier or a plain white T-shirt made from the softest possible cotton, each one outfitted with the necessary declarations of *#Ad* or *#PRGift*.

Other days, our captions would be simpler, Clara and I weaving words that accentuated her online persona, every sentence reminiscent of the easy, breezy luxury and glittering decadence that was her life.

For the first time, I was being paid to write. It wasn't a lot of money – I would've felt uncomfortable accepting more, given all that Clara had done for me – but it was reliable. And, considering that I was no longer paying rent, I was better off than I ever had been.

I told myself that it didn't matter that I was only writing captions, pretending to be somebody else. It didn't matter that this writing wasn't my very own, that the words weren't pulled from the very depths of my heart and soul. I was still being paid to tell a story. Did it really matter if it was Clara's? My own time would come.

Chapter 16

As time rolled on, the last lingering chill of winter melting into the buttery warmth of spring, the time came to plan the next party. There wasn't an official schedule, Clara explained to me, but generally she threw one big party per season – and the last one had been New Year's Eve.

We were in the coffee shop, both of us ignoring the enquiring glances in our direction. I was getting used to it; since the New Year's Eve party, Clara's significance on campus – and, therefore, mine too – had only grown.

Vanessa, meanwhile, had faded into the background. In a press conference in late January, attended by a few members of the local media, police revealed that they had found two noteworthy emails on Vanessa's personal laptop, both of which might indicate her whereabouts. The first was an unsent email to her faculty head, querying the process for leaving her course. The second was a confirmation email for a one-way train ticket to London.

It seemed like Clara's suspicions were correct: Vanessa had planned to drop out of university, and had left Havington of her own accord. As a result, the police came to the campus less, focusing instead on other lines of enquiry – like who Vanessa might have visited in London, or where she might be staying. In a matter of days, *#FindVanessa* slowed to a stop, and the *MISSING* posters began to droop, wet and soggy in their leaky plastic casings.

Although I was occasionally frozen with guilt that I hadn't gone to look for her at the party, I told myself that Vanessa had been planning to leave all along. Inviting her to the party clearly hadn't changed her mind. It was a shame that I hadn't been able to say goodbye, but I hadn't actually *done* anything; her train ticket was already booked. If she wanted to be found, she would be found.

I forced myself instead to look ahead, to ignore what regrets I had and instead start planning for the future. Start planning for the next party.

As I leaned back in my comfortable coffee-shop seat and nibbled the top off a white-chocolate-and-raspberry muffin, a hint of an idea flashed in my mind. 'What about an equinox party?'

Clara pointed at me with a perfectly manicured finger, the nail painted a pearly pink. 'Go on,' she said.

'It's towards the end of the month,' I said. 'The twentieth, I think? It's the first official day of spring. We could have . . .' I wracked my brain. 'Crystals. Candles. Lots of foliage and flowers.'

Clara's eyes lit up. 'I like it! We could set it up by the river.'

'Perfect,' I said.

'We could swim in the river under the moonlight.' Clara's gaze was dreamy. 'It'd be so beautiful.'

'It'd be freezing!'

'It's not a sacrifice if it's *fun*,' Clara retorted.

I peered at her over my muffin. 'Who said there needed to be a sacrifice?'

'That's not a thing for the equinox?'

'Literally, no.'

Clara sighed. 'Shame.' She ran a fingernail round the edge of her mug, rubbing off a smudge of lipstick, and when she caught my eye we both burst into spluttered laughter.

The initial idea began to solidify, buoyed by a back-and-forth between me and Clara that was almost constant. Despite being in one another's presence for hours a day, we still ended up sending each other paragraphs of ideas at midnight from our respective rooms – links to inspirational photoshoots, decorations, even just lists of words that established Clara's desired aesthetic: *shimmer, dusk, elixir, rose, mist, constellation, energy, starlight, nature.*

The next step was to work out who, exactly, to invite.

'What shall we do about the guest list?' I mused over breakfast one morning, a week or so after I'd first proposed the equinox party.

Clara, in her pyjamas, was nursing her usual cup of coffee. 'What do you mean?'

'Well, it looks like more people want to come. More than at New Year's, even.' I knew that that had been Clara's biggest party thus far, aside from her sweet sixteen. (I could only imagine how raucous an affair *that* had been.)

'How do you know?'

'People are asking. Online.'

'I don't think anyone's ever *asked* to be invited before,' Clara said.

I sat up. 'You're kidding, right?' I said. 'Everybody wants to be invited to your parties.'

'Do they?' Clara was playing it cool or fishing for compliments or utterly oblivious. I decided the first and last options were the most likely; after all, she received no shortage of compliments.

'Do you even *read* the comments when you post something?' I asked her, half scolding and half playful. 'I mean, seriously?'

'Sometimes,' she said. 'Not all of them, though.'

'Go and have a look,' I said. 'But believe me: everybody wants to get an invitation to one of Clara Holland's parties.'

There was a pause. 'Maybe we should widen the guest list,' Clara said. 'Allow plus ones. What do you think?'

That *we* again. It made something warm and dark deep in my ribs open, like a flower unfurling. 'I think it's a good idea,' I said. 'That way, it's still exclusive. And you should be able to trust everyone, if they're friends of friends.'

'I don't care about trusting them,' Clara said unexpectedly. 'I care how they make me look.'

'You have to be able to trust that they won't go crazy or trash your house, though,' I pointed out. 'Or post a million pictures on the internet.'

'That'd hardly be a disadvantage, considering my career.'

My expression must have changed in some minute way, because she folded her arms. 'What?'

'What do you mean, what?' I said.

Her expression clouded. 'You smirked.'

I blinked at her. 'No, I didn't.'

'You did. When I said *my career*. Do you not think this is a career?'

'Of course I think it's a career,' I said. 'It's just that – well, it could be *more* of a career.'

Clara waited, silently, for me to make my point. Poised to strike.

I scrambled to explain that I hadn't meant it as an insult. 'I just think you could use everything that you've done so far as an influencer, as a model, to launch even more of a career. You know? Brand partnerships, charity work – you could write a book. You could do anything.'

Clara's irritated countenance became one of wonder, her face transforming like the dawn breaking over the landscape. 'I'd love to write a book!' she said. 'An autobiography. Or, like, a fictionalised version of my life.'

'Yes!' I said. 'You'd be brilliant at that.'

'Or . . .' Clara looked at me, her excitement fizzing like the

152

bubbles in a glass of champagne. 'You're a Creative Writing student. And you're so clever at writing captions! Maybe we could write it together? Me and you, with both of our names on the cover. I could narrate, and you could write.'

My stomach clenched, soured. *I don't want to write a book with you*, a voice in my head whined. *I want to write my own book, my own story, with my* own *name on the cover.*

I hadn't written – or even tried to write – any of my own novel in weeks. My life had become consumed by university assignments and, let's face it, my commitment to Clara. And, somehow, Clara expected me to write a book on her behalf? What was *wrong* with her? But, then again, I was the one who'd suggested it; I could hardly be upset. If anything, I should have been pleased that she liked my idea, that she valued my input.

'Sure,' I said, hoping that she didn't detect the hint of reluctance. 'That would be fun.'

'We'll start it after the party,' Clara said decisively. 'We've got enough to keep us busy until then.'

And I, perfect little follower that I was, pushed down any protest that rose up inside me and nodded in agreement, smiling all the while.

As I'd been trying, and occasionally failing, to balance my university commitments with my life with Clara, she had, apparently, not had the same concerns.

One Monday morning a couple of weeks later, still relatively early in the semester, she waltzed into the kitchen, all golden hair and cheeks flushed from the cold, while I was making my first coffee of the day. She wore a black velvet headband studded with pearls, her hair creating a halo of light round her face. She looked positively angelic. I, meanwhile, was still in my pyjamas.

'Coffee?' I asked.

'Yes, please,' she said. She slid on to one of the kitchen-island chairs, tossing her miniature leather backpack on to the counter beside her. I noted a familiar triangle logo on the flap: Prada. Naturally.

I grabbed another mug, and set the machine going. 'Where've you been?' I asked. 'It's barely nine thirty.'

'On campus,' she said. 'I had a meeting with my academic advisor at eight thirty. She was concerned about my performance and my attendance.' She rolled her eyes.

I ignored the stab of guilt. My own academic advisor had been sending me probing emails about my increasing number of absences too, to which I had yet to reply. I was irritated at the concern. I'd barely missed any at all, really – four or five, maximum.

'What happened?' I asked Clara now.

'Oh, it's all resolved,' Clara said breezily. 'Ninety-eight percent attendance for last semester, and a healthy sixty-five on my last assignment. They couldn't give me too high a grade, obviously, since I only handed in my notes. But it's a solid two-one, so I'll take it.'

I frowned. As far as I knew, Clara had only attended one or two lectures and seminars since I'd known her. Her time on campus was largely spent in the library or the coffee shop, supposedly for research purposes – but mostly, I felt, for being visible, for playing the part of the well-dressed, dedicated student.

'But you haven't been going,' I said. 'Right? So how can—'

'Chloe,' she said, almost pityingly, 'anything can be arranged, if you ask nicely enough.'

I stayed quiet.

Clara sighed. 'Look,' she said, 'I would've written a brilliant essay. That much was clear from my notes, so they just . . . didn't require the actual essay. It makes sense, doesn't it?'

'I suppose,' I said grudgingly.

'And as for my attendance – all of the lecture notes are online, anyway. Why would I go?'

'I thought a big part of journalism courses was learning from industry experts,' I pointed out. 'Like, actual journalists.'

'My mum's been talking to people she's worked with at *Vogue* and *Harper's Bazaar*,' Clara said, taking the steaming mug of coffee when I offered it. 'I can just do a summer with one or the other. Or both of them. It's whatever.'

It's whatever. If only everything in life could be so simple.

'I'm going to go and get changed,' she said, brushing past

me with an affectionate squeeze of my shoulder. 'Thanks for the coffee.'

I chose not to remind her that it was her coffee, made with her coffee machine, in her house. Instead, I leaned into the touch and smiled, but, as I watched her walk away, I was left with a sinking feeling of unease.

Chapter 17

The twentieth of March, the day of the equinox party, dawned bright and blue. It had been cold overnight, and the lawn was speckled with dewdrops that glittered in the sunlight.

I'd stolen a towelling white robe from Clara, monogrammed with our shared initials, and I sat in the orangery with a latte, gazing out of the window at the distant hills shrouded in mist.

The stylists and caterers weren't due until the afternoon, and, though it was a Friday, I decided I didn't have anywhere to be. I'd decided to have a relaxing morning, and then go for a long walk. I hadn't explored much of Clara's parents' land yet, but she'd told me that there was a footpath down by the river, close to where we'd be hosting the equinox party that evening.

I drained my mug and went indoors, rinsing it in the sink as I passed through the kitchen and into the hallway. Clara was in the living room, wearing a baby-pink athletic set, holding an impossible position as she followed the commands of an on-screen Pilates instructor. Her skin was covered in a sheen of sweat, her hair tied back. She wiggled her fingers at me.

'Where are you going?' she asked, breathless, as she released her muscles from the taut position, preparing to move, slowly and smoothly, into another.

'Just to get changed,' I said. 'I think I'll go for a walk. I want to get some air before tonight. I was thinking I might go down to the river, follow the footpath along for a bit.'

'Cool,' Clara said. She reached down and touched her toes without bending her knees. 'Walk east,' she said. 'And you'll get to the temple.'

'The what?'

'There's an old Roman temple. Actually, no, it's not really Roman. It's a folly, built by some old, eccentric landowner to look like one. It's pretty, though. You should go and have a look.'

'I think I will,' I said, my interest piqued.

I didn't have hiking clothes with me – my stout boots and waterproofs and fleeces were all at home – but, upstairs, I slipped on my trainers and a soft, hooded jumper in an approximation of outdoor clothing. I wasn't going to be climbing mountains, anyway.

Clara was still at her Pilates as I came back downstairs, the instructor's voice cool and calming. I darted to the pantry to grab a can of Diet Coke, and then exited Deneside Manor via the orangery. I closed the doors gently behind me.

The morning air was still cool. The grass was beginning to grow again, the sparse, muddied patches left over from winter slowly coming back to life. Morning birdsong filled the air, indicating that spring was well and truly here – even if the temperature hadn't quite caught up yet.

As I approached the woodland, my trainers sliding over the mud, I noticed that the spaces between the trees were bright with daffodils, the last waning snowdrops dotted here and there in little bunches. The trees were budding, and everything smelled of new life.

The ground sloped steadily downhill, and I followed a rough path towards the river. It was grassed over, studded with roots and rabbit holes, the entrances to the deep burrows where, I imagined, families of rabbits were curled up warm and tight, undisturbed by my quiet presence.

When I reached the river, it was full from the recent rain, dark and thick with peat from the hills. I walked along the bank, upstream, heading east as Clara had suggested.

And then I saw it. The temple.

Despite its history as a folly, the temple had a resplendent yet forlorn air, which suggested it belonged to long-forgotten gods. It was a hollowed-out egg of once-white marble, its domed roof supported on carved marble pillars that were being choked by ivy. The side closest to me, half facing the river, featured an arched opening partially covered by an ivy shroud. Whatever lay inside was wreathed in shadow, and my skin prickled in anticipation.

I pushed my way through throngs of brambles, my thick sleeves preventing scratches, but the sharp barbs still clinging to the fabric and tugging my hair as I passed. I felt strangely pursued: Little Red Riding Hood in the frightening dark woods. I knew that I was letting myself get carried away, my imagination running wild, as it always had since I was a child. There was no danger here – aside, perhaps, from the river.

The temple was shaded when I stepped inside, the air cooler beneath its roof than it was outside. The marble floor was dark and dirty, littered with dried leaves and a bird corpse. The bird was long dead, a mere pile of bones and stray black feathers. I poked it, gingerly, with the toe of my trainer.

Despite the decay, the feathers and bones of the bird and the dead leaves, the temple was peaceful. Sunlight reflected on the running water, creating dappled patterns on the temple's walls. The overhanging ivy swung in a light breeze. I could imagine bringing a book here in the summer, or a notebook and pen. This would be the perfect place to jot down some thoughts or dreams, or just about anything else that I could think of. I could see myself here on a hot day, putting down my pen and then slipping into the welcoming cold of the river, the waist-deep water a balm on my sweaty skin.

But, today, I didn't have time. Besides, it was far too cold to go swimming. I shuddered at the thought, and then remembered that a big element of Clara's equinox party was for guests to swim in the moonlit river. She'd been particularly struck by the image, and I was still hoping I'd be able to persuade her otherwise.

I left the temple and set off back downstream, glancing

over my shoulder one final time at the eerily wonderful structure. I wondered whether the wealthy landowner who'd had the temple constructed was responsible for any other features on the land. The statue of the woman in the fountain, the one that was in a state of neglect with her thick coating of moss, seemed to be of a similar material and style. Perhaps the same person had arranged for her to be built too. If so, I was certainly grateful.

The birds continued to sing, the woodland vibrant and alive as I walked on. I passed the bottom of the garden, where I'd first entered the woodland, and continued along the riverbank. A rabbit darted in front of me, and for a moment I stopped to watch an agile nuthatch flit up and down a tree, its orange chest bright in the shadows. I even saw a heron, standing stock still in a slower-moving pool, its neck poised, ready to strike.

By the time I set off back to the house itself, I was outstandingly relaxed. Unfortunately, it wasn't to last.

'Chloe!' Clara said, sounding relieved as I stepped through the door to the orangery.

Caught off-guard, I took in the scene in front of me.

Clara was standing in the middle of the orangery, still clad in her workout gear. The wicker garden furniture had been pushed aside, replaced by an enormous table, packaging tangled around its legs.

'They delivered the table,' she said, by way of explanation. 'But they left it here.'

'Did you ask them if they could move it?' I asked.

'Yes,' Clara said. 'They said that wasn't their job.'

To be fair to them, it probably wasn't. But it did leave us in an unfortunate position.

'We could wait for Emily and the others,' I said hopefully.

Clara pouted. 'I told them there wouldn't be any heavy lifting.'

I sighed, understanding our fate. 'We're going to have to carry it, then,' I said. 'Or we'll have to try to, anyway.'

For the second time that day, I entered the woods. This time, I was walking backwards holding one end of the heavy table while Clara, who had a firm grip on the other, directed me. I glanced periodically at my feet, keeping an eye out for the roots I'd spotted earlier. To fall over something now would result in the table landing on me, which wasn't something that I fancied happening. If the sudden weight of it didn't actually break a limb, it'd certainly leave me with one hell of a bruise.

We lugged it through the trees, occasionally stopping and putting it down, its legs sinking into the leaf litter while we caught our breath.

'This is ridiculous,' I said, panting, my hands on my knees. 'Whose idea was it to put a bloody table in the woods?'

I knew that it was mine, but it was worth it to see the way that Clara lifted her head, her furious gaze zeroing in on mine. 'It was *yours*,' she said.

'I know, I know. But who *agreed* to it?'

Clara's mouth opened and then shut. 'You're not invited tonight,' she said, catching on that I was making fun of her. 'You can just stay in your bedroom and watch us all having fun out of the window.'

'You'd never do that to me,' I said. 'You like me too much.'

A long-suffering sigh. 'Yes,' Clara said. 'I do.'

'Come on,' I said, taking hold of the table again, my fingers gripping its underside. 'Let's get this over with.'

We set the table up in the glade that Clara had mentioned, a space that I'd walked through an hour earlier. It was close to the river, but not *too* close; near enough to hear the water flowing, the splashes of little fish leaping. I wondered if the heron I'd seen earlier was still hunting nearby. I gazed up at the branches; they were still bare, cautiously beginning to bud, but in a month or so they'd be a canopy of leaves.

'Okay,' I said as we both stopped to catch our breath. 'What else?'

'The caterers are bringing the food,' Clara said. 'Sam, Linda and Emily are bringing the crystals and candles. Oh, and they're stopping off at the florist for us, to pick up the flower arrangements and crowns.'

'What about glassware?'

'They'll bring that too.'

'Cool, okay,' I said. 'So we just need to bring the drinks and the cooler boxes down.'

'We can do that,' Clara said. 'It's all coming together.' Then,

'Wait! We need a photo. We need to post something, to ramp up the excitement ahead of tonight.'

I held out my hand ready to receive her phone, more than used to Clara's impromptu photoshoots by now. 'Why don't you pretend you're carrying the table?' I suggested. '"Party preparation in progress".'

'That's perfect,' Clara said, clapping. 'That's exactly what we need.'

She moved to the opposite side of the table, and hooked her fingers beneath the edge. The pose emphasised the lean muscles in her arms, the ridge of her collarbones. With her make-up-free skin glowing and her hair loose and sticking to her sweaty brow, she looked absolutely delectable.

Together, we scrolled through the pictures. I'd taken half a dozen, and Clara selected the image she wanted to post in seconds; she was uncannily used to assessing her own beauty and disregarding any unflattering angles. It was a skill that I imagined took a lot of practice, as I could hardly bear to look at photographs of myself.

The picture she selected, though, was perfect. In it, she was caught in a shaft of watery sunlight filtering through the branches above her head, her smile halfway to laughter.

'What caption?' Clara asked.

'Something simple,' I said. 'What about just *Party pending*, and the eyes emoji? Maybe a little fire emoji too.'

Clara nodded. 'I like that. It's cute.'

I watched as she typed the caption, added a few select

hashtags, and clicked Post. Almost instantly, the comments began to roll in.

Clara turned back to me, and I was struck once again by how beautiful she was when she was so happy. 'Right,' she said. 'Let's go get ready!'

Chapter 18

As the guests began to arrive, I gazed in admiration at what we'd created.

Under Clara's instruction, her stylists had built a sanctuary in the darkness of the woods – the quiet, shaded glade transformed into a grotto of wonder.

The table was dressed in white lace, like a bride, adorned with enormous vases filled to bursting with spring flowers in shades of pink, lilac and blue. They were the kind you would find in an English cottage garden: hyacinths, peonies, bluebells. They glowed in the flickering light of the elegant white candles and tealights in mason jars, the cutlery and white porcelain plates tinted burnt orange and amber by the flames and the setting sun. A flower crown sat on each plate, golden threads woven around the stems, and the blooms gleamed beneath the strings of lights that hung from the branches above our heads like an arrangement of tiny stars. It looked completely magical.

Linda had provided a selection of crystals, which Clara had painstakingly arranged as a centrepiece. There were chunks of rose quartz, raw amethyst, long stems of selenite. I didn't recognise the others.

'This one's white aragonite,' Clara explained to me, indicating a milky stone in the centre of the display. 'That's celestite. And that big one's called desert rose. See the shape?'

The crystal was a deep sand colour, with flat petal-like formations fanning out from its centre. I ran my fingertip over it, lightly, feeling the edges against my skin. 'I love it.'

'Maybe, after the party, you could keep it,' Clara said.

Secretly, I'd already decided that I would.

At Emily's suggestion, we'd used the leftover fairy lights to create a path that stretched from the patio outside the orangery to the edge of the woodland. Now, we watched as the guests strode through the grass in their equinox party finery.

There was an otherworldly feeling to the proceedings as, one by one, they entered the woodland. Clara, ever the hostess, greeted them all with hugs and kisses on both cheeks. I, meanwhile, could only stare.

Everyone had taken our equinox theme to heart. I spotted a pink tulle minidress studded with rosebuds; a shimmery maxi dress embroidered with tiny colourful flowers and white sequins; an ankle-length chiffon affair in lilac with enormous puffed sleeves. However, none of these young women in their wonderful gowns, elaborate hairpieces, expensive jewellery and sparkling brooches could hold a candle to Clara.

For this party, a celebration of the beginning of spring and the revival of the natural world, she'd chosen the polar opposite of the glamorous outfit she'd worn on New Year's Eve. She wore a simple white satin dress, midi-length, with thin, delicate shoulder straps. She was barefoot, with minimal make-up, her hair in effortless, natural waves. At some point while we were surveying our handiwork, leaves and twigs had got caught in the strands. I'd gone to pull them out, but Clara had shaken her head, pulling away from me, her eyes shining and cheeks flushed.

Of course, my own outfit mimicked Clara's: a silky dress that brushed my ankles, teamed with a pair of barely-there sandals. My hair, like hers, was loose.

I picked up a glass of champagne fizzing with raspberries, and drifted around the edge of the party, smiling at the faces I recognised, nodding at the ones that I didn't. Already, the party looked like something out of *A Midsummer Night's Dream*, an otherworldly gathering of fairies in the woods.

Vanessa's face swam to the forefront of my mind, the way that she'd spun in her silver dress at the New Year's Eve party. I pushed it away. Across the clearing, Clara placed a flower crown on a guest's head. She threw her head back, laughing at something that the girl had said, and admiration swelled in my chest.

And then I felt a presence beside me. It was Ayanna.

'I hear you've moved in with her,' she said. She wasn't looking at me, though; she, too, was watching Clara.

'I have,' I said.

She turned to face me, her expression unreadable. 'Are you sure that's a good idea?'

'Why wouldn't it be?' I asked. 'I love living here. We have so much fun. We're going to write a memoir together.'

'Clara's memoir,' Ayanna said. It wasn't a question.

'Well, yes,' I said. 'If it was my memoir, it'd be about a page long.'

'Don't say that,' Ayanna said. 'You shouldn't put yourself down.'

'It's true, though,' I said. 'The most interesting thing that's happened to me in forever is meeting her.'

'Is that why you put up with it?'

I frowned. 'I don't *put up* with anything.'

Ayanna's voice was hard. 'So you don't live your life on Clara's terms?' she asked. 'You don't live in her shadow, doing what she wants, when she wants?'

Her words stung. 'I don't mind,' I said.

'You should mind,' Ayanna said. Something seemed to dawn on her. 'She's already trying to manipulate you, isn't she? How many lies has she told you?'

'No,' I said hotly. 'And none. She tells me the truth – even if it makes her look bad.'

Ayanna's lips twitched. 'She didn't tell you she was offered places at Oxford and Cambridge, then? That she turned them both down to come to Dern?'

I stayed silent. She *had* told me that.

'Clara is a wonderful person, when she wants to be,' Ayanna said, softer now. 'Sometimes, she's even inspiring. But, well . . . to be honest, she's a bit of a fraud, Chloe. You can't even apply to both Oxford and Cambridge – you have to choose one of them! And you must see she doesn't work hard enough to get into somewhere like that. The only university she applied to was Dern, because her parents owned this house, and because her mother knew someone on the faculty who could pull a few strings for her. And I know this for a fact, because we were dating at the time.' She shook her head. 'Clara knew that she'd be found out at a bigger university, that everyone would see through her glossy veneer. At Dern, she's a big fish in a little pond, and that's the way she likes it.'

'Look,' I said, struggling to absorb this new information, 'I know she can be difficult. I know she's done some questionable things. Maybe she *has* lied to me, once or twice – whatever! But she's not like that any more. She's told me everything, Ayanna, even the truth about the rumour.'

'Oh, the thing with the model?' Ayanna said. 'That's something, at least.'

Fear slithered down my spine. 'What are you talking about?'

'The rumour that she pushed a model down a flight of stairs to steal her spot at a magazine shoot,' Ayanna said. She paused. 'What are *you* talking about?'

'I'm talking about the girl with the nut allergy,' I said faintly. 'At boarding school, when she was thirteen. Someone told me that she gave a girl peanut oil, and when I asked her about it she said that it was true.'

Ayanna briefly closed her eyes. 'God,' she said. 'That's horrendous.'

'You didn't know?'

'No. I didn't.' Ayanna exhaled deeply, visibly pained. 'People spread nasty rumours – I know that. But *multiple* nasty rumours – especially when Clara herself has said that one of them is true – is bad news. That's . . . a potential track record of assault we're talking about.'

'I don't believe that,' I said. 'Just because she admitted to making one bad decision when she was a kid doesn't mean that every other rumour about her is true. Because that's what that model story is, right? Just gossip? Clara didn't actually tell you that it happened?'

'No,' Ayanna said. 'She didn't.'

'So, it could just be a rumour, then,' I said. 'An *actual* rumour. One that's not true.'

Ayanna's gaze was pitying. 'Sure, maybe,' she said, glancing around us, at the gathered girls. 'I think it's time for me to get going.'

'You're not staying?'

'No,' she said. I could tell she was preoccupied by Clara, by everything we'd discussed. 'Strangely enough, I'm not really in the mood. I'm going home.' She looked at me significantly. 'You should do the same.'

'But I am home,' I said, under my breath.

I watched her walk away until I couldn't see her any more, her tall, slender figure disappearing into the crowd.

Clara didn't seem to have noticed the tension in our conversation at all. In fact, she was facing the opposite direction, her hands gesticulating wildly as she told a story. A little gathering of girls, all of them in floral dresses, their flower crowns perched on their heads, listened intently, their eyes like saucers. I knew that it was the exact same way that *I* looked at Clara.

Maybe Ayanna was right and I *was* in too deep. Clara had caused real harm to someone, at least once – twice, if the rumour Ayanna had told me was true – and she didn't seem to regret it. Why would she? She hadn't faced any consequences; she was still universally beloved. It made me wonder: would she face any consequences if she did something like that to me?

I wanted to believe that she loved me, that she'd never hurt me. But, at the same time, I hadn't yet outdone her. I'd allowed her to have control, to be the star of the show at every party we'd hosted – because that was who she was. I'd shrunk myself down, letting all eyes fall on her. An accessory to her stardom, like the headpieces she wore or the floral arrangements she ordered. But what if I wasn't her accessory any more? What if I didn't spend every hour of every day with her, didn't let her dress me like a little doll? What if I didn't attend all her parties, a supporting actress in my own story? Would she allow it? Would she embrace my uniqueness graciously, or insist that

I move out? Would she poison me? Push me down the stairs in the entrance hallway, my head cracking on the chessboard tiles, a new centrepiece for her party, Clara's name on even more people's lips?

Just then she turned to look at me, saw me standing on my own, and beckoned me over, a smile spreading across her face.

'Girls, this is Chloe,' she said. 'My partner in crime, and the most loyal friend a girl could ask for.'

I knew, in that moment, as my heart swelled at her praise and the other girls gazed at me with something quite like awe, that I could never leave her.

If I had – if I'd walked out that night, following Ayanna's lead, then maybe everything would have ended there; I'd have escaped, unscathed, from Clara's orbit. But I didn't. I stayed. Despite Ayanna's warnings, the way that fear shuddered across my skin when she'd told me about what had happened between Clara and the model, I didn't want to let her go.

If I wasn't living here with Clara, I thought selfishly as I poured myself another drink from a near-empty bottle of champagne, *where would I be?* Who *would I be?* I would probably be back at Ivy House, living quietly in the shadow of Vanessa's disappearance, making cups of tea in my room to avoid my flatmates. I would be a nobody.

Here, though, I was *somebody*. I was loved, appreciated – almost revered even, sometimes. And, while I might see myself as a burnish to Clara's gleam, she clearly didn't. She kept me close for a reason, and she'd given me countless opportunities –

opportunities that I never would have had anywhere else. So what if she was self-centred occasionally and liked to help me choose what to wear? So what if she wanted me to help her write her memoir? I danced at her parties, ate her food, drank her champagne. I lived in her *house*. The very least that I owed her was my loyalty.

And I *wanted* to be loyal to her. It wasn't just a matter of owing her, or because of our friendship. I couldn't deny the way I felt about her. Clara fascinated me, bewitched me, intoxicated me. I'd never felt like that before, about anyone. And I couldn't – didn't want to – let go of that feeling.

With that in mind, I tried to dismiss what Ayanna had told me. I let her words of warning fade into the background, a faint buzz, and focused instead on what I could see with my own eyes: the Clara I knew, being generous and funny and all kinds of beautiful, dancing to a Lorde song somebody had put on, her glass held high as she half sang, half shouted along to the lyrics.

I drained my own glass, poured another: a gin and tonic this time, topped with slices of fragrant strawberry, the fruit adding a touch of sweetness. The warmth of the alcohol seeped through my veins, bringing with it a newfound happiness, a confidence that all was right with the world, and that I was exactly where I was supposed to be.

So when Clara said, 'I have an idea!' I ignored any reservations that I had. I was right by her side, as attentive as a butler, anticipating when I would be needed, how I could help.

Unsteadily, Clara climbed up on to a chair, and then on to the table. She wavered, slightly, before straightening up. A few people gasped, myself included, as a light breeze moved her dress dangerously close to a candle. But, before it set her alight, she leaned down and picked it up, holding it beside her face like a torch, her cheekbones in stark relief. Somebody switched the music off.

'This modern world,' Clara said loudly, so that everyone could hear, 'has no idea what true happiness is. It isn't *material*, like expensive cars, or designer bags, or the next video-game console. It's being able to do this – to appreciate beautiful things and people, to spend time with the people that you love.' She looked out across the crowd, her eyes fixing on every face, searing. 'All of us here tonight are immensely privileged. Look at me; I've never wanted for anything in my life. I've had all the clothes, the make-up . . . all the experiences and luxuries that money could buy. But I've never been truly happy.' Her expression grew pained, her grip visibly tightening around the candle. White wax dripped over her fingers, down on to the table. There were nods, murmurs of assent. 'My parents believe that money is the root of everything – even happiness. When I was a child, they'd try to buy my love and affection. They'd make sure I always had money, that they bought me plenty of expensive gifts. They paid for boarding school, throwing money at the problem of our relationship in the hope that their money could fix it for them.' Clara swallowed. 'But I've learned that love and happiness is so much more meaningful than that. Love and happiness is being surrounded by like-minded people, it's having the freedom to be who you are, wherever you are.'

The crowd held their breaths. I held mine.

'This is the start of a new life. A beautiful, new life,' Clara proclaimed. 'For all of us. Your love has shown me the light – that I deserve to be happy, and be loved. And to love you all in return. So I am opening up my life, my home, to you all. Indulge in true happiness. Join me here, and be yourself.' She smiled, breathless. I could have sworn that her eyes were filled with tears, shining in the candlelight. 'Stay the night, or come back tomorrow – in a week, in a month. And stay with me. If there's room, you'll be welcome. Everybody deserves to live like this – to be truly happy, to be truly loved. Together, we'll create the lives that we deserve.'

I felt like I'd been punched in the stomach.

Clara's passionate declaration was met with whoops, cheers, the shatter of glass as somebody, inexplicably, tossed a champagne flute in the air. She shut her eyes, smiling all the while, her face tilted upwards as if the love and happiness she spoke of was shining down on her, warm like a sunbeam.

Chapter 19

'Were you serious last night?' I asked.

It was the following morning, and Clara was sitting cross-legged on the kitchen island in a set of satin pyjamas. We still hadn't brought the chairs back up from the wood, but that hadn't stopped her from setting the coffee machine running and brewing her usual morning iced latte. She made a hot one for me, and I held the chunky pink mug, marbled with gold, with both hands.

Clara had dark circles under her eyes from the late night, but rather than making her look gaunt and tired they made her look subtly gothic, like a dark goddess. 'Of course,' she said, in answer to my question. 'Why?'

'You really want more people to live here with us?'

A line appeared between her eyebrows, the most minuscule of frowns. 'There's plenty of room,' she said. 'And we'll have a communal fund for groceries, toiletries, that kind of thing. Can you imagine it? A house full of girls, all of us looking out for each other.'

I started to speak, and then I stopped. How could I possibly vocalise what it was that I wanted to say – that I wanted it to just be *us*, that *I* wanted to be the girl who lived with Clara Holland – without sounding absurdly, horribly jealous?

Clara read my mind. 'Nothing's going to change between us,' she said, nudging me with her elbow. 'We'll still be *us*. We'll still have this.'

'With more people.'

'More people like us,' Clara said. 'I meant it, Chloe. You know I love our life, the rhythm we've got into, the parties – all the little luxuries that we indulge in together. But imagine another five, ten of us, all living and loving and celebrating together. We've got an opportunity here, to share our world with girls who deserve it.'

I was sulking, unconvinced. 'Can't they get it for themselves?'

'How?' Clara said. Her words were sharp. 'Not everybody is lucky enough to befriend someone like me by chance.'

I cringed. I'd hardly earned this lifestyle; I'd been in the right place at the right time – that was all. And so I had no grounds to complain if Clara wanted to open up her home to more girls, to share her space and resources.

'You're right,' I said, shamed. 'I just thought we had something special here, you know?'

'We do,' Clara said. 'Of course we do. But that doesn't mean we should keep it to ourselves. We should share what we have.'

'I know,' I said. 'I was being selfish. I'm sorry.' Then, 'Can I ask you something?'

Clara raised an eyebrow. 'Go on.'

'At the first party I came to, all of the guests were girls,' I said. 'Women. Last night too. But New Year's Eve was mixed. Why?'

'I wanted New Year's Eve to be a party for everyone,' Clara said. 'But sometimes I think we women just need and deserve a space of our own. To be ourselves, and to spend time exclusively with other women. And, anyway, I told the girls I invited on New Year's Eve that they could only bring a man if they'd vouch for him – tie their reputation to his. Sort of like a guarantee.'

I took this in. 'Did you – have you had a bad experience, or something?'

Every girl I knew had had a bad experience.

But Clara just smiled. 'Our life as women *is* our bad experience, Chloe,' she said. 'Think about it: pretty much every bit of external pressure that you've ever felt – to somehow look beautiful when you're waking up in the morning, to be a career girl *and* a stay-at-home parent, to get married before you turn thirty or else you're a colossal failure – was put upon you by the patriarchy, one way or another. And I don't want our girls to feel like that when they're here. I don't want them to be *reminded* of that. I want our parties – and the manor itself – to be a place for us to relax, to let go, to be free. I want it to be a paradise.'

I studied her, her skin and hair golden in the morning sun. 'Where has all this come from?' I asked.

Clara shrugged. 'I don't know. I suppose I've just finally realised what I want to do with my influence.'

'And what's that?'

'Make women – girls, like us – happy,' she said. 'I want them to feel safe and accepted and adored.'

It sounded selfless, generous. I truly believed that she genuinely wanted to make a difference. Until she added, dreamily, 'And be adored in return.'

We had been the first to wake up. And, as the hours passed, the hands on the clock jerking closer to noon and beyond, the guests who'd stayed over began to materialise. They appeared in the kitchen, some still wearing the shirts or dresses they'd been wearing the night before, their make-up smudged on their face, helping themselves to the contents of the pantry and to Clara's coffee machine, using the last of my favourite vanilla lungo pods.

I silently stewed over their presence, wondering which of them would choose to stay, to encroach on my life here with Clara. And I couldn't help but notice that the crystal I'd fallen in love with last night was nowhere to be seen.

Clara had asked everyone who'd like to join us at Deneside Manor to add their name to one of two lists. There was an online one for her followers who were further afield (she'd posted something on her social channels at midnight about her offer, the wording she used suspiciously close to the speech she'd given, which made me certain she'd written it beforehand) and a paper one for last night's party guests, which was stuck to the fridge with magnets shaped like strawberries. There were four spaces on each, and, naturally, it was up to Clara to determine who she believed would be a good fit. There were already more names than there were spaces.

As I peered at the paper list, I noticed that several names were jostling for space right at the very bottom of the sheet: an informal reserve list, in case Clara deemed any of the other applicants unsuitable. Or, I supposed, if any changed their mind and decided to move out.

Why would they, though? I wondered. *Why would any of them ever want to leave?*

Clara's plan was set in motion, and eight new girls made Deneside Manor their home. They moved in a week after the party, arriving in taxis and cars loaded with their possessions: feather-dusted table lamps and boxes of battered books, delicate ornaments and picture frames and well-worn shoes. The driveway was cluttered with their vehicles: battered Ford Focuses and bubblegum pink Fiat 500s like a swarm of locusts covering every bit of available space.

I'd spent the days after the equinox party sifting through applications with Clara. She'd trusted me to bin the unsuitable ones – tear-stained proclamations of love from fourteen-year-olds, applicants whose obsession with Clara seemed a bit *too* intense – but, otherwise, I'd had no involvement. She had the final say, of course, and she'd simply proceeded on her own, weighing each applicant against her own secret specifications. And, once she was satisfied, she'd handed me a list of names to contact.

On moving day, Clara had chosen to welcome our new housemates with a champagne reception, so I left her to greet them all while I poured rosé champagne into neat glasses, garnishing each one with a half strawberry. I was nervous; all these girls were beautiful and talented and lovely, both inside and out. Would I fit in with them? Would Clara come to like them more than she liked me?

I forced my face into a smile as I carried a tray of drinks into the orangery, attempting to look breezy and relaxed, comfortable and at home. There were six girls there already, all of them unique, exquisite. And, as I entered, they turned to look at me. I felt like I had the very first time I'd been a guest at one of Clara's parties, not so long ago – exposed and vulnerable beneath the weight of their combined gaze, waiting to be judged.

'I know you,' one of them, who I'd later learn was called Alexis, said warmly. 'You're Chloe! You're Clara's second-in-command, right?'

The other girls were all watching. This was my moment, my chance to establish myself as not only one of Clara's followers, but as her most loyal follower. And, because of that, as somebody to be friends with.

'That's right,' I said. I had their attention, and I added, in my best Clara impression, 'I can't even describe how delighted I am to join Clara in welcoming you all to Deneside Manor. I've lived here for a little while now, and it's . . . well, it's paradise. And I'm sure that all of you being here will only make it even better.'

There was some delicate applause, which, for a moment, I thought was half-hearted, or maybe even sarcastic. But as I looked back at the girls, who were all listening to me, I realised that it was genuine enthusiasm. They were electrified just *being* here, and their smiles couldn't be bigger.

'Beautifully put, Chloe,' said a familiar voice.

Clara strode into the orangery with all of the grandeur of the leader that she was, her head held high and the cashmere jumper and jeans she was wearing clinging to her figure. This was Clara in casual mode: eye-catching as always, even with her hair slicked back in a bun and Uggs on her feet.

She took a flute from the tray, and held it up. 'By joining us here today,' she said, with a warm glance in my direction, 'you have already done something amazing, something that was never expected of you.'

The new girls quietened, all of them listening attentively, adoringly, as Clara spoke.

'As young women,' Clara continued, 'we're taught to hate each other. From childhood, we're encouraged to be jealous of one another, to tear each other down. We fear girls more beautiful, more successful than ourselves, and this manifests in hatred. And who decides who is beautiful? Who decides who is successful? Who determines these metrics? It's not us.' The girls murmured in agreement. 'For so long, the *patriarchy* has separated us into factions, pushed us to turn on each other, on our fellow women. To so many men in this world, we're either ugly and dull or beautiful and whorish. And, if we dare to ignore these labels, if we dare to love ourselves anyway? We're conceited, stuck-up, feminist *bitches*. And who benefits from this?' Clara gazed at each of us in turn, and I imagined that her eyes lingered on mine just a little longer than everybody else's. 'In this house, the patriarchy doesn't exist. All of us are beautiful, powerful, independent women, and in this house we can throw off our insecurities. We can remove the masks that we're forced to wear for the rest of the world. Together, we're one.' Clara's tone turned lighter, and she raised her glass. 'To all of us,' she said. 'To fresh starts.'

Around us, the girls lifted their glasses too. 'To fresh starts!' they echoed.

Over the afternoon, we all got to know one another. The plentiful champagne softened the edges of any pre-existing anxieties, and it wasn't long before we began to bond.

The new girls ranged in age, with the youngest to join us eighteen, the same age as me. Her name was Bella, she told us with a bright smile, and she worked part time in Tate's coffee shop, a busy spot on the Havington main street. She'd been one of the girls to apply online. I watched as she followed Clara's every move with devoted, puppy-like eyes, and wondered if that's how I appeared when I looked at Clara too. I shuddered at the thought.

Four of the girls had come to the equinox party the previous week: wealthy, well-dressed, confident girls with polished fingernails and glossy hair, who moved in the same social circles as Clara: Alexis, Sophie, Lily and Lottie.

The other three girls, the ones who'd added their names to the online list alongside Bella, were from elsewhere around the country. Mia seemed to be from a similar background to mine – not well off, but not struggling either – whereas the other two, Millie and Christie, admitted they'd grown up envying girls like Clara. Millie unashamedly declared herself to be from a 'shithole'.

Despite the girls' surface differences, one thing was clear: each of them believed that Clara was going to be their saviour. This, I thought, was presumably the reason that Clara had selected them, along with the convenient fact that they were all gorgeous.

I watched as Clara integrated herself into every conversation, welcoming her new houseguests, hugging and kissing cheeks. After a while, she began to gently direct them to their bedrooms, encouraging them to relax before the chef prepared our evening meal. I helped as much as I could, lugging suitcases and cardboard boxes up the curved staircase and along the hallway, explaining which bedrooms had en-suites and which ones didn't, where the other bathrooms were and where they could find logs to restock the baskets beside their fireplaces. I advised on Wi-Fi passwords and the location of Blu-tack, sourced extension cables and batteries.

I was flattered that, as Deneside Manor's first resident other than Clara, I'd taken on an authoritative role. The girls looked to me, listened to me, and the satisfaction was warm in my chest. I was Clara's second-in-command, and so I mattered to them. Most of all, I mattered to Clara.

As the girls settled into their assigned rooms, pinning up posters and laying out duvet and pillowcase sets, Clara and I lingered in the kitchen together. I poured the last of a bottle of champagne into two mugs, and we perched on the edge of the kitchen table, gazing towards the orangery, cluttered as it was already with half-empty champagne flutes and stray hair accessories.

'Is this what you wanted?'

Clara clasped her mug between two hands, as if nursing a hot drink, and let out a long, satisfied sigh. 'Yes,' she said. 'This is exactly what I wanted.' She didn't look at me as she spoke, her voice soft, confessional. 'I always wanted a sister when we came to stay here during the summer,' she said. 'Someone to talk to in this big, empty house, someone to play with. Someone who *understood*. For the last few months, I've had that with you.' She smiled. 'And now I have so many more sisters. This is *good*, Chloe. I feel like I'm doing something good.'

'You are,' I told her. 'You're doing something wonderful.'

I meant it. Clara *was* doing something good; she was trying to create a utopia, a place where young women could support each other, somewhere that they could belong and be themselves, distanced from the multitude of pressures hanging over their heads like the blade of a guillotine.

And I wanted to love this idea with all my heart, to lavish praise on her for such a philanthropic undertaking, but I just couldn't.

Despite myself, I started to warm to the new Deneside Manor. Once a quiet haven, it was now chaotic and loud, but wonderful too. It was just like I'd hoped my flatmates at Dern would be: a warm, welcoming sisterhood. As the days passed, we got to know each other better. The ten of us would sit in the living room, sharing blankets and bars of chocolate as we watched a film – usually one chosen by Clara – or we'd loll in the orangery, drinking glasses of wine and talking as the sky darkened outside.

It was on these evenings that I learned more about the girls that I was living with. I'd been intimidated by Lottie, Lily, Sophie and Alexis when we'd first met, talented, wealthy and beautiful as they all were. But I learned that they, too, had big dreams and insecurities, goals and fears that kept them up at night. Lottie desperately wanted to be an singer, Lily a lawyer. Sophie had been seeing a therapist for bouts of bone-deep anxiety since she was small, and Alexis regularly butted heads with her parents over her lack of interest in a position at the family business (a well-known technology firm). It was a strange kind of relief, to understand that even girls as stereotypically perfect as the four of them were just as human as the rest of us.

187

However, it was Christie and Bella who I grew closest to. They reminded me of myself before I met Clara: sweet, slightly nervous, fearful that they didn't belong. I made it my responsibility to make sure that they knew they did.

'The other girls are all just so gorgeous,' Christie said to me one evening. She was nineteen but looked younger, with a heart-shaped face and cute round glasses. The girls were all in the living room watching a new fashion competition show that Clara swore would be the next big thing, and, when I'd left to make a cup of tea, Christie had followed me. We spoke while the kettle boiled, everything she said hushed as if she could hardly bear to admit it. 'They're so successful. And *rich*.'

'You were chosen,' I said. 'Clara picked you from literally hundreds of applications.'

'But why?' she asked. I knew she was reaching out for validation, but I couldn't give it to her. I didn't know myself.

All I knew was that we, collectively, fitted into the scene that Clara had conjured up, the innocent camaraderie of a group of young women living together in a beautiful house.

Bella, too, was initially uncertain about where she fitted in and why she'd been chosen. A Havington local, she'd moved out of her parents' house to join us at Deneside Manor. Like the rest of us, she had big dreams – and hoped that Clara and her many connections would help her to achieve them. We bonded over discussions of our favourite books, and she mentioned how envious she was that I'd got into Dern.

'I'm just taking a year out,' she explained. 'Working as a barista, saving up money. I might apply again next year. But this opportunity . . . it's just, *wow*. I feel so lucky to be here, with all of you.'

'Me too,' I said. I looked around at the girls – all of us together, smiling, laughing – and I knew I meant it.

Two weeks later, a set of rules appeared on the fridge in Clara's handwriting. She'd simply replaced the previous sheet, the list of potential guests, and used the same strawberry magnets to fix the rules to the fridge. Each one was noted down in her neat, blocky handwriting, dotted with smiley faces and tiny, doodled hearts.

1. Replace what you take – food, drinks, toiletries. If someone else bought it, *ask* before using it.
2. Attend *all* parties.
3. Follow *all* dress codes for parties (included with invitations!).
4. Leave bedrooms unlocked. If you're staying here, you've been assigned a bedroom. You MUST leave it unlocked for safety purposes.
5. Be kind. :)

Note: Girls who don't abide by these rules will be asked to leave. xo

As I was reading, I felt a warm hand on my shoulder.

'Look at this!'

I spun round. It was Clara, of course, flushed, her hair damp from a bath or shower. She thrust her phone in my face. I blinked, and it took me a moment to make sense of the blurred image, the spiky black text. I took the phone from her, waited for my eyes to adjust. It was a headline.

INSIDE: CLARA'S CULT FOLLOWING, the bold letters screamed.

Clara's lip curled. 'Can you believe it?' she said disdainfully. 'Listen to this.'

She took the phone back, scrolled down and began to read aloud. '*Clara Holland's parties run rife with rich-girl hedonism. But is there something more sinister underneath?*' She glanced at me, maybe making sure that I was paying attention, before she continued. '*On the surface, Holland's parties are identical to any other gathering of eclectic young professionals. The guest list is a who's who of bright young things, including prominent artists, singers, writers, models, activists, wannabes, and hangers-on of the common-and-garden variety. However, rumours have begun to fly in recent months — both among her hundreds of thousands of online followers and on the campus of the prestigious local university which she attends.*'

'Wow,' I said, taken aback. 'As if.'

'I know!' she said, her eyes flashing with righteous fury. 'I can't believe they're accusing us of being a *cult*. Because why *else* would young women come together? What is this, a witch hunt?'

'It's not really surprising, though, is it? It's the *Daily Sun* – they're complete misogynists.'

'True,' Clara relented. 'I just hate the idea that they're seeing what we're doing here and twisting our intentions, moulding them to suit their own toxic agenda.'

'What *are* our intentions?' I dared to ask.

I half expected Clara to refuse to answer me, to pout and sulk over the fact that I didn't know, by heart, what it was that we'd chosen to stand for. But, frankly, we hadn't *chosen* anything. It wasn't like we'd held a focus group and come to the conclusion that a) we were going to invite other girls to live with us, and b) we were going to do it for these specific reasons. Everything that had happened had come from a single speech that Clara had made, the carefully incubated idea hers alone.

'Our intention is to provide somewhere where young women, girls like us, can be *free*,' Clara said. She spoke carefully, her tone measured, as if this particular phrase, too, was something that she'd rehearsed beforehand. Perhaps she had. 'Somewhere they can be free to be who they are, and where they can shrug off all the expectations and the assumptions and the fucking *mundanity* of the patriarchal society that we live in.' Clara was glowing, her eyes shining with fervent belief. 'We're cultivating the *ultimate* girl gang. We want to live life like the party it is, to live together like we're having a permanent sleepover. We're empowering and supporting each other, and we're building a society. A *society*, Chloe – of strong, beautiful, independent young women.'

It was clear that she meant it, every word accentuated with her sheer enthusiasm and her pride. But, as lovely as it was, I was struggling to believe that there was really something *radical* about her plan. When all was laid bare, she was a pretty, privileged girl opening up her lovely home to girls just like her. How was she empowering anyone by inviting her followers, who already worshipped her, to live with her and worship her even *more*? Surely, the only young woman she was empowering in this scenario was herself?

'It's a trashy newspaper,' I said eventually. 'It's full of rubbish. But it *is* a national one. Maybe we should be careful, just in case.'

'Be careful? How?'

I hesitated. 'Well, we could get rid of the rules. Maybe? In case people ask questions.'

Abruptly, Clara turned on me. 'Seriously? That's what you're worried about? We have a house full of amazing, intelligent women – a community of brilliant girls who came here of their own accord, who are *desperate* to have what we have. They *want* to be here. And if anyone asks them about it, that's exactly what they'll say! It's obvious that we're not a cult, rules or not. So will you please just stop overthinking it?'

Her point made, she stormed off. I recognised, with a sinking feeling, that she was upset with me. The thought of

192

having displeased her made nausea roil in my stomach, even though what I'd said was important. What if she made me move out, replaced me with somebody who listened to her, who believed in her, who could follow her rules more closely? There would be no shortage of girls eager to take my place.

She was right, anyway – of course we weren't a cult. And nothing was going to happen. Why would it?

Chapter 20

But everything changed in the days and weeks after the first article came out.

Her previously honoured guests, the famous and the super wealthy who'd attended her parties in haute couture and who'd arrived on New Year's Eve in Lamborghinis and Bentleys, stayed away from the manor. Presumably, they'd been put off by the headlines that seemed to multiply every day, their publicists concerned about their proximity to a budding scandal.

That didn't seem to matter to Clara. After all, she was adored by so many more people now. She didn't need powerful connections. She *was* the connection.

Deneside Manor began to fall into disarray. The replacement housekeeper had quit, the chef too. The garden became a tangle of weeds, the orangery a veritable jungle. There was girlish clutter on every surface: lipsticks, eyelash curlers, stray earrings. In the kitchen, foil takeaway containers were left open, their contents scattered across the kitchen table. Half-eaten peaches and nectarines seeped juice across the countertops. Bare feet tracked mud and dust across the hardwood floors, the tiles, the carpets. The once quiet manor became thoroughly lived in, and it became all the more intriguing to outsiders because of it.

Clara would often host small gatherings, intimate socials with nibbles and cocktails that were far less extravagant than her seasonal parties. Afterwards, the assorted hangers-on – those girls who didn't quite live with us but desperately wanted to – would lounge on the sofas and the rugs like flies stuck in honey. They would stay until the early hours and then, reluctantly, venture out into the night to travel home by taxi.

Due to the random nature of these gatherings, there was no longer any way to keep track of who should be in the house and who shouldn't. People walked in at odd hours, and the front door was very rarely locked. Sometimes, I lay awake at night, listening to the low murmur of voices downstairs, the clinking of glasses and the sound of light footsteps coming and going. Whenever somebody passed by my door, I held my breath. I knew that they could easily open it, and it seemed inevitable that, at some point, they would.

Clara insisted that it was a non-issue. She enforced a system based on mutual trust, on an understanding that nobody would make off with her parents' antiques or set fire to the living-room curtains or drink all the stockpiled Moët in the pantry. It was never discussed what might happen if somebody did any of those things. Privately, I assumed it would result in their exclusion from the manor. In Clara's world, though, it simply wasn't a possibility worth considering.

Whenever I raised my concerns with her, she'd brush them off. 'It's fine, Chloe,' she said, over and over. 'I like it this way.'

I don't, I wanted to say. And yet, every time, I stayed quiet, shamed into silence. What Clara wanted mattered most – just like Ayanna had said.

For the first time, I began to feel a distance between us. Previously, Clara had always been concerned about me, keen to ask me for my input – or even just to spend time together coexisting in the same room, no conversation, just reading. It felt like the more I tried to grab on to Clara, to keep her interest focused on me and remind her that this had all started with the two of us, the more she pulled away, excited about her new venture, her new followers.

And her followers *were* growing. The cult article had spread rapidly online. And, as much as I hated to admit it, the old adage of *all press is good press* appeared to ring true. Every day, Clara's online following was a little bit bigger, the comments a little more devoted. Girls our own age, younger than us, older than us, begged to stay at Deneside Manor, pledged their love and loyalty, said that even if it *was* a cult they didn't care; they wanted to be in it. Clara was gentle when she reminded her younger followers that they needed to be adults to live with us, to join in our drinking and our parties – but she added names to waiting lists and lapped up the flattery.

I took it upon myself to rile up the other girls, to renew their excitement about Clara. Sometimes, during the unplanned gatherings or the casual drinks, tempers would fray. We were a house full of hormones, of different backgrounds and beliefs and goals; conflict was not only likely, but unavoidable. At these times, I became the gel that held the group together.

If I caught wind of a barbed comment or a moment of tension, I'd take the opportunity to make a rousing speech. 'Girls,' I said, on one such occasion, as several of us lounged together in the living room, 'don't you understand how lucky we are? It might not feel like it, sometimes, but Deneside Manor is a *paradise*. There's always another girl to help you, to care for you. Someone who'll help you to apply the perfect amount of eyeliner or blush, to braid your hair or who might be able to suggest ways to deal with that sexist guy at work.' I glanced towards Bella, who'd previously asked for advice on how to deal with a male colleague who wouldn't stop interrupting her during staff meetings. She nodded in acknowledgement, in acceptance. 'Here, one of us is always around to look over your job application, to point out where you've sold yourself short, and later offer champagne and celebrations or tears and hugs when you're accepted or rejected. We're the ultimate girl gang, remember? Everyone wants to be *us*.'

Reminded of the positives, of the exclusivity of living at Deneside Manor, everything quickly became right again, harmony swiftly restored with sheepish apologies. And I knew it wasn't about me, not really, but it made me feel powerful all the same.

On that particular occasion, Clara had nipped out of the

room and the girls had taken the opportunity to gripe and complain out of her earshot. She'd returned while I was mid-speech and stood at the door, watching me, silently smiling with approval. But her eyes were stony.

Meanwhile, on campus, Clara was simultaneously a beacon and a pariah. I'd grown used to the curious looks, the knowing whispers, that surrounded us as we walked together, as we bought our coffees. Overnight, though, after the article, it escalated. People began to approach us and greet us by name, telling Clara how much they admired her – both university staff and students alike. Once or twice, I was enveloped in a completely unexpected hug, Clara looking on like a proud parent as I tensed and tried to accept the affection and the compliments without cringing. It was an odd feeling, knowing that people who I'd never met had seen my face. Sometimes, courtesy of Clara's Instagram, they'd even comment on what I'd had for breakfast, the outfit I'd worn yesterday, the book I'd been reading in the background of one of Clara's pictures. When that happened, I'd be momentarily stunned, reminded of just how attentive Clara's followers were.

At the same time, other people seemed to have grown more suspicious of Clara, and of me by association. They'd cast wary glances in our direction as they passed us on campus, studiously avoid browsing the same shelves in the library. Some of them, usually girls our own age, even vacated nearby tables if we sat down inside the coffee shop to chat, picking up their bags and their drinks and moving to sit elsewhere. This behaviour bothered me, but not enough for me to voice it to Clara. Besides, she barely seemed to notice it at all; she was too preoccupied.

Clara had begun to call her followers Goldens, nicknamed so because they liked to copy the accessories that she wore – which were, of course, predominantly gold. Gradually, Clara's other wardrobe choices began to spread; both Dern's campus and my Instagram feed experienced a sudden influx of white broderie anglaise dresses, flowing maxi skirts, cute little flower crowns and flashes of gold.

Inside Deneside Manor, too, we'd begun to dress like Clara.

It had been unintentional really; apparently, all of us were simply desperate to mimic our idol. This not-so-subtle copying – our clothes various shades of ecru, cream and sparkling white, with hints of denim and leather and glitter – started out as an innocent trend, yet another extension of Clara's influence. However, this copycat styling quickly progressed to becoming a dress code, a uniform; something to be enforced, not just enjoyed.

One morning, Christie bounded down the stairs and into the kitchen wearing a red cropped T-shirt and jeans. Her hair was in two stubby plaits, each tied with a hair bobble that resembled a pair of cherries: red plastic balls with tiny green stems, which clicked against each other as she walked. She was chattering away about the forecast as she poured herself a glass of orange juice, and it took her a minute before she realised that nobody was responding to her. Instead, the Goldens who were sitting at the table – Mia, Alexis, Sophie, Lottie – all stared at her derisively, their lips curling. Standing by the coffee machine, I looked on, taken aback by how quickly the informal dress code had seemingly become mandatory. Clara would always dictate the dress code for parties, of course – but this was all the Goldens. Christie left the kitchen a moment later, her cheeks the same colour as her top. The next time I saw her, she was in all white. Even her cute cherry hair bobbles had gone.

Away from Havington, people didn't seem to know what to make of Clara. It was easy to write her off as just another influencer – just another thin, blonde white girl living in her rich parents' house. She wasn't anything special. There were hundreds of girls just like her online. And yet even her harshest critics couldn't deny that there was something *about* Clara, something magnetic in the way that she seemed to exert real power, genuine influence, over the girls and the women who were loyal to her. She recommended a beauty product; it sold out. She asked people to donate to causes she cared about – Havington's animal rescue centre, a scheme to help young children learn to read – and the money from her followers flowed in. It felt as if she could ask them to do anything, give their money to anything, and they would. She was unstoppable.

Every day, I scrolled through the comments, overwhelming myself with Clara's reach and wondering what on earth she had dragged me into. But, of course, she hadn't dragged me into anything; I'd followed her willingly. I'd been the first Clara-obsessed resident of Deneside Manor, hadn't I? I couldn't hold it against people for falling in love with her. I'd fallen for her too. My feelings for Clara were something that blurred the lines.

What made this time bearable was the memoir.

As Clara had decreed, we began shortly after the equinox party, just as the first Goldens came to live with us. Every day, or at least every other day, Clara and I would get together – sometimes in the orangery, more often in Clara's bedroom. It was the one place where it was understood that nobody went without an invitation, unlocked or not. Desperate for alone time with Clara as I was, I never missed a session.

Clara would sit cross-legged on her bed, and I'd sit on the dressing-table chair, and she'd talk. I'd type as she did, ignoring things like spelling and punctuation. And then, after an hour or so, we'd go our separate ways and I'd redraft what we'd written – what *I'd* written – into something legible. I'd then email it to Clara, who'd read it. She'd send me her feedback (remarks on anything from grammar to turns of phrase), which I'd then action on the document. When she was happy, sometimes after three or four versions, she'd come and find me and give me a hug, her arms warm and her skin smelling of vanilla, and it'd be just like old times.

Three weeks after Clara's followers arrived at Deneside Manor, we finished the first few chapters. They were primed, polished, every single word perfect – or, at least, what Clara deemed to be so. As I flicked through the pages, rereading paragraphs here and there, I couldn't help but feel frustrated. This wasn't the kind of book that I'd ever imagined I'd write; I'd spent all this time, all this effort, on somebody else's dreams. But, I told myself, at least it *was* a book.

The early chapters described Clara's childhood: dark, lonely winters in a London townhouse; bright, solitary summers in the country house we all lived in, sitting on the landing with her legs dangling through the railings, listening to the soirées her parents hosted down below, the muffled laughter and clinking of glasses. She described the many trips abroad, sulking by rooftop swimming pools in Monaco and villa pools in Tuscany, the ever-present stink of chlorinated water weighing down the air, as thick and as heavy as her boredom. She'd read the same books over and over again, their pages damp and wrinkled and bleached by the sun, while her parents drank negronis and martinis and Aperol spritzes and acted as if she'd never been there at all.

As I dutifully wrote down Clara's words, translating them into something that I hoped would eventually be intimately confessional but still readable, I began to understand something about Clara that I hadn't quite before. There was a simmering, seething energy beneath her kindness, her generosity, her excitement and enthusiasm. It seeped into her every word as she lamented finally feeling like she belonged at one boarding school and then being torn away to attend a more prestigious one; her parents' disappointment at her constantly mediocre

202

grades, remarks that cut to the bone about beauty not equalling brains – 'Pretty rich, coming from two people who work in high fashion,' she'd interjected bitterly – her resulting fastidiousness and determination to succeed no matter what.

The overarching discovery that I made during those long afternoons, my fingertips racing across my keyboard in time to Clara's syrupy voice, was that Clara knew, had known all along, that she deserved better, that she deserved love and adoration. And she would make sure that she got the adoration that she believed she deserved – no matter what, or who, stood in her way.

Chapter 21

Later, as I reviewed the early chapters of Clara's memoir, one thing became clear to me. Clara was telling a story – *her* story – but throughout it she kept the reader at a distance, at arm's length. If I hadn't known Clara already, I realised, while reading back the latest paragraphs about her childhood, I wouldn't be able to grasp very much about her personality at all.

The Clara that we'd described throughout the memoir was a combination of caricatures, leaping from one to the next depending on what the particular scene or recollection required. One moment, she was a lonely child, a solitary figure surrounded by chaos. The next, she was a precocious little girl, her family's darling and beloved by all who encountered her.

Was this because of my lack of skill as a writer? Or was it because Clara's story was inconsistent? I wasn't sure.

Not for the first time, I felt hot resentment welling up inside me like floodwater, threatening to overflow. What was I *doing* here? I was supposed to be spending hours toiling over my own words, not perfecting Clara's. Frustrated, I saved the draft and then closed my laptop, shutting the lid harder than I meant to.

I sat silently for a moment, morose like a sulking child. And then I opened it again.

These *were* my words. I'd conducted the interviews; I'd written up Clara's story. Once it was published – and it *would* be published, I was sure of it – I would officially be a co-author. I'd be a *real* author, and my days of brainstorming Instagram captions would be over. My options would be endless. All I had to do was see this project through.

Really, I thought, I should be grateful to Clara for the opportunity. She'd trusted me with her story, and I had a responsibility to share it with the world in the best way that I knew how.

I broached the subject with Clara during our next writing session.

'I just think,' I said from my usual seat in the orangery, 'that you need to open up more. Not just about your childhood – about you *now*. Your followers love the glimpses they get into your life, right? We need more of that.'

Reclining on the wicker couch, Clara absorbed this information. 'I don't want to give everything away,' she sighed. I wondered briefly if she was having a crisis about privacy, about her life always being monetised, until she added, 'I want to be able to write a second book.'

I decided that it wasn't the right time to remind her that *I* was the one writing the book, that we were collaborating.

'I know,' I said instead. 'I just think it'd be good to have some more personal, more current stuff in there. You know, like . . . your thoughts. Your dreams. Your plans for the future.'

'My plans for the future,' Clara said thoughtfully. 'World domination? Murder?' She paused, then burst into laughter. 'God, Chloe. Your face!'

'We probably shouldn't joke about murder,' I said.

'No,' Clara agreed, but she was still smiling. 'We probably shouldn't.'

Something about the easy way she'd said the word, in such a light tone of voice, made my skin creep. I cleared my throat, keen to get the session back on track. 'What if we do a quickfire round?' I suggested. 'And we can use your answers as inspiration for more content.'

'Sure,' Clara said. She leaned back on the couch and crossed her legs, completely unperturbed. 'Fire away.'

I consulted my notes. 'Morning or night?'

'Night.'

'Summer or winter?'

'Summer.'

'Happiness or success?'

'Success.'

'Rich and famous or rich and anonymous?'

A smirk. 'Rich and famous.'

'So, from those . . . I have some follow-up questions,' I said. 'You said you'd choose success over happiness. Why?'

'I suppose, in my mind, success *is* happiness,' Clara said thoughtfully. 'I wouldn't have anything if my parents hadn't been successful. This house, the clothes that I wear, the life that I have . . . and it all makes me happy.'

'What if they weren't successful?' I pressed. 'What if you didn't have any of this?'

Clara's tone was cool when she replied. 'Then what would be the point?'

'What do you mean?'

'I'd have no reason to be happy,' Clara said matter-of-factly. 'Everything hinges on this. This life. I love this gorgeous house; I love the glittering parties. Without them, then what would there be?'

I frowned. Hadn't Clara just weeks earlier declared to a crowd of adoring party guests that happiness *wasn't* material? I wondered whether she'd truly meant it then, had truly believed it, or whether that part of her speech had simply been a tool, an act designed to draw more devoted followers into her circle.

'You'd have everything else,' I told her. 'You'd have your family. Your friends.'

'Be serious, Chloe,' Clara said. 'Do you think any of those wonderful people who come to our parties would want to know me?'

'I would.'

Clara smiled. 'I know.'

Neither of us said anything else and, after a long moment, Clara stood up. 'I need to go and speak to Alexis,' she said. 'Can we finish this part later?'

'Of course,' I said. 'I'll go and write up what we have.'

Clara flashed me a grin. 'Perfect,' she said.

She disappeared inside the house, and I let myself relax. I had a feeling that she was lying about having to go and find Alexis – who'd recently been getting closer to her than I would like – but I wasn't going to call her out on it. I understood; she'd been open, just like I'd asked, even to the point of vulnerability. She'd cracked herself open and handed me what was potentially her biggest insecurity, presented it to me on a silver platter. And, of course, Clara wasn't prone to vulnerability – so once her words were out there, she'd made her escape.

Clara believed that her value – and, therefore, her happiness – hinged on what she offered to the world, and the love she was given in return. Now that her parties no longer sparkled with the beautiful and rich and famous, where would she get this adoration from? I knew that it would have to come from the Goldens. But what if that wasn't enough? What if *we* weren't enough?

Chapter 22

Clara had wanted to create a girls' paradise, and she had. And, as much as I'd grown to love it, sometimes I missed the era of Chloe and Clara. I was already nostalgic for those heady early days – even though they weren't so long ago – where it felt as if we were young royals, reigning over our empire. I missed the freedom of twenty acres of house and lawn and woodland and river, the pantry filled with champagne, the strawberries and the sugar, and the glitter in our hair and on our faces, the sticky lip-gloss prints on glasses and the carefully edited Instagram pictures, Clara's sharp cheekbones and her waterfall of hair and the curve of her breasts under her filmy satin dresses.

More than once, in those first few weeks of the Goldens, I'd venture into the living room or the kitchen and find Clara surrounded by the girls, all huddled close like moths to a flame. To them, she was an oracle, one who was there for them, always. She could give them a solution to any problem, heal any pain or torment. At first, I felt sorry for her – it couldn't be easy listening to all of the girls' troubles like that, under pressure to find the right thing to say. Soon, though, I couldn't help but notice that whenever I walked in on one of these impromptu therapy sessions, usually with at least one of the girls in tears, Clara had a little gleam in her eye. And that gleam revealed how much she loved being wanted, being needed. I couldn't take that away from her. I didn't want to.

One afternoon, I emerged from my bedroom to another crisis, this time in the living room.

'They just don't *get* it,' a tearful voice lamented as I passed the open doorway.

I paused, and peeked round the doorframe. Clara and Mia were sitting together on one of the leather sofas. Christie, Bella and Alexis were kneeling at their feet, on the thick, fluffy rug, and Bella was holding one of Mia's hands. Mia clutched it as if it was a lifeline, her knuckles white.

'They told me that they'd support me, but only if I choose a *proper* subject that'll lead to a *real* career,' Mia continued. I could hear the hitches in her breath, a guarantee that there were more tears on the horizon. 'So I said I didn't need their help. And now they keep ringing me, my dad screaming down the phone that I'm making a bad decision and that I'm irresponsible. And I told him that I don't *want* to work in finance, I want to be an *actor*. Like what's so wrong with that?'

Clara's voice was soothing. 'There's nothing wrong with

that at all,' she said. 'Your dreams are your dreams, and if you're willing to fight for them you can achieve them. It's as simple as that. And the world needs actors, so why can't you be one of them?'

Mia looked at her as if the two of them were the only people in the room, blinking away her tears.

'I'm so sorry that your parents don't support you,' Clara said. 'I'm sorry that they don't understand you, that they won't help you become who you were born to be. But we will. *I* will.' She glanced at the other girls, and I realised that this was both for Mia's benefit and for theirs. 'Have you heard of Ayanna Lynch?' she asked. Mia nodded, sniffled. 'Well, Ayanna's a close friend. I can get in touch with her and see if she can help you out. I'm positive she'd be able to take you to set one day. Put you in as an extra, maybe set up an audition. Wouldn't that just prove them wrong?'

Still tearful, but smiling, Mia leaned into Clara, who held her. The girls surrounded them both, one of them stroking Mia's hair.

Slowly, I backed away and carried on to the kitchen. As the coffee machine worked its magic, I couldn't help but dwell on the scene that I'd witnessed. It all seemed innocent enough – the epitome of the cute, supportive girl-gang culture that Clara insisted was her goal – but Clara's behaviour had made me uneasy. Specifically, her offer to speak to Ayanna about Mia. Clara knew that Ayanna had promised *me* a set visit – which she'd been unable to pull off due to time restraints during filming. Had Clara simply forgotten that inconvenient detail, or had she chosen to ignore it? By making such a promise, even if it was one she couldn't keep, she'd successfully drawn her girls in even closer, showed them the power that she could wield. I thought back to Mia's tears, the way that she'd sunk into Clara's side with exhausted, grateful relief, and it made my stomach twist, uneasy.

A week later, three new rules appeared on the fridge.

6. Beware of journalists/reporters mining for gossip.
7. No prioritising outside friends or family over the group. Our family comes first! :)
8. Always love and respect our leader, and trust in what she has to say.

I frowned. What was Clara doing? Did she not realise how these rules could be misconstrued? We were already fighting off headlines as it was after the first 'cult' article went viral. And the girls at Deneside Manor no longer spoke to their friends; they ignored calls from their parents. All they wanted was *Clara, Clara, Clara*. If any outsiders saw the house rules, this would surely bring Clara's critics crawling out of their holes. There seemed to be a newly formed horde of armchair commentators online, all of them fixated on Clara and the Goldens. They posted their hot takes and insults without a second thought. I often imagined their fingers clattering across their keyboards, their fingertips leaving grease spots on the screens of their phones, as I read their assessments of Clara.

@cityboy1432_: I'm not criticising her. I'm saying she's vapid, self-obsessed, and nobody cares what she has to say. Those are facts.

@phillyannalise: She's literally just another blonde girl with rich parents who's acting out because she's bored?? Nothing more to say lol.

@2944372819: Okay but who is Clara Holland? What has she actually done?

@dean_tunstall10: If she's a cult leader . . . I'm joining a cult #ThatGirlIsHOT

@whispers_newaccnt: Soooo a friend of a friend goes to uni near where she lives and apparently she's got all these rules she's making people follow if they want to live with her? Including what to wear. Like this is a literal cult lol.

I closed the app. How could Clara *stand* it? Then it occurred to me. She overcompensated. They didn't love her yet? She'd *make* them.

I had to look for her; I had to speak to her. But nobody knew where she was.

'Her car's still there,' Alexis told me. She was standing by the door to the orangery, smoking a cigarette.

'I can see that,' I said. Then, feeling snippy even as I said it, 'Can't you do that outside?'

She rolled her eyes, but did as I asked. I was fairly sure I heard a muttered remark under her breath as she stalked away, something that sounded a lot like 'bitch'.

I knew that I was being unnecessarily spiky, but Alexis's behaviour had begun to grate on me. I was tired of the way she fawned over Clara, the way she clung to her whenever I was around. *Maybe*, a tiny, traitorous voice in my mind suggested, *it's because she reminds you so much of* you.

I pushed the thought away and went outside to where Alexis was now smoking on an upturned flowerpot.

'Can you tell Clara that I've left?' I asked. 'If you see her, obviously. I've got a seminar.'

She smirked. 'Sure,' she said. 'I'll tell her.'

I chose to ignore her tone, which indicated just how pleased she was that Clara had left me behind. Instead, I nodded wearily and then turned away, leaving the house through the side gate with my backpack slung over one shoulder. The bus stop was nearly a mile away. I sighed, and set off.

I was ten minutes late to the hour-long seminar. I'd run from the bus stop, my backpack slamming against my back almost

214

hard enough to wind me, feeling completely humiliated. After all, people knew who I was now. Jogging across campus rather than arriving with Clara in her Mini was a significant downgrade.

I burst through the door, breathless, and twenty faces all turned to look at me. I was horrified to see that none of them had eyes or mouths; they were blank ovals, slightly blurring as they moved.

Suddenly, a mouth appeared in one of the faces, a yawning black hole which opened and shut as words came out of it. My stomach lurched.

'Chloe?' the oval said. 'Is everything okay?'

All at once, the room swam into focus.

It was Lisa, one of the PhD students who occasionally led the seminars. She was looking at me with such kind concern that my eyes filled with tears.

Everyone else was looking at me, too, their expressions ranging from concern to surprise to disdain.

'I'm so sorry,' I said. 'I think I need to leave.'

And I turned and fled from the room.

'I thought you'd have gone home,' Olivia said. 'Or back to Clara's. Wherever.'

I'd gone to the café in the Art block, somewhere that I was sure Clara wouldn't go. I needed to calm down, to breathe. Fifty minutes later, Olivia sat down in the seat opposite me, her face a map of worry, and slid a cup of coffee across the table. The act of unforced kindness made me want to sob.

'I just needed some space,' I said. 'Things at the house have been . . . a lot.'

'What do you mean?'

So I told her. She already knew a little of what had happened at the spring equinox party, when Clara had climbed on to a table and made her declaration. I told her about how every bedroom was filled within a week, how people who didn't even live at Deneside Manor spent all their time there. I told her about the rules.

'We're supposed to be wary of people who might see us as sources,' I said finally. 'To refuse to speak to anyone who might sell stories and gossip to the press. And we're not supposed to prioritise anyone on the outside over the Goldens, either. That's the latest rule.'

Olivia gaped at me. 'You're kidding,' she said. She saw my expression and put a hand over her mouth. 'Oh God. You're serious. It's really that bad?'

'I mean . . . it's not *that* bad,' I said hurriedly, backtracking. 'I think she just phrased it weirdly – that's all. I think what she *meant* is that she wants us to be committed to being part of the group. We're like a little family, after all. And as for the press thing – that's pretty sensible, really. No one wants to do anything that could harm Clara. We love her.'

'Holy shit,' Olivia said.

'What?'

'Do you have a little earpiece in or something? Did she tell you to say that? Because that sounds a *lot* like damage control.'

I laughed. 'She's still herself. She's still great. She's just so much more . . .' I trailed off, unable to find the right word.

'Clara?' Olivia supplied.

'Like a *more intense* version of Clara,' I said.

'Do you think,' Olivia pressed gently, 'that it might be time to end this friendship?'

'I don't know,' I said. 'I love her. I really do, Liv. But this whole Goldens thing – she's just so *into* it, with her rules and her dress codes and everything. And it makes me worry for her.'

Olivia placed her hand on mine. 'It's not your responsibility, though. She's an adult.'

I sighed. 'But I was the first. I was the first girl to move in with her, to follow her around like a little puppy. And now there's a house filled with girls who're all doing the same thing. I encouraged her!'

'That doesn't mean it's your fault,' Olivia said. 'Something like this was bound to happen sooner or later, anyway.'

I peered at her. 'Why's that?'

She began to list things off on her fingers. 'She's charismatic. Her followers are devoted to the point of worship. She makes people want to *be* her. She's like a symbol – they think that if they live like her, or even with her, then they'll become her.'

'That doesn't mean she was always destined to lead a *cult*.'

'Well, no,' Olivia allowed. 'But she's this famous influencer, and she's still always wanted more. Like you – she couldn't just be friends with you, invite you to her parties. She had to *have* you. And she has to have them too.'

I felt my skin prickling, a flush creeping up my neck. 'She doesn't have me.'

Olivia snorted. 'Oh, she has you, right where she wants you.'

'Not really,' I protested. 'I'm still here, aren't I?'

'Fine,' Olivia said. 'You're here. But if she rang you right now and asked you to go straight back to her house – if she *demanded* it – what would you do?'

I knew exactly what I'd do. I'd go outside and I'd wait for Clara to pick me up, or else I'd get the bus and walk the mile back up the single-track lane to the front gates of Deneside Manor. And the worst part was that I wouldn't mind at all, because a little part of my brain still believed that Clara cared about me above anything else. Above her followers – above, even, herself. But I couldn't say that to Olivia.

It didn't seem to matter, though; from the way that she was looking at me, her eyebrows furrowed and lips pursed in a combination of affection and pity, she already knew.

'Look. I'm not an expert,' she said, 'and I'm not going to try to tell you what to do, or what not to do, but, from what you're telling me, what Clara's doing is dangerous. She's separating people, isolating them. And that never leads anywhere good.'

'She's not a bad person, Liv. She just wants to do well, to succeed – to make these girls happy. I guess I just need to convince her that bringing in a load of rules isn't the way to do it.'

'You need to convince her quickly, then,' Olivia said darkly. 'Because if you don't, sooner or later, something bad is going to happen.'

I arrived home just before five, having spent the afternoon in the Art block café with Olivia. When we'd left, she'd unexpectedly pulled me into a hug.

'Text me,' she'd said. 'If you need anything. Anything at all. Okay?'

'Okay,' I'd promised. 'I will.'

I'd taken the bus back to Deneside Manor, walked up the tree-lined driveway (it seemed to get longer every time), and I was barely through the front door when Clara appeared in front of me. 'Where have you been?' she asked.

She was incredibly calm, but her eyes were fiery. I tried not to look over her shoulder, where some of the girls were observing the proceedings with curiosity.

I let my backpack fall from my shoulder, and held it by one strap as it rested on the dusty tiled floor. 'I went for coffee with Olivia after my seminar,' I said. 'What's wrong?'

Her lips were a tight line. 'I thought you'd seen the rules.'

'I have,' I said. 'I wasn't—'

'You were prioritising an outside relationship over the group,' Clara said. She enunciated each word carefully, as if she was speaking to a very young child.

219

'What do you mean?'

'You went out with Olivia,' she said. 'You should have been here.'

My mind was reeling. I'd defended Clara's rules to Olivia, given them a rational explanation – but I'd been wrong. Clara wasn't just asking the Goldens to show their commitment and dedication. She really did expect us not to see our friends or family.

'I didn't know you needed me,' I said faintly. '*You* weren't even here. I looked for you, before I left.'

'That doesn't matter,' Clara said. 'What matters is that when I need you, I know where you are. Or that I can, at the very least, actually reach you.' She looked at me, disappointed. 'I'm your *family*, Chloe. I've changed your life. You wouldn't be the person that you are without me.'

Suddenly, I didn't care that we were being watched. I heard the warning in my own voice as I said, 'And what person is that?'

Clara smiled, but it didn't reach her eyes. 'A special one. You're loved, Chloe. You're admired. You're envied. Do you think that anyone would envy you if you still lived at Ivy House? Do you think they'd envy you if you were besties with sweet little Olivia and completed all your coursework on time? Do you think anyone would care?' She shook her head, slowly, all faux pity. 'But here, people care about you. *I* care about you. My *followers* care about you.'

'Your followers care about *you*, Clara,' I said. 'I'm not important.'

'That's not true,' Clara said. For a moment, I thought she was going to pay me a compliment, but then she continued. 'You're like an accessory, Chloe. You bring the whole outfit together. Every Batman needs a Robin. Every Barbie needs a Midge.'

Her words stung. 'And what if I don't want to be your Midge?' I asked.

She tilted her chin up in challenge. 'You can do what you like,' she said. 'You can stay, or you can go. But you will *always* be my Midge.'

It wasn't a promise. It was a threat.

She turned on her heel and strode away. The girls who'd been lurking scattered as she passed through them, deliberately avoiding looking in my direction.

I realised, then, what had happened. I was Clara's most loyal follower and I had, in her mind, strayed. She'd made an *example* of me. I wondered if she'd meant anything that she'd said at all.

I waited a while, and then went to find Clara in her bedroom. She'd changed into a loose pink T-shirt and grey joggers, and was running a bath in her en-suite. The room was already enveloped with fragrant steam, her dressing-table mirror misted with condensation. The vanilla scent, so intrinsically Clara, made my chest ache. She glanced up at the sound of the door shutting.

'You caught on,' she said, instead of a greeting.

'I think so,' I said. 'So that was . . . what? A performance?'

'Not entirely,' she said. 'I'm still unhappy with you.'

I rolled my eyes. 'I'm allowed to have friends, Clara.'

'We're your friends,' Clara said. For the first time since we'd spoken in the hallway, she sounded vulnerable. Childlike. 'I'm your friend. Why do you need anybody else?'

'Because I do,' I said. 'Olivia's the only friend I have on my course. And she's lovely. She's funny—'

Clara's expression hardened. 'Fine,' she said. 'You can invite her to our next party.'

I reached for words, but couldn't find them. 'I . . . what?'

'Invite her to our next party,' she repeated. 'If she wants to be one of us, then she can. But if she doesn't, I don't want you spending time with her any more. She'll mess with your head, tell you that you don't need us. That you don't need me. But you do.' She stepped closer to me, until our noses were practically touching. I could smell the summery scent of her perfume, the cherry lip gloss she was wearing. 'You know that you need me,' she said. 'You couldn't live without me.'

Her proximity was intoxicating, her breath on my lips like honey. And without thinking I leaned in, closing the distance between us, my hand moving to her waist.

She stepped back.

I felt as if I'd been drenched in ice water as she turned away from me. I could feel my cheeks flushing, chest heaving, but Clara looked completely unaffected. Instead, she busied herself setting out little jars of skincare products on the lacquered surface of her dressing table. Her nonchalant air wasn't cruel;

it was as if she hadn't even noticed that I was going to kiss her. And that was so much worse.

'We're agreed, then?' she said, without looking at me. 'Olivia comes to the next party.'

I swallowed, hard, to get rid of the lump in my throat. 'I'll ask her.'

Chapter 23

I didn't know how to broach the subject with Olivia.

After all, she'd told me – in no uncertain terms – that Clara was bad news. And here I was, planning to drag her into the fray.

If I was a good friend, I knew, I wouldn't have even considered it.

No, Clara, I would have said. *I'm not bringing Olivia here so that you can play your mind games with her.*

But her breath had been so sweet on my tongue, and I'd so nearly kissed her, and I wanted nothing more than for Clara to adore me like I adored her. I wanted her approval so much that I felt it inside like a physical ache. And the only way to get that was to reassure her that Olivia wasn't a threat, that Olivia was my friend and, even if she didn't particularly care for Clara, she wasn't a danger to her either.

And maybe, an idealistic portion of my brain supplied, Olivia might even learn to love Clara as much as I did.

Clara had set the date for the next party without consulting me, something which I interpreted as either a slight because my opinion didn't matter as much any more, or another aspect of the public punishment for my perceived betrayal. Either way, this was to be the first spring party, the balmy air of early May sweet-smelling and filled with potential.

I heard her discussing it with some of the girls one morning as I entered the kitchen, closer to midday than usual due to a late night writing an essay. The deadline had been at midnight, and I'd used every last second to try to create something remotely worth reading before pressing the submit button. The Chloe of a year ago would have been appalled, but I couldn't bring myself to care. I had enough to worry about, and getting stellar grades across the board was, for once, not a priority.

'What about a "girls gone wild" theme?' Christie suggested. 'Like the parties Americans have for Spring Break? Inflatables, pitchers . . .'

I knew that Clara wouldn't go for it. It was tacky. And as much as she saw herself as an icon, a modern-day superstar, she detested anything that she saw as being too *Americanised*. If it wasn't old Hollywood (gilt and glamour, red carpets, flashbulbs) or East Coast elite (old-money families, summer houses at Cape Cod and in the Hamptons, tennis lessons at the country club) she wasn't interested.

'Inflatables?' she repeated with a disbelieving sneer. 'I don't think so.'

Cowed, Christie looked away. And, as she did, she caught my eye. It was a pleading look, the kind that said they'd been discussing ideas longer than I could possibly imagine, and yet they were still having little success pleasing Clara. I was feeling charitable, so I intervened.

'I like "girls gone wild",' I said. 'As a theme.'

Clara looked up at me, her pen grasped lightly in her hand. I noted that the sheet of paper on the table in front of her was still blank. 'You do?' she said testily.

'I just think we need to adapt it a bit,' I continued. 'Girls gone *wild*. Back to nature, digging into our roots.' I saw Clara's posture straighten, and smiled to myself. 'Imagine it, Clara. A daytime party in the garden, in the woods. The sun shining, the insects buzzing. We could lay out blankets and cushions by the river, pack picnic baskets and cooler boxes with baguettes and cold meats, pomegranates, chunks of mango and strawberries. We could blend summery cocktails, decant them into glass bottles, stand them in the river to keep them cold. If it's warm enough, we could even sunbathe and swim. It'd be the height of springtime perfection.'

I waited to let my words, the images that I'd evoked, sink in. I knew that Clara would go for it. After all, that's why she loved me – I knew what she liked, what she disliked and, above all, the message that she wanted to convey with every party that she hosted. She was quickly becoming a controversial figure, the girl at the helm of wild parties and inexplicably cultish behaviour, but this was her chance to change that. At its heart, this was a pared-back garden party: simple, wholesome fun. Who could complain about that?

'*Yes*,' Clara said. 'Yes! I like it.' She clapped her hands. 'Let's make it happen.'

I didn't say anything else. I left the room without a backwards glance, leaving them to their planning. I'd done what I needed to – I'd reminded Clara just how important I was. And, therefore, just how important it was that she made Olivia feel welcome.

The other side of this, of course, was convincing Olivia to make an effort with Clara.

Unfortunately, the following week was a reading week, a full week with no lectures, no seminars and no compulsory events. It was scheduled to give students the opportunity to catch up on their studies, to devote a week to getting ahead with their subject-specific reading lists or to finish assignments that needed a bit more perfecting.

After what had happened last time, I didn't dare go behind Clara's back to meet Olivia in person – especially when I didn't have a reason to be on campus. I considered asking her permission, but the thought of actually having to *ask*, as well as the possibility of her saying no and having to abide by that, filled my mouth with a sourness that tasted like shame.

I called Olivia instead.

'Hey,' I said when she picked up after the fourth or fifth ring. 'It's me.'

'Chloe?' she said. I could hear laughter in the background, the buzz of conversation. It muffled slightly as, presumably, she put a hand over the microphone. 'I'll be back in a minute, guys.

Yeah. Two secs.' The background noise quietened. 'Sorry about that. House party.'

'No worries,' I said. 'It's funny, actually. I wanted to talk to you about—'

She caught on straight away. 'I don't think so, Chloe.'

'You don't even know what I was going to say.' My voice was infuriatingly whiny, even to my own ears.

'Yes, I do,' she said. 'You were going to ask me to do something Clara-related. And my answer is *no way*.'

'I'm inviting you to Clara's next party. That's all.'

'No, Chloe. I mean it. I'm not doing anything to indulge that girl in her absurd little fantasies.'

I was surprised at the venom in her tone. 'You used to love her,' I said. 'Remember? What happened?'

'*She* happened,' Olivia said. 'I was a huge fan of her online persona – this wonderful, funny girl with amazing clothes. But now I know the real Clara. I've seen what she's done to you. What she's doing to you.'

I rolled my eyes to an audience of no one. 'She isn't doing anything to me.'

'She's making you into another her.'

'No, she isn't,' I said, but I felt a flicker of pride at the idea. 'And even if she was, what's so bad about that? I *want* to be like her.'

'Why, though?' Olivia asked. 'I know you love the big house, all the parties, everything Clara's given you. But Clara and her friends aren't inherently worth more than you just because their families are rich, you know. They're not better people. You don't have to be someone else to fit in with them.'

I didn't say anything. How could Olivia understand? I *wanted* to be someone else.

I heard her sigh. 'Are you still there?'

'Yeah,' I said. 'I'm still here.'

'You know you're one of my best friends,' Olivia said. 'I wouldn't be saying this if I really didn't feel that I had to.'

'The thing is, Liv,' I said, 'Clara's one of *my* best friends. I need you to get along.'

'But why?' Olivia asked. 'Why do you need us to get along?'

I could sense her frustration, the thin, viscous layer of it simmering beneath her outwardly calm words. On top of that, though, there was something else: sympathy. And, with that, impending defeat. Olivia was too kind.

'Because I love you both,' I said. 'And . . . look. I think it'd be really good for you to get to know her. You want to be an editor, right? At a big publishing house? Clara has connections. You know she does – you just said it yourself. She can help you.'

There was a long silence as, presumably, Olivia considered what I'd said.

'When is it?' she asked eventually.

I told her the date.

'I can't come that night,' she said. 'I'm going home for the weekend.' A pause. 'But look – the next time she has a party after that, let me know. And I'll come. For you.'

'You're the best, Liv.'

A long-suffering sigh. 'I know.'

She hung up.

I knew that I should have felt ashamed. I should have been riddled with guilt at what I'd done, the way that I'd tried – and succeeded – to manipulate the only other friend that I had.

But, instead, I felt an all-consuming thrill. Olivia was going to come to one of Clara's parties. Olivia was going to see the other Chloe. Not studious little Chloe who she saw at university, the lonely and lost girl she had study dates with and sat next to in lectures. She was going to see *Golden* Chloe, beloved by familiar faces and strangers alike. The quieter, yet no less compelling, foil to Clara's charisma.

And I couldn't wait.

Chapter 24

The Monday after reading week, buoyed by a belief that the world thought that she had enough influence to be a cult leader and the thrill of planning yet another party, Clara arrived on campus wearing a cream cashmere cardigan, light blue jeans, heavy buckled biker boots and a golden tiara.

When I'd peeked into her room that morning, she was still fast asleep, wrapped in her blankets, her hair a mass on the pillow. No doubt she'd be nursing a gin-induced hangover, and so, I deduced, she was unlikely to make her nine o'clock seminar. I'd left her a note, a chirpy Post-it with *Got the bus! See you later :)* scrawled in Sharpie. I'd stuck it to the lamp on her bedside table and set out alone.

The bus rattled along pot-holed single-track roads, pausing almost constantly to pick up or drop off passengers: a gruff farmer wearing a battered wax jacket, a young mum gazing fondly at her sleeping baby in a pushchair, a heavily made-up older lady carrying a bag full of shopping and a walking stick topped with a plastic mallard's head. Despite having my headphones plugged into my ears, playing the tinny chatter of some podcast or other, I entertained myself by making up stories about my fellow passengers instead. The farmer had won an award for his memoir, which was a soulful, heart-rending tale of growing up in the hills and revitalising his parents' once-dwindling sheep farm, all the while looking for love. The mum had spent all morning walking her child up and down Havington's Main Street and, although she was blissed out with happiness that he was finally asleep, she'd completely forgotten to buy the toothpaste that she'd gone there to buy in the first place. The older lady, I decided, was the matriarch of a powerful family, her dark eyeshadow and thick black liner and bright lipstick all leftovers from her family's heyday in the sixties – the days when she was the most beautiful and powerful woman around, and could frighten any hardened criminal by simply brandishing her green, duck-headed cane.

It occurred to me that, finally, my imagination was coming back to life. I'd been so occupied with writing Clara's memoir that I'd forgotten all about writing my own stories, and I was suddenly consumed with longing. I wanted nothing more than to go back to Deneside Manor, to shut myself away with my laptop and to release the words that were desperate to pour out of me. *My* words. *My* story.

But, of course, I didn't have the time. I never had the time.

I still didn't feel properly awake when I reached campus. Even more so when I saw Clara leaning against the railings outside the library and realised that she'd most likely left half an hour after I had and still beaten me here.

'You left early,' she said.

'I left on time,' I told her. 'I didn't think you'd be coming in today.'

She laughed. 'Neither did I,' she said. 'But I remembered I have an assessment. That's why I'm wearing this.' She indicated her hairpiece, a tiara covered with vines and roses subtly entwined around its base. It glittered as a stray sunbeam touched down, dozens of tiny stones embedded in the golden surface.

'It's beautiful.'

Clara didn't seem to have heard me. 'It's eighteen-carat gold,' she said with pride. 'And the stones are opals and diamonds. The diamonds aren't the most incredible quality, but they have such a lovely sparkle—'

'Beautiful,' I said again, interrupting her. I was irritated, both at the fact she'd had a lie-in and still arrived before me, and because she'd chosen to wear a literal tiara to university. *Who does she think she is?* a tiny, bitter part of myself seethed. I swallowed it down and tried to make amends. 'Is it lucky or something? Is that why you're wearing it for your assessment?'

'Nah, I just wanted to,' Clara said. 'I am the golden goddess, after all. Have you seen that's what people are calling me now?'

I shook my head.

'They're calling me a goddess because of what I wear,' Clara continued. 'And golden because, well, gold is my signature. My make-up, my accessories – I *knew* that it would catch on. I'm actually trending!'

'Good for you,' I murmured, but too quietly for her to hear.

We started walking together, towards our respective buildings.

'Do you mind getting the bus back later?' Clara asked. 'Sorry – you know I'd give you a lift, but I don't know how long I'll be here.'

'That's fine,' I said. 'Is it an open-ended assessment, or . . . ?'

'No,' she said. 'It's only an hour. But I need to go to the town hall afterwards.'

'The town hall?' I repeated. It was the last place I'd expect Clara to go.

'I've been letting Alexis borrow my car, and she's racked up a ton of parking fines,' Clara explained. 'So now *I've* got to go and sort it out.' She rolled her eyes, but the gesture was fond.

'I thought you could pay those online?'

'We won't be paying them,' Clara said cheerily. 'My father knows everyone who's anyone at the town hall. They're all drinking buddies. And most of them have known me since I was tiny, so . . .'

'Oh,' I said.

As we passed through the courtyard, I saw people glancing at us – at Clara – smiling and laughing and whispering. And, for the first time, I truly, properly grasped Clara's impact on the outside world.

She was no longer Clara Holland, eighteen-year-old daughter of fashion industry professionals and a semi-successful social-media influencer. No, she was Clara Holland, notorious social-media personality, the exclusive party hostess and alleged cult leader, who treated this town as if it was her kingdom, as if all the people who lived here were her subjects. She was confident in the knowledge that they would give her what she wanted, whenever she wanted it.

Later, I tried to pinpoint exactly when she'd performed her metamorphosis, the moment when she changed from an influencer to who she was now: this perplexing gossamer thread of a human, every inch of her glittering gold. She was a girl who thought, who truly believed, that she had earned and deserved the term *goddess* as a moniker. She was untouchable. And, as I watched her preen and smile her coy little smile, I knew that she knew it too.

Despite the rest of the world's obsession with Clara, her own parents didn't seem particularly interested in her. I'd never asked, but I assumed they knew about the parties, about the girls moving in. About the cult rumours. Clara rarely spoke to her parents, but when they did speak it was always over the phone or via a scheduled video call.

'Mum doesn't have time for texts,' Clara had told me one day when we'd been writing her memoir. 'She's usually too busy to reply, so I just don't bother.'

I'd nodded like I'd understood, but the thought of Clara's own mother not being able to spare ten seconds to send her even an emoji chilled me to the bone.

Tonight, they were video calling. The other girls were downstairs having a binge-watching night, an event that involved duvets dragged from beds, a selection of throw blankets and a lot of popcorn. I'd declined their invitation (blaming a headache when actually I just wanted some time alone), and Clara had said that she'd join them later – after she'd spoken with her parents.

And so I lay on my bed, a book that I'd given up on reading spreadeagled beside me. My door was open, and so was Clara's; her voice carried from down the hall, as did her mum's. Clara must have had her on speakerphone. I tried not to listen in, but their voices carried and it was impossible not to. I could hear almost every word.

I began to zone out after a while, the one-sided conversation very much an itinerary of Clara's mum's work schedule, which was packed – but not, I noted somewhat protectively, too packed to reply to the occasional text from her daughter.

And then I heard something that made my ears prick up.

'Darling,' Clara's mum was saying. 'I'm not worried. How could *you* lead a cult?'

'It's just . . . that's what they're all talking about online—'

'I promise you that I'm paying no attention to gossip on *social media*.'

Clara's mum said *social media* in the same way that somebody else might have said *gangrene* or *toenail clippings*: with barely disguised disgust. Considering that Clara's life revolved around social media, I knew this must've hurt.

'It's true, though,' Clara said, doubling down. 'Some of it, anyway. It's not like what they're saying, but we *are* having these incredible parties. And the girls that have come to live here are all lovely. If you think about it, it's actually kind of revolutionary . . .'

Clara's mum was tiring of the subject. 'Sweetheart,' she said with a sigh, 'you don't have to try to convince me. I know that there's nothing to worry about with all of this cult talk.' A chuckle. 'We both know you couldn't lead your way out of a paper bag!'

There was a brief, almost stunned silence. I winced.

'Well, darling, it's time for me to go,' Clara's mum said lightly, as if she hadn't just insulted her daughter. 'We've had a lovely catch-up, haven't we? And I'll speak to your dad – we'll pop a little something into your account. You'll need it for your *cult*.' I heard her laugh, a jarring sound. 'Speak soon, okay?'

'Okay,' Clara said, but the enthusiasm, the energy, had gone from her voice. 'Speak soon. Love you.'

There was no reply. The call had already ended, her *love you* spoken to the empty air.

It wasn't surprising that Clara was so desperate to be the centre of attention, why she basked in the love that her followers threw at her like so much confetti. I'd just heard, in real time, how she'd tried to get her mum's attention, to hold her interest, but her efforts had been in vain. If anything, it seemed like Clara was just another thing to be dealt with, another task to check off her list. *Video call with daughter. Tick.*

All Clara wanted to do was impress her parents. Maybe, I thought, that was why she threw such elaborate parties. She was trying to speak their language, to do something to get their attention – to make them look at her and really see her as something more than an obligation.

I wondered whether the upcoming party, in all its floral, shimmering glory, would be enough. I doubted it.

Chapter 25

Another sign that our situation was changing came just a few days later.

It was early evening, a crescent moon high in the sky and coating the world with silver. I'd had a long, luxurious bath with plenty of fragrant oils, then put on a pair of comfortable pyjamas, and was making my way down to the living room when I heard raised voices.

'I'm sorry!' a girl was saying. 'Don't make me leave. I'll do anything!'

I wondered, briefly, who she was talking to – until Clara spoke, her words measured and cool. 'I appreciate your apology,' she said. 'But it doesn't change anything.'

'It was a mistake,' the girl said. 'It won't happen again.'

By now, I'd reached the bottom of the stairs. Standing by the front door was Lily. Tears streamed down her perfect face.

A little way away from her were the other girls, huddled. And, in the centre of them, Clara.

'What's going on?' I asked.

They all looked up at me.

'Lily stayed with her boyfriend last night,' Bella explained. 'And she's been with him all day today, too, even though we needed her here.'

I looked at Clara, quizzically. 'What did we need her here for?'

Her answering glare was fierce. 'It doesn't matter,' she said. 'She should have been here. Everyone has read the rules, and the majority of us have abided by them – myself included.'

'I haven't seen him in weeks,' Lily whispered. 'I just missed him so much. I'm sorry. It won't happen again.'

'You're right,' Clara said. 'It won't.' Minutely, I relaxed. Until she continued, 'You have two options. You can either break up with him and once again commit yourself to our group. Or you move out.'

Even from my position on the staircase, I could see Lily's lip trembling. 'We've been together for five years,' she said helplessly.

I frowned at Clara, who looked back at me, her chin tilted, daring me to say something. I shrank under her gaze. She broke eye contact, her attention back on Lily.

'Then you've made your choice,' Clara said simply. 'Mia, will you please go up with Lily and help her pack her things?'

Lily started to sob. Clara didn't so much as glance at her as she walked away towards the living room. The girls who'd gathered trailed after her, somewhat reluctantly, looking over their shoulders. Lily's closest friend in the house, Lottie, hesitated for just a second before she wiped her eyes and followed them. Only Mia stayed behind.

'Come on,' she said, putting a hand on Lily's shoulder. 'Let's get it over with.'

Together, they passed me as they went upstairs, but I stood frozen to the spot. Clara had done it; she'd really done it. She'd shown her hand, wielded her power. She'd actually *banished* someone.

I thought back to the rules, the neat, smiley restrictions stuck on the fridge door. Nobody else would break them after this – that much was for certain.

Chapter 26

On the morning of the party, I woke with a pit of dread deep in my stomach.

This wasn't entirely unusual. As the date had grown ever closer, I'd felt the pressure increasing. I was Chloe Hughes, second to the one and only Clara Holland. If the world's eyes were on Clara, they were on me too. I had to look beautiful, elegant, just like she did – but no better, of course. The bridesmaid could never look more beautiful than the bride.

I stared at myself in the mirror as I brushed my teeth, then tied my hair up in a loose ponytail to keep it away from my face. My skin was smooth but dull, the circles beneath my eyes newly pronounced. I massaged a pea-sized amount of serum into my skin using my fingertips, and then layered a hydrating moisturiser on top, followed by concealer. *There.* I looked more awake already. Maybe, at the right angle and in the right lighting, even pretty.

I'd never be a natural beauty, a fact which still stung, despite the years I'd had to accept it. I'd spent the last decade comparing myself to every other girl or woman I saw, all of us pitted against each other in a strange, silent competition in which none of us had agreed to take part.

It didn't matter whether it was an edgy-cool girl I'd idolised at school, a glitzy older woman I'd walked past in the street, or an actor or singer or model who I'd seen on social media. The self-judgement was instant, automatic; the habit of measuring my beauty and my worth against any other woman's so deeply ingrained I did it without even knowing what I was supposed to be striving for, what that pinnacle of beauty I was so desperately trying to attain even *was*. And yet, while these standards had never been so explicitly defined, I knew that I didn't make the cut. I knew it with such certainty that insecurity ran through my veins, self-flagellation an act as natural as breathing. I'd looked at myself in the mirror as a thirteen-year-old, a fifteen-year-old, a seventeen-year-old, all the while thinking of how beautiful I *could* be if only . . . if only . . .

Now, it seemed that I had the answer.

If only I was a girl like Clara.

Clara spent the entire morning by the river with the Goldens.

I watched them from my window as they emerged from the woodland from time to time and came back up to the house. After a brief interlude of rattling cupboards and slamming doors somewhere in the depths, they'd reappear, heading back down towards the river with their arms full of whatever Clara had chosen: rugs, pillows, flowers.

Even from a distance, it was clear that Clara wasn't being much help at all, standing there directing the girls as they carried things across the lawn instead of doing anything herself. I decided I'd stay where I was for the time being, out of the firing line.

Things had fallen apart after what had happened with Lily. Deneside Manor had been tense, Lottie glaring at us all with red-rimmed eyes, and we'd barely discussed the next party at all. By the time the atmosphere eased and the Goldens collectively began to buzz about the party, both the stylists and Clara's usual caterers were fully booked.

Clara had decided to take matters into her own hands, which had inevitably led in turn to this rush. I wondered whether she'd acknowledged – even to herself – why this had happened, why things had slid.

Eventually, in need of breakfast, I braved the kitchen. Four of the girls were there when I went in, looking somewhat dishevelled, all of them drinking smoothies or tall glasses of water.

'Where've you been?' Alexis asked me, rather accusingly. 'We've been decorating all morning.'

'I know,' I said. 'Sorry. I had some last-minute coursework to finish.' I held up the book that I'd brought down with me. 'How did it go?'

'It was a lot of work,' Christie said between sips of a bright green smoothie. 'I think Clara is happy with it all, though. She's still down there. Everyone else has gone for a shower.'

'Except Mia,' Sophie added. 'She went to the deli. Clara put a huge order in last night, since we won't have the caterers. She really thinks of everything, doesn't she?'

'She does,' I agreed. It was disconcerting, how little Clara had needed from me. I'd grown used to us planning her parties together, brainstorming aesthetics and dress codes in an excitement-fuelled haze. But she had the Goldens to do her bidding now. Did she even need me at all any more? I pushed the thought from my mind.

'I'll see you guys later, okay?' I said. 'I've still got some reading to do.'

'See you,' Christie chirped.

I grabbed some pancakes from the pantry, and then went out into the garden. I did still have some reading to do, that wasn't a lie, but it wasn't anything to do with my degree.

The book was one I'd borrowed from the university library, with the justification, if asked, of needing it for an essay. *Cults Today*, it boasted. *How* you *could be vulnerable to a cult!*

It was a bit more fictionalised than informative, which wasn't what I was looking for, but it was also the only cult-related book that hadn't been filled with troublesome stories and gory black-and-white images, the only one that hadn't pushed me almost directly into the throes of a panic attack.

In case Clara became suspicious of my intentions, I'd replaced the dust jacket with one from a children's classic I'd found in my bedroom. Paranoid? Maybe. Or maybe not.

This paranoia was probably why, when a shadow fell over

me after I'd read a chapter, I was so startled that I nearly dropped the book.

'*God*, Clara,' I said, shutting it abruptly. 'Where did you come from?'

'We've been decorating.' She was faintly breathless, a sheen of sweat across the V of skin exposed by her low-cut tea dress and the arches of her collarbones. I had the urge, inexplicably, to lick it. 'Do you want to come and see?'

'The girls told me,' I said. 'Of course I do.' I tucked the book under the garden chair I'd been sitting on, brushed off my jeans.

'You're not wearing those, are you?' Clara asked as I stood up, eyeing my jeans with suspicion.

'No, Clara,' I said. 'I couldn't even imagine it.'

We began to walk across the lawn, downhill towards the woodland and the river. It was getting too long, the grass growing unevenly, with patches of white clover, creeping thyme and Irish moss dotted throughout it like patchwork.

'Good,' she said. 'I've picked a dress out for you. It's in your wardrobe.'

Inside, I bristled. *Why do you always have to choose what I wear?* I wanted to ask.

Logically, I understood that there was nothing stopping me from choosing my own dress. I could open those wardrobe doors, push whatever dress she'd selected for me aside and pluck out one of a dozen or more that I wanted to wear, that I'd chosen of my own accord from Clara's own extensive wardrobe.

I could buy my own dress. I could say, *Actually, Clara, I'm wearing jeans – and there's nothing you can do about it.*

At the same time, I knew that I had to choose my battles. Disappointing Clara wasn't on the cards. I needed her – her power, her connections, her charisma, her friendship. Her very *self*.

So instead I smiled. 'Exciting,' I said, trying to sound enthusiastic. 'What colour is it?'

'Pink,' she said. 'It'll suit you.'

I didn't doubt her.

We were in the woods now, everything sun-dappled and newly green. What had only a few weeks ago been tight buds clinging to the bare branches were now leaves, still unfurling, filling the air with their sweet, musky scent.

The spell was broken when we reached the clearing, the space by the river where we'd had the equinox party not so long ago.

'Clara,' I breathed. I turned in a circle, taking it in. '*Shit.* You've outdone yourself.'

She was glowing. 'Do you really think so?'

'Yes!'

It was true. She had. Bohemian-style rugs and tapestries had been laid across the hard earth between the trees, the edges of each touching to form a carpet. Floor cushions and throw pillows were scattered everywhere, more than a dozen of them, in a mixture of plump velvet and soft corduroy and overstuffed gingham cotton, like an old dress. She'd had silver trays placed on tree stumps and in gaps between the rugs, each one holding an array of hand-painted clay and porcelain bowls. They were all empty, awaiting Clara's choice of nibbles. No doubt it'd be decadent: olives, figs, grapes, cubed feta and slices of Manchego, delicate curls of paper-thin prosciutto and thick slices of chorizo.

There'd been similar food at the first party I'd attended. I remembered being impressed to the point of being overwhelmed by the laden table, the huge array of meats and cheeses all for the taking. That had been in the late autumn, early winter; now here we were, with spring in the air.

However I felt about Clara, however much I loved and hated her in equal measure, I couldn't deny that she'd changed my life. And I knew I'd always have some level of gratitude for that, even on the days when she was at her most strange and moody, when she was compulsive to the point of being neurotic. I'd always care about her.

I loved her even now, as she turned to me with an unreadable expression. 'Is Olivia coming?'

'Not tonight,' I said. 'She couldn't make it. She said she'll be at the next one, though.'

Clara looked doubtful. Perhaps she knew that I'd had to persuade Olivia to come, to use the promise of Clara's own connections to convince her. But, if she suspected anything, she didn't call me out. Instead, she nodded sagely. 'I hope she does,' she said, with all the grace of the goddess she so wanted to be, that she believed she was. 'It's an honour to be invited.'

'It is,' I agreed.

We stood there a few moments longer. I shut my eyes, listening to the undulating flow of the river, the song of the birds in the trees above our heads.

And then her lips were on mine.

I gasped into the kiss, my hands moving to her waist, her shoulders, as she pulled me close, her hands in my hair, tugging lightly on the strands. She tasted of coffee and cherries, the stickiness of her lip balm on my own lips sugary sweet.

I'd had crushes in school, of course: the occasional beautiful boy, an eye-catching girl. But I'd never really understood the bone-deep attraction people had spoken about, this urge to grab and hold and touch, to pull somebody close enough so there wasn't an inch of space between your two bodies. Now, suddenly, I did.

'Is this okay?' Clara said, softly, against my lips.

'Yes,' I breathed, barely able to find the word in my blissed-out brain.

One of her hands stayed in my hair, and the other moved down to my other hand, to link our fingers. 'We're perfect together,' she murmured. 'I want you to stay here. With me.'

'I will,' I said. 'You know I will.'

'Promise?' she asked. Her eyes were enormous, her pupils dark and wide.

'Of course.'

She kissed me, gently, once more. And then stepped back.

I blinked at her, confused. 'Did I do something?'

'No,' she said. 'You're perfect. But we need to get ready. I'll see you back at the house?'

I blew out a long breath. 'Yeah. Yeah, okay.'

She left me standing in the woods. I pressed a fingertip to my lips, wondering if I'd dreamed what had just happened. But the red-pink smear of shimmer on my fingertip, the trace of Clara's lip balm, indicated that it was real. It was very, very real. Clara had kissed me.

Chapter 27

I couldn't find Clara when I got back up to the house.

The downstairs was empty, the kitchen an echoing cavern without the constant conversations, the snacking and making of cups of tea.

Upstairs, on the other hand, was a flurry of activity. Girls were everywhere; they called to each other from their open bedroom doors, traded eyeshadow and lipsticks, asked to borrow hair straighteners and earrings and nail polish.

'If you're not sure,' I heard Alexis saying to Christie, 'you can borrow one of mine. I've got a blue one, if you fancy it — it'll really bring out your eyes.'

Across the hallway, Sophie's door was open. 'What if we both wear pearl earrings?' she said to someone. 'We'll look so cute.'

'Yes!' Bella's voice agreed fervently. 'Love that. Let's do it.'

I smiled to myself. It was beautiful, in a way, this world inside a world that Clara had created.

The dress that Clara had chosen for me was a pink, ruffled minidress embroidered with tiny silver flowers. It would look good with a denim jacket for when the temperature dropped in the early evening, I decided. Once again, Clara's taste was impeccable.

I listened to the sounds of the girls as I got ready, the conversations and laughter, someone singing. I showered and shampooed and conditioned my hair, and then, with my damp hair pulled back from my face with a silk hair tie, started to put on my make-up. I mimicked Clara's, of course: the light, dewy combination of sheer foundation and well-placed touches of highlighter and bronzer, eyelashes long and fluttery. It was bare skin but better: the bronzer giving me a glow as if I'd been out in the sun, the highlighter emphasising my cheekbones. I added a dusting of glitter across my collarbones and then spritzed myself with a woody, floral scent I'd ordered online because I'd once spied a similar bottle on Clara's dressing table.

I sprayed my still-damp hair with a defining serum and scrunched it, a small handful at a time, allowing the product to accent my natural waves. I tried not to look too hard at my reflection as I pulled the dress over my head and then added the denim jacket on top; it wouldn't do to have a crisis of self-confidence, not when the first guests were sure to be arriving.

As if on cue, I heard the doorbell ring. I slipped my feet into the sandals and then fixed a smile on my face.

There was a knock on my bedroom door. I knew it was Clara.

When I opened it, she looked me up and down. A warm, fond smile crept on to her face. 'Ready?' she asked.

I wanted to ask her about the kiss. I wanted to ask if she really cared about me. I wanted to ask why she'd left me in the woods, walked away from me while my lips were still tingling. But I didn't.

'Ready,' I said, and joined her in the hallway.

The guests who'd attended the equinox party were familiar with the route across the lawn and down into the woods. The newcomers – and there were only a few, each one having received an exclusive invitation – didn't need directing; they just followed the swell of people, a line of ants heading into the woods.

I let Clara be the star, of course, naturally beautiful in her white dress, the gold of her jewellery glinting against her skin. I watched from inside the orangery, jealousy curling in my chest, as she greeted her guests on the patio, hugging each one as if they were her best friend in the entire world.

It was a relief when my phone rang, Olivia's name flashing on the screen.

I could see through the window that Clara was still suitably occupied, so I answered the call and then ducked into the kitchen. 'Hi,' I said.

'How's it going?'

My answer spilled out of me before I could overthink it. 'Something happened,' I said. 'Clara kissed me.'

I heard Olivia's slight intake of breath. 'When?'

I leaned against the kitchen island. It was filled with huge jugs of lemonade studded with halved strawberries, all waiting to be taken down to the river. It was a good excuse to be indoors, if I needed one.

'Earlier today. In the woods. She was showing me all the decorating she'd done for the party, she asked about you and then she just . . . kissed me.'

'She asked about me?'

'She asked if you were coming tonight,' I said. 'I told her that you'll come to the next party.'

There was a silence. Olivia started to speak, then stopped.

'What?' I asked.

'You don't think she was . . .' Olivia paused. 'You don't think that's *why* she kissed you, do you? Because you did what she asked?'

I thought back to the kiss, my nerves lighting up as I did.

We're perfect together, Clara had said, her breath warm on my lips. *I want you to stay here. With me.* I'd told her that I would. *I will. You know I will.* I'd even promised as much.

And then Clara had pulled away. She'd gone back up to the house, left me with stained lips and a fluttering pulse. Had she been *rewarding* me?

'Do you think she likes you?' Olivia asked. 'Romantically?'

'I don't think so, Liv,' I said. 'I do love her. I'd die for her, you know? But she doesn't love me like that. I don't love *her* like that.'

I wasn't entirely convinced about the last part, but I didn't say as much to Olivia. This I wanted to keep to myself until I'd figured it out, unravelled my complicated feelings like a tight ball of string.

'Well,' Olivia said, 'I guess we'll just have to see what happens, won't we?'

'Right.' With one hand, I poured myself a glass of lemonade. The ice cubes clinked as I brought it to my lips. It was sweet and bubbly, blissfully cold. For a moment, everything seemed like it might just work out.

'Oh,' Olivia said, 'before I go, are you going to Vanessa's memorial service? I wasn't sure if you'd heard about it.'

Vanessa's face flashed in my mind, her spiky bob, the way she'd looked, walking away from me in her silver dress the last time I'd seen her. 'Why are they having a memorial service?' I asked, her words not sinking in.

'Her parents have requested her funeral be family members only, which is totally fair enough; they've had a horrendous few months. So the university's arranging a service of its own to pay tribute to her.'

I froze. It felt impossible to decipher Olivia's words, even though I knew exactly what they meant. 'Her *funeral*?' I repeated. It sounded as if I was hearing my own voice underwater; it had a muted, dreamlike quality to it. 'Why would they arrange a funeral for her?'

There was a horrible silence. 'She's dead, Chloe,' Olivia said slowly. 'They found her body like . . . a week ago, in the river.'

I set down my glass of lemonade, a little splashing over the side, as the blood left my face. I was sure that I could feel it, even, all the tiny vessels and capillaries draining as the blood travelled to my heart, which was thumping hard in my chest. 'She's dead?'

I heard a rustling on the other end of the line; Olivia sitting down, maybe. 'You didn't know?'

'I didn't.'

'Fuck,' she said. 'It was all over the news. I thought you'd know. *Fuck*, Chloe, I'm so sorry.'

Vanessa was dead.

I didn't know how I'd missed it. As far as I was aware, after the police had found the booking confirmation for Vanessa's train ticket, the *#FindVanessa* posts had slowly faded into the ether. She hadn't wanted to be found – or, at least, that was the assumption.

But Vanessa had never made it to London. She'd been here all along.

'How?' I croaked finally. 'How did it happen? Do they know?'

'There's nothing official yet,' Olivia said. 'I don't think they've done the autopsy. But the police have said they don't think her death was suspicious. They're not looking for a third party.'

My head spun. 'They think she killed herself?'

'I suppose,' Olivia said solemnly. 'That, or she fell in. They found her near the bridge. It's happened before.'

256

'So why didn't they look in the river to begin with? They have police divers, right? For this exact purpose?'

'Well, sometimes bodies get . . . stuck, apparently. They get caught on branches or rocks, stuff like that. So they can't always see them until they' – Olivia swallowed thickly – 'float.'

I slumped heavily against the kitchen island. 'I'm going to be sick.'

I forced myself to take a deep, slow breath. And then another. In and out, in and out.

'I really thought you knew,' Olivia was saying. 'I didn't mean to spring it on you.'

Gradually, my heart resumed its normal pace. 'I just don't understand how I didn't,' I said, once I was calm enough to speak. 'Surely there have been articles.'

'There have,' Olivia said. 'Loads of them.'

Something about this situation didn't sit right, a niggling in the back of my mind. *Something's wrong.*

'Hold on a sec,' I said. I glanced around. The kitchen was still deserted. 'Let me put you on speakerphone.'

I heard Olivia's hum of assent, and pulled my phone away from my ear. I opened the internet browser, then typed in *Vanessa Hancock* with shaking fingers. I tried *Vanessa Hancock missing*, then *Vanessa Hancock Havington*. And then I tried *Vanessa Hancock river*. Nothing. All nothing.

I opened my social-media platforms one by one and typed in the same search terms. *Zero results found,* mocked the text on one. On another, *Better luck next time!*

257

'There's nothing there when I search her name,' I said, out loud, partly to Olivia but mostly to myself. 'Not a single result is coming up. Not on the internet, not on socials. Why isn't there anything there?'

I heard Olivia tapping at her keyboard. 'I've got thousands,' she said. 'Headlines, videos, all sorts.'

'Read some of them out.'

I scanned my phone for the same headlines as she read them aloud, slowly scrolling down the search results. I could imagine them there, stark and glaring at me . . .

HEARTBREAK AS BODY DISCOVERED IN RIVER AT HAVINGTON

BODY OF MISSING STUDENT FOUND IN RIVER, DROWNING SUSPECTED

UNIVERSITY CHANCELLOR PAYS TRIBUTE TO FIRST-YEAR STUDENT

TRAGIC VANESSA'S FAMILY TO SAY GOODBYE IN PRIVATE SERVICE

But, although Olivia's words echoed around the kitchen, none of the headlines appeared on my screen. I was struggling to absorb what I was seeing – or, rather, what I wasn't. Firstly, there was the battering ram of finding out that Vanessa was dead. Not just missing – she was *dead*. And then, as I recovered from that gut punch, there was the question of why I hadn't known. Why was every result with Vanessa's name missing from my phone?

A sick feeling dawned on me.

'I'm just going to try something,' I said.

I swiped to the internet settings on my phone, and switched Wi-Fi off. The 5G signal here was poor, Clara had warned me when I first moved in; I was unlikely to get a connection. She'd been quite insistent about it, actually. At the time, I hadn't thought anything of it. Now, I wondered.

After a few seconds, my phone connected to whichever tower was closest. The signal was there. And this time when I searched Vanessa's name all the results that Olivia had seen appeared.

Olivia must have heard me gasp.

'What?' she asked. 'What's wrong?'

'I turned off the Wi-Fi,' I said. 'And I can see everything. Everything you've just read out, it's all there.'

Olivia realised what had happened before I did.

'Clara put a filter on it, didn't she? Why would she do that?'

She was right. Clara must have added a parental protocol to her Wi-Fi account, one that had allowed her to block any mention of Vanessa's name the way that somebody might ban content relating to drugs or sex.

I was trembling with an unfamiliar yet no less potent combination of shock, hurt and sheer fury. How dare she try to hide something like that from me! I'd *lived* with Vanessa. I'd *known* her. I deserved to know that her body had been found. Surely Clara had known that this wouldn't last forever, that somebody would mention Vanessa's name? Or had she been simply hoping that they wouldn't? Had she been hoping that they'd have a quiet, unremarkable memorial service at the university, and that anybody who saw me afterwards would delicately avoid the issue because – and there it was again, that painful fact – I'd known Vanessa?

I didn't answer Olivia. I couldn't. But, as she stayed on the line with me, I methodically opened the settings on each of my social-media apps. And there they were: the phrases that had been muted from my various feeds. Not by me, of course. They stared at me, accusingly, from the screen. *Vanessa Hancock. Vanessa + Havington. Vanessa + Found. Vanessa + Body.*

It wasn't just the internet. Clara had changed the settings on my social media accounts. I didn't even know how she'd accessed them. She'd either hacked my accounts by guessing my passwords, or she'd stolen my phone. And, I thought, if that was what she'd done, she would have had to have been very careful. My phone was always close to me, either in my pocket or on the bedside table. The only time it wasn't near me was when I was in the shower.

Was Clara really so calculating? Was she truly capable of sneaking into my bedroom while I was in the shower or asleep, unlocking my phone, and methodically blocking these phrases? Or was this all too far-fetched?

Of course it isn't, I thought. *Not for Clara.*

'You need to talk to her,' Olivia said.

'No kidding,' I said. I tried to keep the words light, easy, but my voice betrayed my true feelings by cracking on the last syllable.

'Go and find her,' Olivia pressed. 'Seriously. You can bring me with you, if you like. Turn off speakerphone, but keep the call going? I'll be right here.'

I was reluctant, fully aware of what challenging Clara on something like this might imply, particularly if it wasn't true and she somehow wasn't the person responsible. But I knew I had to do it.

'Okay,' I said. 'Yes. You're right. I'll go and talk to her. Stay quiet.'

I tucked the phone into one of the pockets in my jacket, safely hidden from view.

When I reached the party in the woodland, Clara was dancing. She was mid-twirl when I saw her, the tiered skirt of her dress floating around her hypnotically. The other girls she'd invited – some that I recognised, some that I didn't – laughed and spun next to her, holding each other's hands and glasses of champagne and whatever they'd brought from the kitchen or dug out of the cooler box, its deep pit of ice a yawning cavern of promise.

The newcomers were obvious. They were the ones who were having the most fun, or at least trying to look as if they were, a hectic, possibly drug-induced flush high on their cheeks, each one still astounded that Clara had invited them.

The music was pounding an entrancing beat, something that sounded like a darker version of the indie pop Clara favoured. As I listened, I picked up on the lyrics, eerie in Florence Welch's soulful voice. They told of sacrificing human hearts, blood-covered dance floors, mermaids with long hair and sharp teeth, and I shivered.

'Clara,' I said loudly, to be heard over the music, 'I need to talk to you.'

The other girls glanced my way, recognising me, their scrutiny intense and familiar. It was the way in which I looked at other girls, the way I'd best learned to measure my beauty against theirs. A childish habit that had lingered since my pre-teens, like biting my fingernails. It was oddly flattering, in a way, but I couldn't dwell on that right now.

'I need to talk to you,' I repeated as I got closer to Clara, still whirling around in the centre of the clearing with her arms outstretched. She didn't seem to have heard me. After all, she was surrounded by her guests, all of them frowning slightly with fervent concentration. Her skin was shimmering, a mix of sweat and glitter, her head thrown back as she danced. I noticed that the liquid in her glass was clear. Was she drinking straight gin?

I reached out, touched her shoulder. 'Clara?'

She startled, her eyes shooting open. They appeared unfocused, just for a second, as if she needed a moment to remember who and where she was. And then they were filled with recognition. Love.

'Hey!' she said. She took one of my hands in hers. 'Where've you been? I missed you.'

I tried to see her as Olivia did, through a more cynical lens. *She's being a manipulative bitch*, I imagined Olivia saying, even as Clara's thumb grazed the back of my hand gently, affectionately.

I decided to just come out and say it, to use the element of surprise to my advantage. 'I know about Vanessa,' I said. 'Vanessa Hancock.'

To Clara's credit, she didn't seem particularly perturbed by my revelation, although she did stop dancing. She took a long swig of her drink – it had to be water, surely? – and dabbed her lips dry with the back of her hand, so as not to smudge her lipstick. 'Oh, right,' was all she said. 'The girl that drowned?'

'Yes, the girl that drowned,' I repeated bitterly. 'I lived with her! You know how upset I was when she went missing. Why did you block her name on your Wi-Fi? Why did you put filters on all of my social-media accounts so that I couldn't see anything about her?'

Clara looked at me with her huge doe eyes. 'I did it because I thought knowing what had happened would hurt you,' she said, her voice soft and persuasive. 'And I was right. Look at you.'

My eyes had filled with tears, almost without me realising, and they'd begun to escape, rolling down my hot cheeks. 'By not telling me,' I said, 'you robbed me of my chance to grieve her. To come to terms with her death. *That's* why I'm so upset, Clara. You never gave me the chance to find closure.'

'You hated her,' Clara said. 'She was cruel to you. Why would you need closure?'

'Because we made up!' I reminded her. 'We had a truce. I invited her to your party!'

Clara seemed to consider this. 'Oh,' she said. 'Well, no harm done.'

I blinked at her. For the first time, I understood what people meant when they said they saw a mist of fury. I was so upset that the world around me was blurred, the only clear point the girl in front of me who didn't seem to be at all bothered by what she'd done.

'No. Harm. Done?' I repeated, so low that the words were nearly a growl. 'You manipulated me. You wanted to stop me knowing a girl I used to live with had *died*! In what world does that translate to "no harm done"?'

My voice had risen just as the song changed, the last few words shouted into the near-silence of the woods. Whoever hadn't been listening before certainly was now, the gathered Goldens' eyes wide and their mouths little ovals of surprise. They were too intrigued to be polite. They simply stared, their gazes flicking between Clara and me, trying to understand what was going on.

'I'm leaving, Clara,' I said, pushing past her, back the way I'd come. 'I'm done with all of this.'

'You can't leave,' she protested. 'You belong here. This is your home.'

I whirled round to face her. 'I don't care, Clara. I'm taking my things, and I'm going. I don't want to be around you for another second.'

I didn't give her the chance to say anything else.

I stormed through the woods towards the garden, the girls behind me no doubt stunned by what had just happened. I wondered how long it would take to reach social media, the news of Clara and her most loyal follower having a spat at one of her famous parties.

I crashed into the house, through the orangery and the kitchen. I slipped my phone out of my pocket. The call was still going. Lovely, reliable Olivia.

'We're done,' I told her.

'What?'

'I told Clara I'm leaving,' I said. 'I'm going to pack my things.'

'Where are you going to go?' Olivia asked.

I hadn't thought that far ahead. Luckily, I still had part of my student loan put aside, saved from the rent that I'd no longer had to pay. Plus, there was the fee Clara had been paying me to manage her social media. If I didn't have this money, I realised, I'd be in a far more difficult position.

'There's one of those budget hotels on the edge of town, right?' I said as I climbed the stairs towards my bedroom. 'I'll stay there for a few weeks.'

'And then what?'

I flung open my wardrobe. 'It's not too long until the semester ends. I'll go back to my parents' for the summer. That was always going to be the plan, anyway, before I moved in here.'

I set my phone aside, back on speakerphone, as I dug through my wardrobe. So many dresses with embroidered bodices and flowing skirts, so many pairs of expensive stiletto heels. So many things that weren't *mine*. I pulled out *my* clothes, my jeans and T-shirts and my little satin peplum blouses, my Converse trainers and my ballet flats and my chunky boots. This was who I was, not the kind of girl who wore a diamond tiara to university, who favoured designer heels for a party in her own garden.

I stuffed my clothes into my backpack, then emptied the bathroom. Once the backpack was full, I grabbed a Kate Spade tote bag that I vaguely remembered borrowing from Clara and shoved my laptop and all of its assorted cables into it, followed by my books.

I was surprised that Clara hadn't come after me. I'd expected her to be shocked at first, and then, after realising that I was serious, bereft. I'd pictured her following me into the house, clinging to me and begging me not to leave.

That she'd done none of these things spoke volumes.

Maybe our relationship really had meant more to me than to her, like it had meant more to Ayanna. The thought made my chest ache with sadness and humiliation, and my eyes prickled with tears.

'I've booked you a taxi,' Olivia said. 'It shouldn't be long. I'll meet you at the hotel.'

'Thanks, Liv,' I said. 'You're the best. Did you know that?'

'Yes,' she said simply.

There was no sign of Clara as I crept back down the stairs, rather pointlessly, since there didn't appear to be anybody inside at all. They were all still outside, enjoying the sunshine and their drinks, luxuriating in the feeling of being at the very centre of their idol's little world.

I said goodbye to Olivia and sat outside on the front steps to wait for the taxi. I looked out at the view, at the hazy distant roofs of Havington, the dark outline of the university's clock tower. I'd expected this to feel like an ending, the significant completion of one era of my life leading smoothly to the start of another.

Oddly, though, it didn't. Instead, it felt like there was something else still to come.

One last encore.

Chapter 28

I didn't tell Mum and Dad that I'd moved into a hotel.

Whenever they called or texted me, which was often, I pretended that I was still living with Clara. We talked about her latest party (they'd seen the photos online – luckily, none of them featured the argument) and my university workload, with me fashioning scenarios that I knew they'd approve of, like studying with the other girls in the garden, the way that we all helped each other with our essays. Clara would have been pleased with the girlish little utopia I described, with only the occasional fragment of truth thrown in, such as how we were always running out of coffee pods.

The hotel was close enough to campus for me to walk to my lectures, meeting Olivia on the way, and I realised how much I'd missed campus life. I'd missed being surrounded by students in various states of stress, sprawled in the grassy quad holding pints in plastic cups, lugging backpacks to and from the library and smiling all the while.

I still received more curious glances than I was comfortable with, particularly since I was usually on my own, but the attention had certainly died down. There were plenty of girls wearing light colours too, gold hairpieces and glittering claw clips fixed carefully into their hair. But they didn't approach me. Most of them, in fact, acted as though I didn't exist, which made me wonder what Clara had told her followers about my abrupt departure.

Olivia came round when she could, usually after a lecture or a seminar. We'd lie on the queen-sized bed, its starched white sheets nothing like the soft ones I'd grown used to at Deneside Manor, comparing notes or laughing about a comment someone had made.

The room came equipped with a kettle and a mini fridge, and with these tools I concocted a reasonably fulfilling daily routine of cereal for breakfast, a sandwich for lunch and some kind of rice or noodle pot for tea – the kind where you just had to add hot water. I made sure to choose the allegedly healthy ones, so that I felt like less of a slob.

I began to visit the Ivy House launderette, sneaking in whenever somebody left the door open. I'd spend my pocket change on detergent and softener, then sit with a book while my load of clothes tumbled around in the washing machine. After a few chapters, I'd heave the wet bundle over into one of the big metal dryers, which were enormous and circular like aeroplane engines and nearly as loud.

But I wasn't happy. On the outside, I smiled more, socialised more. I even went for a drink at the students' union with my course mates, including Olivia, one afternoon. I copied her order of a wild berry cider, but as I sipped it and tried to savour the blackcurrant and cherry flavours, I longed for the fizz of champagne on my tongue.

I put on a brave face during the day, but at night, when I was alone, I wept. I missed the life that I'd built. I missed padding down to the kitchen each morning, making a latte with the expensive coffee machine, picking through the pantry to select one of the many expensive jams or jellies for my toast. I missed lounging in the orangery, the warm dirt and citrus scent of it, the mildewed cushions soft beneath my back. I missed the noise and the camaraderie; I missed Bella and Christie, and Lottie and Sophie and Millie. I even missed Alexis and Mia. I missed the way we'd all cosy up to watch a film together in the living room with blankets and popcorn, the way there'd always be someone to laugh with at the breakfast table on a morning, or lend you a pair of earrings or give you a pep talk when you needed one. I missed the Goldens.

But most of all I missed Clara.

I'd lie on the bed and scroll through her account, obsessing over every new picture that she posted. I'd scrutinise everything, from where she was and the caption (had she already enlisted another Golden to help her write them?) to her smile, and whether she looked genuinely happy or not. I was broken. Why wasn't she?

Sometimes, I'd run into the other Goldens. Bella served me in Tate's with sad, wide eyes and awkward, stilted conversation. Mia strode past me on Main Street without even glancing in my direction. I could tell they'd been instructed not to speak to me. I'd officially been shunned.

Even Alexis, who clearly relished being Clara's shiny new second-in-command, didn't say a word when she saw me outside the bookshop with the red door one morning – but I did see her lips curl up into a self-satisfied smile.

Thankfully, though, I never came across Clara. I didn't quite trust myself not to grovel at her feet.

I'd been staying at the hotel for three weeks when she finally reached out.

Olivia and I were studying together in my room, preparing to hand in our last assignment of the year. She was sitting at the desk, tapping away at her laptop, and I was stretched out on the bed, rereading some notes I'd taken that I was hoping might be useful for the point I was trying to argue.

'The problem is,' I said, holding up my notebook, 'I write down notes at the time, but I don't elaborate on them. So now I have no idea what I'm reading.'

As I spoke, my phone began to vibrate. I glanced at the caller ID. *Clara.*

All other thoughts left my head.

Olivia must have seen the change in my expression, because she stopped typing. 'You don't have to answer it, you know.'

'I know,' I said, 'but I want to hear what she has to say.'

I pressed the call answer button, and pressed it to my ear. 'Hello?'

Clara was crying. 'Chloe?' she said. 'I'm so glad you answered! Are you okay?'

I tried to be curt, even as my heart leaped at the sound of her voice. 'I'm fine.'

Although it was cruel, I couldn't deny how good it felt to hear her crying over me, the little hitches in her breaths confirming what I'd always hoped. Clara did care about me.

'When are you coming home?' she asked. 'I miss you. I need you here.'

More words that were a balm to my insecure, jealous self. Clara missed me. And not just that – she *needed* me. To say it out loud was vulnerability on another level. Or, of course, this was simply more manipulation. After all, she still hadn't actually apologised.

'I don't know, Clara,' I said. 'You haven't even said you're sorry.'

'I *am* sorry,' she said. 'I thought I was doing the right thing, but I clearly wasn't. I just want what's best for you. That's all I ever want. I love you, Chloe. I care about you.' She made a little noise, a sob or a snort. 'I really am sorry. I'm so fucking sorry.'

I could see Olivia looking at me and it was hard not to feel judged as I relented. 'I know, Clara,' I said. 'It's okay. I mean, it's *not*. Obviously. But I accept your apology.'

A series of sniffles. 'Okay. Okay, thank you, Chloe. I promise you, I really did just want to help.'

'I know you did,' I said. 'But you understand now how you did the opposite, right?'

'Yes,' she said, barely a murmur. 'I understand.'

The line went quiet.

'Are you still there?' she asked.

'I'm here,' I said.

'When you want to come home,' she said, 'you don't have to text. You still have your key. And I'll just see you when you're ready, okay?'

'Yeah,' I said. 'Okay, Clara. I will.'

I hung up.

Olivia had closed her laptop, and was now staring at me. 'So?'

'She wants me to move back in with her.'

'Yeah, right,' Olivia scoffed. 'As if you're ever going back there.'

I winced.

Olivia's face slackened, her righteous fury on my behalf fading into horror in an instant. 'You're not actually thinking about it, are you? Chloe, you can't be serious.'

'What am I supposed to do?' I asked. 'I can't stay here forever. My student loan's about to run out, and I won't get another payment until September.'

'Get a job! Plenty of students have them.'

'It's not like I haven't tried,' I said. It was true; I'd sent out dozens of CVs, but the fact was that there simply weren't many jobs that I was qualified for in Havington, and the competition between students for the few jobs that there were was intense. The shopping centres on the outskirts weren't an option either as they all required a car to get to: the buses were both sparse and unreliable, and I didn't drive.

Olivia was quiet. 'You want to move back in with her, don't you?' she said. 'You *miss* her. After everything she's done, you still want to go back to her.'

I thought of the kiss, of the way that Clara's lips had felt on mine. And just now on the call she'd sounded so hurt as she'd begged me to come home.

'She did it to protect me,' I said. 'She didn't want me to get hurt.'

In my desperation, I wanted to believe, more than anything, that it was the truth. That Clara had only done such a terrible, despicable thing because she didn't want me to find out about Vanessa's death through a push notification or a trending hashtag. I wanted to believe that, eventually, Clara would have chosen a time to tell me.

'Keeping you in the dark isn't protecting you, Chloe,' Olivia said. 'It's abusing you.'

'She thought she was helping!' I protested. 'And she's apologised. You should have heard her on the phone, Liv. I've never heard her cry like that before.'

Olivia shook her head, pity etched into the lines on her face. 'She's manipulating you,' she said, 'just like she always has. And you won't let yourself see it. Please don't go back there. Please. For me.'

'You know I have to,' I said.

Olivia got up, collected her books and laptop in her arms.

When she looked at me, I was startled to see that her eyes were glistening with unshed tears. 'You don't have to,' she said. 'You *want* to. Please, Chloe. Can't you see what she's doing?'

I didn't reply.

She stood there in the middle of the room, dressed in her trademark all-black outfit even in the height of summer. Her red hair was shorter than it had been when we'd first met, her sleek, wavy ponytail now a shoulder-length bob.

We'd been through so much conflict, the majority of which, even I had to admit, had concerned Clara. But it had been Clara who had brought us together too, back when we'd first seen her in the campus coffee shop, when I'd returned her monogrammed scarf and Olivia had lit up at the sight of her. How much had changed.

A tear escaped and she swiped at it, roughly, with her sleeve. 'Okay,' she said. 'Okay. I'm just . . . I'm going to go.'

Olivia glanced at me one last time over her shoulder before she left, but I couldn't meet her gaze. The door slammed behind her.

Two days later, I was back at Deneside Manor.

Chapter 29

When I returned, three weeks and two days after I'd left, I slotted seamlessly back into life at Deneside Manor.

I'd let myself in with my key, as Clara had told me to, my bags in hand. Really, that was a sign in itself that I'd had no intention of staying away forever. If I had, I would've posted my key back through the letterbox the day that I'd left.

It was ridiculous how much I'd missed the place: the chessboard tiles in the entryway, the summery, zesty smell of the orangery, the *Vogue* magazines and satin scrunchies and lipsticks scattered around every room.

It was a little anticlimactic, in all honesty.

When Clara saw me standing in the kitchen making a coffee, she wrapped her arms round my waist from behind and rested her head on my shoulder so that I inhaled the sweet, familiar scent of her.

'I'm glad you're here,' she said. And that was all.

Life went on.

I still thought about Vanessa. I weighed our every interaction leading up to New Year's Eve, wondering whether things would have turned out differently if I'd gone with her to find Clara that night. Maybe we would eventually have become friends, and I grieved for the unknown, for what we might have had.

And I missed Olivia. She no longer sat with me in lectures; in fact, she rarely came to lectures at all. I handed in my last assignment of my first year at Dern alone, and then treated myself to an iced caramel macchiato to celebrate. Afterwards, Clara picked me up, and I lay back on the familiar white leather passenger seat of her Mini Cooper and watched the countryside in full summer bloom flash by.

However, it wasn't long before I learned about the events of the night that I'd left. And that was the beginning of the end.

I found out at the end of June. I'd delayed moving back home with my parents to – in my own words – enjoy being a student with no responsibilities for a little while longer. It was the start of a heatwave, the temperature slowly climbing, the leaves crisping on the trees and the lawn sun-bleached.

The girls were all exhausted from the heat, lazing around on the sofas, setting out blankets on the grass, sipping drinks through striped paper straws from glasses whose sides ran wet with condensation.

I'd dressed that morning in white mom-style shorts and a racerback vest and was in the kitchen blending a frozen red-berry smoothie (with relative caution, given my all-white outfit) when Christie approached me.

'She's in an awful mood today,' she warned. 'I'd keep out of her way.'

There was no ambiguity around who she meant.

'Any idea why?' I asked. I carefully transferred my smoothie to a glass, held up the jug in offering.

Christie shook her head. 'No, thanks,' she said. 'I'm not sure, but she's been slamming the cupboard doors all morning.'

'Where is she now?'

'In the garden.'

Wonderful.

'Thanks for letting me know, Christie,' I said. 'Whatever it is, you know it's nothing to do with you, right?'

She sighed, a long-suffering kind of sound. 'I know, Chloe,' she said. 'Thanks. She doesn't know how lucky she is to have you.'

She patted me on the arm in a way I interpreted as being slightly sympathetic, and then carried on through the kitchen, out into the orangery. I waited a moment, sipping my smoothie while I let Christie's words sink into my skin. *She doesn't know how lucky she is to have you.* I needed them to form a layer of armour for the inevitable spat I was about to have with Clara. Then I took a deep breath, and went outside.

Clara was sitting alone on a sunlounger that somebody had dragged on to the grass from the patio. She wasn't relaxing, though – I could see her foot bobbing, the tightly coiled energy in it. She must have heard my footsteps, because she swung her legs round to face me, pushing her sunglasses up on top of her head as she did so, and looked up at me with a worryingly manic glint in her eye.

'Look at this,' was all she said. She leaned down, picked something up and then thrust a pile of pages in front of my face. A newspaper.

I took it from her and, as I did, noticed that she had a collection of papers spread beside the sunlounger. There appeared to be a wide range, from broadsheets to tabloids, local press to national.

'Since when do you get newspapers delivered?' I asked stupidly.

Clara didn't appreciate my question. She stabbed her finger at the newspaper in my hand, leaving a dent in her wake. 'Read it,' she demanded.

HAVINGTON HYSTERIA: IS A TEENAGE GIRL LEADING THE NEXT TOXIC CULT?

Everyone has heard of Clara Holland.

The British model-slash-influencer, 19, has hit the headlines in recent months for the parties she hosts at her parents' Georgian country house. Rumoured to be both opulent yet utterly wild, Holland's parties are incredibly selective – with only people she personally favours making the cut for an invitation.

However, if you follow the party scene, you may have heard other reports.

We spoke to one of Holland's guests, under condition of anonymity, who alleged that her most recent party, which took place last month, featured both drug use and ritualistic behaviour in the woods.

As well as being pressured to participate in rituals, all attendees are supposedly asked to follow a set of rules – including verbally accepting Holland as their leader. If they don't? They're forced out of the party, and, if they happen to belong to the 'lucky' few chosen to live at Holland's manor, they're forced out of their home too.

I didn't know what to make of it. I glanced back up at Clara, waiting for her guidance on how to react.

'Well?' she said. 'Aren't you concerned?'

'They're calling us a cult,' I said. 'That's nothing new.'

Clara let out an aggrieved sigh, as if I'd completely missed the point on purpose.

'Read *between* the lines, Chloe,' she said. 'Somebody who lives with us is leaking details to the press. We have a spy. A fucking spy!'

I tried to be reasonable, to keep a level head in the face of her irrationality. 'You post so much about the events online,' I pointed out. 'Couldn't they just be getting this information from your posts, or some other people's posts, maybe?' I scanned the article. 'There's nothing in here that's a secret, really. They might just be bluffing, saying they have a source when they don't.'

Clara snatched the newspaper back from me. 'Are you on my side or not?'

'That's not fair,' I said. 'You know I'm always on your side.'

Clara's gaze was steely. 'You don't like Olivia better?'

I gaped at her. 'What are you talking about?'

She folded her arms, her chin raised in challenge. 'I know that she told you to leave.'

'She didn't tell me to do anything,' I said. '*I* wanted to leave. I was upset.'

Clara ignored me. 'You're more loyal to her than you've ever been to me.'

'Where is this coming from?' I asked. 'I'm literally right here. It's you that I'm loyal to. I haven't even spoken to Olivia since I moved back in.'

It was true. We hadn't so much as texted, and I felt her absence like a hole in my chest, the memory of our fight still raw round the edges.

A devious expression crept across Clara's face. 'What if she's the spy?' she said. 'What if she's the little snake who's been gossiping to the press?'

'She's never even been to a party here,' I reminded her. 'So how could she be the spy?'

'Maybe she snuck in. The night she made you leave.'

It didn't seem to matter that I'd already told her I'd chosen to leave of my own accord. There was an air of triumph about her now, her eyes gleaming. As far as Clara was concerned, she'd solved the mystery.

'Olivia did *not* sneak in,' I protested. 'Anyway, she'd never do something like that. Ever.'

Deep down, I knew that Olivia was perfectly capable of being a spy – in theory, at least. But our spy clearly had a reasonable level of access and in-depth knowledge, which Olivia didn't have. Unless . . . A chill ran through me. Unless *I'd* been the source of her information?

I pushed the thought aside. The suggestions of cult behaviour would surely raise red flags with any reasonable person, which meant that the spy could conceivably be any one out of literally hundreds of Clara's previous guests. Olivia was just one of many potential spies.

Clara was watching me intently. 'Are you sure about that?'

I knew that she couldn't see into my brain or read my thoughts, but sometimes it really seemed as if she could. I could feel her eyes boring into me, examining every inch of my face, every tiny change in my expression. Once upon a time, I would have been flattered to have been at the centre of Clara's attention, her focus beaming down on me like a spotlight. Now, though, I was struggling to remember why I'd ever wanted it in the first place.

'I'm sure,' I said. 'You're being paranoid, Clara. You're letting all of *this* rubbish' – I gestured at the collection of newspapers – 'get into your head. I'm going back inside.'

I turned to leave.

Her voice was cold when it came from behind me. 'Am I paranoid?' she asked. 'Or am I right?'

I didn't look back at her as I walked away, her gaze burning into my neck, but I was trembling.

I had to talk to Olivia, and I had to talk to her soon.

First, though, I needed to find out what had actually happened at the party. The article that Clara had shown me had mentioned drug use and ritualistic behaviour as evidence that she was leading a cult. The occasional joint being passed around counted as drug use, of course. But ritualistic behaviour? I had no idea what that could mean.

I decided to hunt Christie down, since she was one of the only Goldens who seemed comfortable even lightly criticising Clara. I'd learned the hard way that the others, if gently nudged in the direction of an unfavourable comment, even if it was a joke, would stare at you as if you'd asked them to hack one of their legs off with a chainsaw. Which was to say that they were loyal to a fault, and blind loyalty wasn't what I needed right now.

Christie was in her room, one of the smaller ones that looked out over the fields at the side of the house. The door was closed. I knocked, a couple of times, then leaned close.

'It's Chloe,' I hissed. 'Can I come in?'

The door opened a sliver, Christie's face peeking out. 'Oh,' she said. 'Hi. Yeah, of course.'

As I closed the door behind me, I couldn't help but take in Christie's room. There was a book on her unmade bed, the pillows propped up as if she'd been reading there. The bedroom itself was plain, the only furniture an old bedframe and a heavy armoire. The personal knick-knacks on the bedside table were sparse: a hairbrush, a red lip gloss, a pair of earrings shaped like ladybirds.

I noticed, then, that the book she'd been reading was *Rebecca*. I suddenly remembered talking about books with Olivia the day we met. We'd both named it as one of our favourites, and I had to swallow hard before I could speak.

'So, hi,' Christie said again. 'Are you okay?'

'I'm fine,' I said, my voice only a little hoarse. 'I just wanted to talk to you.'

She settled back down on the bed. When I looked at her questioningly, she nodded her permission and I perched on the end of it, beside her socked feet.

'What do you want to talk to me about?'

'The last party.'

'Oh,' she sighed. 'What do you want to know?'

'What happened after I left? I want to know why it seems to have led to an . . . well, an *explosion* of media coverage. Clara showed me a newspaper article just now and it mentioned "ritualistic behaviour".' I air quoted the words. 'What does that even mean?'

'Well,' Christie began, 'it was definitely weird.' She paused for a moment. 'After you left, Clara was *furious*. It was fine at first, we all just kept drinking and dancing, but as the sun set she asked us all to get in the river. She wanted us to dunk ourselves under the water, right up to our noses. I went completely under! My hair was soaked.'

I'd expected Clara to be angry, but I hadn't expected fury. 'Why would she ask you to do that?'

'She said it was a test of loyalty,' Christie explained. 'That we were cleansing ourselves for our new lives.'

Did this count as ritualistic behaviour? I was pretty certain that it did. I thought back to when we'd been planning the equinox party, and Clara's little quip about sacrifices. It hadn't taken her long. Besides, even without the ritualistic connotations, asking a group of undoubtedly drunk or high girls to stand in a fast-flowing river and dunk their heads under the water was dangerous. So incredibly dangerous. And as for the cult accusations . . . that could only have fuelled the rumours.

'Okay,' I said. I stood up, my knees wobbly. 'Thanks, Christie. That's so helpful.'

She was watching me. 'Is Clara in trouble?' she asked. 'She didn't force any of us to do it. Really. If there was anyone who didn't want to, she said they could just leave.'

'The party?'

Christie shifted. 'Well. The house too, I guess.'

I didn't say that that sounded like forcing to me. *Do as I say, otherwise you lose your home and your friends, your sisters.*

'She's not in trouble,' I said instead. But the *yet* that followed hung in the air, unspoken.

Chapter 30

Being back in Havington was dizzying. It was like standing in a funfair hall of mirrors, with Clara looking back at me from every surface.

She was in the styling of every girl's hair, their choice of broderie anglaise blouse or flowing skirt, the gold necklaces fastened round their throats, their arms clinking with glittering bangles, fake versions of the Cartier ones that Clara liked to wear. Some of them even wore long white dresses. Was her influence really so strong that these girls – these beautiful, intelligent, determined young women – wanted to give up their own identities just to be like her?

And yet, as these girls strolled around town, each mimicking Clara in her own dedicated way, their idol was being completely eviscerated.

The newspapers that Clara had collected weren't the last of the media commentary surrounding the Goldens. With information about her latest party continuing to spread, she was being heavily criticised online too – by everybody from fellow influencers who'd once looked up to her (one girl even posted a tearful video apologising for being duped by such a fake) to once-committed followers. Clara was accused of being a new kind of cult leader, of brainwashing, of risking bringing the girls who lived with her to both physical and psychological harm. And the fact that these other girls were dressing like her, visibly worshipping her, disturbed me.

Outside the coffee shop, I braced myself. It hadn't been easy to get Olivia to meet with me.

Although I knew that she was staying in Havington for now, busy securing her accommodation for September and working a summer job at the students' union, she'd ignored all of my calls. I'd messaged her repeatedly, and she'd read them, but she'd never responded.

I understood why. I'd chosen Clara over her, again. She'd tried to help me as best she could, and I'd pushed her away. But I hadn't had a choice. Or, at least, that's what I kept telling myself.

Eventually, I'd just texted her a huge paragraph.

Liv, I'd said, *I know you don't want to speak to me right now, and I completely understand. But Clara thinks someone's spying on her to feed stuff to the press about the Goldens (that's what she's calling them now btw) and she's convinced it's you. I told her that it definitely isn't, but she doesn't believe me. We need to talk. Phone me, text me, whatever. I just need to talk to you.*

Olivia texted back within ten minutes. *Are you free this afternoon?*

Yes, I'd replied. *Tate's Coffee on Main Street?*

287

Her reply flashed up on the screen a second later. *As long as you're buying.*

Done.

The campus coffee shop had been my haunt during term-time, but I'd gradually become fond of Tate's after Bella had introduced me to it. It was an independent coffee shop, quirky, with mismatched furniture and an old-fashioned glass-fronted cake display cabinet made of walnut. The pictures that lined the walls were all painted by local artists, many of them landscapes of the area, and had white price tags hanging from their frames. Bella wasn't working today, which made it a safe place to meet.

Olivia was sitting at a table for two by the window, her hair glowing burnt orange in a shaft of sunlight. She must have been there for a while, must have got there early, as there was an empty glass in front of her leaving a wet ring on the wood. She was tapping away at something on her phone, and only looked up when I sat down.

'Hey,' she said tiredly.

'Hey,' I said. 'Thank you so much for meeting me.'

'It sounded important,' Olivia said. 'Kind of like my welfare depended on it.'

'Fair enough,' I said. 'She's just so . . . *paranoid*, Liv. I'm worried about her. She's convinced that people are spying on her. Even the girls who live in the house.'

'And where do I come into this?' Olivia asked, stone-faced.

'She thinks that you've been speaking to the press,' I said. 'Telling them about her parties, about what's going on on the inside, because you're angry with her. She thinks that you're the reason the press coverage has amped up lately.'

Olivia considered this. 'Well,' she said, 'I have been speaking to the press.'

I broke out in a cold sweat. 'What?'

'Obviously, I was angry with her,' Olivia said matter-of-factly. 'For how she'd manipulated you. How she *is* manipulating you. And I could see that other people were getting suspicious too, starting to figure out who she really is. So when you went back to stay with her I emailed a guy I know at the *Havington Herald*. He was *super* interested in what I had to say.'

'I told Clara that you'd never do anything like that,' I said. 'I said you'd never dare.'

Olivia shrugged. 'Then I don't know what to say to you. Because I did.'

My fingers drummed on the table between us, my anxiety made physical. I'd hoped that the repetitive action would soothe me, or at least release some of the tension. But it didn't. 'What did you tell him?' I asked.

'He'd heard rumours already,' Olivia said. 'I didn't really tell him anything new.'

'What did you *tell* him, Olivia?'

'I told him that Clara is manipulative, that she's desperate to be loved and genuinely wants people to see her as some sort of avant-garde cool new cult leader. I told him that she'd allegedly poisoned a girl when she was thirteen, and that, frankly, I suspected her in what happened to Vanessa too.'

A chill ran through me. 'Vanessa drowned.'

Olivia leaned across the table. 'Yes,' she said. 'She drowned. *After* she left Clara's party. And don't you think it's convenient that there's no record of her actually leaving? Don't you think it's strange that there isn't any CCTV footage of her in Havington that night at all? Only eyewitness accounts?'

'The eyewitness accounts are reliable,' I said. 'The police obviously think so.'

'They saw a girl with short blonde hair, wearing a silver dress,' Olivia said, rolling her eyes. 'You could step out of here right now and spot ten of them.'

'What are you saying?' I managed. 'What exactly are you accusing Clara of?'

'Nothing,' Olivia said. 'Not yet.'

I opened my mouth to protest, but she held up a finger. 'I'm not interested, Chloe. Look, whether she was involved or not – people need to know what she's doing to those girls, how she's using them and manipulating them. They need to know what she's doing to *you*. Her little protégé.'

It would have been so simple, at that moment, to give in. I wanted to. I wanted to sigh, to slump forward, to admit that *fine, okay, yes*, Clara's behaviour *was* beginning to scare me. I wanted to tell Olivia that I'd heard from the Goldens that

Clara's actions had escalated, that she'd outright encouraged them to baptise themselves in her name. But, despite everything that had happened, Clara's hooks were still deep in my skin. The memory of her lips on mine, her arms round my waist, the way she looked at me from beneath her eyelashes. And, even as I contemplated telling Olivia the truth about what was really going on, I could feel those hooks tugging at my heart, pulling at it.

'Clara was right,' I said, although my voice trembled. 'You're not good for me.'

Olivia's briefly shocked expression faded into one of dull acceptance, of defeat. 'I thought you'd say that,' she said. 'I knew Clara would put words in your mouth.'

I swallowed hard. 'I'm going back now.'

'Okay,' Olivia said resignedly. 'When it all falls down, and the little world she's created crumbles around you, you'll know that I had your best interests at heart all along.'

I shoved my chair back, the legs screeching on the floor as I stood up. 'We'll see.'

Olivia wasn't even looking at me. She'd pulled a menu towards her, and was perusing it with practised nonchalance. 'Yes,' she said. 'We will.'

I stormed out of the coffee shop without a backwards glance. I tried to keep my expression calm, unbothered, as I strode along the pavement, but I was shaken. Could Clara really have had something to do with Vanessa's death? Of course not; Olivia was jealous, that was all. She was just reaching, searching for a way to tear me away from Clara's side. It simply wasn't going to happen. Not now, not ever.

Still, the idea of it instilled an itchiness deep in my bones, the knowledge that, if Olivia's suspicion got out, it would ruin everything that I'd grown to love. It would ruin Clara.

I wondered, briefly, whether I should go to the police – to get ahead of the narrative. *But*, a frightened voice whispered in the back of my mind, *if Clara was involved, won't they suspect you too? You invited Vanessa that night.*

I shoved the thoughts away. As I did, my phone began to vibrate in my pocket. Maybe it was Olivia, already ringing to apologise for her harsh words, to try to fix our friendship before it was irreparably damaged.

But when I took it out *Mum* was flashing up on the screen. I took a deep breath, and forced a smile on to my face before I answered.

'Hi, Mum!' I said.

'Chloe,' Mum said, 'what are you up to?'

She sounded tense – not a good sign.

'I'm in Havington,' I said. 'I just met Olivia for a coffee.' It wasn't a lie.

'So Clara's not around?' she said. 'Good. I need to talk to you about her.'

Oh, no.

'I love that you've made such a good friend,' she began. 'You know I follow you both on social media, and it looks like you're having so much fun.' *Here it comes.* 'But I've been reading things. Articles in the newspaper.'

'You should just ignore them, Mum,' I said. 'It's all rubbish.'

'Well, the thing is, Chloe, I don't think it *is* all rubbish,' she said. 'The articles say she makes you dress all the same, follow strict rules and take part in rituals. And I've seen all of that on her Instagram.'

Damn. I should have asked Clara to block her.

'It's her house,' I said. 'Obviously we follow her rules. We dress like each other because we want to – we all share clothes and stuff. And the rituals are just a bit of fun. These reporters are making a big deal out of nothing.'

For a second, I thought I had her convinced. And then she said, 'We had a letter from the university too. About your attendance.'

'They don't send letters to parents,' I said.

She hesitated. 'It was addressed to you.'

'So you opened my post,' I said, 'and now you're trying to hold it against me? You know that's illegal, right? I'm an adult.'

'You are an adult,' Mum said, 'and I know I can't tell you what to do, but I don't think living with Clara is good for you. You used to have such an incredible work ethic, such big dreams! And you haven't even been going to your lectures?'

'Mum—'

'I think you should move back into halls,' she interrupted.

'That's all. If you're not careful, you're going to fail your exams. You'll fail your first year, and that's a year of your life that you'll never get back. And all for what? Parties and rich friends?'

'It's good for me, Mum,' I said, growing defensive. 'University's not just about grades. It's about networking, making connections. Clara's mum's in fashion – she can get Clara an internship at any magazine she wants! They're good people to know.' I sniffed. 'And, anyway, I'm writing. Properly writing, for the first time in ages.'

'What are you writing?'

'Clara's memoir.'

I knew it was a mistake as soon as I said it.

'And is that her dream or yours that you're missing out on university for?'

I didn't know what to say.

'Look, Chloe.' Mum sounded tired. 'I just want what's best for you.'

'I know.'

'So will you consider it? Moving back to halls?'

'Yes,' I lied. 'I'll consider it.'

'Good,' Mum said. 'Thank you. I love you.'

'I love you too.'

We said our goodbyes and I ended the call, then tucked my phone back into my pocket. Obviously, I wasn't going to consider it. Why would I move back to the damp, cold halls and lose everything that I'd gained? Mum didn't know what she was talking about – how could she, from a few articles and some social-media snapshots? She didn't know anything about me, about my life with Clara.

I boarded the bus back to Deneside Manor, utterly drained but feeling confident in my decision to defend Clara to both Olivia and my mum. Nobody knew Clara better than I did, after all. Nobody.

And yet, as I gazed out of the window at the sunlit passing fields, my mind lingered on what Mum had asked.

Is that her dream or yours?

Still reeling from my conversation with Mum, I didn't think about Olivia's suspicions for the rest of the afternoon. It was only when Clara cornered me in the orangery that her words came screaming back.

I'd flopped down on one of the bistro seats with a chunky novel, keen to catch some sun while I could. I'd just finished the first chapter when she came in from the garden, looking delectable in a summery pink satin tea dress. She leaned against the doorframe, in a move that I calculated as being far less casual than she wanted it to appear.

'Alexis was in town earlier,' she said. 'She said she saw you at Tate's with someone.'

Fucking Alexis.

'Yeah?' I said, feigning indifference as I flipped the page.

'Yeah,' she said. 'Some girl with red hair?'

There was a pregnant pause.

When I looked up at Clara again, she was watching me expectantly, her eyes hard.

'Fine. Yes, I went to meet Olivia,' I said finally, closing my book. 'But it's not what you think. Really. I wanted to talk to her about this whole "going to the press" thing.'

Clara sat down in the other bistro seat, and turned it to face me. Across from each other, our knees practically touching, we were centimetres apart. 'It was her, wasn't it?' she asked.

'No,' I said. 'It wasn't.'

Clara smirked then. 'You're a terrible liar, Chloe,' she said. 'I can see the guilt written all over your face.'

'It wasn't her,' I insisted. 'She told me that she sent stuff to a journalist a while ago, but it was just a local guy from the *Havington Herald*. I don't even know how much of that he used.'

'Enough to trigger a thousand and one headlines elsewhere,' Clara said.

'Look, Clara,' I said, 'I'm pretty certain those aren't anything to do with Olivia. For a start, she's never even come to a party. How could she describe everything so vividly to a journalist if she hasn't been to one?'

Clara considered this. 'Maybe she isn't working alone,' she said. 'Maybe she has somebody on the inside.' She peered at me. 'It's obviously not you, because you weren't here either.'

I was a bit offended by that, by the idea that I could ever betray Clara in such a way, but I chose to let it slide. 'Who do you think it is, then?' I asked her.

296

'I don't know,' she said. 'It could be anyone.'

'So how do we single them out?'

Clara didn't answer at first, but, gradually, a smile crept across her face. It wasn't a real smile, a warm one; it was the cold, sharp-toothed grin of a shark. A warning in itself.

'Whoever it is, they want a story,' she said darkly. 'So we'll give them a story.'

Chapter 31

Clara's grand plan: to host the biggest, wildest party yet.

'It seems kind of counterproductive,' I admitted when she told me her idea over morning coffees in the kitchen. We'd recently fallen back into the old habit, something that pleased me more than I'd ever admit to her. Sometimes, we were joined by other Goldens – occasionally Alexis, sometimes Mia or one of the others – but, more often, it was just the two of us. Those quiet moments in the morning, the combined aromas of the coffee brewing and my pancakes toasting, the open kitchen window contributing a burst of dew-dropped freshness from the garden, were something I looked forward to as I fell asleep every night.

To receive Clara's singular attention was an honour made more perfect by the circumstances: the warm glow of the morning sun, the creaminess of my latte, the sweetness of the blueberries studded into each forkful of pancake.

However, today wasn't particularly relaxing. Instead, there was a thick undercurrent of tension as Clara explained what she intended to do.

'Look,' she said, 'the press is convinced that we're a horrid feminist cult, poisoning the minds of our innocent members. So we're going to open our doors, invite a select few journalists in, and we're going to show them that we're a supportive, powerful collective.'

'And you think a party's going to do that?'

'We have a reputation for throwing extraordinary parties,' Clara said. 'Our parties are our foundation. They're what attracted the Goldens to join us in the first place, the sense of exclusivity and belonging and excitement that only we could provide. What better way is there to show the world who we are?'

I didn't say anything. In a way, what Clara was proposing did make sense. But was drawing the world's attention to us really such a good idea?

'You don't have to look so worried,' Clara said, with a roll of her eyes. 'I'm not just some stupid little girl who doesn't know what she's doing.'

'I know that,' I said. 'I guess I'm just confused. I thought you wanted all the attention to quiet down.'

'I want the coverage to be on our own terms. Our rogue Golden, whoever she might be, has been feeding vicious lies to the press. This is our chance to change their perspective. I want the world to see who we really are. Who *I* really am.' She finished the last of her coffee, then took my hand. 'I just want you to know I really appreciate everything that you've done for me since we met. I wouldn't have all of these beautiful followers without you. I wouldn't have found my calling.'

Something flashed inside me, a shiver of guilt. Was it true? Was I partially responsible for all of this? It took everything in me not to pull my hand away. Clara squeezed it in a quick, affectionate little gesture, and then pushed back her chair.

'I'm going to go and ring Emily's team,' she said. 'And book them in. We'll discuss the guest list and decorations later, okay?'

'Sure,' I said. 'Of course.'

I sipped my coffee in silence, alone, watching the sunlight play over the tiled floor.

Clara presented her idea to the Goldens in the living room that evening, all of us piled on the sofas and beanbags and on the floor in our pyjamas as if we were having a sleepover.

'We're going to do something big,' she said. 'Right now, all eyes are on us.'

At this, the gathered girls grinned and preened.

'For weeks now,' Clara continued, 'critics have accused us of being something dark, a dangerous force. A *cult*. They think we're influencing vulnerable young women, urging them to be mindlessly loyal, when, actually, we're doing the exact opposite.' Her gaze moved from girl to girl, warm with love. 'We empower each other. Here, we're equals. We're women supporting women, helping each other to succeed, to thrive, to achieve our dreams.'

The girls around me were nodding fervently, smiling.

'We need to show the world that being a Golden is a celebration of sisterhood,' Clara said firmly. 'Which is why I propose this. We're going to host a *monumental* party. This party will be the most significant event we've ever held. It'll have a huge guest list, extensive catering, and the biggest bonfire Havington has ever seen. And we're going to invite the journalists who've written such vitriol to join us.'

There were a few scattered whoops, a clap or two. Clara nodded in response. She knew that she had the Goldens right in the palm of her hand. She just had to seal the deal.

'And you, my beautiful, loyal Goldens,' she said, her every word hitting its mark, 'you're going to show them what we do here, how powerful *you* are. You're going to light the bonfire, you're going to throw your flower crowns into it, and you're going to shrug off your self-criticism, your impostor syndrome, your self-rejection. You're going to shrug it all off like an old snakeskin, and then, together, we're going to fucking dance around that bonfire and celebrate *all night long*.'

The room erupted. Around me, girls leaped to their feet, hugged each other. Then they crowded around Clara and hugged her too. When I got up and joined them, Christie threw an arm round me, Lottie kissed me on both cheeks and Sophie pulled me towards her, and suddenly I was at the centre of the circle, with Clara's hand in mine.

The girls, the Goldens, looked at me the same way they looked at her, their faces seeking my love and my favour. And who was I? I was no one.

Just a few months ago, I would have basked in their attention, let it soak into my skin like a nourishing balm. But now I only felt an uncomfortable twist of the stomach, the spotlight on me too hot, too bright.

Maybe Clara's plan would work. Maybe the reporters and newsreaders and photographers would be pleasantly surprised at how empowering being a Golden was. Perhaps they'd come to appreciate the thought-out symbolism behind each and every ritual, how each one was the casting-off of insecurity, of self-hatred, of the weight of being a teenage girl in this decade. The weight of being a teenage girl in *every* decade.

It seemed more likely that they wouldn't, though. They already knew the story that they wanted to tell, however true or untrue it might be. And, when the inevitable fallout came, what would happen to these girls? Where would they go? Desperate to find the same sense of community, how vulnerable would they be to being preyed upon by a *real* cult, a more dangerous one that wasn't founded on a teenage girl's ego?

But, for now, they had tonight. They had hope. And I supposed I had to allow them that.

The day before the party, excitement and anticipation had officially hit fever pitch. The headlines had died down, but the online commentators, the many, many people on X and TikTok and Reddit who seemed to care so much about Clara's every move, were ramping up. For once, their suspicions were correct: something *was* coming.

At the same time, Deneside Manor was a flurry of activity. Clara and I had brainstormed and decided the colour scheme: a combination of white, gold and pink. The trio of colours would dictate the decorations, the tableware, the lighting and, of course, the outfits, make-up and hairstyles that would be worn. Sam, Linda and Emily were, by all accounts, thrilled to be preparing for a new 'Clara party', and had already come up with some wonderful ideas combining crystal beading and gold leaf.

Meanwhile, I took on my organisational role once again. I rang round the local suppliers to arrange for the delivery of logs and fire starters for the bonfire, and liaised with the caterers who'd provided the food for the equinox party. With surprisingly little persuasion, they agreed to provide more substantial charcuterie grazing platters for the usual cost – with the caveat that, naturally, we had to mention them on Clara's social-media accounts.

I'd left my bedroom door open as I spoke to them, and Clara wiggled her fingers lightly at me as she passed. I tilted my head to indicate the caterers on the other end of the phone.

'Of course,' I said. 'Wonderful. Thanks so much. We look forward to seeing you too.'

I hung up.

'All sorted?' she asked.

'Yep,' I said. 'They'll be here at six tomorrow, which should give the stylists enough time to set up before the earliest guests arrive. Eight o'clock, right?'

Clara considered this. 'I think that's what Mia wrote on the invitations, but you know what people are like. They might come earlier; they might come later.'

I nodded. Then I took a deep breath. 'One last time. Are you sure this is a good idea?'

'I am,' Clara said. She was calm as she answered, almost as if she'd anticipated this very question. That, or she'd been asking it of herself often enough to no longer be concerned by it. 'We have nothing to hide, Chloe. We don't hold people here against their will; they stay because we inspire them. And there's nothing wrong with celebrating that.'

'The bonfire, though,' I said. 'Burning the flower crowns. Don't you think it could . . . send the wrong message? Like we're antagonising the people who're saying all these horrible things about us?'

'So what if we are?' Clara said. 'They don't know anything about me, or about you, or about any of the girls here. No matter how much they like to act like they do.'

Her confidence was impressive. This was a girl who was being vilified by the press, by thousands of people online, receiving the most ugly of comments, and who, while she was discussing it, had taken a nail file from my bedside table and begun to file her fingernails. She inspected the neat oval of one, and then started filing the next.

'It's all going to work out the way it's supposed to, Chloe,' she said. 'Just you wait and see.'

Chapter 32

Have you ever woken up on the day of an event you've been feeling apprehensive about – an exam, say, or a funeral – and forgotten all about it?

For a moment, you lie there, still caught halfway between dreams and reality, slowly returning to the real world. Gradually, your mind catches up with all the things set in store for you that day. And then you remember, with a stab of sheer dread, what you have ahead of you.

That's how I felt about the party. The very thought of it made me queasy, my reluctance so strong that I had to force myself to crawl out of bed. I knew why I was so anxious about it. Clara's words were echoing in my mind. *It's all going to work out the way it's supposed to, Chloe,* she'd said firmly. But what if it didn't? What if it all went wrong? What if this was the last day of the Goldens?

I showered slowly, washing every inch of my body and then my hair, delaying the inevitable moment when I'd have to go out and face the rest of the Goldens with a smile. Unfortunately, though, there was only so much hot water. When the shower began to trickle with cold I had no choice but to get out, shivering.

It was far too early to start getting ready for the party so, bare-faced, I pulled on a T-shirt and a pair of joggers to go down for breakfast. Or, rather, brunch – it was well past noon.

The kitchen was fizzing with excitement, girls gathered on and around every surface. There were tall glasses of juice and smoothie on the counter, some half drunk, plates of cooling toast and tiny glass jars of spreads: amber marmalade with bits of deep-orange peel, a thick raspberry jam and a large jar of local organic lavender honey.

They all looked at me as I went in, and I was able to see the moment their bright-eyed, eager expressions faded into mild dismay. Clearly, Clara hadn't made an appearance yet this morning. It was her they were waiting for.

Once they'd recovered from their initial disappointment, though, the girls were happy enough to see me. Bella, in particular, bounced like a puppy at my elbow, offering me a coffee, tea, toast.

'Bella,' I laughed, 'I'll get my own. Seriously! Thanks, though.'

Despite my good-natured refusal, she still hovered as I put a vanilla latte pod into the coffee machine, and topped up the milk frother. As the machine rattled, she asked, 'Are you excited for tonight?'

My smile was so false that my cheeks ached with it. 'Of course I am,' I said. 'Are you?'

'*So* excited,' she said, with all the giddiness of a girl looking forward to her prom night. 'I've already picked out what I'm wearing! Christie said I could borrow her dress, the one with the pink and gold. What do you think? Do you think that's on theme?'

'If there's gold in it,' I said, adding a not insignificant amount of sugar to my coffee, 'then it's on theme. Don't worry, Bella. You'll look amazing.'

'What's Clara chosen for you?'

I used to love that everybody knew that Clara was in charge of my party outfits, but now it was starting to feel a bit humiliating. Infantilising, almost. To them, it was a status symbol. To be singled out to wear something that Clara had selected, especially for me, indicated to the other Goldens just how much Clara thought of me, how much she appreciated me. It was becoming increasingly clear that they, too, wanted to be styled by Clara. I nearly snorted at the thought. If that was the case, it'd be like living in a life-sized doll's house, all of us just little dolls for Clara to dress up, to play with and discard as she pleased.

'She hasn't decided yet,' I said to Bella. 'She'll probably put it in my room later. She's got a lot on her mind right now.' I turned to address the rest of the girls. 'Which means everyone needs to give her space, okay? I know you're all excited, but I don't want anyone pestering Clara. Okay? She'll come and speak to us all when she's ready.'

Everyone except for Alexis nodded. I stared at her until she rolled her eyes, but nodded too.

'Great,' I said. 'That's settled, then.' I picked up my vanilla latte, the surface thick with foam, and took a long sip. Sweet, sweet caffeine. 'I'll see you all later.'

I didn't wait for a response this time, just waved and headed through the door into the orangery, then out into the garden. Bella was right on my heels. I tried not to be frustrated by the way that she looked at me with wistful, admiring eyes. We were the same age, for God's sake.

'What's up, Bella?' I asked as I kept walking.

'I wanted to check something with you,' she said. 'Out of earshot.'

'Out of whose earshot?'

Her eyes flitted back towards the kitchen. *Ah*.

I sat down on one of the sunloungers we'd dragged into the garden, making space for Bella to sit beside me. 'Go on,' I said. 'What's worrying you?'

'Clara asked me to text everyone an invitation,' she said. 'And she gave me a list of names and phone numbers.'

'Okay,' I said. 'So what's the problem?'

'Olivia Pembroke.' Bella whispered Olivia's name as if it was a swear word, or a magic spell – as if saying her name out loud meant that she would appear, right here, in front of us. 'She's on the list.'

'Olivia is?' I frowned. 'Have you mentioned it to Clara?'

'Yes,' she said. 'And she said to invite her. I just . . .' She wrung her hands. 'I know you both used to be friends, and now you're not, and Clara doesn't even really like her, so—'

I interrupted her rambling. 'If Clara says it's okay, then it's okay,' I told her. 'Really.'

'Are you sure?'

'Of course I'm sure,' I said.

'Okay,' she said, pushing herself to her feet. 'Thank you. I just really, really wanted to make sure.'

'I know,' I said. 'You did the right thing. Thanks, Bella.'

She gave me a quick, grateful smile before she set off walking back towards the house, presumably to send the last invitation on her list.

I couldn't understand why Clara had invited Olivia. She wasn't one for forgiveness, so *what was this invitation for*?

As Clara had predicted, Olivia had confused me; she'd inserted doubt into my mind as swiftly, as cleanly, as a needle. Clara had been selfish, yes, and she had upset me inadvertently by trying to protect me from the news about Vanessa. She was more than a little controlling when it came to the Goldens, and her goal for tonight's party – to gain recognition on her own terms – did concern me. And, yes, there were the rumours. But I knew that she cared about me. She would never hurt somebody I loved. It just wasn't her.

She just wanted to set the record straight, to show Olivia that what she had here, her cluster of Goldens, wasn't sinister. It was perfectly lovely, in fact, and everyone was happy. That would make far more sense.

I sat with my hands clasped round my latte, the summer sun warm on my neck and the swallows and swifts soaring above the trees. I should have been happy. I had everything: wonderful friends who admired me, a beautiful home, endless opportunities that I could access just by using Clara's name if I chose to do so.

And yet, as I sat there, looking out at the garden that would be transformed in just a few hours into an otherworldly scene, I had the feeling, deep down, that something terrible was about to happen.

By six o'clock, the stylists had been and gone, the caterers were setting up and Clara still hadn't delivered her chosen dress. So, once I'd styled my hair and put on my make-up, I decided I had to take matters into my own hands. I ignored my own advice, my urging of the Goldens to let her be alone, and went to her bedroom. I rapped, twice, on the door.

'Clara,' I called. 'It's me. Do you want me to just pick a dress?'

'No!' Clara's voice, through the door, was thick. 'Come in. Quickly.'

I pushed it open and slipped inside, then closed the door behind me. 'Clara,' I said again. 'What's—'

Clara had been in her en-suite, but she chose that moment to come out. She was covered in blood. My mouth dropped open.

'What happened? Are you okay? Are you hurt?' I asked, the words falling over themselves as they rushed to pour out of my mouth.

'I'm fine,' Clara said. 'It looks worse than it is. I had a nosebleed.' She held her arms out at her sides, showing the blood-soaked sweetheart neckline of her white silk gown, the red smears on her arms. 'Don't you think it's just perfect?'

I blinked at her, uncomprehending. 'What's perfect?'

When she smiled, it was savage, her teeth glistening red. 'The blood. It's so *animalistic*, isn't it? Tonight's all about sacrifices and baptisms and burning, right? About rituals? There's nothing the matter with a little bit of blood, as long as it's your own.' Clara ran her hands down her body to her waist, sensually, her fingertips leaving blood smears on the fabric in their wake. 'What are you wearing tonight?'

'I don't know,' I said faintly. 'I thought you were going to choose for me.'

Clara didn't seem to be listening. She was studying herself in the mirror, admiring her blood-streaked dress, the palms of her hands, the skin there rust-coloured. 'Oh, yeah,' she said absently. 'I did pick something out. It's on the side of my wardrobe.'

As she'd said, the dress was there, waiting for me, the coat hanger carefully hooked over the top: a sleek ivory satin, with a corseted bodice and a skirt that I imagined would end just above my knees. It was understated and elegant, everything that I wanted to be and everything that Clara already was. At least, when she wasn't covered in blood. I swallowed, hard. Was I imagining the tinge of iron in the air?

311

It was impossible to compare the Clara I was with, in that moment, to the Clara I knew. *My* Clara was an elegant, intelligent girl who made me laugh, who'd invited me into her home and let me borrow her clothes. She was the girl whose parents didn't seem to particularly care about her, the girl whose only company for weeks at a time were her party guests, a whole host of people who adored her at night and who disappeared like mist by morning. *This* Clara, this beautiful, savage girl with blood on her lips, wasn't *my* Clara. And, still, I couldn't help but love her.

Clara was watching me. 'It's white,' she said meaningfully. 'Like mine.'

'You want me to wear a matching dress?' I asked. Even as I spoke, I cringed at the fervency in my own voice, my desperate need for her validation plain in every syllable.

'I do,' she said. Her voice in return was a warm murmur, a whispered prayer. 'You're going to look exquisite. Absolutely exquisite.'

I was self-conscious as I shrugged off the robe that I'd stolen from her, the one with her – our – initials monogrammed on the lapel. I was only wearing my underwear beneath, my strapless cream bra and no-show knickers both more practical than sexy. Nothing ruined a sleek silhouette more than a wayward bra strap, after all.

I'd expected Clara to subtly turn away as I undressed, the habit ingrained from pre-teen sleepovers and school changing rooms, but she didn't. She just watched me, slightly smiling, as if it was a perfectly normal thing to do when your friend was nearly naked in front of you.

I couldn't help but notice the way that her eyes skimmed my body, hungrily roving from my ankles to my collarbones and lingering around my hips, my breasts.

I knew that if I'd shrunk beneath her gaze, if I'd moved away or shown any displeasure at all, she would have given me space. But I didn't.

Instead, I relished her attention. Sparks lit up my skin everywhere her eyes touched, leaving goosebumps in their wake. I wanted her to touch me more than I'd ever wanted anything in my life, but I didn't know how to ask.

Luckily, I didn't have to.

In an instant, she was pressed up against me. One of her hands brushed my lower back, her touch like a thousand tiny lightning bolts, making me shiver and gasp. The other gently cupped my jaw, and we stopped, just for a moment, and looked at each other. Her pupils were enormous, and I realised with a stab of surprise and then desire that she wanted this as much as I did. She wanted *me*.

And so this time I was the one who leaned in.

Clara's lips were soft as they pressed against mine, and I could taste her blood – iron and something else, sickly sweet – on my tongue. I couldn't get enough of it, the taste of her. I kissed her over and over again, our lips moving in sync, until my own felt bruised.

Clara nudged me backwards, towards the bed. I allowed

her to direct me, our lips parting briefly as I felt the mattress against the backs of my bare thighs. I let myself fall, sinking into the soft duvet, and Clara lay beside me, propped up on one elbow.

She met my gaze, silently asking, and I nodded, giving her permission to continue. Satisfied, she leaned over me and kissed me again, deeply, as she explored my body. Her fingertips ran along my collarbones and then down, my skin tingling at her feather-light touch.

All the while, my own hands traced soft patterns on the skin above her dress, mapping out her shoulder blades, the delicate curve of her neck. She gazed down at me, her cheekbones dusted with colour and her eyes alight.

My mind was clouded with a heady combination of love and lust, and I wondered why I'd ever doubted her; she would never do anything to hurt me. She loved me. She really, truly loved me.

Her touch moved gradually lower, her fingers running along the waistband of my underwear. My eyes fluttered closed as they slipped beneath.

And then there was a knock at the door.

'What is it?' Clara called. She didn't stop as she spoke, continuing her gentle explorations.

I bit my lip.

'People are starting to arrive.' It was Bella, her voice tremulous. 'Are you nearly ready? What should we do?'

Clara looked down at me, her expression mischievous. 'I

won't be long,' she said to Bella. 'Could you and the girls just show them into the garden, for now?'

'Yeah, of course,' Bella said. She sounded relieved to have been given official instructions, and I allowed myself to breathe out, slowly, as the sound of her footsteps in the hallway faded.

All at once, the sounds of a Goldens party filtered through the door: the bustle of girls getting ready, faint music, laughter. Our bubble was broken.

'We should stop,' Clara murmured.

The words caught in my throat, and I had to try twice to dislodge them, to say them out loud. 'Do you want to?'

'No,' Clara said. 'But we can't keep everyone waiting, can we?'

She sat up, and I was gratified to see that her cheeks were flushed, her hair a little mussed.

'You're right,' I said. 'You don't have to wait for me, though. You're the hostess.'

'We both are,' Clara said. 'Of course I'll wait for you. And we'll go down together.'

As we prepared to make our grand entrance, we looked at one another's reflections in Clara's floor-length mirror.

She was a vision, of course. People often describe women as *visions*: ethereal brides in sheer veils; celebrities clad in haute couture walking red carpets; fallen goddesses shrouded in silk, their make-up dark and sultry and their hair fixed in place with animal bones. But Clara truly was a vision, streaked with red.

315

An animalistic possessiveness rose up in me, my love and my desire for her hot in my throat.

Her hair was glossy, her perfume floral with a hint of something dark. The lights above us gleamed and the satin on my body shimmered. When she held out her hand, I could hardly believe my luck.

Her slim fingers held mine tightly, the metal of her rings smooth against my palm, still sticky with her blood. I imagined a connection between us, an electricity, a sharp undercurrent of something truly unique. I hoped that she could feel it too, this thing that linked us. It felt like fate. Unavoidable.

I could still feel the ghost of Clara's touch along my waist, my hipbones, as we finally left her bedroom and descended the curving stairs together.

I wanted to imagine that the Goldens who'd gathered in the hallway below, gazing fervently upwards, were all looking at me. I knew that it was Clara. It was always Clara.

As we reached the bottom of the stairs, her sea of admirers closed in around her, all beaming smiles and extended hands, all of them wanting to touch her, to be chosen by her. I watched her absorbing all their attention, her adoration, her elated smile stretching from ear to ear.

And, gently, lovingly, I let her go.

Chapter 33

It didn't take long before the house and garden were buzzing. I'd never seen so many people at Deneside Manor. It seemed as though word of Clara's ultra-exclusive party had spread far beyond its intended borders, and dozens more people than I'd expected were descending eagerly on the house. To my surprise, some of the people who'd avoided Clara for months, the ones who'd been scared off by the cult accusations, were back. Clearly, her allure had been too much for even them to resist – especially when the invitations came with promises of free bottomless alcohol and a hint of scandal.

I recognised some of the guests from my very first Golden party, before Clara had even coined the name. Alessandra, the model who Clara had told me had been on the cover of *Vogue Italia*, hugged me, and so did Dove, the activist. Once she'd let go, she held me at arm's length.

'Look at you,' she said, grinning. 'Running the show!'

I laughed. 'I'm not running anything; I'm hanging on for my life.'

'Maybe so,' Dove allowed. 'Clara's basically a runaway train at the best of times, isn't she? But you've had a hell of a year, haven't you? A positively meteoric rise in the ranks.'

I shrugged, faux nonchalant. 'I guess that's what happens when you're super clingy.'

It was Dove's turn to laugh. 'Well, if you've got any tips,' she said, 'I'd love to be invited into this inner-circle thing you've got going on.'

'You were part of the *original* circle,' I said. 'You belong here even more than I do. You don't need an invitation.'

'You're just lovely, you know that?' Dove said. 'I can see what Clara sees in you. You're loyal to a fault.'

I smiled. 'I try,' I said.

She hugged me again. 'I'm going to go and get a drink,' she said. She glanced around at the milling guests, more of whom were arriving every minute. 'Before the champagne runs out and somebody starts a riot.'

'Sensible,' I said. 'I'm sure I'll see you later, anyway.'

'Oh, absolutely,' Dove said. I watched her walk away, weaving through the throngs of people.

The crowd was making me uneasy; we'd only ordered enough food and drink for the people who were supposed to be coming, the people who'd been invited, not the masses that had somehow found their way here. How had they even got in? I imagined them climbing over walls, over fences.

The pit of dread in my stomach had returned, and I had to force air into my lungs so as not to hyperventilate. I practised breathing slowly in and out, rhythmically. All these people, the various influencers and rich kids, the hangers-on, would see the bonfire, the enormous burning. What would they think? Would they understand? Would they take part in Clara's rituals? Or were they just here for the spectacle of it all?

There was another fear to contend with too: there were men here. Some of them were young, stylish, on the arms of the various darlings who Clara had no doubt invited. But others didn't seem to fit the scene: they were older, wearing puffer jackets and sturdy boots. Oh, God, were they press? Photographers? There were more of them than I'd imagined. Far more.

I envisioned them watching through critical eyes, snapping pictures, sending them to their colleagues or contacts in newsrooms at tabloids and gossip magazines across the country. That was what Clara wanted, wasn't it? She wanted to reclaim the press coverage, for the world to see how empowering and positive being a Golden was. But, looking around at the horde of guests, I couldn't help thinking that she was more out of control than ever before.

I pushed the thought from my mind. It was fine. It was *all* going to be fine.

It was at this moment, as I convinced myself that everything was going to work out, that I saw her. Olivia.

She looked uncertain, uncomfortable, as she moved through the crowd, her movements tense and unsure, as if she was somewhere different to everybody else, somewhere with much stronger gravity. She'd seen me already and I made a beeline for her.

'What are you doing here?' I asked.

Olivia's face, which had been open and earnest, slammed shut. 'What?'

'Don't get me wrong, it's lovely to see you and everything,' I said, backtracking, 'but you shouldn't be here.'

'If I shouldn't be here,' Olivia said slowly, 'why did you invite me?'

'*I* didn't.'

Olivia glanced over to her right, and I followed her gaze. Clara was at the centre of a group of girls, all of them hanging on her every word. As we watched, she said something and they all laughed.

'Right,' Olivia said. Her voice wobbled. 'Of course. So you didn't actually want me to come? *She* did?'

'I didn't think you'd want to,' I said. 'You know, since you hate Clara so much?'

'You're right,' Olivia said. 'I didn't. I didn't want to come at all.'

I rolled my eyes. 'Why are you here, then?'

Olivia bit her lip, hard enough to draw blood. 'I thought you might want to apologise to me.'

'You think *I* owe *you* an apology?' I spluttered. 'Are you joking?'

Olivia glared at me, and folded her arms across her chest. 'No. I'm not,' she said. 'I've tried to be a good friend to you,

Chloe. I've done my best to pull you away from Clara, from her toxic, *horrible* influence. And you've just thrown my kindness back in my face. Over and over again.'

'You have no right,' I said, 'to say anything about Clara. You don't know her like I do.'

I thought about Clara's soft lips moving against mine, her gentle touch on my waist, how it felt when her fingers moved lower.

'You're right,' Olivia said, her voice growing louder. 'I don't. And I have no desire to, either. You know what? I'm done trying to save you from her.'

'I didn't ask you to save me from her,' I snarled. 'I *don't need* saving.'

'You do,' she said. 'You do, Chloe, and the worst thing is you can't even see it.'

Her words lingered in the air between us like a fog.

'I think you should leave,' I said quietly.

Olivia shook her head, seemingly in disbelief. 'Fine,' she said. 'Whatever. But when the time comes, and you finally comprehend the deep, *deep* hole you're in, you can climb out of it all by yourself.'

I gritted my teeth, but I didn't reply. What more was there to say?

'I get it,' she said. 'Bye, then, Chloe. Take care of yourself.'

I couldn't tear my eyes away from her as she walked back towards the house, hitching her dress up as she crossed the lawn. It was only a few seconds before I lost her among the crowd, but it felt like forever. Like I'd watched our friendship end in slow motion.

I wanted to run after her, to grab her by the hand, to ask her to reconsider. Why couldn't we all just be friends? Olivia would love Clara, once she got to know her, wouldn't she?

Realistically, I knew neither of them would be open to it. Clara would never associate with somebody whom she'd suspected was a spy, someone with whom she'd be forced to compete for my loyalty. And Olivia had made her stance very clear: she wanted nothing to do with Clara. Or me.

I'd chosen my side.

Chapter 34

The night rolled on and I tried to forget about Olivia. *I'm done trying to save you from her*, she'd said. Her words were like barbed wire, curling tighter round my brain every time I thought them, their sharp edges digging in.

At the party, though, there was plenty to distract me. I helped myself to a glass of strawberry gin and lemonade, and a handful of olives, and watched while Clara glided around. She was a fantastic hostess, seemingly everywhere at once, greeting and flattering and plying her guests with drinks. I could see the looks on everyone's faces, the same dizzying worship that I felt when I saw her, the headiness of her attention on you and you alone. She could make you feel like the most important person in the universe with one glance, one well-placed touch.

The bonfire was starting. I'd noticed it earlier, of course; the pyramid of logs and sticks in the middle of the lawn, with straw threaded throughout to help the flames to spread. The garden was night-time quiet, the insects gone and the twilight calls of the birds in the woods the backdrop to every conversation.

I stayed at a distance, at the edge of the wood, as the assorted guests and the Goldens gathered around the bonfire. Clara stood beside it, poised, looking every inch the goddess. Her dress was still streaked with her blood, and she wore an elaborate headpiece that I hadn't seen before. It was formed from twists of gold, deep-green foliage and a pair of antlers. Real, spiked deer antlers. She looked like a malevolent goddess, a forest queen: someone unearthly, a cut above the rest of us. Someone to be worshipped.

I studied her as if I was observing a stranger as she knelt down to light the kindling. As she straightened back up to her full height, the flames licked across the wood, climbing higher and higher. She turned towards the crowd, the bonfire's rich orange glow lighting up one half of her face, the other left in shadow. I saw her smile, darkly. And I was glad that she couldn't see me, from the cover of the trees, watching.

I jumped, startled, as I felt a sudden presence beside me. Ayanna.

'It's so messed up,' she said. 'All of this. I feel like I don't know who she is any more.'

She wasn't looking at me, didn't seem to require a response; her attention was on Clara, who was now speaking to her besotted audience. Her voice was faint, so I couldn't hear the words, but I knew the general gist. I'd heard her speeches before.

'I looked into the rumours,' Ayanna continued. 'The one that you told me about, and the one that I'd heard myself.

Everything I found suggests they're both true.' She turned to me, her expression unreadable. 'Did you know that Clara's being investigated for her suspected involvement in Vanessa Hancock's death?'

Vanessa Hancock's death. The words hit me like a battering ram. My pulse pounded in my head, my vision blurring.

'That's right,' Ayanna said coolly as she absorbed my stunned reaction. 'At first, when I contacted the press, I was just concerned about her behaviour. But after Vanessa's body was found and new evidence came to light, I felt it was my duty to report it. Clara does have a track record, after all.'

Ayanna's words from our conversation months ago ran through my head. *That's a potential track record of assault.* Even if she *was* capable of that, could Clara really be guilty of something worse? I didn't want to believe it. I couldn't. Not without proof.

'What new evidence?' I asked.

'A video,' Ayanna said. 'A friend sent it to me. Would you like to see it?'

She slipped her phone from her beaded clutch bag, swiped until she found what she was looking for and held it out to me. I took it with shaking hands. The screen was a dark blur of shapes, revealing nothing. There was no going back now. I took a deep breath and pressed play.

There were just shadows, at first. Then the camera tilted, and colours and lights and people swam into view. The camera, presumably a phone, panned round, revealing that the person recording was at the edge of a mass of people dancing: a chaotic kaleidoscope of glittery dresses and champagne flutes and fairy lights. I realised, with a spike of horror, that I recognised those decorations. I recognised those dresses. This was New Year's Eve. This video had been recorded on the night that Vanessa went missing.

'Keep watching,' Ayanna murmured.

I couldn't tear my eyes away. The people in the video were all facing one way – towards the DJ, I knew, from the angle. I was amongst that crowd, somewhere. Right at the front. Perhaps, at that very moment, wondering where Vanessa had got to.

The camera spun again, flashing briefly over the woods, and then the video ended. This time, Ayanna didn't have to say anything. I played it back. Just the last five seconds.

The very end of the video showed two girls, together. Both blonde. One in a white, tiered tulle dress with long hair, leading. One in a silver sequinned dress with short hair, following. Walking into the woods. Towards the river.

'Isn't it strange,' Ayanna said, 'that they found Vanessa's body downstream of here?'

I could see it as clearly as if it were happening right in front of me. Vanessa fervently thanking Clara for her invitation to the party. A gracious Clara suggesting that they go somewhere private to talk. Vanessa, tipsy on champagne and delighted by Clara's attention, happily agreeing. Clara taking her into the woods, to the water's edge. It would only have taken one stumble. Or one push.

326

'Why would Clara do something like that?' I demanded. 'It doesn't make any sense.'

Slowly, though, it began to dawn on me that it *did* make sense. It made complete, horrifying sense.

Earlier on New Year's Eve, Vanessa and I had agreed to a truce. When Clara had picked me up, I'd been thrilled – so thrilled, in fact, that I'd told her all about it during our drive back to Deneside Manor. Up until that point, all she'd known about my flatmates was what I'd told her: how snotty they'd been when we'd first met, how they'd deliberately excluded me and how they'd then begged me to score them an invitation to one of Clara's parties. Maybe, I thought uncomfortably, I'd even exaggerated Vanessa's poor behaviour. I'd painted her as the villain, from the way she'd made assumptions about me from my accent, to the way she'd seemingly encouraged the other girls to completely blank me.

It was their treatment of me that had pushed me to attach myself to Clara so quickly. I could see that now. First, I'd clung to Olivia, and then, faced with the possibility of another new friend – one who could make my snooty flatmates jealous – I'd latched on to Clara like a limpet. If I'd become friends with Vanessa on New Year's Eve, if we'd grown close, would I have been so desperate for Clara to care about me, to notice me? Maybe not.

And, to Clara, our truce may have seemed like a threat: the risk of my attention, my utter devotion to her, being pulled elsewhere. Could that have been enough for Clara to consider a threat? Maybe. After all, Clara herself had told me that day that, if she'd been me, she would've ruined Vanessa's life for being so horrible. Was it really so much of a stretch to imagine her *ending* Vanessa's life instead, and thereby ensuring that she could never steal me away from Clara's side?

'If the police have this,' I asked, indicating the phone clutched in Ayanna's beautifully manicured hand, 'then why hasn't she been arrested? Or questioned?'

To my surprise, Ayanna smiled. 'Oh, she will be,' she said. 'Soon. They're still gathering evidence – and on a *lot* more than that one incident.'

My stomach lurched.

Ayanna looked at me, searchingly. 'If I were you,' she said, 'I'd pack everything and leave. Tonight. And tell the other girls to do the same.'

The other girls. All at once, the gravity of the situation dawned on me. Every single girl here was in danger. The Goldens, the guests – we'd all come to Deneside Manor, drawn in by Clara's honeyed promises, to be happy and free and young, to drink and dance and run wild, safely hidden away from the eyes of the patriarchy. But everything that we'd believed in – the empowerment, the loyalty, even the girl we worshipped – had been built on lies and manipulation and death.

And then a gut-wrenching wave of fear washed through me.

'Olivia,' I said. 'I told her it was Olivia.'

'You told her *what* was Olivia?' Ayanna asked.

I fumbled for the words. 'I met my friend Olivia for coffee, even though Clara didn't want me to. Liv told me that she'd sent an email to a local newspaper, about Clara and the Goldens. We both thought the coverage had stemmed from that. And I told Clara.'

My knees turned to water as I was struck by the gravity of what I'd done, and I sank to the ground. Clara had tried to kill a thirteen-year-old girl. She'd maimed a model. And, if Ayanna was right, she was responsible for Vanessa's death.

I thought hard. If it was true – if Clara really *had* been caught up in a fit of jealousy that had driven her to murder – then Olivia, who was my only other friend and outspoken in her dislike of Clara, had already been at risk. And, by telling Clara that Olivia was the whistleblower, there was every chance that I'd put her in grave danger. I'd led her to Clara like a lamb to slaughter.

'I need to find Olivia,' I said.

Adrenalin flooded my veins as I scrambled to my feet. Ayanna reached out a hand to help me, and I took it.

'Do you know where she is?' she asked. 'Oh, God . . . is she *here*?'

'Yes,' I said. 'We had a fight. I told her to leave.'

'And did she listen to you?' Ayanna's dark eyes implored me to think back, to remember the details. 'Did you actually *see* her leave?'

'I saw her walking back towards the house,' I said. 'And then . . . I lost her in the crowd.'

Ayanna's expression hardened. 'We've got to find her,' she said. 'Before Clara does.'

Chapter 35

We decided that Ayanna would start the search inside the house, moving from top to bottom and then out into the gardens, while I'd start amongst the crowd and call Olivia's number as often as I could until she picked up. First of all, though, I had to show Ayanna who she was actually looking for. She gave me her phone and I typed in Olivia's Instagram handle, my fingers trembling over a picture of her smiling face when the page finally loaded. I handed the phone back, and Ayanna and I parted ways with tight-lipped smiles so as not to arouse suspicion. Then I ran up to my room to retrieve my own phone.

It was still plugged in where I'd left it charging on my bedside table. I picked it up with trembling fingers, and frantically swiped through my contacts list until I found Olivia's name. As it rang once, twice, three times, I focused on inhaling deeply and exhaling slowly, trying to trick my adrenalin-filled body into calming down.

'Hi!'

Olivia's voice was loud in my ear, cheerful, without a care in the world. Relief washed over me.

'Olivia,' I said. 'Where—'

She continued speaking, as if she hadn't heard me. Which, I quickly realised, she hadn't.

Hi! It's Olivia. I can't come to the phone right now, so leave me a message.

It was her voicemail. I stared at the screen, aghast. I hung up, and pressed call again. Once. Twice. Three times. And then her voicemail again.

This wasn't going to work. Either Olivia had blocked my number or she was deliberately ignoring the call after seeing my name flash up on my screen. Either would be a fair assumption, given how we'd left things. In my mind, I saw her eyes shining with tears, her hopeless expression as I'd told her to leave.

She had to be safe. She *had* to be okay.

I typed a hurried text to her.

Liv, can you please answer the phone? It's really important. I'm worried about you.

I sent it, then tore back down the stairs and out into the garden. Now that Clara had finished her welcome speech, the party was in full swing.

It was frightening.

Someone, I had no idea who, had brought masks – masquerade masks, Venetian masks, masks that covered only part of your face, like in *The Phantom of the Opera*. Shiny faces gleaming gold leered at me from every direction, and the sight of them made my stomach churn.

Olivia, Olivia, Olivia, I thought. *Where* are *you?*

I fought through the throngs of people, scrutinising every unmasked, shadowed face, trying to work out if Olivia was still here, somewhere, amongst the crowd. My heart pounded in time with the music, the party growing ever louder, ever wilder.

Almost without realising, I came to the woods. They stretched out in front of me, dark and foreboding like something out of a fairytale, the trees, the thorny briars and twisting vines that encased Sleeping Beauty's castle, I, a helpless rescuer with no weapon strong enough to defeat them.

Even so, I kept going, spurred on by the thought that Olivia could have somehow ventured into the woodland and become lost, maybe even hurt. She didn't know the woods like I did. My dress caught in the undergrowth, the fine material snagging on brambles, and I heard a ripping sound as I tugged it free. Twigs brushed my hair as I ducked beneath low-hanging branches, haltingly making my way towards the river. If I hadn't seen Olivia by the time I reached the water, she was most likely not in the woods at all.

And then I thought about the video that Ayanna had shown me, Clara leading Vanessa into the woods. Had they come this way, followed this same path that night? It would've been a lot less overgrown then, in the dead of winter. I swallowed the bile that rose in my throat and continued on.

Up ahead, I could see something gleaming, opal-like,

between the trees. I stumbled on, tripping over roots, my bare arms scratched bloody by tiny barbs, until it came into view. It was the folly – the Roman temple – its domed roof rising up and glowing in the evening light. I almost laughed with relief.

Until I heard a stick snap behind me.

'What are you doing?'

Clara. I spun round.

There she was, pale against the trees, looking perfectly calm.

'It's not safe here when it's getting dark,' she continued. 'You could get hurt.'

There was no sign of malice in her tone, no fear. Only gentle, almost parental, concern. I disregarded it.

'Where's Olivia?' I asked. I was faintly pleased that I didn't hesitate, that I sounded as fierce as I'd intended, my voice cold.

'I don't know,' Clara said. 'You asked her to leave, didn't you?'

I frowned at her, caught off guard. 'How did you know?'

She sighed in a patronising way, as if I was a particularly dim child. 'That's why I invited her, silly,' she said. 'I wanted to see what you'd do, if you'd allow her to join our circle or if you'd punish her for her . . . indiscretions. I should've known you'd choose the easy option and just tell her to leave.'

'She doesn't deserve to be punished,' I said. 'It wasn't her.'

'Not all of it,' Clara allowed. 'Christie and Ayanna bear some responsibility too.' I flinched at the mention of their names, and Clara smiled. 'Yes. Lovely *Christie* is our spy from inside the house. Apparently, she thought it was "all going too far" and she was "scared". Poor girl. And as for Ayanna . . . One of the girls overheard you both talking. I should've known she'd be involved somehow. She's the reason we're swarmed with people tonight.' She bared her teeth. 'All of these tabloid photographers and journalists roaming around the grounds, desperate for an exclusive. They were invited by *her*.'

'Clara,' I begged. 'You have to stop this. This vindictive, scary, cult-leader thing . . . It isn't you.'

We stared at each other. Her gaze was steely, her eyes glittering like those of a snake about to strike. 'Isn't it?' she asked. She was confident, verging on cocky, a blood-covered queen in her antler headdress. She had both nothing and everything to lose.

I clenched my fists, my chest heaving. We were standing less than a metre apart; I could close the gap between us in a single pace. I wanted to kiss her. I wanted to kill her. Her response to what I said next would confirm which of the two I wanted the most.

'Did you kill Vanessa?'

Clara's smile was feral. 'No,' she said. For a half-second relief swept through me. And then she added, 'But when she fell into the river, I didn't hang around to help her. It's lucky, really, that she was already planning to drop out. Nobody suspected a *thing*.'

And there it was. My worst fear had been realised. Clara, the girl I loved, who I idolised, who I'd kissed mere hours earlier, was a monster.

'Where's Olivia?' I asked again, this time with gritted teeth.

'I don't know,' Clara replied, again. 'But I'm getting tired of this game, Chloe. Let me ask you a question.' She smiled, darkly. 'What would you sacrifice to stay a Golden?'

I stared at her, blankly, uncomprehending. 'What?'

'I want you to choose,' Clara said. 'Between me and Olivia.'

My lips moved, but no sound came out. I knew what she wanted; she wanted me to pick her. She wanted me to prove myself to her, to pledge my loyalty once and for all.

But, for the first time, that wasn't what I wanted. *She* wasn't what I wanted. I wanted Olivia.

I wanted Olivia in her dark hoodie and Doc Martens, her hair pulled back from her face in the same way that it had been the first day we'd met, the way she'd smiled at me so hopefully, how relieved she'd seemed when I'd sat down beside her. I wanted our library study sessions, our takeaway coffees from the cart, our shared lecture notes and hunts for books from the reading list. I wanted to thank her for coming with me to the hotel, for supporting me when Clara had betrayed me and for pushing me to leave Deneside Manor – even when I'd thrown all that kindness, that bravery, back in her face.

But here, alone with Clara in the woods, I knew that I couldn't say it. Not out loud – not to her.

'Clara,' I said. 'Of course I choose you. I'll always choose you.'

Her eyes were wide, hopeful. 'Always?' she asked, child-like.

'Always,' I said, the lie falling from my lips like poison. 'I don't need anyone else.'

At that, she seemed to relax somewhat, the tension in her spine, her shoulders, dissipating.

It occurred to me then that if Clara was here with me, it meant that she wasn't with Olivia. It meant that Olivia was safe. And if I could keep her here, if I could play for time, I could give Ayanna a chance to find Olivia, to warn her.

'I don't need anyone else,' I repeated. 'But it doesn't matter. None of it matters. Not any more.'

Clara folded her arms. The young girl had vanished; the bloodied goddess, capable of murder, had returned. 'And why not?'

'Because Vanessa's death is your fault. You took her into the woods, drunk. You watched her drown. You left her to *die*. And with all of these journalists swarming around, somebody's going to find out sooner or later. They're going to find out about everything else that you've done too. All of this, everything you've built?' I gestured wildly in the direction of the party, the bonfire. 'This is how it ends.'

It was a shock when Clara laughed. 'This isn't how it ends, Chloe,' she said. She took a step closer, the distance between us now a hair's breadth. Her voice was a whisper. *'This is how it starts.'*

We looked at each other, the silence of the woods broken only by the distant laughs and whoops of the party guests. There was a metallic bang as something exploded, presumably after being thrown into the bonfire.

Clara reached out and took my hand. Her fingers were cold, scabbed with dried blood. The air was warm, spiked with honeysuckle and woodsmoke.

'Stay,' she said. 'Stay with me.'

Everything in me screamed to shove her, turn my back on her and run. But I had to stay close to her, at least for now. For Olivia's sake.

'I'm only staying for the girls,' I said.

'For the girls,' Clara repeated, and I could sense the underlying smugness in her tone. She was letting me think I'd won. 'Of course.'

Together, we walked back to the party.

As we emerged from the trees, it was clear that the guests had gone completely wild. The Goldens in particular were something else; they spun around the bonfire, masks slipping from their sweat-slick faces, their arms tightly linked. A swathe of material soared into the flames and burst into sparks. A scarf? A dress?

I eyed the table. It was empty. The wooden slabs that had been packed with olives, slices of cheese and cured spiced meats earlier in the evening had all long since been picked bare by dozens more passing fingers than we'd catered for. Beside them, the bottles of Moët stood empty. The vodka, too, was gone. And there was no sign of the gin at all.

I looked around, taking in the scene. By the flowerbeds, a girl in a wonderful red dress was throwing up, another girl holding back her long, dark hair. There were couples everywhere, kissing and touching, pressed together, fingers tugging on hair and exploring other, more personal places.

A girl that I didn't recognise tottered towards us, and I braced myself for confrontation. Luckily, she hardly seemed to notice that Clara and I were there; instead, she slid one of the empty serving boards closer towards her, and set out neat lines of a white, powdery substance. She leaned in and snorted one using a paper straw and then picked up the board and walked away with it.

There was a volley of flashes outside of my peripheral vision. The photographers were feasting on the debauchery. I could only imagine the headlines that would run tomorrow.

'Clara,' I said urgently, 'everyone's drunk. Or high. This isn't safe.'

'Oh, but isn't it beautiful?' Clara said breezily. 'Look at how happy they are, Chloe. They're all free, all powerful.' She raised her voice so that everybody could hear. 'My wonderful Goldens! Tonight is about us: *us*, and nobody else.' Clara looked every inch a goddess, with her high cheekbones and her righteous rage, flickering in the firelight. 'Let's set this world on fire, and show them who we are!'

The girls clapped and cheered, sparks floating up into the dark velvet sky behind them. Clara melted into the crowd, surrounded by hands reaching out to caress her skin, her hair, her dress, as if some of her magic might rub off on them. They worshipped her, they loved her. But she was wrong. They weren't free and powerful. They were tied to her, their lives hinging on her every want and whim, trapped believing in a goddess who was anything but holy.

I would stay at Deneside Manor long enough to find Olivia, I told myself, and that was all. After that, I'd be gone.

For, now, though, I had to play along. I had to be a Golden, one last time.

I lingered at the fringes of the party, feeling like an anthropologist, or maybe a historian – somebody with the strange privilege of observing a society at the last moments before its collapse. The garden was a tangle of madness packed with silhouettes, their faces hidden behind masks, all of them drinking and dancing with an air of dangerous, thrilling decadence.

And among it all, of course, there were the Goldens. They were frenzied and feverish, their unceasing energy fuelled by their love for Clara, their love for each other and, no doubt, plenty of illicit substances. The sky had begun to glow with the faint stirrings of dawn, the guests departing with sideways glances and mutterings about Clara and her cult, and the photographers and reporters moved in ever closer – and still the Goldens partied on.

It was what I imagined a bacchanal must have been like: all these girls, so beautifully out of control, so uncaring about what anybody thought of them. They spun around the bonfire, holding hands, their hair and limbs kissed orange in the light of the flames, and I hoped that they were having fun. This would be the last time.

I was distracted from my musings by Mia. 'Chloe!' she sang, drawing out the final syllable as she approached. *Chlo-eeee*. She was coated in glitter, a daub of crimson blood bright on her cheekbone – presumably from her worship of Clara. 'What are you doing here all by yourself?'

'I'm just taking a breather,' I said. I'd hoped I'd sound believable, but it didn't matter; she wasn't really looking for an answer. She wasn't even looking at me. Her gaze was trained somewhere over my shoulder, her eyes unfocused and slightly wild. I turned my head to see what she was looking at, but my view was blocked by a smiling Bella.

'Don't you want to join us?' she asked, her eyes shining. 'Come on! Come and throw some things into the fire. It'll make you feel better!'

Oh, Bella. The youngest of all of us, freshly eighteen, who'd followed Clara's Instagram account for years, who'd charted her route to online stardom as if it was a path that she, too, could follow. Bella, who looked at Clara as if she was the sun or the moon, as if she was simply too much to behold. Bella, who, alongside Mia and Alexis, would go to prison for almost a decade for what she did that night.

I didn't want to join them. I wanted to separate myself, to distance myself as it all fell apart. But I had to appear to be Clara's second-in-command, her most loyal follower. I had to look as if I wasn't worrying about Olivia, who still hadn't called me back, or Ayanna, who wasn't answering my texts.

'Sure!' I said. 'Let's go.'

I held my hand out to a delighted Bella, who led me towards the bonfire. Smoke hung heavy in the air, thick and cloying. Up close, the heat was unbelievable: I could feel it hitting me in waves. Sweat broke out on my skin, partly because of the temperature and partly from anxiety, as we joined the other Goldens.

I could see now that the girls weren't as blissed out, as goddess-like as they'd looked from a distance. Their glittery make-up had smeared across their maskless faces, and their hair was knotted with twigs and stray blooms from the flower crowns they'd long since cast aside. Their feet were bare, dirty, and their arms and dresses were ash-streaked, dark from burning things. Where was Clara? I craned my neck, unable to see her. She'd been here only moments ago. Hadn't she?

Sparks flew as the girl closest to me tossed a sheaf of papers into the flames. The paper curled and blackened at the edges, and Bella's grip on my hand tightened as a cheer went up.

'What are you burning?' I asked, raising my voice to be heard over the girls around us.

'My university dissertation,' she replied with a dazed grin. 'I don't need it. Not any more.'

Somewhere in the distance, a camera flashed.

My resolve weakened. It was only a matter of time before the police arrived, before Clara was arrested and the darkness inside her was exposed to the world. Within days, anyone who cared would be able to read all about the sordid happenings at Deneside Manor. And they'd see the pictures of the girls, *these* girls, with their dresses and their masks and their flower crowns, all of them tainted with the stink of blood and smoke. They'd forever be remembered as Goldens, those girls who worshipped Clara Holland. And so would I.

'I think we should stop,' I said, the words taut with urgency. 'I think we need to stop this.'

'What?' Bella asked. 'What did you say?'

I didn't get a chance to repeat it. Arms wrapped softly round my waist, and I looked over my shoulder to see Clara. She kissed me on the temple and then let go, stepping back to address her followers.

'Chloe's right,' she said. 'It's time to let the fire die down. We'll go inside, get some rest and then return in the morning to reflect on what we've done tonight, and what we've learned.'

It was surprising how quickly everything calmed at her command. Her followers murmured their agreement, the fierce, unrestrained Goldens once again normal girls with smudged eye make-up. They spread out to gather their things, collecting half-drunk drinks, discarded heels, silver necklaces, anything that had made dancing difficult. As they headed for the orangery as one, their arms linked, Clara and I remained, gazing at each other.

I couldn't comprehend her gentle treatment, her sudden, affectionate touch. A month ago, I would have relished it. Now, it made my blood run cold.

'You chose me,' she said.

'I did,' I said.

'I want you to remember that.'

Clara smiled at me, then: a real, genuine smile. She raised her hand in the direction of a lone photographer. A dismissal.

'Come on,' she said to me. 'Let's go.'

Before I could say anything, she set off towards the house. She followed the same path as the Goldens without looking back, leaving me to trail behind.

Chapter 36

Last inside, I closed the glass doors of the orangery behind me. Whichever guests were still lingering outside could party to their heart's content, until the bonfire crumbled into ashes. We were done.

Clara and the other girls had retreated to their rooms. No doubt the Goldens would be wiping off make-up and rinsing the smoke from their hair, then settling down to sleep in preparation for the inevitable hangover they'd wake up to in a few hours' time.

I, meanwhile, sat cross-legged on my bed, my dirty feet leaving marks on the bedspread. I couldn't go back out to search for Olivia now. Wherever Clara was in the house, I had no doubt she would be watching me. She'd be *waiting* for me to disprove my loyalty, to break my promise, and then what would happen? I knew it would be nothing good.

In desperation, I called Ayanna.

When she picked up, she sounded breathless. 'Did you find her?'

'No,' I said. 'Clara found me. I had to stay with her. And

now the party's over – we've all come back up to the house. I don't think I can leave.'

'Damn,' Ayanna said. 'How far did you get?'

'The gardens and the woodland,' I said. 'I don't think she was there.'

'I didn't see her in the house, either,' Ayanna said. 'I checked every room. Chloe, I really think if she was here, we would've found her by now.'

'She still isn't answering her phone, though.'

'She might've just run out of battery,' Ayanna said reasonably. 'Look, since everyone's leaving, I'll stay in the garden till the crowd thins out. In the meantime, keep texting and calling her.'

'I will,' I said. 'And, Ayanna? Clara knows you invited the journalists. And she knows you've been warning me too. Don't trust anyone.'

'I'll be careful,' Ayanna said. 'Just stay where you are, okay? Don't make Clara suspicious. I'll text you if I see Olivia.'

'Okay,' I said. 'You're a star, Ayanna. Thank you.'

She made a *mwah* sound, and hung up.

Now that the call had ended, I switched back to my texts with Olivia. The messages lit up the screen, all of them from me and all still unanswered.

03:29: I know you're mad at me, but please pick up. It's an emergency. x

03:50: Please text me back. x

04:03: I'm so sorry if you're at home and in bed, but I NEED to know you're okay. x

04:17: I know this probably looks like a total overreaction, but please text or ring me back. It's important. x

04:32: Please, please, please text me, Liv.

As I texted and waited, and texted and waited, I heard doors slamming along the hallway, whispered conversations, the sound of running water. And, gradually, it all faded into silence as Deneside Manor slept.

I received a text from Ayanna, at four forty-five.

Hi, love. Heading home. I was literally the last person to get a taxi, and I didn't see Olivia anywhere. Maybe try her at home in the morning? x

I tried to convince myself that Ayanna was right. Of course Olivia had gone home; I'd told her to, after all. She was probably in her flat right now, curled up in bed, fast asleep. In a few hours, she'd wake up to a dozen missed calls and twice as many texts, and be utterly confused. I stared at my phone, willing it to light up with Olivia's name on the screen, her message accentuated with a ton of question marks. *What is going on??* she'd have written. And everything would be okay.

I lay back on my pillows and stared up at the ceiling, imagining the moment. I'd done what I'd said I'd do: I'd played my role. I'd been a loyal Golden for the last time. And now that everybody was asleep it was time for me to leave. It was time for me to choose Olivia.

I packed my bags as quietly as I could, freezing whenever I heard a sound from elsewhere within the house. I didn't want Clara to come in and find me like this, getting ready to run after I'd promised to stay. The earliest bus was at six o'clock sharp, and I knew I had to time my arrival at the bus stop carefully: I dreaded the thought of waiting there in full view of the house if I was too early or too late.

'Chloe?'

It was Clara's voice, on the other side of the bedroom door. I glanced around wildly, threw my duvet over my half-packed suitcase, then went and opened the door a crack. I rubbed my eyes to feign sleepiness.

'Hey,' I said. 'What's going on?'

Clara was still wearing her bloodied dress, and in the light pouring in from the hallway she looked like a vampire bride.

'I want you to see something,' she said.

I opened the door fully. 'Can't it wait?' I asked. 'I'm exhausted, Clara.'

'No,' she said. 'It can't.'

She had a strange, earnest expression on her face. I told myself to act normal, to not arouse her suspicion. It wouldn't be too difficult to catch a later bus.

'Okay,' I said wearily. 'Fine. Show me.'

I followed her out into the hallway.

Together, we descended the stairs, a somewhat tense re-creation of the moment we'd entered the party hand in hand less than twelve hours earlier. She led me along the hallway, and into the kitchen. I realised, then, that we were going outside.

The bonfire was still smouldering on the lawn, a stark pile of blackened logs and ash reminiscent of a funeral pyre, when I followed Clara out of the orangery.

I was still wearing the stained white satin dress, and I was barefoot. The morning dew chilled my toes, and wet grass brushed against my calves as we walked across the lawn towards the woodland at the end of the garden. Neither of us spoke.

The ground gradually sloped downhill, the trees growing denser the closer we got to the river. To the temple. It was there that Clara led me, strands of her blonde hair snagging on branches as we passed, sticks snapping underfoot.

It started to rain, warm droplets running down my face, my arms, my back.

When we reached the overhang at the water's edge, in the shadow of the crumbling temple, Clara stopped. Silently, she looked down into the rushing torrent, the shallows choked with reeds and vegetation. She tilted her head, indicating something that I should see. I followed her gaze.

There was a body in the water.

It was Olivia.

She was floating, on her back, her eyes closed. I collapsed to my knees. I wanted to wail, to scream, to cry out her name, but the sounds stuck in my throat.

I scrambled into the water, my bare feet sliding in the mud, and gripped Olivia's shoulders, helplessly propping her up so that her face was above the water. She was pale, so pale. Bloodless.

Operating on mindless instinct, half-remembered first-aid videos flashing through my mind, I pinched her nose, put my lips to hers, and attempted to blow air into her mouth, desperately trying to revive her.

It was no use. Her skin was icy, mottled with purple from the cold, and her muscles had long since stiffened. She was dead. I couldn't help her.

My tears dripped on to her forehead as harsh sobs wracked my chest, and her body slowly rose and fell in my arms as the water flowed around us both.

It was then that understanding came over me like a tsunami, a gradual building and then a roaring force that destroyed everything in its wake. I let go of Olivia, something in me unspooling as I did, and struggled to my feet. I lurched, unsteadily, towards Clara.

'What did you do?' I asked, hoarse. I could hear my own

horror and anger tightly coiled around every word like barbed wire. 'What did you *do*, Clara?'

Clara was calm, composed. She seemed completely unperturbed by the situation, by the grief tearing through me as I'd cradled my friend's dead body.

'You chose me,' she said.

I stared up at her. 'What?'

Clara glanced down at Olivia's body, right there below us in the water. She was expressionless, her lips a straight line. 'Right here, in the woods,' she said. 'You chose me, and not her.'

All the air left my lungs as Clara's words hung in the air between us, and I had to fight to get the words out. 'You did this,' I said. 'You're a fucking *monster*!'

Clara said nothing, didn't even try to deny it, which made me angrier.

'You're a twisted, jealous, *delusional* fucking monster!' The volume of my voice rose until I was shouting. 'Olivia wasn't taking me away from you – she was trying to protect me from you. She said you were dangerous, and she was right.'

'And yet,' Clara said coolly, 'you chose me over her.'

'What does that matter?' I spat.

'It matters,' Clara said, 'because she *knew*.'

If I'd felt on the verge of collapsing before, it was nothing compared to the reaction that Clara's words triggered in me now. Stars burst across my vision, darkness wavering at the edges. 'What?'

Clara's lips twitched. She was enjoying this.

'You see,' she said. 'After you told poor Olivia to leave, I asked some of the girls to show her another way out of the grounds. A way that was a little more private, away from the crowds.' She glanced at the Roman temple. 'Of course, she didn't make it that far. I had the girls hold her in the temple until I was ready. I had to find something first. Do you remember that crystal you fell in love with that time? The big, heavy chunk of desert rose?'

I closed my eyes.

'Well, I brought the crystal to the temple, ready to get rid of our little *loyalty* issue, and who should I hear stumbling about in the woods outside?' She shook her head, tutting at me. 'I came out, and there you were. And I thought, *Oh, this could be fun.*'

For a moment, I struggled to understand what Clara meant. And then, unbidden, flashes from Olivia's point of view swam in front of my eyes. Dragged to the temple and held there by the Goldens, she would've known that I was her only hope. She would have heard my footsteps, Clara speaking to me just metres away, oblivious to the fact that I could have saved her.

She would have heard Clara asking me to make my choice: her, or Olivia. And she would have heard my answer, even though it wasn't the truth. I couldn't imagine what that had done to her, trapped there, hearing me choose Clara over her and then walk away.

'She cared about me,' I said softly. 'She cared about me, and she died thinking I'd betrayed her.'

'*I* care about you,' Clara said. 'I love you. Don't you understand? She's out of the picture now, Chloe – we don't need to worry any more. Nothing's going to take you away from me.'

Inexplicably, I laughed. The sound was harsh, as if it had been torn from my throat. 'This isn't what love is,' I said. 'Love is what Olivia and I had. Love is selfless, Clara – not self*ish*. Love doesn't cause pain. Love doesn't hurt anyone. If this is your idea of love . . .' I couldn't look at Olivia, still lying in the water, cold and alone. 'Then I don't want it. Not a single piece of it.' I staggered away from the riverbank. 'I'm going to call the police.'

I floated back up to the house in a daze. I barely acknowledged the raindrops as they soaked my hair, my skin, my dress. Olivia was dead. Clara had killed her.

I thought back to the previous night, to Olivia's dismay that I hadn't been the one to send her the invitation. Her disgust when she'd looked at Clara, laughing and covered in blood. The way that her sorrowful eyes had gleamed in the evening light as she'd told me never to speak to her again, and walked away from me, back up towards the house. If I'd walked with her, not let her get lost in the crowd, she would still be alive. The thought made me gag, and I had to stop, to rest for a moment with my hands on my knees, until the sudden, intense nausea faded.

It felt like an eternity before I made it into the orangery, my bare feet leaving muddy prints across the tiles.

'Chloe?' Christie was there, right by the kitchen door. 'Chloe, what's happened? Where've you been? It's so early!' She took a proper look at me, at the state that I was in. 'My god, you're drenched!'

She rushed to me, shrugging off her cardigan as she did so, and wrapped it around my shoulders. I was shaking, with cold or with shock, or both. Outside, the thunder clashed like an entire orchestra of cymbals.

I couldn't speak. I stumbled past the girls, all of them in their pyjamas, tired-eyed. They were looking at me with the kindest, sweetest concern, their brows furrowed, their mouths turned downwards, but I didn't trust them. Which of them had done Clara's bidding? Which of the girls had taken Olivia prisoner?

My mobile phone was sitting on the kitchen counter, right where I'd left it. As I picked it up, Mia stepped forward, a hand outstretched.

'Chloe,' she said, 'don't do this.'

I pulled away from her. 'Did you know?' I snarled. I could feel the Goldens looking between us, their confusion palpable. 'Did she tell you what she was going to do? What she did?'

'It doesn't matter,' Mia said stonily. 'It's over now.'

Her words – delivered so simply, so matter-of-factly, as if we weren't talking about murder – sickened me. Behind her, among the Goldens, there was a sudden clamouring. *What happened, Chloe? What did* who *do? Are you talking about Clara? Where* is *Clara?*

I held Mia's gaze as I dialled the emergency number with trembling fingers. I let her see.

'Yes,' I said. 'You're right. It's over.'

Her eyes widened as she realised I wasn't bluffing. 'Chloe, please,' she said, urgent now. 'Don't. You'll ruin everything.'

I hit the call button. 'It's already ruined.'

Mia looked as if she wanted to say more, but she didn't. She turned away from me instead, and pushed through the girls. They watched her go, whispering. I didn't know where she was going, and I didn't care. She could try to warn Clara, but it wouldn't make any difference. It was too late.

'Hello,' said a man's voice. 'Emergency service operator. Which service do you need?'

'Police,' I said. 'And an ambulance. I think.'

The call connected.

'Police,' said a different voice, this time a woman. 'What's your emergency?'

I couldn't look at the Goldens who remained as I answered. 'I'm at my friend's house,' I said. 'She's killed someone.'

Chapter 37

If Clara had truly intended to get away with Olivia's murder, she should have done the same thing that she'd done to Vanessa. She should have framed Olivia's death as an accident.

It wasn't as if she didn't have a series of convenient 'accidents' under her belt already. She'd previously used a peanut allergy and a well-timed push at the top of a staircase to defeat girls that she saw as her enemies. What was another quick shove to a girl with that kind of history?

Clara, though, had got cocky. She'd plotted and schemed, convincing herself she was untouchable. She'd brought in accomplices, and together they'd discussed how to persuade Olivia to go to the temple, how they'd hold her there, how Clara would kill her and how they'd dispose of Olivia's body. After, of course, Clara had shown it to me.

That was the one thing that Clara hadn't accounted for. In her delusion, she had genuinely believed that my loyalty to her, to the Goldens, would be stronger than my grief for my friend. I had promised, after all.

* * *

The trial lasted weeks.

Once, Clara's devoted followers had shared pictures of her glamorous lifestyle and hedonistic parties. Now, they gushed over the outfits she wore to court: a pink tweed blazer and skirt co-ord set worn with white tights; a black velvet dress with a matching headband and shiny loafers; a houndstooth miniskirt teamed with a fluffy black jumper. In every picture, she looked perfectly innocent, positively demure, her hair sleek and her cheeks rosy.

I was grateful that the judge didn't seem particularly impressed by her cute, stylish outfits. Nor did she seem impressed with the hotshot lawyer Clara's parents had hired.

Over a period of days, the judge listened, expressionless, to a combination of witness testimonies and Clara's answers to the prosecution and defence. It was during this time that I learned what had really happened on the night of the party. Mia, Alexis and Bella had caught Olivia on her way back up to the house, warned her that reporters and photographers had gathered outside the manor's front gates, and offered to show her an alternative route out of the grounds. When they'd reached the temple, Mia explained tearfully, Olivia had become suspicious. Panicking, the three of them wound a silk scarf round her mouth to gag her, and pinned her to the ground when they heard footsteps and voices outside. This had been Clara and me arriving, when Clara asked me to choose between her and Olivia. The lie that Olivia had heard, the lie that had effectively signed her death warrant, would haunt me forever.

Not long after, Clara and I had left to return to the party. And then, after allowing herself to be worshipped, Clara had gone back to the temple. There, as calm and composed as anything, she'd kept Alexis by her side and instructed Mia and Bella to distract me. I now understood why Mia had been so distant, constantly looking over my shoulder, as she spoke to me. And I understood why she had a smear of blood on her cheek. It hadn't been Clara's after all.

The forensics team had found the desert rose crystal in the undergrowth, still spattered with blood and brain matter. It wouldn't have been easy, they told the jury, to bring it down with enough force to crack Olivia's skull. Clara had been determined.

Alexis had helped Clara to drag the body to the river. But in their horrified, excited state they'd missed something crucial. Olivia was still breathing. Shallowly, yes; but she was still alive. If anybody had found her then, if Alexis had made the decision to call an ambulance hours before I finally did, she might have lived. But, together, Clara and Alexis watched as Olivia sank beneath the water, air escaping from her lungs. Her autopsy confirmed that she'd died by drowning.

Once Olivia was underwater, Clara had turned away and brushed the twigs and mud from her dress. She'd been unconcerned, according to Alexis; she'd been excited to get back to the party.

And then she'd come and found me, wrapped her arms around me and kissed me so tenderly.

Eventually, it was my turn to take the stand. The media coverage surrounding the trial was extensive, and much had been made on social media about Clara's second-in-command, the dark-haired girl who she'd been seen with around campus and who featured in almost every recent photograph. It was a shock to everyone who'd followed the story, I think, when I wasn't charged. I'd lived in the house. I'd associated with the girls involved. My fingerprints were all over Olivia's body.

But, as it turned out, at some point Clara had spoken up for me. She'd insisted that I'd had no knowledge of her plan whatsoever. I was strangely grateful for that, for how she didn't want to take me down with her, even as she allowed all the other Goldens to dig their own graves.

And so I appeared in court only as a witness, called upon to describe, from the beginning, my friendship and life with Clara – how it had started off so wonderfully, and how it had all come apart, piece by piece. Unsurprisingly, my parents, sitting in the public gallery, were horrified to discover how much I'd hidden from them. I couldn't bear to look at them as I answered questions, first from the prosecution and then the defence. Instead, I looked at Clara, the catalyst for it all.

When the other girls had taken the stand, Clara hadn't seemed particularly concerned. Bella, Mia and even Alexis had all downplayed the extent of her manipulation, her threats. The girls who had gone into detail – usually trembling with fear, in tears or both – had earned either a blank face or a half-smile, as if Clara was holding back something that would destroy every bit of their testimony. Who knows? Perhaps she was.

But with me, though, she was attentive. I saw her gaze flicking to the lawyers and back to me, quick and anxious, as they grilled me on how I'd come to know Clara, at what point I'd moved into Deneside Manor, and the overarching nature of our relationship. I answered each question without embellishment. We'd met at university, when I'd found her scarf. She'd invited me to a party, and I'd comforted her when she was upset. I'd moved into Deneside Manor in January. We had become more than friends.

It was difficult to meet Clara's eyes when I admitted that to the court. I'd expected her to be furious – forgetting that she couldn't actually do anything to hurt me any more. But, to my surprise, her lips twitched into a smirk.

And so the trial went on.

Olivia's parents weren't particularly well off, but they'd received enough sympathetic donations to have hired a well-known lawyer, a real piece of work, from the city. She'd managed to dig up evidence that I hadn't even known existed – like how Clara's boarding-school teachers had ignored her classmates when they'd insisted that the allergy-triggering incident had been deliberate. Then there was the fact that the coroner hadn't even considered foul play with regard to Vanessa's death. And that when Olivia had gone to the police, days before she was killed, to report her concerns over Clara's erratic behaviour, she had been thornily dismissed with a warning that, next time, she'd receive a fine for wasting police time.

Clara was found guilty. She was to be sentenced to a minimum of twenty-five years for Olivia's murder and her role in Vanessa's death, with additional sentences for incitement, for conspiracy to murder and for false imprisonment. It was unlikely that she'd ever leave prison.

Following the verdict, the mood towards me on social media changed. I'd loved her, and I'd wanted to support her career – the half-written memoir (part of the body of evidence used in the trial) only confirmed that. My only crime was being a loyal friend. How was I supposed to know that it would end like this? That all the innocent sessions of laying tables and arranging flowers and hanging up string lights would lead to bonfires and rituals and murder? I'd been manipulated by Clara, just like everyone else. I'd been trapped. And none of it was my fault, they said. None of it was my fault. I still didn't quite believe it.

Bella, Mia and Alexis were sentenced separately, and somewhat less severely. They'd moved into Deneside Manor hoping for camaraderie, friendship, support. And instead their lives had been shattered. It was no excuse, of course, but it was agreed that all three of them would have been unlikely to commit such a crime if it hadn't been for Clara.

As for the other girls, like me, it was all over. Clara was in prison, yes, which was some form of justice. But now they – *we* – were left to pick up the pieces.

The worst part was that I missed her, even after everything she'd done.

I lay on my side in my childhood bed, my knees curled to my chest, and imagined that Clara was there with me. I imagined her stroking my cheek, my hair, whispering about the next party. How it was going to be the best party ever, and how everything would go back to the way it was, and how everyone would love us. Love me. I often fell asleep like that and, when I did, I dreamed of her too.

At home, my parents still didn't really know what to do around me.

They knew that I'd been a victim of Clara's overarching control, drawn in by her friendship and kept close – kept *in line* – by her mind games. But they also knew that I'd been an enthusiastic follower, that I'd ignored their pleas to come home more than once in favour of staying with Clara. They didn't hold me responsible for what had happened, of course – but sometimes I'd catch one or the other of them looking at me with a vaguely puzzled expression, as if I was a completely different Chloe to the one they'd raised, to the one they'd always known.

And, maybe, I was. After all, we're shaped by what we live through, by the people that we're surrounded by. I spent the better part of a year being best friends with a girl who'd become a cult leader and a murderer. A girl who'd murdered the only other friend I'd had out of misguided jealousy. I would never be the same again, and I didn't expect to be.

In September, I re-enrolled at Dern for my second year. My parents had been reluctant to let me go, and tried to persuade me to switch to a university closer to home. I'd made a deal with them, promising to live on campus in a different accommodation block. I'd be far from the memories of Ivy House and Vanessa, and far from Deneside Manor, now shuttered and dust-sheeted by Clara's parents, to be left empty until it was, inevitably, sold to someone who had a morbid fascination with girls like Clara.

My parents and I had bonded again over the summer. Their uncertain glances, their whispered comments, had gradually changed into open-ended questions, and we'd had a long, hard talk one night, which had left the three of us in tears. The next morning, Mum had made me a coffee for the first time in weeks, and Dad had patted my shoulder. I'd known, then, that everything was going to be okay.

I took the train back to Havington almost exactly a year after I'd arrived there for the first time. I pulled my suitcase along the platform, and then out on to Main Street. I saw Olivia everywhere: striding along beneath the old-fashioned streetlamps, sitting in the window of Tate's Coffee, browsing in the tiny, independent bookshop with the red door. I felt responsible for her death, and I almost welcomed the torture of her memory as punishment. I had to come back to relive what had happened here, the tragedies that I had helped cause. This was my penance.

My parents had set me up with a therapist, one of the conditions of me returning to university. She was based in Havington, her home office a short walk from campus. She reminded me a bit of Debbie from the coffee shop: she was middle-aged and plump, with dimples in both cheeks when she smiled. And she smiled a lot during that first hour, her every word filled with reassurance.

'You didn't know, Chloe,' she said, emphasising my name as if to remind me of it, to remind me that I was still a whole person without Clara's influence. 'How could you have known?'

She was right. I couldn't have known. But maybe I should have.

I'd known that Clara had poisoned a girl, and I'd known that she'd pushed another down the stairs. I'd known that the last place Vanessa had been seen was at Clara's party. The pieces were all there; I just hadn't put them together. Maybe I hadn't *wanted* to put them together. And that was something that I was going to have to hold on to for the rest of my life. While everyone else moved on, I would not. I didn't deserve to.

Even so, life continued around me.

My new accommodation at Dern was the polar opposite of

Ivy House. Poppy Halls was relatively new, barely a decade old, and had recently undergone a full refurbishment. Part of me missed the artist's garret energy of Ivy House, the thick stone walls and deep-set windows – but a larger part of me shivered at the thought of the memories those walls held.

The three other girls that I lived with were friendly. Niamh and Ella were both bookish, mild types who preferred a night in. Esther was more of a social butterfly, a pub-quiz, paint-ball-club, ordering-shots kind of girl. Together, we blended well.

Niamh and Ella tended to keep to themselves, but if Esther managed to persuade them to go to a students' union pub quiz – or, on the rare occasion, to Havington's only nightclub – they'd always make sure to invite me. More often than not, I'd turn them down with a smile, cite an assignment deadline or a much-needed early night. Usually, it was the truth. I threw myself into my studies, determined to make up for my dismal academic performance last year, and it wasn't long before my grades started to shine again.

Sometimes, often when it was raining outside and I was feeling morose, I wondered where I'd be right now if I hadn't applied to Dern, if it hadn't been my dream university. I would most likely never have come to Havington; I certainly never would have met Clara. I would have been just another girl, scrolling through my feed and seeing her pictures. I would have admired her long, glossy hair, her chiselled bone structure, her elegant style. I might have even clicked on her profile, chosen to follow her account. I would have watched her highly publicised downfall from a distance.

And maybe, just maybe, I would have wondered why anybody would get themselves involved with a girl like her in the first place.

Chapter 38

That isn't to say that Clara's story ended when she went to prison.

Those of us who'd once been so loyal to her were no longer her followers. No longer her friends. Her many celebrity connections had kept their distance during the trial and subsequent sentencing. Many of them claimed to have never even met Clara, only to have pictures of them together, posing at any one of a dozen or more parties that Clara had hosted, thrown back in their faces. The Internet would never forget. And neither would they. Nobody would let them.

Occasionally, I would open my laptop and click my way through the maze of folders to the file that housed Clara's memoir. It was still a relatively rough draft, the earliest chapters polished but the rest an amalgamation of bullet points and quotes. I would skim what I'd written, the screenshots I'd taken from Clara's social-media accounts, the photographs of the two of us pressed cheek to cheek. I couldn't quite bring myself to delete them.

One day, maybe, I would use this draft. I would break it apart, tear it to pieces, and use it to create something new. I knew now that the world didn't need another self-indulgent memoir, a promotional puff piece. What the world wanted was the real thing: Clara's meteoric rise and spectacular downfall, every sordid detail of how her popularity had transformed into notoriety. And who better to tell that story than me, the girl who'd been there all along, right at the heart of everything?

It was December when Ayanna finally got in touch.

Hi, babe, she wrote. *Sorry to pop up out of the blue. I just thought you'd want to see this.*

Below her message was a link. Cautiously, I clicked on it.

I was taken to a website, a cursory two pages built by somebody who knew what a website should look like, but who apparently had little experience in building one. There was a title at the top, in bold pink. *#FreeClaraHolland*, it declared. Beneath, a caption. *We know that Clara is innocent. We'll defend her until the day we die.*

I texted back: *Wow.*

I know, right? she replied, in under five minutes. *These followers of hers are crazy!*

Crazy? Maybe. Or maybe they just needed to feel like part of something, to feel special. Like Clara. Like me.

Maybe, like us, they were desperate for love, for recognition, for success. Maybe they were desperate to be adored. They'd just looked in the wrong place for it, and perhaps they would be haunted for the rest of their lives as a result of that mistake.

Poppy Halls was far warmer than Ivy House had been in the winter. Its walls weren't as thick, but the insulation was better. No wind rattled the windows. I was sitting at my desk, carefully writing a list of names on a sheet of thick, creamy paper, when there was a soft knock at my door.

'Chloe?' Ella said, her voice muffled by the wood. 'There's a parcel for you. I've left it in the kitchen.'

'Okay,' I said. 'Thanks! I'll come and grab it.'

I slid my legs off the bed, stretched luxuriously and glanced outside. It was snowing.

I padded through to the kitchen in my thick-knit socks, my joggers and T-shirt – an oatmeal colour threaded with gold. Some habits would never die.

The parcel on the table was the size of a shoebox, wrapped in brown paper and tied with string. My first thought was that my parents had sent me an early Christmas present, maybe some of their old decorations to hang up around the flat or some chocolates to share with my flatmates.

I tugged at the string and slipped the paper off, and then tore open the sellotaped box inside. And I could only stare.

Bound with a ribbon tied into a bow, there was a scarf.

A cashmere scarf in pink, grey and cream wool, with the letters *C A H* monogrammed in a light pink square. And, as if that wasn't enough to make my heart skip a beat, there was something else on top of the coiled scarf. A small, red box. I opened it, barely able to breathe. Inside, sitting on a crimson cushion, was a gold bracelet. It was of a similar style to the ludicrously expensive ones that Clara had always worn; a beautiful gold bracelet that secured with a clasp. Trembling, I picked the bracelet up from its setting and turned it round in my hands.

There was no note, of course. But there was no mistaking who it was from.

I thought back to the website that Ayanna had sent me, to the *#FreeClaraHolland* hashtag. Clara had fewer followers now, but if anything they were more loyal, more committed, more determined. She had exactly what she wanted.

I paused, allowing myself to take a series of deep, calming breaths. I considered how my life had changed. My grades were improving, I was newly confident, I was slowly bonding with the girls in my flat and some of the students on my course. My therapist was pleased with my progress, and my relationship with my parents was beginning to heal. I'd made all of my social-media accounts private.

But something was missing. It had taken a while for me to understand exactly what it was, the sense of absence and loss. I didn't just miss Clara. I missed the Goldens. And so I'd begun to curate a list of people. My *own* list, made up of wonderful, genuine people – the kind of people who'd really *get* the Goldens, who'd understand what we were trying to do.

I would do it better than Clara. I would be a better leader; I wouldn't let the power go to my head, let my ego take control. Nobody would die under my reign.

I slipped the bracelet on to my wrist and fastened the clasp, the metal warm against my skin.

Acknowledgements

I've been so incredibly lucky to work with such a fantastic team on *The Goldens*.

Thank you to everyone at HarperCollins *Children's Books* and the Harper Fire team, especially my wonderful acquiring editor Natalie Doherty and my brilliant editor Megan Reid. Thank you also to Charlotte Winstone, Laura Hutchison, Nick Lake, Tom Bonnick and Jane Baldock.

Thank you to the team at Flatiron Books and the Pine and Cedar imprint – especially my fabulous editor Christine Kopprasch and her amazing assistant Kate Lucas.

I'd also like to thank my international publishers and editors for being so invested in Chloe, Clara and the Goldens, and for bringing their story to readers across the globe.

Thank you all for pouring so much time, effort, support and love into my debut novel. It's been an absolute dream to work with you all.

Thank you to my superstar agent Chloe Seager – you've quite literally changed my life. Thank you also to the Madeleine

Milburn Literary Agency as a whole. It's an honour to be one of your clients.

Thank you to my inspiring writing group, the North East Novelists, and to New Writing North for bringing us all together.

Thank you to Lucy, for many, many writerly conversations over more than five years of friendship, and for being one of my biggest cheerleaders. I'm so proud I get to call you a colleague.

Thank you to Laura, this book's very first reader, who is both my fabulous future sister-in-law and an extremely talented author.

Thank you to Ellie for the breakfast dates, the many book-related conversations, and for resisting reading this book until you could buy your own copy.

Thank you to Grace for all your excitement when I was writing this book. I hope you enjoy it!

Thank you to Nanna and Grandad, for letting me use all of your typewriter paper to write 'novels', and for always encouraging me to tell my stories.

Thank you to Mam and Dad for years of taking me to the library, for buying me literally hundreds of books, and for always, always believing in me – no matter what.

Thank you to my fiancé, Jack, for your unwavering support, your patience, your encouragement and, most importantly, your love. Thank you for always being there.

Thank you, lastly, to our spaniel, Albie. You give the best cuddles.